Chrissy

THE
EDGE
OF
NEVER

Sarah Bailey xxx

SARAH BAILEY

The Edge of Never © 2024 by Sarah Bailey

Please note the spelling throughout is British English.

Cover Art by Sarah Bailey

Published by Twisted Tree Publications
www.twistedtreepublications.com
info@twistedtreepublications.com

Paperback ISBN: 978-1-913217-56-3

*This book is dedicated to
the younger version of me.
The one who didn't know they were
non-binary, asexual and autistic.
The one who didn't know it was safe
to be who they were deep down inside.
This is for you, little Sarah because
you deserved better from this world.*

GLOSSARY

One of the main characters in the story is Scottish and speaks a mix of Scots and English. I've made every effort to make the phrasing/dialect as authentic as possible to the area the character is from.

This is by no means an exhaustive list of Scots, only the words and phrases I've used throughout the book.

Aboot – about
Am – I'm/I am
Aye – yes
Cannae – can't
Dae – do
Didnae – didn't
Dinnae – don't
Eejit – idiot
Get – git
Glen – a valley
Gonnae – going to
Guid – good
Hadnae – hadn't

Havnae – haven't

Hasnae – hasn't

Hoose – house

Hullo – hello

Mah – my

Mahself – myself

Mibbe – maybe

Mooth – mouth

Munro – a mountain in Scotland with a height over 3,000 feet.

No bother – no problem

No – not/no

Noo – now

Oor – our

Oot – out

Polis – police

Shouldnae – Shouldn't

Tae – to/too

Wannae – want to

Wasnae – wasn't

Werenae – weren't

Wee – little/small

Wouldnae – wouldn't

Willnae – won't/will not

Withoot – without

Ye/yer/ye're/yers – you/your/you're/yours

Ye've/ye'd/ye'll – you've/you'd/you'll

Yerself – yourself

ONE

Kit

ou'd think standing on the edge of the cliff would leave you with your life flashing before your eyes. Not me. I was contemplating my life, sure, but not in the sense that I'd decided it should end. It was a case of wondering how the fuck I got here.

The decisions I'd made and why I'd made them haunted me. Made me realise my adult life had been a series of mistakes leading to an epic finale that only drove me to hate everything. Perhaps that was being a tad dramatic, but I wasn't in the mood to be reasonable about what happened to me.

I needed time to contemplate what next. To stop my life from disintegrating in front of my eyes. To get far away from the shitstorm as possible. I wasn't a coward, but there was only so much one person could take. And I was way over the limit.

The wind whipped my almost shoulder-length dark hair around my face as I stared out at the ocean before me. Mist shrouded the horizon and the space around me. My arms looped around my stomach, drawing my coat tighter against the chill in the late January air. The new year was meant to bring a new beginning. However, the ongoing fucked up situation in my life had marred it. It left me reeling and ready to disappear into nothingness.

A scream lodged itself in my throat. The need to let out my frustration was on the tip of my tongue. I held it back, opting to remain silent in my pain. No one cared about how it affected me. How I was drowning in misery and failure. It wasn't about me. Maybe it never had been.

Two arms banded around me, pulling me backwards. I stumbled but caught myself before I fell into them.

"What the fuck are you doing?"

My whole body tensed at the sound of her voice. I spun around and faced the woman who dragged me back from the cliff's edge.

Sienna had a deadly expression on her pale face. Her red hair was tucked into the hood of her jumper and her brown eyes were full of anger.

I didn't understand why she was here or how she'd found me.

"Seriously, what the fuck, Kit?"

I unstuck my tongue from the roof of my mouth.

"What do you mean?"

She waved a hand at the ocean behind us.

"Are you kidding me? You looked like you were about to jump."

I rubbed my arms.

"Oh."

"Oh? Is that all you have to say? Oh? Jesus fucking Christ, Kit. You scared the shit out of me."

I stepped further away from the cliff and turned to the side, not wanting to see the reproachful look in her eyes. She'd read the whole situation wrong, but it shouldn't surprise me. Sienna had a habit of doing that.

"I wasn't going to jump."

"Then what the hell were you doing?"

I let out a breath. Telling her the real reason I was standing out here felt impossible after what happened. She should already know, anyway. None of this had been easy. Yet my feelings weren't a priority for her. I couldn't remember a time when they had been.

"I came out here to think, not commit suicide. You should know I have no intention of doing that."

"Funny, I don't think I know what you're capable of any longer after the way you've been acting recently."

My hand clenched into a fist at my side. Her words stung. Just because I hadn't been there for her like all the other times she'd been in crisis mode, it didn't mean I'd changed. I was still me. Still Kit. But I was sad. So fucking sad that it hurt to breathe sometimes. You don't go through a tragedy without it scarring you somehow. Without it leaving a mark.

"The way I've been acting?" I pressed my other hand to my chest and looked at her again. "I lost a baby, Sienna. How do you think I'm supposed to act after that?"

The flash of pain in her eyes made me sorry I'd brought it up.

"My baby. You lost my baby. He wasn't yours."

The stabbing sensation in my chest made me flinch. While she was right, it didn't make it any easier. It didn't stop the ache in my gut and the damage to my heart and soul.

"I know he was yours, but I carried him for you and Law. I…"

My voice cracked. Talking about it didn't get any easier. No one tells you how fucked up you'd feel after a miscarriage. It didn't matter that he wasn't my baby. He had still grown inside me. And I lost him. I was the one who physically fucking lost him. Not Sienna. Not Lawrence. But me.

"It still hurts," I whispered.

Her face dropped. She closed the distance between us and wrapped her arms around me.

Usually, I'd welcome her comfort, but today, it felt hollow. My arms remained limp at my sides. I stared off into the distance and couldn't bring myself to tear out of her embrace, despite it reminding me of things I couldn't have. Of a life I could never live because she wasn't mine. She wouldn't ever be mine. And that was the icing on the shit cake that was my life.

I don't remember when my heart started loving Sienna. Probably early in life, considering we'd met at school when

4

we were five years old. I turned thirty next week. Twenty-five years of feelings that I couldn't help but resent. Loving your best friend who knew of your feelings and did nothing but shove her relationship down your throat was probably the worst feeling in the world.

Sometimes I wondered why I loved this woman when she could be so cruel to everyone. Sienna always put herself first. It hadn't changed because I agreed to be her surrogate, only to lose the baby at twenty weeks. Two days after we found out they were having a boy.

Fuck, it hurts. It really fucking hurts so much.

"I don't want you to touch me."

The words were out of my mouth before I could stop them.

Sienna dropped her arms from around me almost immediately. When she backed away, I could see the irritation and confusion in her expression.

"What's that supposed to mean?"

If we were going to do this, I might as well lay it all out for her. We'd been going around in circles for the past four months. Ever since the day that changed everything. And now things had come to a head.

I wasn't surprised, but I hadn't been prepared to do this with her now. I wanted to deal with my feelings away from her because Sienna kept making it worse. She kept making it harder to breathe.

"It means you need to stop touching me. Stop coming near me. Just stop."

"Kit…"

I put a hand up.

"No. You keep talking at me and never listening to what I have to say. I know you're in pain, and I know you're hurting, Sienna. I fucking get that, but what you don't understand is how this affected me. How I feel."

I dropped my hand to my chest. The ache there almost crippled me. I took a deep breath in an attempt to ease it.

"I'm tired."

My voice sounded utterly defeated. It didn't sound like me at all.

"I'm so fucking tired, and lost, and hurting… and I don't want to do this with you anymore. You keep asking me when I'm going to be ready to do it again. Keep pestering me, and yet you don't fucking listen to a word I've said to you. You don't even listen to Law either. We've been telling you that this isn't good for any of us. We all need time, and you won't give that to us."

Her eyes narrowed. Since Sienna wouldn't hear me out, I talked to her husband instead. It had been a mistake, but what else was I meant to do when no one understood what I was going through? How much this whole situation had eroded our friendship until I was hanging onto a fraying string. Sienna kept tugging far too hard. And I was done.

"Don't think it escaped my notice how close you've been getting to *my* husband."

"He's my friend too."

She scoffed.

"Friend, huh? That's rich. I mean, I don't care what the two of you did. By all means, fuck my husband if it makes you feel better. You're welcome to his dick since it's the closest you'll get to me, but don't you dare tell me you need time. You've had time."

I stumbled back. Her words cut like a knife. Throughout my life, I had listened to Sienna bitch and moan about other people. She never directed it at me. I guess that's why I let it go. It was easier than to call her out on it. More fool me for being the meek one who was always outshone by the gregarious Sienna Michaels.

"Law told you?"

"Of course, he told me."

It had only happened once. We were drunk and miserable after Sienna had gone off at us over the baby situation. I regretted every moment of it afterwards. I should have never let my emotions get the better of me around him.

"It was a mistake."

"That's not what he told me. Law's always had a thing for you."

Just like I have a thing for you. Although, I don't know what that thing is anymore.

"So? That doesn't mean I want him."

She raised an eyebrow.

"I know who you want."

"Don't do that, Sienna. Don't use my feelings against me. That's not fair. I've never asked you for anything, so don't."

"And what? I've asked you for everything, have I?"

I wrapped my arms around myself.

"Yeah, you have. I tried to give you what you desired most in the world, but I can't do it again. I don't even want children, but I was willing to put myself through a pregnancy for you. For you, because that's what friends do, but you've been nothing but ungrateful ever since and I'm not going to put up with it any longer."

The way her eyes darkened made me want to run. I knew that look. She was about to unleash hell. And this time it would be all on me.

"You think you're better than me because your body fucking works and mine doesn't. That's it. You're more of a woman than I am, isn't that right?"

I shook my head, unable to believe what she'd said to me. As if I felt that way. That thought had never occurred to me. I felt awful that Sienna had fertility issues. Why the fuck did she think I agreed to help her have a baby? Out of pity? I didn't pity her. I wanted to make her happy.

"Don't you dare say that. You should know better than to call me a woman."

I don't know what hurt worse. The way she was treating me or the fact she'd deliberately misgendered me. Sienna was there when I came out as non-binary. She had supported me when I was struggling with my feelings about my gender. How I didn't identify with either. She came to my defence when people couldn't get my pronouns right. She was my champion when it came to being agender. To have her throw that back in my face was too much.

"You are a fucking woman, Kit. Don't kid yourself."

"My gender is not the same as my sex. You know that. You fucking know."

I took a deep breath.

"I'm done. This conversation is over. I don't want to see you or talk to you when you can't be reasonable or remotely respectful."

I turned away from her with a sick feeling in my stomach and started walking back down the hill towards town. I'd lived in Seaford my whole life, but now I wanted to escape. It was a good thing I'd booked myself a trip away for my birthday. I needed to be far away from Sienna, Lawrence, and this absolute mess.

"So that's it, is it? You're just going to walk away."

I didn't turn around or acknowledge Sienna. There would be no point. I didn't even flinch when she screamed at me that I was a bitch and other obscenities. No, I kept walking away from my best friend, who had lost all of my respect. There was no way we could come back from this. She crossed far too many lines today.

It wasn't until I was safely locked away behind the front door of my studio flat that I broke down and cried until my throat was raw and my head hurt. And I wondered why I had wasted almost twenty-five years of my life on someone who never appreciated me the way I did them.

TWO

Thane

A sigh left my lips as I turned off the engine of my old Land Rover Defender. As soon as I got out of the car, I'd have to put on a brave face and act like a regular human being. One who wasn't drowning in prolonged grief. I was so very tired of those feelings. Of hating myself and everything around me.

After almost two years of being a widower, it was time for me to find a way to live again. Long overdue, really, but it couldn't be helped. There was no time limit on grief. On how it infiltrates every part of your life and makes breathing regularly so much harder. No one tells you how bad it gets nor how much you wish you were the one who died rather than your spouse. Such was my lot. And I had to go on without her, no matter how much it hurt.

Callan was right to insist I do him a favour and be an extra hand for his mountaineering course. I needed to get out of my own head. To move on with my life. I wasn't ready, but who's ever ready to move on from the person they loved? The person they'd built their life with and had never planned on losing?

My forehead rested on top of the steering wheel momentarily. I had to get a hold of myself. Jenna was gone. I was here. This was for the best. Getting back into mountaineering would help. It'd been my first love for as long as I could remember, having grown up surrounded by the Cairngorms. Being outdoors amongst nature was where I felt most at home.

Getting out of the car, I grunted as the cold hit my face. While I was used to winters here, this year was a particularly cold one. The previous year had been mild, which was good for those wanting to get up into the hills. No such luck this year. You had to be wary out on the mountains at the best of times. The weather could turn at any moment. One could not overstate the importance of winter mountaineering courses like the one Callan ran. Too many people went out without taking the necessary precautions or having an understanding of the dangers that could befall them.

Callan often gave me shit about being over-prepared for every eventuality, but it was better to be safe than sorry. I had every reason to ensure nothing went wrong, and if it did, then I'd be ready for it.

After retrieving my bag from the back of the car, I trudged into the lodge that Callan ran the courses out of.

When I arrived in the room, I found it full of people. I spotted Callan at the back, talking to his fellow instructor, Ruairí. My feet carried me through the throng to reach them.

"There ye are," Callan said as I came to a stop next to him.

I didn't apologise for being late. The roads were a bit ropey this morning. I lived out of town on a dirt road off a single track, far away from everyone else. It suited me better. I could choose when I wanted to spend time with people outside of work, which wasn't all that often these days.

"Aye, like I promised."

He gave me a pat on the back, earning him a scowl. Ruairí let out a belly laugh at the sight of it. No fucking surprises there. He thought I was a miserable bastard. And to be honest, since Jenna died, I had been.

"Ye didnae say this grumpy fuck would be coming."

Callan grinned and winked at him.

"Slipped mah mind."

I wanted to tell them both to shut up, but I refrained. Wouldn't do me any good to make a bad impression on the people we were teaching. Besides, Callan would have told Ruairí. They were married, after all. His husband merely liked to give me a lot of shite.

"The group's already getting tae know one another," Callan said to me.

He pointed everyone out, giving me their names, most of which I promptly forgot. There were thirteen of them. Callan and Ruairí could have handled this themselves, but Callan kept telling me I needed to get back out there. He didn't want me going off on my own when I was still grieving Jenna's death.

I almost rolled my eyes when he told me that. What did he think I was going to do? Something idiotic? I'd gone off the rails when it first happened, but I was better now. At least, I wasn't drowning my sorrows in whisky every night. That helped me see clearer. No more self-destructive behaviour. Jenna would have hated seeing me that way. I was trying to be better even though some days getting out of bed was a struggle and a half.

"And that's Kit." He pointed to a person with shoulder-length dark hair and the lightest blue eyes I'd ever encountered behind a pair of round glasses. "They're on their own. Rest are couples or pairs, so they might need a partner at some point."

"They?" I asked, wanting to be sure I heard Callan right, so I didn't misgender them by accident.

"Kit's non-binary."

"Aye, right."

"Ye ready tae get this show on the road?"

"Aye," Ruairí said, breaking out into a smile.

I nodded slowly, rubbing my beard with one hand as I watched Kit stare out of the window at the snow outside. They were off to one side of the room and didn't show any interest in interacting with the others. I knew how that felt. People did my head in more often than not.

Callan got everyone's attention and introduced me and Ruairí before letting them know the order of events. I took a seat at the back, allowing them to do their thing. The morning was dedicated to Callan going over winter safety essentials, such as avoiding avalanches and handling emergencies. The group was very engaged, leaving me time to go through the kit list and check everyone had everything they'd been required to bring.

After lunch, we did navigation and training on using an ice axe and crampons outside in the cold. I was helping a couple who were struggling with their axe when a yelp sounded from behind me. Spinning around, I spied Kit slumped in the snow with a grimace on their face.

"Gimme a minute," I said to the couple.

I set the axe aside and approached them, extending my hand.

Kit stared up at me with those icy blue eyes and a wrinkled nose.

"I tripped."

"Aye, I can see that."

They put their gloved hand out, letting me haul them up out of the snow. Kit only came up to my shoulder. They were small compared to my larger build. Given I worked in forestry and did a lot of hillwalking in my spare time, it wasn't surprising.

Their head tipped back as their eyes landed on me again. I felt a wee bit hot beneath my collar at their intense examination of my face.

This close-up, I noticed the light dusting of freckles across their face. If I was in the habit of finding other people attractive, you could call them pretty, but I hadn't been interested in anyone since Jenna died. If I was honest, it was before then. I didn't look at people that way. And the thought of another relationship made my skin crawl, anyway.

"Uh, thank you. I'm Kit, by the way."

"Thane," I said automatically, even though Callan had already introduced me to the entire group earlier.

They kept staring. I realised I hadn't let go of their hand. Dropping it abruptly, I took a step back, finding being in their personal space a wee bit unnerving. Those eyes of theirs were going to be a fucking problem. I wanted to stare into them to discern the exact colours, but that would be creepy, so I refrained.

"Ye okay noo?" I asked when the silence had gone on for too long.

"Yeah, just not used to this ice axe business… and the snow, I'm not used to that either."

I wondered why they were here if they had no experience with winter mountaineering. Despite this being a beginner course, many in the group had prior experience in snowy conditions.

"Ye wanting some help with it?"

"I mean, you were busy with those two, so it's okay."

They waved at the couple behind us. I glanced at them before my gaze landed back on Kit.

"Ye can join us."

"Oh. I guess that's true."

"Ye dinnae wannae?"

Kit shrugged.

"I kind of came here to get away from people."

I could completely understand the sentiment. People were a pain in the neck. I tolerated very few of them.

"Let me show ye noo, then."

It was my role to assist the group, so I wanted to make sure Kit knew what they were doing. That was the point of the course.

They didn't object to my demonstration of how to hold the axe properly. I waited while Kit mimicked me, correcting them when their technique was wrong. It took a few more tries before they handled it right.

From that brief encounter, I knew Kit would be a problem. Their struggle with getting their crampons on their boots further solidified my suspicions. Callan, thankfully, took the lead on that issue, but I could see the cogs turning in his head as he helped them.

As the day came to a close, and the group left the room, he arrived next to me with a pensive look on his face.

"Ye think the day went well?" I asked.

Ruairí was busy tidying up the room, leaving me and Callan alone in the corner.

"Aye."

"But?"

Callan shook his head and scraped a hand across his chest. Then he turned to me.

"Am thinking Kit needs a partner. They're taking longer than everyone else tae master the necessary skills. It's no bother. We all need an extra hand from time tae time."

Before his next words were out of his mouth, I knew exactly what he was going to say. And I wasn't happy about it. Although I had no issue with Kit, Callan knew I had no patience when it came to people in general. Before Jenna's death, you wouldn't have caught me getting irritated so easily. Now was a completely different story.

"I want ye tae give them a bit of extra time tomorrow when we go oot in the hills tae put their skills intae practice."

"Me?"

"Aye."

"Callan…"

He grinned.

"If ye think am gonnae let ye get oot of this, ye're wrong."

"Am no guid with people who dinnae know what they're deaing."

"Ye are. Ye've just forgotten how."

I scowled and crossed my arms over my chest.

"Ye're gonnae spend the rest of yer fucking life being a grumpy get if ye dinnae start living again, Thane. Am no gonnae let ye keep pushing everything and everyone away. It's no healthy."

If I argued with Callan, it wouldn't do me any good. He had been there for me in the wake of Jenna's death. Had seen how far I'd fallen. And was willing to help me pick myself up, even if it meant pushing me harder than anyone else had the guts to. My family walked around me on eggshells, not to mention Jenna's parents and brother barely talked to me any longer. It was my fault, of course, and it made me feel like shite. They were a reminder of what I'd lost. It was too painful to be around them. It was Callan or

17

nothing at this point. No matter how hard my grief had hit me and fucked up my relationship with my family, I wasn't inclined to destroy the only friendship I had left.

"Am no a get, Callan."

I wouldn't dispute the grumpy part. Even I could admit my disposition had become a hell of a lot surlier since Jenna passed.

"Ye sure act like one."

"Fuck ye."

He slapped me on the back and winked before helping Ruairí get ready for tomorrow's excursion.

"Ye can thank me later," he called over his shoulder.

"Aye, thank ye for being a cunt," I muttered under my breath as I grabbed my bag and walked out of the room.

Tomorrow would be interesting, and I didn't think it would be in a good way.

Fucking Callan. If this goes to shite, then I'm blaming you entirely.

THREE

Kit

The moment I walked into the room where we were assembling to go out for the day, one of the instructors came over and stood beside me. I looked up at him with a frown, wondering what he wanted.

When we met yesterday, I had been a little embarrassed about falling on my arse in the snow. While he hadn't outright said I was an idiot, I had seen it in his dark green eyes. The judgment for my clumsiness. I couldn't help that. Sometimes my coordination would go out the window. The only time I didn't have an issue with it was when I was working. Everything else faded away when it was me and the tattoo gun creating art on skin.

"Morning," I said when he didn't make any move to acknowledge me.

"Ye're with me today," was the curt response I received.

What does that mean?

"Okay?"

Thane gave me a nod and turned his attention back to his fellow instructors as if I didn't need further explanation.

I didn't have time to ask what he meant because Callan started talking about today's plans. I tried to listen, but my attention was firmly on Thane. The scowl on his face said he would rather be anywhere else but here. I didn't know what his problem was since he'd been perfectly polite to me yesterday.

My eyes roamed over his face. It was covered in light brown freckles, at least the parts that weren't obscured by his thick, dark auburn beard. His hair was long and the same colour as his beard, with streaks of a lighter colour running through it. He had braids on the sides of his head above his undercut. They met in the centre where it fell in one long braid down the back of his head. He was tall, broad as fuck, and quite frankly, intimidating. Apparently, I liked intimidating people, judging by my history with Sienna, but I wasn't here to think about her. No, I was here to get away from that shit. Only, being next to this man had my skin feeling hot and I didn't know what to do with that.

I swallowed hard, adjusted my glasses, and turned my gaze away from him to find the group gathering up their packs. People often told me I should wear contacts, but I found them uncomfortable, so I stuck with my glasses.

We weren't going to summit a mountain today, but we were going out to test our newly acquired winter skills. That meant going off the beaten track. Although I'd done hillwalking before, I had only been as far as the Lake District to go up Scafell Pike. That had been four years ago. I hadn't had a chance to summit any mountains since, but I liked to keep fit all the same. I hadn't done any winter walking, hence the need to go on this course. And to get as far away as possible from the mess that was my life.

I filed outside with the rest of the group. Thane kept silent behind me as we set off from the lodge along a track that led into the hills. I should've asked him what was going on, but the annoyed look on his face kept me silent.

The walk was fine for the first half an hour. I shifted my pack on my shoulders. It wasn't digging in anywhere, but I wasn't used to the weight of it yet.

"Did ye pack that right?"

I almost jumped out of my skin at the sound of a voice behind me. My head turned, catching Thane's irritated expression.

"What do you mean? And also, can you maybe not scare the shit out of me?"

"Yer backpack, did ye pack it right?"

Ignoring the scaring me part, I see. Maybe you wanted to scare me. That's kind of fucked up, so maybe not. Who fucking knows with this guy!

"Of course I did. What kind of a question is that?"

"Am just checking."

I rolled my eyes and stomped off behind the rest of the group. As if I didn't know how to pack my stuff and distribute the weight just right.

It took all of two minutes for me to seethe over his words before I stopped abruptly and spun around.

"Why do you care if I packed it right?"

Thane stopped, looked me over, and cocked his head to the side.

"Did ye no hear me tell ye that ye're with me today?"

"I did, but you didn't explain what that means."

He crossed his ridiculously muscly arms over his chest.

Hold on, what am I thinking? Ridiculously muscly? Someone stop my brain from conjuring up such imagery.

"Am looking after ye."

I had to take a second to replay his words inside my head before I could process what he said.

"I do not need looking after."

The way he smirked irritated the hell out of me.

"If ye say so."

"I do."

He dropped his arms and continued walking.

"If ye have a problem with it, take it up with Callan," he threw over his shoulder.

I clenched my jaw shut before it hung open in shock and made me look like a gawking idiot. My gloved hands balled into fists. I came on this trip to get away from bullshit and here I was, landed with a stupidly hot guy who thought he knew better than me.

He's not hot, brain. Look at that hair. Who does he think he is? I mean, the braids are nice, I suppose, and I have always had a thing for red hair, but that doesn't make him hot.

Cursing the world under my breath, I followed the smug bastard. Just because I fell over yesterday, it didn't mean I was incapable of staying upright and mastering the skills on this course. I would show him I didn't need a babysitter. And what had he meant about taking it up with Callan? Did he tell Thane to watch over me? I was the only single person on the trip, but I still didn't need an extra helping hand. I was perfectly capable... wasn't I?

Self-doubt was a bitch. I was a lot less experienced than some people here. Maybe that's why Callan thought I should have someone else watch over me. That shouldn't bother me. After all, he had to think of the group's safety. Maybe having someone keeping an eye on me wouldn't be so bad. If only it wasn't a certain man who was making my skin itch in a way I didn't appreciate.

I refused to say anything to Thane as we made our way higher up the slopes. Callan brought the group to a halt before a particularly steep bit and announced we were going to work on our walking in crampons technique.

When I got them out of my bag, I managed to put them on easily after yesterday's disaster. Last night, I spent half an hour doing it alone in my room after dinner to make sure I didn't embarrass myself. Sometimes I took longer to get things right. I couldn't help that, but it didn't mean I couldn't get there eventually.

I noted the way Thane watched me put them on. His expression remained unchanged, but from the look in his green eyes, I went up slightly in his estimation. That was another thing. He had really pretty eyes. I didn't want to find him attractive at all.

He cut a very imposing figure standing there with his arms crossed against the backdrop of the snowy mountains. The highlights in his hair glinted in the sunlight. The way his trousers clung to his thighs was making my mouth dry. It should be illegal for someone to look that good in walking gear.

Un-fucking-fair.

My cheeks heated, and I abruptly looked away, not wanting to be caught staring. No doubt it would piss him off if he thought I had a crush on him, which I didn't, because I was absolutely not doing this shit again. I didn't need another instance of unrequited feelings. There would be no surviving that. Sienna already broke my fucking soul. She was part of why I was here. And yet... I was kind of grateful I had an attractive distraction, even if he was a bit of a dick.

Ignoring Thane, I watched as Callan and Ruairí demonstrated the different ways to get up and down the slope in crampons depending on the terrain and angle of the slope. It didn't look at all easy or instinctual, but I was hoping I didn't fall over as they asked the group to practise what they'd shown us.

I jammed on my helmet and clipped it under my chin. We were all given them for safety.

The first thing I did was try walking in my crampons normally, which Callan called flat footing. I understood the reasoning behind wanting to engage as many of the points as possible to stay balanced.

It was unnerving having Thane watch me walk around in them as if assessing my every move. It was even worse when I was ascending the hill sideways and when I came back down again.

"No bad," he murmured when I arrived next to him.

"Oh well, thanks, glad I'm not completely inept in your estimation," I said with a sunny smile because fuck him.

"Never said ye werenae capable."

"You didn't have to say it."

Thane raised an eyebrow.

"Didn't I?"

I scoffed but didn't rise to the bait. A verbal sparring session with my so-called babysitter wouldn't do me any good. He wasn't the type to back down from a fight.

Instead of arguing with him, I tried front pointing using my ice axe to help me stay upright. It wasn't easy to keep my foot from sinking down on my heel, but I did my best.

I could feel Thane watching me. I turned my face to check what he was doing, but he wasn't behind me. My head twisted left and right.

"Jesus!"

Thane was right next to me with his front crampons dug into the snow the way mine were. My heels sank down and I bit the inside of my cheek.

"Ye guid?"

"Are you going to make a habit of scaring me?"

His attempt to suppress a smile made me want to throw him down the mountain. Instead, I adjusted my glasses and brushed my hair out of my eyes.

"Mibbe."

"That's not very nice."

"Ye'll learn better if I keep ye on yer toes."

"What makes you think I want to learn from you?"

That fucking smirk of his is going to be the death of me.

"Am yer partner on the course noo and am more experienced than ye. Ye'd dae well tae listen tae me."

Digging my crampon out of the snow, I started on my progress up the slope. He kept pace with me, which annoyed the fuck out of me.

"I thought you were my babysitter," I muttered.

"If ye wannae think of me like that, ye can."

My ice axe dug into the snow with a thud as I came to a stop. This guy was getting on my last fucking nerve. I was going to wipe that damn smug look off his face if it was the last thing I did.

While forgetting entirely that I was precariously balanced on my crampons, I turned half of my body to face him and pointed a finger at his chest.

"Listen here, I don't know what your problem with me is, but I would appreciate less of the smug, judgy attitude, thank you very much... oh!"

My feet slammed back into the ice. That wouldn't have been a problem if I was still holding onto my axe. But I wasn't. My arms waved around as I tried to regain my balance. And I realised I was about to fall backwards right when I was trying to be taken seriously by the very infuriatingly attractive man next to me.

Why the fuck is this my life?

FOUR

Thane

As Kit flailed next to me, almost falling backwards in their attempt to stay upright, I couldn't help but wonder what I had done to deserve this hell. Maybe I should let them fall over. Would serve them right for calling me smug and judgy. However, I wasn't that kind of person, regardless of how much I wanted to see Kit grow red with annoyance.

You want what? Absolutely not. I don't have any interest in them.

Reaching out with one hand, I gripped their arm. I dug my ice axe into the snow to free up my other hand to reach around their pack to hold them steady.

It took Kit a few seconds to realise they weren't going to topple over. They wrapped a hand around my arm. The fear in their icy blue eyes made my heart twist.

What the fuck? Why the hell is their expression affecting me like this?

"It's okay, I've got ye," I murmured. "Noo, twist yer feet around like am daeing."

I dug my crampons out of the snow and turned my feet towards them, sticking them back in the snow.

Kit followed my lead. Only then did they let out a breath and bowed their head. Their hair fell down, curtaining their face. I couldn't see their expression any longer. That was probably a good thing.

Their hand tightened around my arm, leading me to believe they weren't okay, or maybe they were reassuring themselves. I couldn't be sure.

"Ye okay?"

"Give me a sec," they said in a hushed voice.

Kit took several deep breaths before they looked up at me through their glasses. The round shape of them and the angle made their eyes look larger than they were. Or maybe it was because they were wide with dilated pupils. The ring of ice around them made me swallow. Why the fuck did they have to have such beautiful eyes? And since when did I start noticing that kind of thing? It made me even more frustrated with them for merely existing and looking the way they did.

"Are people staring?"

Of all the things I expected to come out of their mouth that wasn't it. My gaze darted about. Except for Callan, no one was paying attention to us. Most of them were further up the slope. My friend was looking at me with a smirk, which I really didn't fucking appreciate. Whatever he was thinking, I was pretty sure it could be nothing good.

"No. They're no paying attention tae us."

Callan kept staring. I didn't want to tell Kit about it. For some reason, I wanted to save them the embarrassment. Why I cared was a question I didn't want to look too closely at.

"Thank fuck. If I fell over again, I would've never lived it down."

Dragging my gaze away from Callan and back to Kit took effort.

"Ye guid noo?"

"You mean am I going to stay upright? I think so."

I nodded at their hand gripping my arm.

"Ye sure aboot that?"

Kit snatched their hand back and gave me a dark look.

"Yeah, I am."

I didn't let go of them, concerned they weren't telling me the truth.

"Ye dinnae want me tae help ye tae the bottom?"

"No. I'm fine. Jesus."

They tried to shrug me off, but my hands tightened around them.

What the fuck was my problem when it came to Kit? I didn't know why they kept rubbing me up the wrong way, and yet I wanted to protect them. If they ended up hurting themselves on my watch, I didn't think I would forgive myself.

Let go of them. They said they were fine.

"Pick yer axe up and I'll let ye go."

With a huff, Kit leaned down and gripped their axe, ripping it out of the snow. They looked at me with a raised eyebrow.

"Happy now?"

"Aye."

It took a second, but I finally let them go.

Kit didn't wait for me to get my axe. They twisted and set off up the slope, front pointing the entire way as if trying to prove a point. They wanted me to think they didn't need me. Stubborn wee thing.

I followed behind them at a slower pace to make sure they didn't get spooked or give me hell again. And to be sure they weren't going to fall over.

When I reached the top where Callan was standing with his dark hair glinting in the sun, I let out a sigh. Kit had already made their way back down, practising front pointing in reverse.

"Wipe that fucking smile off yer face," I said as I resisted the urge to shove him for forcing me into this awkward as fuck situation.

"What smile?"

"Ye know what am talking aboot, Callan, dinnae try yer innocent shite on me."

He dipped his head and kept smirking.

"Ye looked like ye were gonnae lose it when they almost toppled over."

"I fucking was. They need tae pay more attention tae what they're deaing."

Kit was more interested in giving me a hard time than doing what they were supposed to.

"Or mibbe ye need tae be nicer tae them."

"I was being nice."

He rubbed his chest and watched Kit doing their level best to show me they were more than capable of practising on their own.

"No, ye were being a grumpy get."

"The fuck I was. Am taking care of them like ye asked. No mah fault they cannae stay on their damn feet."

Callan shook his head.

"Am sure ye were daeing what ye dae best."

"And that is?"

"Pushing people's buttons."

I growled at him before stomping away. The wee fucker was doing my head right in.

First, he partners me up with Kit, who was definitely sent into my life to irritate me. Then he gives me shite for trying to do what he asked. I wasn't *that* abrasive… was I?

I cared about Kit learning the right skills, so when we attempted to summit the mountain, provided the weather held out, they'd be safe. We all needed to be safe. I wouldn't be able to deal with another outcome. Not after what happened with Jenna. Wanting to protect everyone around me because of it wasn't rational. Especially not people I barely knew. But I didn't care for rationality in this respect. I would keep Kit safe. They were in my care now. I didn't shirk my responsibilities no matter how annoyed a person made me.

31

With that thought, I made my way down the slope to where they stood, staring out over the landscape.

"Ye done proving a point?" I asked as I came to a stop next to them and crossed my arms over my chest.

Kit's pretty ice blue eyes were guarded as they glanced at me.

"And what point would that be?"

"Ye can dae it withoot me."

They snorted.

"I think almost falling over proves I can't." They waved their hand around. "Or maybe, just maybe, the blame should be placed at your door for, you know, antagonising me just a little bit."

The fact they had no issues telling it like it was had me struggling to keep a straight face. I wanted to smile, but giving Kit the satisfaction of knowing they got to me wasn't something I was willing to do.

"Am giving ye practice for every eventuality."

They blinked behind those cute fucking round glasses and wrinkled their nose. Why did I find that endearing? They were a menace to my thoughts. I swear they were going to drive me to distraction and for reasons I disliked immensely.

"Huh, so what you're saying is the most dangerous thing out here for me is you. Is that it?"

"Mibbe."

The way they outright laughed at me made my skin itch.

"Oh, you're something else. I'm inclined to agree right now since I'd rather take a tumble down the fucking mountain than spend another minute near you."

They kept laughing.

I scowled and tore my gaze away from them. That mouth would get them in trouble one day. If you looked at Kit, you wouldn't expect them to be the type of person who spoke their mind. Just goes to show you couldn't judge a person by their appearance. Kit might look small and cute, but their mouth could cut you if you weren't careful.

I didn't care what they thought of me. Only that they got through this course accident-free. That was my priority. If it meant putting up with their sharp tongue, then so fucking be it.

"Mibbe I shouldnae have saved ye from making an eejit of yerself," I muttered.

"Ha, as if. Overprotective boar doesn't do you justice. Reckon you couldn't help yourself if I was in danger."

"Aye, and ye should be fucking grateful for it. Ye can barely stay on yer feet for five minutes withoot needing rescuing. Dae ye even have any experience in hillwalking or did ye think ye could wing it oot here? Is it any fucking wonder Callan thought ye needed a babysitter? Am daeing ye a favour by looking oot for ye, so mibbe ye should quit yer fucking complaining and accept mah help or ye'll end up needing airlifting oot of here or worse. These mountains are dangerous for the unprepared. People die. And am here tae make sure ye're no a part of that statistic."

I turned my eyes back to them in time to see their gaping mouth and indignant expression. Internally, I cursed myself because Callan was right about one thing. I did push people's buttons. Usually, they wouldn't push right back, but Kit had been from the moment we met. And I wasn't sure they'd let up now I'd given them a hard time over their attitude towards me.

"I have… some experience."

"Some, aye? No enough clearly."

Kit had the good sense to look away as their face coloured up.

"There's no need to make me feel so stupid for having shit balance, okay? I can't help that."

They said it quietly with embarrassment tingeing their voice. It made me feel bad, but not enough to apologise for it. I wasn't apologetic in the slightest for putting them in their place. Having a blasé attitude out here was a terrible fucking idea.

"And also, I'm not thanking you for saving me."

"Am no expecting thanks."

"Good. I was just making sure since you said I should be grateful, and maybe you hadn't noticed that I am grateful you saved me from the embarrassment of falling over with being all condescending towards me like I'm a child or something."

"Trust me, I know ye're no a child, Kit."

Just looking at them made me feel a lot of things I didn't care to admit to. My eyes roamed over them, regardless. My fingers twitched and my mouth went dry. I didn't like it. Especially the way their face was going redder. It had me wondering why they were staring so hard.

"What?" I asked, confused by their expression.

"Nothing."

"Ye're staring."

"I'm wondering why you have to be such a dick when you have an accent like that."

I tilted my head, genuinely confused by what they were getting at. Were they trying to say they liked how I spoke? That couldn't be the case since it was clear Kit couldn't stand me. Just as well. I couldn't stand them either.

"Am a dick with an accent?"

"You know what, never mind. Not sure you need the ego boost."

Before I could ask further questions, Kit walked away from me. I couldn't help wondering if they were trying to give me a backhanded compliment or if they had a screw loose. Either way, Kit was a problem. A big fucking problem I couldn't wait to be rid of. And it was definitely all Callan's fault that I had this problem to begin with.

FIVE

Kit

As I packed up the necessary kit into my pack for our summit attempt, I cursed my mind for its continual loop of the moment I almost told Thane his accent gave me heart palpitations. It had been him saying my name that had set me off. I don't know why it sounded so delicious coming out of his mouth. My skin grew hot thinking about him whispering it in my ear, his breath washing over my skin and giving me goosebumps. Yeah, I was pretty fucked because his personality was a complete nightmare. No one should look like him and be so rude. It wasn't fair. I already had one fucked up crush on someone who wasn't good for me. I didn't need another.

I could only be glad he hadn't said my name in the past couple of days. It would've made an already awkward situation much worse. I'd been getting better with my winter skills, despite Thane making smart comments about my lack of experience. He'd been overbearing and downright grumpy for the entire course. I was glad today was our last day together, and I never had to see him, his damn muscles or red hair again.

Shut up about his muscles and hair, brain! I know he's attractive as fuck, but we don't like him. He's mean and rude and hot as sin.

I was my own worst enemy for being attracted to someone like him. Instead of letting it show, I gave him shit right back. He deserved it for the way he spoke to me. There was no way he suspected I thought about him at night when I was alone in bed.

At least he had got my mind off Sienna. I could thank him for that. Secretly, of course. Not sure I could live with myself if I gave him any sign that I appreciated him in any way, shape, or form. Especially not when the first thing he did when I walked into the room was look me up and down like I'd got dressed wrong this morning.

"Before you ask, yes, I've brought every single thing on Callan's list for today. And yes, I packed it as per *your* instructions, so I don't need another lecture about how it's important to distribute the weight evenly."

Thane raised one dark auburn eyebrow.

"Oh, and let's not forget bringing extra layers and food because you never know what's going to happen."

He crossed his arms over his chest.

"Thanks to you, my pack is heavier than ever, but I suppose that's the price I have to pay for safety."

He blinked slowly and continued to stare at me without speaking.

"What?" I barked, already exasperated by him and I'd barely been in his presence for a few minutes.

If he had something to say, he should just say it instead of staring at me as if I was completely nuts.

"Are ye done?"

I huffed.

"Yeah, I guess so."

"Yer jumper is on inside oot."

It took a second for me to wrap my brain around what he said. Then I looked down and saw he was right.

"Oh for fuck's sake."

I struggled to get my pack off and dumped it on the floor before stripping out of my jacket and tearing off my jumper. The room was chilly, which made me shiver. I ignored it as I turned my jumper the right way around. Pulling it over my head, I groaned as it got caught on my glasses.

"Why is this my life?" I mumbled.

As I tried to pull the jumper away from my glasses, I felt two hands on my arms, pushing them down to my sides. I froze as Thane carefully pulled my clothes down over my glasses. My face was hot when he came into view. There was a small furrow between his brows as he straightened out my jumper across my chest and stomach. I couldn't speak when he picked up my jacket and helped me into it, followed by my pack. He tightened the straps for me before stepping back with a nod and a small smile playing on his lips.

I think I've died because why the fuck did this man fix my clothes after witnessing me be a clumsy fool yet again?

Every day I spent in Thane's presence, I managed to do something idiotic. I got it out of the way early today, so I could only hope I wouldn't do anything else.

I rubbed my heated cheeks and turned away from him, trying, and failing to regain my composure.

Thane made me feel too many things I shouldn't. There was a need inside me to show him I was capable. It took me longer to get the hang of things, but it didn't mean I couldn't do them. But why did I need him to see that? He was annoying, constantly made me feel stupid and yet... I wanted him to see that I was good at this. Well, as good as someone with terrible balance and coordination could be.

Pity he can't see me with a tattoo gun. He wouldn't think I was such a stupid idiot then.

Maybe I wasn't cut out for winter walking. Probably better off in the tattoo studio I worked at, but I needed my life to be more than my art. I liked the outdoors. I enjoyed walking and the sense of accomplishment that came with summiting a mountain. Not that I had done many of them, but I wanted to do more. This was my opportunity. And I needed something outside of Sienna that was truly mine.

I wouldn't let Thane ruin this for me. Not when the past four days had been restorative for me. There was something about exhausting yourself physically. The bone-deep ache of tiredness that couldn't be fixed by anything but sleep. I needed that badly, despite my brain fixating on Thane at night like he was the only man on earth. It was better than crying over Sienna. I'd take his grumpy arse any day compared to wallowing in misery.

When I finally looked at Thane again, he wasn't paying attention to me. He stared at something across the room with narrowed eyes.

I let myself take him in. His hair was up in a bun with his side braids tucked into it. I wondered if the short hairs of his undercut would be soft if I touched them. Then I threw that thought away. What the fuck was it about him that had me all twisted in knots? I didn't know what to do with my wayward imagination other than to tell it to get fucked.

My eyes roamed down his body, noting he was in all black apart from the small touches of green on the zips of his jacket and pack. Speaking of his pack, it was the largest I'd seen him wear. We were only going out on a day trip, so it seemed slightly excessive for the occasion.

"Are you carrying a dead body in that or something?" I asked.

Thane's head whipped around. His green eyes landed on me with confusion and annoyance written all over his face.

"What?"

"Well, we're only going out for the day." I waved at his back. "Is whatever you have in there necessary?"

Before Thane had a chance to say a word, Callan slapped a hand on his shoulder. I hadn't noticed him coming up to us.

"Dinnae mind Thane and his constant need tae be over-prepared for anything. Have told him a thousand times he doesnae need tae bring his whole kit up the mountain. This one doesnae listen tae a word I say."

Thane's scowl had me folding my lips into my mouth so I wouldn't laugh.

"Shut yer mooth."

"Am just saying ye should lighten yer load. Carrying the weight of the world on yer shoulders isnae gonnae help anyone."

Callan gave me a wink before he wandered off without waiting for Thane's response.

"Am gonnae throw him off the side of the fucking mountain."

Thane's words were mumbled as if he hoped I wouldn't hear him say them.

"Glad I'm not number one on your shit list today or I might end up in a body bag like whoever that poor sod in your pack is."

He glared at me and pursed his lips.

"Ye can keep yer mooth shut tae."

"You'd get bored if I did that."

He huffed and rubbed his fingers across his forehead, clearly frustrated by everything and everyone.

"Ye can make jokes all ye fucking want, Kit. Am no letting ye die today even if ye decide no tae stay on yer damn feet."

Damn him for saying my name.

I locked my knees to prevent myself from melting into a puddle of goo on the floor. Thane might be a grumpy shit, but his protective instincts were endearing. They were his redeeming feature that kept me from writing him off as a complete prick who wasn't worth any of my time.

"My hero."

The sarcasm dripping from my voice wasn't lost on Thane. He dropped his hand and gave me the dirtiest look imaginable.

"Am gonnae be fucking glad tae be rid of ye after today."

"The feeling is mutual."

Is it though?

Thane let out a breath before he adjusted the straps on his pack and fiddled with something in his jacket. He thrust a hand out to me a moment later.

"Zip yer jacket up and put this on."

In his hand was a dark grey beanie.

My eyes darted up to his face, wondering what the hell was going on.

"Why?"

"Ye complained aboot how cold yer head was yesterday. Ye can borrow this for today."

My heart was in my fucking mouth. I couldn't look away from him with my absolute confusion at the gesture. It hadn't occurred to me he was listening when I grumbled about the cold. The wind whipping my hair around had driven me crazy.

"Just fucking take it, Kit."

He waved it at me. I reached out and grabbed it. My fingers brushed against his rough ones. It made me wonder what he did for a living with hands like that.

42

"Thank you," I whispered, staring down at the beanie like it was the most precious thing I'd ever been given.

Why are you so happy about this? You're ridiculous, you know that, right? He did one nice thing and now you're a puddle at his feet. Get a grip!

Before I could internally scold myself further, Thane took it out of my hands and slid it on my head, tugging it down over my hair to keep it in place. Then he zipped my jacket up for me as if I couldn't do it myself. Apparently, he was determined to ensure I was properly kitted out today.

"There. Ye can give it back later. Just dinnae lose it."

"Wait, this is yours?"

"Aye."

My hand went to the beanie, fingers brushing over the soft weave. He wore this and was okay with sharing it with me.

"I… I'll take care of it."

Thane's cheeks darkened, and he looked at the ground. Another point for his redeeming features. He listened and found solutions without being asked for them. He cared in his own way. And that was almost too much for me to take.

"See that ye dae."

He looked up at me again. The tension in the air was almost stifling. I didn't know what to think or say, and he didn't either.

"All right. Are we ready tae go?" came Callan's voice from across the room, disrupting the moment.

There were general murmurs of agreement. I nodded without speaking since my throat felt all tight.

43

"Aye, right. Let's get moving."

Everyone started filing out. I followed Thane, whose cheeks were still red, but he had a stoic expression as if he didn't want to acknowledge his sweet gesture towards me. I decided not to give him a hard time about it. Wouldn't do me any good to be on his bad side. We had quite the day ahead of us. I wanted to show Thane that I'd learned enough to be safe during the mountain ascent, so he wouldn't have a reason to give me any shit.

Or maybe you just want to impress him, so he looks at you differently.

Brain... do one!

If I could keep my damn thoughts under control, then maybe today would go better than the very low expectations I had. Because a lot of things could go wrong with the very strong possibility of the weather turning. Callan had warned everyone about it the day before. And I just had to hope everything went to plan for all our sakes.

SIX

Thane

My skin itched, but I refused to look at Kit. They'd been staring at me since I gave them my beanie for the day. I wasn't trying to be nice, merely practical. If I had to listen to them complaining the whole day, it would do my head in. They already irritated the fuck out of me without that.

The past couple of days hadn't made things any better between us. They tested my patience at every turn, making me question why I was here in the first place.

I was only on the course as a favour to Callan. I didn't have to be here. My conscience wouldn't let me quit. Our friendship was more important to me than the mild inconvenience of being stuck with Kit. Well, it wasn't exactly mild, but I was trying to remain positive about things. It was our last day. I wouldn't have to see them again after this.

We were about an hour into our trek across the glen towards the base of the mountain. It wasn't accessible by road. We'd left early since, at this time of year, the daylight hours were limited. Not to mention the sun was hiding behind the cloud cover. It made everything duller and darker, but I didn't mind so much. The weather could be temperamental at any time of year around here. We often got four seasons in one day, especially in winter.

"You never answered my question about whether you're carrying around a dead body."

I gritted my teeth. Kit wasn't going to drop the subject of my pack, clearly. I didn't have to explain anything to them, but I was getting sick of them insinuating I carried around dead people on the regular.

"No, am no a killer."

"Okay. What do you do then? You never told me."

I wasn't one for sharing personal information about myself with strangers. Particularly not ones who had a habit of pushing my buttons. However, I had learned with Kit it was better to tell them what they wanted to know. Otherwise, they would pester me for hours and I couldn't abide by that.

"Forestry. I work in forestry."

"So you manage the woodlands?"

"Aye."

I preferred the outdoors to sitting inside all day. Staying active helped keep my dark thoughts at bay, at least during the day. Besides, the preservation of our forests, especially the ancient ones like the Rothiemurchus and Abernethy Forests near where I lived, was important.

"You know, that's exactly the type of thing I imagined you doing."

"Oh aye, and why's that?"

I finally turned to Kit. I wasn't sure if their red cheeks were from embarrassment or the cold.

"Well, you just…"

"I just what?"

"Look fit and stuff. Like you work out or something."

My feet almost came to a standstill at the realisation Kit had checked me out. Self-consciousness had me dipping my head so they wouldn't see my reaction. Maybe their assessment of me had been entirely innocent. It couldn't be anything else. Kit didn't like me. I was sure of that much.

It didn't stop my face from getting warm at the thought of their eyes roaming over me.

What is wrong with you? You don't like this person. Yes, Kit is cute as fuck and seeing them in my beanie is not helping me at all, but I don't like them.

"I dinnae dae anything but work and hillwalking."

"Fair enough."

I caught Kit's grin as they adjusted the beanie. My beanie. *Fuck.*

I had to get my head on straight. Giving them the beanie was a mistake.

"How are ye two getting along back here?" came Callan's voice.

He'd slowed down to check on us since Kit and I were at the back of the group. There was a twinkle in his brown eyes that had me tensing up.

"We're guid," I barked, wanting to dissuade him of any ideas knocking around in his head about me and Kit.

"Kit?"

"Like he said, we're good," they responded with a shrug.

"No finding the pace tae much?"

Kit gave Callan a bright smile. The fact they smiled that way at him when they never did to me was infuriating. Then again, the fact I cared about it pissed me off even more.

"Nope. If I walked any slower, Thane would complain. Got to keep up with Mr Taskmaster over here," they waved at me, "Or I'll never hear the end of it."

Callan chuckled and shook his head.

"Aye. He likes things done a certain way, right, Thane?"

These two needed to quit ganging up on me. I was sick to death of Callan's looks and insinuating words. What the fuck did he think was happening here? I was doing my best to keep Kit alive. That was it.

He should know fucking better. Jenna's death was still too raw. Being with someone else wasn't even on my radar. It didn't matter that she was gone. I couldn't think of anyone else that way. Not with the guilt eating me alive, and my heart in fucking tatters on the floor.

"Did ye need something else, Callan?" I asked, not bothering to hide the irritation in my voice.

"No. Am just making sure ye're keeping up."

And just like that, he quick walked towards the front of the group again, leaving me with a few choice words for my best friend that were not for Kit's ears.

"Have you and Callan known each other long?"

My eyes darted to Kit, who was watching Callan's back.

"Aye, oor parents have lived next door tae each other all oor lives."

"He's kind of like family, then."

I nodded slowly. Callan was the only person I had left, but Kit didn't need to know that. They didn't need to know anything about me, so why was I answering all their questions?

"Ye could say that. What aboot ye?"

Why the fuck did you ask that?

"Me? There's just my dad and my younger brother."

"Did yer mother pass away?"

Again, why are you asking them questions?

Kit wrinkled their nose. It was an endearing habit of theirs.

"No. She's very much alive."

They fiddled with the straps of their pack and stared off into the distance.

The snowy landscape was beautiful. I always appreciated the mountains in the winter. Like the hills, the evergreen pine trees were covered in a light dusting of white. It was peaceful in the frozen wilderness, reminding me I still had things to live for, even if some days I didn't know why being alive was so important.

"But she's dead to me, if that makes sense," Kit finished finally with a sigh.

Prying into what happened with her mother would make Kit question my intentions, no doubt. I left it there. It was fucked up that I had asked them anything in the first place. I had no plans of getting know them further.

"I have an older sister and three nieces."

Why did you tell them that?

"You're an uncle?"

"Aye. I dinnae see them much. They live in Stornoway."

Kit looked thoughtful at my admission.

"Olly moved to Manchester when he turned eighteen, so I don't see him often either. Dad still lives in Seaford. That's where I grew up. Sometimes I wish I'd left too." Their mouth turned down, and they looked lost for a moment. "But I'm sure you don't want to know that, so I'll just shut up now."

Kit put on a smile that didn't meet their blue eyes. Instead, there was a deep sadness in those icy depths. One that made my heart jerk in my chest. The sensation disconcerted me so much that I kept my mouth firmly shut and didn't tell them I was glad they revealed something about themselves to me.

By the time we reached the bottom of the mountain and took a break before starting our ascent, I'd asked myself a million times why I appreciated knowing more about Kit. There was no reason for me to understand them. Their safety was my only priority. At least, it should be. But it wasn't. And I hated myself for that.

50

Kit said nothing as they put their crampons on, and we all started off up the slope. They were clearly lost in thought, and there I was, thinking things I shouldn't be.

What was it about the thought of home that made them so sad?

Why didn't they speak to their mother?

Why had they come on this course?

And why the fuck did they enjoy winding me up so much?

None of those questions would be answered. I wasn't willing to voice them. Kit couldn't know I had any interest in them or who they were.

It didn't bother me to walk in relative silence, but my concern about why Kit was so quiet did. I tried to concentrate on the terrain and keep my footing, but my gaze kept drifting over to them. Running over their expression to garner any imperceptible change in them that would clue me into their melancholic mood. It affected mine. I couldn't stop thinking about how much I missed Jenna. Waking up alone every day was grating on me. I'd been with her for fourteen years, almost half my life. She'd been in it for longer than that, but we only got together when we were sixteen.

No one tells you how difficult it was to go from being with someone every day to having no one. How empty your life would feel without that constant presence. And how no one can replace it because you won't let anyone else in. You can't. Not when the memory of what you had lingers. When you weren't prepared to live without them. When it gets so hard to breathe because grief and loss are choking you from the inside out. People tell you time heals all wounds, but they lied. Or maybe it hadn't been long enough.

The only thing I knew was that I couldn't move beyond this. I was stuck in the past, living with the ghost of my dead wife, haunting me every passing second of each day. And that was why I came out here. To feel alive again. To remind myself that I was here, and I had to keep going even if she wasn't. Too fucking bad it wasn't working.

When I shook myself out of those dark ruminations, my head tipped up to the sky. The clouds had darkened significantly since we started. The wind was colder and whipping around our bodies, making it harder to walk. Especially as we were out on a ridge that had no cover.

Our pace was slow going for the next hour. There were murmurs of concern amongst the group about the conditions. I had my own worries about the situation. The wind hadn't died down at all, and a gentle snowfall had begun.

Callan brought our group to a halt roughly an hour away from the summit. He and Ruairí had a long, hushed conversation with each other. They were thinking of turning back. The snow was getting worse and if we didn't get back down the mountain, we could end up in difficulty.

Kit jumped from foot to foot next to me, trying to keep the cold at bay. They'd put an extra layer on a while back, but it was fucking baltic up here. Even I was feeling it.

"Is it usually this windy up here?" Kit asked me a moment later.

"Can be. Have never been up this way in these conditions before."

"Oh great. That fills me with so much confidence."

I snorted.

"We'll be fine."

"You sure about that?"

"Reckon we're gonnae turn back, so I can only hope we make it back doon."

Kit grimaced and rubbed their cold cheeks with their gloved hands.

"You think they'd let us take a break before we leave?"

I shook my head. Their mouth turned down. They hadn't told me they were struggling despite my being very clear about them letting me know when they needed help.

Callan came over to me to explain the plan. They decided we should head back down before conditions deteriorated further.

I eyed Kit as Callan and Ruairí told the rest of the group. They didn't look so good.

"Come here."

Kit moved closer and let out a wee yelp when I tucked them into my side to shield them from the wind. They looked up at me from underneath my arm.

"Thane, I'm not sure I can start back yet. That was hard going, you know. I thought I was going to fall over several times."

I should have been paying more attention to Kit. They were my responsibility, and I hadn't been doing a very good job of keeping an eye on them today.

"Let me have a word with Callan."

I beckoned him over. Callan's expression was cautious as he arrived next to me.

"We need tae get going," he said before I could get a word in.

"Am gonnae stay here with Kit. There's some shelter amongst those rocks up ahead. They cannae get back doon withoot a breather. And I cannae leave them up here alone. We'll hold everyone else up if we keep going."

Callan looked between us before he nodded slowly.

"Aye, right."

I knew my way back down the mountain. I wasn't going to let anything happen to Kit.

We talked more about the plan and what I would do if we got in trouble, and then he gave me a slap on the back.

"Ye keep them safe."

"Ye know I will."

He gave me a tired smile before he went to gather up the group and let Ruairí know what was happening.

I tugged Kit towards the shelter of the rocks I'd pointed out to Callan. Making them take their pack off, I set mine down too.

Kit took a seat on a rock and bowed their head. I sat beside them, keeping the wind off them, and dug into my pack, bringing out a thermos. I handed it to them.

"Drink some of this."

Kit took it without complaint. Their eyes lit up after they took a sip.

"Is this hot chocolate?"

"Aye."

They smiled and handed it to me, so I could have some too. Sugar and warmth were much needed right then. And the hope that once Kit had a rest, we could make our way down. The weather wasn't getting any better. It would be hard going, and we'd have to rely on each other. I didn't know if that was going to end in disaster or not. Guess we would just have to wait and see.

SEVEN

Kit

The last thing I expected was for Thane to insist we took a break and let the rest of the group make their way back down. The weather had got steadily worse for the past few hours. A lot of the group had been determined to keep going, regardless. They wanted to make it up to the summit. I hadn't felt the same way.

The wind speed and the snow were making it tough to walk. I relied heavily on my ice axe to stay upright.

Thane was lost in thought for a long time and hadn't noticed my struggle. My need to prove I could do this stopped me from telling him I needed a rest. That I wasn't sure I could go on. Stupid, really. I wasn't normally this stubborn. Thane brought out qualities I didn't know I possessed. At least I was standing up for myself around him. I rarely did that with Sienna.

Don't think about her. You're up a mountain. You came here to forget not to dwell on your fucked up friendship with Sienna.

"Ye ready tae get moving?" Thane asked, pulling me out of my musings.

I rubbed my hands over my thighs.

"I guess so."

I wasn't, but I knew we couldn't stay up here for much longer. Despite my warm clothing, it was freezing cold, my lungs ached, and I wanted to be anywhere but on that mountain.

Thane stood up and put his hand out to me. I placed my gloved hand in his, letting him pull me upright. We got our packs back on. I continued to wonder what was in his but refrained from asking. The noise of the wind made it difficult to hear each other without shouting.

With my ice axe in one hand, I set off ahead of Thane, following in the fading footsteps of the group. It was slow going. The wind was blowing the snow into us as we descended backwards down a slope, using our crampons to front point. My concentration was on my feet to make sure I stepped right.

As I reached the bottom right before where we would have to go across the ridge, I heard a loud noise that was a bit like thunder. I looked to my right and saw an enormous cloud of snow sliding down the mountain barely a few feet away.

"Oh fuck."

Two hands grabbed me and dragged me backwards. I barely kept my footing as Thane pulled me away from the falling snow. And I fell into him a moment later. He let out a grunt and tumbled into the snow, tugging me with him. I collided with his body as he hit the ground. The next thing I knew, he rolled me to the side and covered me protectively, holding onto me like both our lives depended on it.

The rumbling sound of the snow tumbling down the mountain was deafening when combined with the howling wind. I clutched Thane's jacket, burying my face in his chest to hide from the disaster happening next to us. I had no idea if we were going to get caught in it or not. And that was the most terrifying part.

After what felt like hours but could have only been minutes, the sound died down. I pulled my face away from Thane's chest. He had his head turned towards the ridge and was watching the snow make its way further down the mountain.

"Was… was that an avalanche?"

Callan had given us training about avalanches during the course. I never expected one to happen right next to us. He hadn't mentioned there were any warnings about avalanches in the area, but then again, the forecast hadn't been entirely accurate either. Snow wasn't on the cards, but here we were stuck in a blizzard.

Thane turned his gaze towards me slowly. There was a grave expression on his face. It made me shiver.

"Aye."

The finality of that one word made my throat tight. If we left any sooner, it would have caught us. There had only been a few feet between me and the ridge. Thane saved my fucking life by keeping me away from it. The realisation made me dip my head back into his chest and let out a sound of distress. Thane, to his credit, held me while I shook in his embrace and tried to regain my composure.

I could have died. Fuck. Fuck!

"We need tae get up, Kit."

I nodded, loosening my hold on him as he pulled away. He got up to a kneeling position first, his eyes darting around us before pushing himself up to standing. I let him tug me to my feet, digging my crampons into the snow to keep steady.

Thane rubbed his face with one hand and squinted at the ridge. I brushed off the snow clinging to my clothes, waiting for him to say something.

"We cannae go that way."

"No?"

"Tae dangerous noo."

I could barely see across the ridge with the snow coming down, but I didn't trust it after the avalanche. In fact, I didn't trust anything about this fucking mountain at that point. The weather and the cold had me wishing it didn't exist.

"What are we going to do, then?"

There was no way I could navigate us out of this. Thane had all the experience. He promised Callan he would keep me safe. And I believed him. He wouldn't let me or his friend down.

Thane didn't immediately respond. I didn't push him. He needed time to think about our next steps. Instead, I glanced around and tried not to imagine what would have happened if we had been in the avalanche's path. And I really fucking hoped the rest of the group hadn't got caught in it. I decided it would be better not to voice that concern to Thane right then. We were already in enough trouble ourselves without worrying about what had happened to them.

A moment later, Thane reached around and unclipped a small bag from his pack. Unzipping it, he dug out a map in a clear sleeve to keep it dry and studied it for several minutes. Then he looked around before staring down at the paper. He let out a huff, shoving it back in the small bag and clipping that to his pack again.

"We have tae take another route doon."

He didn't exactly look confident as he said it.

"Is there a problem with that way?"

"Aye, but ye let me worry aboot that."

His words didn't fill me with confidence. I had no choice but to trust him. He was my only way out of this situation.

"Okay."

He nodded and pointed back up the slope we just come down. I followed him this time. Thane kept looking back to check that I was okay.

My legs hurt after hours of walking and the cold was seeping into my bones, but I didn't stop or complain about it. Judging by Thane's lack of confidence in the route we were taking, I imagined it would be a long time before we made it back.

He told you not to worry, but how can you do anything but? This is bad. Really fucking bad.

My eyes were firmly on Thane, watching each step he took and doing everything he did. There was no way I wanted to give him any further cause to be concerned about me. I might be flagging, but I could do this. I had to. The only way out of the situation was through it.

We didn't speak much as we made our way up further towards the summit. Thane took a sharp left at the rocks we'd sat on to take our break. As I couldn't see much further than his back, I had no idea what we were in for.

A little while later, he put his arm out to stop me in my tracks. His gaze darted over to me, but mine was on the sheer drop a few feet in front of us. I couldn't see the bottom because of the weather and the cloud cover. It scared the absolute shit out of me. I could have walked into that if he hadn't stopped us.

"I need tae get a rope oot mah pack tae tether us together," Thane shouted at me above the wind and snow.

I didn't like the sound of that.

He didn't wait for my response. Thane hauled his pack off, removing the waterproof cover from it. I shivered as he dug through his pack, bringing out a rope and a few carabiners.

What the hell else does he have in there?

There'd been no training with ropes on the course since we weren't doing any climbing. Callan hadn't been joking when he said Thane was over-prepared for anything. I didn't think that was such a bad thing under the circumstances.

Thane attached us together using the rope and carabiners and made sure we were both secure. It made me nervous as fuck about what was coming next, but I said nothing.

"Ye'll need yer axe for this bit and watch yer footing."

"Is this the part you were concerned about?"

He grimaced.

"One of them."

"That fills me with so much confidence."

"The rope will take yer weight if ye fall."

And now I wanted to scream.

"You better be joking."

If I didn't think we were fucked before, his expression made me pretty sure we were now.

"Am no joking."

"I'm going to pretend you didn't say that."

"The rope is a precaution, Kit. Am trying tae keep ye safe."

"Yeah, yeah, let's just get going before I freak out."

Thane squeezed my arm before releasing me and turning to our right. It was then I saw where he intended to take us. I swallowed, forcing my feet to move towards the ledge that wrapped around the mountain with the sheer drop to our left.

"You have got to be kidding me," I muttered.

Thane didn't hear me as he stepped onto it. I kept close, not wanting to find myself dangling down the side of this mountain with only Thane to hold me up. I mimicked him as he dug his axe into the side of the mountain to hold steady against the snow coming down.

"Is there not a safer way?" I called out to him.

"If we're gonnae get doon the mountain intae the glen before it gets dark, then ye have tae trust me when I tell ye this is the fastest route."

But not the safest.

The whole way along the ledge, I tried not to look off the edge. Keeping my eyes on Thane helped me get through it. He was sure and steady in his steps. Being tethered to him by the rope gave me more reassurance than I thought it would. He would save me if anything bad happened. I worried about myself given my lack of coordination and balance, but somehow, we made it across without incident.

Thane took out his map and studied it again while I caught my breath and celebrated the small win. Score one for us.

The snow hadn't let up at all. The sky darkened further during our trek across the ledge. Without asking Thane, I got out my head torch and attached it to my helmet. I'd put it on over the top of the beanie he gave me before we started our ascent for safety.

Thane put the map away and rubbed his face with his hand. His expression remained guarded, but his unease was evident in his demeanour.

"Am gonnae be honest with ye. I dinnae know if it's best tae keep going or stay put until the weather clears up."

"It doesn't look like it will anytime soon."

He nodded and sighed.

"Aye. That's why I wannae get further doon the slope."

"Then we keep going."

"Are ye sure ye're okay tae?"

I shrugged. The prospect of being stuck on the side of the mountain was far worse than the exhaustion I felt.

"It's freezing cold, I'm tired, but I want to get off this mountain so badly, I'll do anything to make it happen. Take of that what you will."

Thane closed his eyes for a long moment, rubbing the bridge of his nose with his gloved fingers. When he dropped his hand, he opened his green eyes and gave me a half-smile.

"We'll keep the rope on. Visibility is shite. I dinnae want us getting separated."

"No complaints from me."

If I had my way, I would wrap myself around him to make sure I didn't get lost, but that wouldn't be practical at all. Also, I didn't think he would appreciate me hanging off him like a limpet. It didn't matter if I wanted to soak up all his warmth to ward off the chill. We had a job to do. To get down this mountain. And the only way to do that was to keep going.

"Then let's get moving."

So I followed Thane down the slope, knowing it would take all my energy reserves to make it out of here in one piece with the hours of walking we had left to go.

EIGHT

Thane

In all the times I'd walked in the winter, there had never been an occasion when conditions had been quite this dire. Our progress down the mountain was far slower than I wanted it to be.

I'd only taken this route once before in the summer months. The landscape didn't look the same covered in snow with a blizzard surrounding us. I had a hard time navigating us through it. Of course, my phone had GPS, but it was spotty as fuck up here where we had no signal. The bad weather made it infinitely worse, so there was no point in me attempting to use it.

I'd learned how to navigate with a map when I was young, but this was testing all of my skills. Especially since I had to keep an eye on Kit at the same time.

To Kit's credit, they were being quite the trouper, but I could tell they were exhausted. In all honesty, I was too. The walk up the mountain had taken it out of me. I was using my almost depleted reserves to get us out of this.

It was hard not to let Kit see the extent of my tiredness. They were relying on me. I had to be the strong one for both of us. I told them earlier I wouldn't let them die out here, and I intended to keep to my word.

When we finally made it down into a glen sandwiched between two mountains, the sun had long set, and we were navigating by the light of our head torches. It was on the opposite side of the mountain we needed to be. However, I had no other choice but to take us down this way.

A part of me knew we might have to stop and stay here until morning, but the need to push on to get Kit somewhere warm and dry drove me forward.

My plan was to cross the stream less than a few metres ahead of us and then take a break. We could eat something, regain our strength, and reassess our situation.

I paused when we reached it, bringing Kit to a halt beside me. They eyed the water with scepticism written all over their features. The water level was higher than I'd seen it in the summer, and it was flowing quite fast. What was usually a stream now looked more like a small river.

"Are you going to tell me we have to cross this?" they asked, looking up at me with wide eyes.

Kit had taken their glasses off a while ago because the snow was making it too wet to see. It meant they had to stick a lot closer to me since they told me they were short-sighted.

"Aye."

They let out a sigh and scrunched up their face.

"Well, that's just great."

We were running out of time, energy, and options. This was the only route we could take if we had any chance of getting close enough to civilisation to get ourselves out of this.

"Here, ye see those rocks." I pointed out several large ones sticking out of the stream. "We'll use those tae cross."

Kit squinted their eyes at them.

"I need my glasses."

I nodded and waited for them to extract their frames from a pocket in their jacket. Kit slid them on their face and eyed the stream again.

"They don't look very stable."

"We take it slow. Ye go first and I'll follow."

We remained tethered together. I didn't want to take the rope off for fear we'd lose each other in the blizzarding snow. It had slightly lessened now we were on a lower elevation, but it was making visibility poor and our journey far more perilous.

Kit visibly steeled themselves and stepped out onto the first rock. Their leg stretched out to the next one. They put their arms out to balance themselves as they brought their other leg across.

When they got to the next rock, I stepped onto the first one. They were wet, which made them slightly slippery. Neither of us had bothered to take our crampons off since we would have to put them back on again when we reached the other side. It made balancing more difficult.

I did my best to hold steady as I hopped from rock to rock after Kit. They made it onto the other bank with relative ease. They put their arms up in the air in celebration.

"Thank fuck for that."

I smiled for the first time in hours at their relief.

As I stepped to the next rock, my foot slipped. It twisted around unnaturally. The pain shot up my leg, causing me to let out a yell as my balance failed and I toppled over into the stream.

The moment I hit the freezing cold water was like having a blast of ice to the face. It was a complete shock to the system, leaving me stunned in the deeper-than-expected water.

"Thane!"

Kit's voice echoed around my skull, followed by the jerk of the rope around my body when it went taut. It kick-started my brain back into gear. I flailed in the water for a moment before feeling the rope tugging against me. Whipping my head around, I found Kit dragging themselves backwards across the snow to pull me out of the water.

"Thane!" they screamed again.

I pushed at the freezing cold water with all my might, trying to swim against the current towards them. It took some effort for them to drag me close to the edge. Then they ran towards me, grabbing a hold of my hand and pulling me up onto the bank.

I coughed, spitting out the icy water that had got in my mouth and tried to catch my breath.

"Jesus Christ, are you okay?"

Kit squatted down next to me and put their hand on my shoulder.

I looked up into their terrified expression and shivered.

"Am cold."

"I should think so, considering you just fell into a stream. Fuck. I thought I was going to lose you."

"Am… am still here."

They nodded slowly, then stood, and put their hand out to me.

I was so fucking cold and wet, I barely had any time to assess what had happened to me.

Taking their hand, I let them pull me to my feet. My ankle immediately buckled under me. The pain was so intense that I thought I might blackout.

Kit tucked themselves under my shoulder to keep me upright. Their eyes were on my feet.

"Did you get hurt?"

"I think I twisted mah ankle."

They let out a long breath before curling an arm around the bottom of my pack, allowing me to lean on them. My arm went around their shoulder.

"Thane, I hate to break it to you, but you're soaking wet and I'm pretty sure if you stay in those clothes, you're going to get hypothermia. But if we take them off now, you're going to be bare to the elements and that's going to make it worse, so I have no fucking clue what to suggest."

My body shook, so I knew what they were saying had merit. I was just having a hard time concentrating on a solution.

"There's... there's camping equipment in mah pack."

"That's what you've been carrying around?"

I nodded and closed my eyes, trying to ward off the pain in my ankle.

"Okay. Let me take that off and get it out."

My eyes popped open. I looked around us. We were far too close to the water. That wasn't safe.

"No, no here. Have tae... tae move away from the water."

My teeth chattered as I spoke.

"Okay. What about over there, near those trees?"

Kit pointed towards something in the distance. I blinked in an attempt to focus my eyes on it.

"Aye... but no right under the trees. Dinnae want the... the snow falling from the branches on tae the... on tae the tent."

Kit nodded before adjusting their hold on me.

"Let's go. Lean on me as much as you need."

The walk towards the trees was slow going. I was hard-pressed to keep my footing. Every time I put weight on my bad ankle, I grunted from the pain. I dealt with it. There was no other choice.

When Kit finally drew us to a stop, I was barely holding on. My brain felt fuzzy, and my movements were sluggish.

Kit made me sit in the snow before tugging my pack off my back and dragging it around my front. Then they fiddled with the carabiners that were holding the rope attaching us together. Kit removed the rope from around me, so we were no longer tethered. They slid their own pack off their shoulders as they straightened and pointed to my backpack.

"You need to show me what's what."

I could barely move my fingers to pull off the waterproof cover.

Kit shook their head and did it for me before opening up my pack. They dug their hands in and pulled out a long bag.

"Tent?"

I stared at the green bag for a moment, trying to remember what the tent bag looked like before nodding slowly.

Kit stood up and got the contents out. I couldn't do anything other than watch them struggle in the snowstorm with the tent poles. My body was slowly going numb from the cold. My limbs felt stiff, and my teeth wouldn't stop clacking together.

My eyes were drooping by the time they got the tent pitched. They used their boots to stamp the pegs into the ground through the snow and got the tent secured, all without my help.

"I'm going to need you to keep your eyes open, Thane. We have to get those clothes off you."

I nodded again, but I didn't really register what they'd said or that they were rifling through my pack.

"Okay, I take it this is the sleeping mat and bag."

They didn't wait for me to respond, disappearing inside the tent for a while. When they returned, I stared up at them without really seeing them.

"Come on, time to get up."

Kit pulled at me. I tried to move, but it was a struggle.

"Am I going to have to drag you into the tent?"

"Am… am trying."

I caught Kit rolling their eyes before they circled me, took hold of my jacket at my shoulders, and tugged me, dragging me through the snow in a circle to spin me around. Then I found myself pulled backwards towards the tent. Pain shot through my ankle, jolting me out of my dazed state.

"Fuck," I growled, shaking my head to clear my mind.

"Glad to hear you're still alive."

I wanted to protest, but Kit stopped and rounded me again.

"Get into the tent."

Placing both hands behind me, I dragged myself backwards. I lifted myself up into the inner part before my arms gave out.

Kit moved into the small antechamber, dragging both of our packs in, and dumping them down before they knelt on the groundsheet in front of me.

"Unzip your jacket," they demanded as they went to work on the laces of my boots.

They got them off me in record time while I struggled to get my gloves off. They pulled my socks off and eyed my ankle with a concerned look. Then they crawled up my legs and took over for me, tugging my gloves from my fingers. It was all I could do to watch them unzip my jacket and move my arms to help them take it off. They unclipped my helmet and removed my head torch, chucking that into the tent to give us more light in there.

"Do you have extra clothes in your pack?"

"Aye… somewhere."

My mind was all scrambled, so I couldn't tell them where I'd put my extras.

Kit nodded slowly and moved over to my pack, digging through it until they found a blue dry bag. I had a pair of thermal layers and underwear in it for emergencies.

They returned to me and unzipped my fleece, throwing that in a pile with my jacket. Then they made me put my arms up to take off my shirt, followed by my thermal layer, leaving my chest bare.

I shivered harder in the exposed icy air. Before I could say a word, Kit was unbuckling my belt and unzipping my waterproof trousers. They were careful of my ankle when they removed them from my legs. Next came my thermal layer. I stopped them when they reached for my damp boxers.

"What… what are ye daeing?"

"Taking these off."

"Am no getting naked in front of ye."

Kit let out an exasperated sigh.

"Listen here. I couldn't give two fucks about seeing what you're packing right now. I'm more concerned about keeping you alive, but if you want your dick to freeze off, then by all means, stay in your wet boxers."

They can't see me like this. What the hell would Jenna think? I can't do that to her.

"No, ye cannae see me," I mumbled. "Only mah wife has seen me naked, and ye're no her."

Kit blinked at my statement. I didn't know why. All I could concentrate on was keeping them from seeing me in the buff. It wasn't right.

When I continued to hold them off, Kit breathed deeply and turned away to dig into their own pack. They threw a ribbed towel across my crotch.

"There, that'll hide everything. Now, please take them off so I can put you in dry clothes before your temperature drops even further."

The concern in their expression had me obeying. Pushing myself up, I tugged my boxers down past where the towel was covering me. Kit did the rest, getting them off my legs and over my sore ankle.

"Right, get inside properly and we'll dress you, okay?"

Pulling myself backwards while holding onto the towel was difficult, but I managed it as I settled next to where Kit had laid out the sleeping bag on top of the mat. I noted they'd pumped it up since it was an inflatable one.

When they came into the inner part of the tent, they'd stripped out of their boots and jacket. Kit zipped us in before kneeling at my feet and helping me into dry underwear and a thermal layer. I put my arms up for them to tug the top layer over my head. Then Kit got me into the sleeping bag, zipping it up and pulling the drawstring around the hood tight.

"You're going to stay there until you're warm again. I'm just going to organise things in here."

I didn't have it in me to respond. My body continued to shake from the cold despite being in dry clothes and wrapped up in a sleeping bag. It was designed for the coldest of conditions.

I heard Kit moving around in the tent, but I couldn't open my eyes to watch them.

"It's… it's so cold," I groaned, my teeth chattering again.

A hand slid over my forehead.

"Fuck, your skin is freezing. Hold on, don't pass out on me."

"I cannae… cannae stop shaking."

The hand left me and there was some shuffling next to me.

"Shh, it's okay, Thane. I'm going to get you warm."

The sound of a zipper followed by a rush of cold had me trembling harder. Then a solid form wrapped itself around me before something else covered us. The zipper noise came again. Whatever was on top of me rubbed my arms and settled down after a minute. A hand gently touched my chest, and a head leaned against my shoulder.

I cracked my eyes open the best I could, staring down at the dark brown head of hair directly in my line of sight.

"I've got you, Thane. You're going to be okay," came Kit's voice.

I had to be out of it because there was no way in hell Kit would have climbed into the sleeping bag with me. They didn't like me. I didn't like them.

That was the very last thought I had before my consciousness gave out and darkness took me under.

NINE

Thane

*C*oming back to awareness was like climbing out of a thick layer of mud, slow going and sticky. I felt my body being weighed down and my ankle throbbed with pain. But I no longer felt cold. I wasn't shivering.

I wiggled my fingers and found they weren't numb. A good sign. I was alive after falling into that fucking freezing cold water. That was something.

"Thane?" came a tired voice that was far closer than I expected.

My eyes flicked open to find it was pitch black. Something moved on top of me.

"Are you awake?"

The gears in my brain started to engage and register there was a body on top of me. A warm, very much alive body that felt good against me, which was an incredibly fucked up thing to be thinking under the circumstances. My focus should be on why the hell they were on top of me, not on the way their curves pressed against me, and how I wanted to trace them with my fingers.

What the actual fuck? Stop it!

"Kit?"

"Oh, thank fuck." Their head shifted on my shoulder. "You had me scared out of my mind. I thought you were going to die for a moment there."

Their words stopped me from asking why they'd crawled into the sleeping bag with me. There wasn't exactly much room for two people in it, even with Kit being a lot smaller than me.

"Ye thought I was gonnae die?"

They shifted their hand across my chest and worked the zipper down to free us from the confinements of the bag.

The next thing I knew, Kit straddled my lap and reached up for something. Light flared in the tent as they turned a head torch on that hung off a hook on the roof.

I squinted and groaned.

"Sorry, that's kind of bright, but figured we need some light in here."

After blinking a few times, I stared up at Kit, who had stripped down to their thermal layers that showed off all their... assets. Why the hell did I have to notice that? My brain was playing tricks on me, and it wasn't funny.

Kit's hands rested on my chest in a rather intimate fashion that had me swallowing hard.

78

"When I got you in here and wrapped you up, you continued to complain about being cold and your skin was freezing. I figured the best way to warm you up was to give you my body heat."

They shrugged, as if saving me from freezing to death was an everyday occurrence.

"I was scared when you passed out, but you were still breathing, and I could feel your heart beating under my palm. So I waited until you were warm and got out to organise everything in the tent. That only made me cold as hell, so I got back in with you so I wouldn't freeze."

They removed their hands from my chest and rubbed their arms. The chill in the air made a shiver run through me.

"Now you're awake, I need to look at your ankle, so we'll have to put up with the cold for a bit."

Kit shifted in my lap. I gritted my teeth against the movement.

Can they get off me now?

All I could focus on was their body pressed against me in places it shouldn't be.

"Are you still with me, Thane?"

I let out a breath and steeled myself. I had to stop thinking about them like that. It was fucking dangerous.

"Aye."

"Okay, good."

They finally shifted off me. Instead of feeling relieved about it, I wished they had stayed. Their warmth was welcome, even if the feel of their body wasn't.

Who are you kidding? You like how they feel against you. Stop lying.

Kit shuffled about the tent, leaving me reeling from my wayward thoughts. I must still be delirious from earlier. There was no way in hell I found Kit attractive and wanted to feel more of them. It couldn't be the case. No one had made me feel this way. And Kit was the very last person I would ever wish to be with. They pissed me off too much. Yet a wee, distant part of me wanted them in a more intimate way. It felt deadly to acknowledge that fact, wrong even.

The only person I had wanted for most of my life was Jenna, at least, wanted in the sense that being in a relationship with her made me happy.

Jenna might be gone, but it didn't make me miss her any less. It didn't make me want to move on, despite knowing I eventually had to. Callan had reminded me of that enough times to make it stick in my head. Only I didn't know how to let go. To truly lay Jenna to rest after all that had gone on in the moments before I lost her for good.

"Right, you ready?"

My eyes darted towards Kit, who knelt by my feet. They'd put their glasses on while I wasn't paying attention.

I nodded, worried if I spoke, I would blurt out something I'd regret. No matter what I did, I couldn't shake my reaction to them being pressed up against me. It was an entirely alien feeling.

Kit carefully extracted my ankle from the sleeping bag. I hissed at the pain.

"Sorry."

"It's okay," I whispered, even though it wasn't. None of this was.

I stared down at my swollen, red ankle as Kit examined it with a furrow between their brows. They moved it from side to side, then up and down.

"Fuck."

Kit gave me a sympathetic look and placed it back down on the sleeping mat.

"I'm no expert, but I'm pretty sure it's just a sprain."

"It fucking hurts."

"I have some paracetamol in my pack, but you're going to have to rest it for a while."

Kit shifted away to where they'd put our packs and started digging through theirs.

"Kit."

"Yes?"

"How long was I oot for?"

They sat back on their heels and opened the packet of painkillers they'd extracted.

"I don't know."

"Ye havnae checked the time?"

They popped out two pills and grabbed a water bottle before shifting closer to me. I put out my hand for the paracetamol and took the bottle from them.

Kit had a tense expression on their face while I swallowed the pills.

"No."

"Mibbe ye should."

They bit their lip and fiddled with the drawstring on the sleeping bag.

"The thing is, I may have left my phone at the lodge because I was busy making sure I packed my bag to your standards and, well, it slipped my mind. I only realised when we stopped at the base of the mountain, so it's not like I could go back for it or anything."

I let out a sigh, unsurprised by this.

"Get mine then. It's in mah go bag with the map."

They kept fiddling with the drawstring, their fingers tightening around the elastic.

"You had your phone in that?"

"Aye."

Kit's eyes darted all around the tent. It set me on edge. There was something they didn't want to tell me. Something bad.

"What's wrong?"

"So… um, when I was organising stuff earlier, I kind of noticed it was missing. The bag, I mean. I looked everywhere for it, but it's not in the tent, and I wasn't about to put all my gear back on to go out in the snow as I was worried about you, so um… yeah, I'm pretty sure it's lost somewhere out there."

The weight of their words settled over me. My go bag was missing. My phone and the map were gone. Our lifelines to the outside world. Callan carried a personal locator beacon as standard on all his excursions. I didn't think I would need one for this trip. Now I was sorely regretting the decision to go without.

I closed my eyes and tried not to panic over the situation. My body felt weak after being in that water and walking all day. My ankle continued to throb, and I had no fucking clue what we were going to do.

How the fuck did anyone stay calm after everything we'd just been through? The avalanche cutting us off from the faster route. The weather draining us of all our energy. Me almost dying from hypothermia. Now we were stuck in this glen with no way of getting help because I was injured. It was all too much.

"Fuck."

"Fuck indeed."

When I opened my eyes, Kit had a concerned look on their face. I couldn't lose my mind over it even if I wanted to. Then it occurred to me I still had my watch. I pulled my arm up and stared at the clock face.

"It's eleven."

"No wonder I'm starving. We missed dinner."

"Ye didnae eat anything?"

"I was far too concerned about you to be worried about me."

I dropped my arm and frowned. They should be taking care of themselves. And they were likely as exhausted as me at this point. I didn't know how they were still going.

"Ye need tae eat."

"So do you."

"Am no gonnae argue with ye there. I have rations in mah pack, but I didnae bring many."

Four main meals and two breakfast ones, to be precise. Even then, I thought I was being conservative. I couldn't imagine Kit had brought much for a one-day excursion. We would have to be careful about food, as I had no fucking clue when we'd be able to leave this tent. Nor whether anyone knew we were missing yet. Callan would notice we were gone at some point, but who knew how long that would take.

I struggled to sit up. Kit immediately took hold of my arm to help me. Their touch burned through my thermal undershirt, making my skin tingle in a disconcerting way.

"Do you want me to get something?" they asked when I rubbed my face with both hands. "You look as exhausted as I feel, so we can go through what we have tomorrow."

After blowing out a breath, I decided I didn't have it in me to argue with them about any of it. I was tired as fuck and needed sleep if I was ever going to make a plan for what to do next.

"Aye. Ye dae that."

Kit squeezed my arm and moved away.

I only let myself react to their touch when they turned their back. My body shuddered, and I clenched my fists because I remembered we only had one sleeping bag. I was going to have to spend the night with them pressed against me. It would be the only way we would both stay warm.

Why is this happening to me? I don't need this dilemma when we're in a shite situation and I shouldn't even be thinking about them as someone I could find desirable. It's not like I even understand desire anyway, so how do I know if this is it?

Kit dumped a packet into my lap and sat next to me on the sleeping mat. I stared down at what they'd given me. It was one of those flapjacks with fruit and chocolate in it.

"This is what ye brought with ye?"

Kit raised an eyebrow right as they were biting into their own one. I waited for them to chew and swallow.

"What's wrong with it?"

I shook my head and opened my packet, stuffing half of it in my mouth. Getting into an argument about appropriate food to bring with you when mountaineering wouldn't be productive when we were both tired. In fact, it would only make matters worse.

"It's no a proper meal," I muttered after I finished mine off.

"Well, I'm sorry it's not a five-course spread, but no one told me that's what I had to bring up the mountain with me."

I huffed and crinkled up the packet. It didn't exactly quell my hunger, but it would be enough to survive the rest of the night.

"Noo ye know for next time."

Kit snorted before their eyes darted to my mouth. Their nose wrinkled in that endearing way of theirs and I hated myself for staring at their mouth too. Then I sucked in air when they reached out towards me. Their fingers brushed over my beard before picking something out of it.

"You had a crumb."

They flicked it away and their eyes darted off to the side as a blush spread across their cheeks.

My eyes were still on their mouth, watching the way their lips parted slightly and the fullness of the bottom one.

"We should probably get some sleep. Well, at least, I should since you were out for a while."

"Aye."

I made no move to lie down. Why couldn't I stop staring? Why were they so close in the first place? What was wrong with me?

"Thane?"

Shaking myself, I handed them the empty packet and settled back down, wincing at the ache in my ankle.

Kit shifted away, putting both our packets down before they hovered over me as if wondering how we would go about this.

"Just get in," I all but barked, wanting to get it over with.

"Well, you're kind of big, so I'm going to have to lie on top of you again."

"Aye. I know."

And I didn't like it.

Kit swallowed and crawled onto me before reaching up and turning out the head torch. I couldn't breathe as they settled over me and zipped up the sleeping bag to keep the warmth in. It was a tight fit. I could feel them everywhere, but since they weren't as tall as me, their feet didn't knock into my ankle, thankfully.

Kit put their head on my shoulder. We stayed like that for a moment until I realised that they were lying on my arm, and it would be numb by morning if I didn't move it.

Carefully, I extracted it from below them and wrapped it around their back instead.

Kit let out a breath at the contact but said nothing.

"It was uncomfortable with ye lying on it," I said by way of explanation.

"It's fine."

It wasn't. We both knew that, but what else could either of us do? Nothing.

"So… this is a really weird time to bring this up, but uh…"

"What?"

"You're married."

I stiffened at their words.

"What?"

"I didn't know, as you don't wear a wedding ring. I just assumed… I don't know what I assumed, but I know this is awkward, but we're only doing it to stay warm."

When the fuck did I tell them about Jenna? I don't remember saying anything.

Our situation was awkward for a multitude of reasons, but none of them had anything to do with me being married. And I certainly didn't want Kit jumping to the wrong conclusions either. However, I wasn't going to rehash my entire tragic fucking story to them, either. I didn't want to think about Jenna right then. Not when Kit was pressed against me. It would only exacerbate my guilt.

"It's fine, Kit. Dinnae worry yer head over it."

"But won't your—"

"She's dead."

The finality of my words rang through the tent.

Kit went stiff as a board, making me feel even worse for saying it like that, but I wanted to end this conversation.

"Ye can rest easy. No jealous wives for ye tae worry aboot."

"That… that wasn't what I meant," they whispered. "I'm sorry, Thane. I shouldn't have said anything."

"Aye, well, there's nothing else tae say, so ye should sleep."

It was clear Kit didn't like me dismissing it that way by their wee hum of disapproval, but they didn't make another sound after that.

I took it as my cue to get some sleep myself. And hate everything about what I'd said to them.

TEN

Kit

Despite being thoroughly embarrassed by thinking Thane was married only for him to tell me his wife had died, I fell asleep quickly from utter exhaustion. Now, in the morning light, I was still tucked up in the sleeping bag with him. The thought of getting out filled me with dread. It would be freezing, and I didn't much feel like moving until I absolutely had to.

Each of his breaths made me rise and fall with his chest. His heart was beating steadily under my palm, reassuring me he was okay after fearing for his life last night. And I was very aware of something else going on with his anatomy that I was desperately trying not to think about.

Listen, it's not his fault. It's just a thing that happens in the morning. And I'm not going to say anything when he wakes up. That will make it even more awkward between us. As if it isn't bad enough already.

When I asked him about being married, it was out of curiosity, since he was most vehemently opposed to being naked in front of me. I mean, I didn't blame him. We were relative strangers, but I was far more concerned about saving his life.

The thought of him being married niggled at me though, especially as we had to spend the night in the valley between two mountains. If he had a wife, then I imagined she would be very worried about him. But the fact he was a widower made me feel even worse. It was clear he didn't want to talk about it.

Who can blame him? He doesn't know you. It's obviously a difficult subject.

I felt for him. Grief was no fun. It broke parts of you that would only heal with time… if at all. Now I wanted to hug him and tell him it would be okay, that I understood how painful it was to lose someone precious to you, but he wouldn't welcome that. I doubt Thane would welcome much from me, considering he made it clear he didn't like my company. He tolerated me because he had to. And now we were stuck with each other for the foreseeable future. It was just my luck to be trapped with someone who never wanted to be around me.

I didn't know what to do with his jealous wife comment either. Did he think I had designs on him? Or that I even considered for one second that what we were doing could be inappropriate? It hadn't crossed my mind. Survival was my focus. And now he fucked it all up by making it about something else. Something I wasn't prepared for.

Let's face it, you've been fighting your attraction to him this whole time.

Being attracted to someone didn't mean I had any interest in acting on it. It would be a complication I didn't need. My life was already messy enough without throwing him into the mix.

"Are ye awake?"

His voice startled me. I turned my head up to find him staring down at me.

"Yeah."

Thane adjusted his hold on me. I had almost forgotten his arm had been curled around me all night. I folded my lips inside my mouth when his fingers brushed over the base of my spine.

Don't react. Don't react. Don't fucking react.

My body betrayed me. A shiver made its way down my back, making me shift my hips.

Thane let out a grunt at the movement.

I wanted to die. Involuntarily rubbing myself against his hard dick was not how I wished to start this morning off.

No, you'd rather intentionally rub yourself all over him, so he realises you don't hate him. And you wouldn't say no if he reciprocated by rubbing against you.

Not waiting for him to make another sound, I unzipped the sleeping bag and practically flung myself out of it. My cheeks were hot. I pressed my fingers to them as I kept my back to him. I didn't even care about the cold, despite it hitting me like a ton of bricks.

"Ye okay?"

"Yup, totally great."

I inwardly cringed at myself. My voice sounded unnaturally chirpy.

"I just have to go… um… relieve myself."

Thane moved. I could hear him, but I didn't dare look.

"There's a shovel in mah pack."

"A shovel?"

He let out a huff.

"Aye. Ye might need it depending on what ye need tae dae."

I immediately got the gist of what he was saying. All I needed to do was to pee, but if I needed something else, then I would have to bury it. We had to be responsible while wild camping, even if this hadn't been our intention and we were in the middle of nowhere.

Instead of replying to him, I hurriedly dragged my clothes on, still feeling awkward as fuck about everything that had happened between us. After I finished tying my boots, I unzipped the inner tent and started to get out, when Thane's voice brought me up short.

"Make sure ye're far enough away from the tent and the stream."

"Okay," I said through gritted teeth.

Don't treat me like I'm stupid, Thane. I'm not going to pee right outside.

When I got outside the tent, the snow had piled up overnight, almost half burying our little camp. I would have to do something about that, but first, toileting and possibly eating because I was fucking starving. No doubt Thane would have something to say about rationing our supplies. I agreed with him on that, since I had no idea how long we would be out here. With his ankle and his clothes all wet, we wouldn't be able to leave immediately. And without the ability to contact the outside world, I didn't know if rescue would happen either. Surely, Callan would have realised we hadn't come back by now.

I didn't dwell on that as I stomped my way through the snow away from camp and the stream. My focus should be on getting us set up for a few days, so we could be as comfortable as possible in our predicament. Although, how I could ever be comfortable sharing a sleeping bag with that blasted man was a mystery to me. It would be too cold to do anything else, but I disliked it all the same. Being so close to someone you found hot as hell, even if you didn't much like their personality, with only a small layer of clothing between you, was unfair. Just plain fucking unfair.

When I found a suitable spot, I kicked at the snow to make a hole, then I did my business while freezing my arse off. Once I finished and filled the hole, I looked around properly. Last night it had been dark, but in the dim morning light, I could see everything around us since the snow had stopped. There were dark clouds overhead, obscuring the sun, so the landscape looked rather sinister, but it was beautiful in its own way. There were snow-covered pine trees above me as we had set up camp next to a wooded area.

A hunger pang ripped through me. It was time to get back to the tent and find out what Thane's plans for feeding us were. He was the prepared one in this situation. All I had left was snack food. I had brought more than I needed, but I wanted to make sure I kept my energy levels up. Too fucking bad I forgot to do that yesterday when I was exhausted from walking in dire weather conditions. It didn't matter. It would help us survive. At least we were near a stream. The running water would be safe to drink.

I trudged back, hoping the awkwardness between us would be dispelled by now. That was most definitely wishful thinking. I unlaced my boots and set them down in the porch area, along with my jacket and waterproof trousers, before going into the main area. I paused at the entrance as there were piles of things everywhere.

"Um, what are you doing?"

Thane had his injured ankle propped up on the built-in pillow of the inflatable sleeping mat. He had things in his hands, but he stopped to look up at me.

"Taking stock of oor supplies."

Turning, I zipped up the inner tent. Then I had to step over his wet clothes I'd left out to dry and nudge a pile out of the way to take a seat next to him.

"What's the verdict?"

He placed a couple of things down and set his hands on the mat next to him. One of them was nudging my thigh. I didn't move, wondering if he noticed and trying not to think

94

about the warmth radiating off him. After being in the cold, I could have wrapped myself around his solid body and taken all of it.

"Depends on what ye have."

I realised he hadn't dug through my pack, just his own. Mine was sitting at the end of the sleeping mat closest to me.

"Nothing substantial."

"Show me."

Resisting the urge to roll my eyes, I dragged my pack closer and dug everything out. I made a pile of crisp packets, a couple of chocolate bars, and a few more flapjacks.

Thane's eyebrow curled up.

"In my defence, I ate the lunch I brought with me yesterday. It's not like I expected to get stuck on a mountain."

He grunted. That was all the response I got. And maybe that was for the best. His judgemental attitude often rubbed me up the wrong way. We didn't need to get into a verbal sparring match today. I would rather call a truce so we could get through this together.

"Three, mibbe four days of food accounting for the both of us," he finally said after a few long minutes of silence.

"Is that if we're careful?"

"Aye… unless ye wannae spend all day thinking aboot how hungry ye are on top of being cold."

"No. Not really."

He shrugged.

"Three days it is, counting today."

I let out a breath. That wasn't much. I didn't know how long Thane would need to rest his ankle or how long his clothes would take to dry. I didn't like the look of those clouds, so putting them outside wasn't an option. At least, not today.

"Do you think there's any chance we'll get rescued before then?"

"Cannae be sure. Callan would alert mountain rescue if he thought we were missing, but we're relying on him tae dae that."

The missing part of Thane's words was that the avalanche we witnessed may have taken up the group's attention. That our predicament may have gone unnoticed. Neither of us wanted to voice the possibility out loud.

"Okay. I guess we'll have to rely on ourselves to get out of this."

"Aye."

He didn't sound very confident about that fact. And I wasn't feeling very good about our chances. I had minimal survival skills, and Thane, who knew what to do, was hurt. The odds were not exactly in our favour. I wanted to curl up in despair, but I couldn't do that.

"Right, well, we should probably eat something," I said, giving both my thighs a slap. "Then I can go get us some water and... uh, help you if you need to go do your... business."

My eyes searched his face. Thane's cheeks went red as he looked anywhere but me. It reminded me of when he gave me his beanie to wear for the day. The way he flushed over that.

"If you need to go now, we can do that."

He rubbed the back of his neck, which was going red too.

"No, after we eat is fine."

If he thought by helping him, I meant anything other than lending him an arm to move away from camp and maybe dig a hole, then he was barking up the wrong tree. I wasn't going to stand there and watch. That would be fucking weird.

Deciding it was better not to ask what was going through his mind, I waved at the food.

"What will it be?"

Thane pointed at the small camping stove.

"Hand me that and I'll dae it."

Arguing with him over it would be futile. His ankle was injured, not his hands. Besides, giving him something to do was probably a great idea. Then he couldn't judge me for doing it the wrong way.

I got Thane the supplies he asked for and then set about organising the tent again, so we had space to move while Thane made breakfast. If the tent was a mess, it would bug the hell out of me. Disorganisation always made me a little antsy. Especially when I was stressed. Plus, I had a habit of losing things, so to combat that, I kept my space as tidy as possible.

"Are ye quite done?" Thane asked after a while.

I sat down next to him.

"Yup."

He looked around at my handiwork before shaking his head. The corners of his mouth twitched. He was definitely trying not to smile at my manic tidy session.

"Here… we'll have tae share."

He waved the bag of reconstituted food at me along with a fork. I took it, not caring about the fact our mouths would be using the same utensil.

You don't care because you'd quite like his mouth on yours, tasting you the way you'd like to taste him.

I told my brain to go fuck itself while surreptitiously watching Thane as we ate, taking turns to use the fork. The bun he'd put his hair up in yesterday was messy now, but, in a way, that made him more attractive. I liked the messiness. Made him seem less perfect. There was no doubt in my mind that Thane was as flawed as me. And maybe I would find out just how much while we were here.

ELEVEN

Kit

When we got done eating, I put my outdoor clothes on and eyed Thane, who looked distinctly uncomfortable. He knew what was coming.

"Okay, there's one thing I need to know, and that's whether I have to go dig a hole or not."

Thane's mouth twitched, and he rubbed his forehead with his fingers. We had to get over the awkwardness of such personal questions. With him being injured, I had no other choice but to help him get around. That meant dealing with our normal bodily functions. Being practical about it was for the best. I'd already seen him mostly naked and felt the rest. He could see pretty much everything about me since my thermals were body-forming.

While I didn't identify with a gender, I wasn't going to deny I had female anatomy. After all, I'd been pregnant with Sienna and Law's baby. My physical appearance always mattered more to other people than it did to me. I felt like my true self identifying as a person rather than a man or a woman. Maybe that didn't make sense to other people, but it did to me.

Thane dropped his hand and let out a huff.

"Dig a hole."

I tried not to smile at his response. The silly man needed to get over himself. I was trying to make things easier on him, not create further tension between us.

"No problem. I'll be back in a bit."

While I had been organising things, I'd placed the shovel and toilet paper Thane had brought near the front of the tent. I picked those up on my way out, zipping everything up so the cold air wouldn't get in. My goal was to find a suitable spot that was accessible for someone who couldn't put too much weight on his injured ankle. No easy feat, but I was determined to try. Thane shouldn't have to suffer any more than he already had after last night's ordeal.

As I walked through the trees, I noted the clouds had darkened further, leaving the landscape looking rather grey. It would be too much to ask for the weather to clear up. It would force us to stay in the tent. Well, force me, anyway. Then I would have to spend the entire day in close proximity with Thane. I didn't know how I would cope. While we'd been on the course, I could get away from him in the evening. That option wasn't available now.

"Maybe if he wasn't so judgy, I wouldn't be reluctant to be near him," I muttered to myself as I walked, careful to avoid any fallen logs sticking out of the snow.

As I paused to look at one of them, a plan formed in my head about how I could utilise it for Thane. If I dug a hole next to it, then perhaps he could use that to hold on to.

Deciding that was the best course of action, I placed the toilet paper on the log to keep it away from the snow and set to work digging through the snow. The ground was semi-solid when I got to it, but I was able to dig down far enough to make a suitable hole.

"Right, hopefully, he'll appreciate this."

I wasn't holding out any hope that he would. Thane hadn't appreciated anything I'd done for him, including saving his life last night. I don't even think he'd thanked me for that yet. The stubborn man probably thought I'd done a terrible job. Well, he could suck it up. He had to rely on me now. It might grate on him, but he grated on me, so it was only fair.

I stomped back to the tent, trying not to let my agitated state show. If he didn't want to thank me, then he didn't have to. But he could be a little less of a dick. If he was nicer to me, I would be less conflicted about finding him attractive. But I wasn't going to hold out any hope on that score. He made his feelings about me very clear. Our dislike was mutual, despite the underlying tension between us. That part was something I refused to entertain.

Thane had got himself off the mat and was attempting to put his wet boots on over his swollen ankle when I arrived back.

"Need help with that?"

"No," he ground out.

He pulled on his spare dry fleece when he was done, having left the laces of his boots undone.

I put a hand out to him. He let me pull him up without a fuss. His grunt of pain made me wince. I hated that he was hurting. When we were done with this, I'd give him more of my painkillers to counteract our little excursion.

Thane leaned heavily on me the entire way to the hole. It took us twice as long to get there than it had taken on my own. I said nothing as I handed him the shovel before turning my back and walking a little way off to give him some privacy. If he needed anything else, he would have to ask.

After a minute went by, I hummed tune to counteract any noises and shifted from foot to foot. I hadn't put all my layers on, but it wasn't too cold. Thane was in less than me, so he wouldn't be enjoying the bracing air. We weren't going to be out here for long, so he could deal, even though I didn't want him getting cold. Last night scared me. I couldn't go through that again.

"Kit."

I spun around to find Thane was done. He had managed to stand by himself, something I wanted to give him a hard time over. If he got himself even more hurt, I wouldn't be happy.

Making my way over, I kept a neutral expression on my face, knowing an argument wouldn't do us any good. The dirt hole was covered over. I kicked at the snow, burying it further without looking at him. Then I picked up the toilet paper and shovel, putting them into my pockets.

"Come on, put your arm around me. I have hand sanitiser back at the tent."

Thane did as he was told. He winced as we set off, and he had to put weight on his injured ankle again.

"Ye brought hand sanitiser but no proper food with ye."

"I carry a small bottle at all times. I like having clean hands. So if you're going to give me a hard time over that, then don't."

"I wasnae," he muttered.

I rolled my eyes since he couldn't see me do it. A cold, wet substance landed on my nose, making it twitch. I looked up to find it had started snowing again.

Well, that's just fucking great.

"If you weren't going to give me a lecture, then what was the point in saying that?"

"I dinnae lecture ye."

I scoffed. As if that was true. He had told me I was doing everything wrong several times over the course, looked at me as if I was stupid, and treated me like a child who couldn't take care of themselves.

"Really now? You're not going to tell me I dug that hole wrong?"

"No."

"That's a first."

He huffed. I took a peek at his face to find him scowling. Those dark green eyes were full of annoyance. Well, I was pissed at him too. I was trying my best, and I got no thanks for it.

"Ye're going tae fast."

"Well, I'm sorry that I want to get you back to the tent quickly to keep you from getting cold again. Woe is me that I'm concerned about your health after you almost died on me."

"I didnae asked ye tae save me."

I almost stopped dead in my tracks. How fucking dare he say that to me. What the hell was wrong with him? I didn't have to go out of my way to help him, but I had. I cared enough about his stupid arse to keep him alive.

"Would you rather I left you in that stream to freeze to death? Did you know I almost fell in trying to drag you out? You're a lot fucking bigger than me, so it wasn't easy. We would both be dead if I'd gone in with you, so the least you could be is grateful rather than being a fucking prick."

Everything inside me was screaming at me to stomp away and leave him there to find his own way back to the tent. Instead, I silently seethed by his side. I wasn't that petty or cruel. I didn't have it in me to leave Thane to fend for himself. Maybe that made me soft-hearted, but I didn't like to see other people in pain or struggling. Sienna always told me I was too nice for my own good.

Why are you thinking about her again? Fuck Sienna.

I didn't owe her my thoughts, time, or attention. After the way she treated me, she didn't deserve any of it. And I didn't want her in my life any longer.

"Kit."

The way he said my name had me flinching. I liked it too much, and I really didn't want to like anything about Thane at that moment. Not when I was angry at him for making me care.

"Don't," I snapped. "Don't say my name."

The moment the words left my mouth, I wished them back. I wished I could rewind time, but life didn't work that way.

"Am no allowed tae say yer name?"

The way he sounded so hurt by my statement left me with an odd feeling in my chest.

"No, no, you're not. How am I meant to stay mad at you if you're saying my name with your damn accent? I want to be angry at you, so just shut up and let me be."

Why do you have word vomit around this man? It's like you can't fucking help yourself.

The only saving grace was I hadn't blurted out that I was wildly attracted to him. There would be no coming back from that. It would likely be the most embarrassing moment of my life since he would have to reject me, and it would be a whole stupid thing.

Thane didn't say anything the rest of the way back to the tent. I wasn't unhappy about that. Maybe he realised he pushed me too far. Was it so bad I wanted to feel like I had actually done something right when I saved his life? That I wanted to feel appreciated for it? Maybe I was an idiot for wishing he would say something nice to me for once.

As soon as we got back, I made sure he got into the tent okay, and then I gathered up the water bottles to go fill them at the stream to get away from him. As I walked, I tried to breathe and re-centre myself. It was hard when I was angry and feeling a little hurt by his words. The fact he didn't ask me to save him.

What did he think I was going to do? I couldn't leave him in the water. He was my only way out of here. I had no idea what direction to walk in or how to get back to civilisation. Though whether Thane knew now we'd lost the map, I had no idea. He still had more knowledge of the area than I did. Besides, the biggest reason I had to save him was that I didn't want him to die. I wanted him alive and, well, because I liked him despite myself.

Once I filled up the water bottles at the stream, I was still upset. The snow was coming down harder, but I would have rather stayed out here than be near him. Remembering I needed to clear some of the snow from around the sides of the tent, I walked back. I didn't go inside.

Setting the water bottles down, I let out all of my frustrations on the snow, kicking at it to move it. When that stopped working, I used the shovel to clear a path around the tent. I'm sure Thane heard me doing it, but I didn't care what he thought. He didn't get a say in this.

By the time I was done, my arms and legs ached, and I was thoroughly out of breath. Unzipping the porch, I stepped inside and took off my outer layers. Then, with a huff of air, I made my way into the inner bit, zipping it up before I turned around to face him.

Thane was sitting up with his hands folded in his lap. His green eyes met mine. I sucked in a breath and willed him not to say anything because I was liable to snap again. Then we would be in trouble.

Thane had other ideas. Ones that caught me off guard and knocked the wind right out of my sails. And I didn't know whether to laugh, cry or curl up in his lap.

"Ye're right. I havnae been fair tae ye. Am sorry. Thank ye for saving mah life."

TWELVE

Thane

Kit froze by the entrance of the tent with two water bottles in their hands and blinked several times. They hadn't been expecting my words. I barely expected them either. However, while they were stomping about outside doing fuck knows what, I had time to think about the things they'd thrown at me. I couldn't stomach the idea they'd risked their life to save mine.

Last night had been a bit of a blur. It didn't register with me how close to death both of us had come. The avalanche had happened a few feet away from us. Then I'd fallen in that fucking water. If Kit had gone in with me… I didn't even want to consider it. Losing another person, even if we weren't close, wasn't something I could handle.

Kit set down the water bottles before staring at me with wide eyes.

"You're… you're apologising to me?" they whispered as their hand rubbed the space where their heart lay.

They were half bent over since the tent wasn't tall enough for them to stand up in. I couldn't help running my gaze over their body. The sight of them in their thermals made something stir within me. Something I hadn't felt for anyone… not even my wife. My dead wife. Fuck. I needed to stop this train of thought.

"Ye think am no capable of saying sorry?"

"Yes… I mean, no… I mean, sort of."

Fighting back a smile, I shook my head and rubbed my mouth with the back of my hand.

"Am no always just a dick with an accent."

Kit snorted. Their face flushed, although it had already been tinged pink from the cold. Clearly, they were thinking about what they said to me earlier. How they told me not to say their name. All but admitting it did something to them. I had my own thoughts about what that could be.

"Yeah, okay. Can I get in there next to you? It's fucking cold outside."

I nodded even as my skin prickled at the thought of being close to them again. Not like I would deny them warmth, but fuck, I didn't know how to handle my reactions to Kit. They were messing me up.

Kit took off their glasses before climbing over me and squeezing themselves into the gap between me and the tent wall, getting all tucked up in the sleeping bag. They shivered, making me feel bad that they were cold. After all, they'd kept me warm last night. I should do the same for them now.

Despite my reservations, I carefully shifted down on the sleeping mat, mindful not to jog my ankle too much as I turned on my side. It ached like a bitch, but I ignored it. There were more important things at stake than my pain.

"Come here, I'll warm ye up."

I flinched at my choice of words. They sounded sexual. I hadn't intended them that way. Maybe it was because I'd been having wayward thoughts about Kit. They flooded me with guilt and self-loathing.

Kit had pissed me off the entire time I'd been around them, and yet… and fucking yet… I found myself wanting to hold them against me. To protect them from the elements despite me being the injured one. To show them I had a caring bone in my body. One I had lost over the past two years, but I was trying to find it again. They made me want to find it.

But why? What the fuck is it about Kit that makes me feel this way?

"Are you sure?"

"Wouldnae have offered if I wasnae."

"Well, okay."

Kit moved closer, pressing themselves against me. I curled an arm underneath them so they could fully share in my body heat.

They let out a harsh breath when I tucked them up in my embrace like it was nothing. But it felt like something. It felt like a great deal of things I couldn't afford to entertain.

It took Kit a few minutes to settle before they wrapped one hand around my waist and placed the other on my chest.

It was the first time I'd willingly held another person this way since Jenna. It was almost alien to me. To want that with anyone else but her. I could kid myself into thinking it was merely to keep Kit warm. Keeping up that pretence wouldn't do me any favours. And yet the guilt kept flaring. Moving on from Jenna wasn't possible. I certainly couldn't do it with a person who pushed all of my buttons the way Kit did.

"Why did ye come on this course?"

I asked it as a way of distracting myself from my racing thoughts. If I was going to get my shite together, I had to find a way through this situation without doing something I'd regret. That meant keeping my mind occupied.

Kit let out a nervous chuckle.

"Um, that's kind of complicated."

"In what way?"

"I mean, the simple answer is that I've always enjoyed walking. Dad always used to worry when I'd take off on these long walks along the coastline when I was younger. I still do. It helps clear my head. It always feels so overcrowded, like my thoughts don't shut off. Then I go for a walk and I'm okay, you know. I sort through things in a way I can't when there's all this noise around me."

Their fingers absently stroked along my waist. I tried not to let it affect me.

"I walked up Scafell Pike a few years ago, but I wanted more experience before I attempted another mountain, so I booked this trip as a treat for my birthday."

They shrugged a wee bit and shifted against me. A grunt got stuck in my throat at the movement. Kit was going to be the death of me.

"Yer birthday?"

They sighed.

"Yeah. It's tomorrow actually. Didn't think I'd be bringing in the big three-o stuck in the mountains in the snow."

Well, fuck.

There wasn't much I could do to make our situation any better, but I'd made a start by deciding not to provoke them any further today. I couldn't promise that I wouldn't do it at all, given the way Kit reacted to some of the things I said. But I could try. Spending their birthday stuck with me in this tent wasn't exactly going to be fun. The least I could do was not make it worse.

"What's the complicated answer?"

It took a long time for Kit to respond. I wanted to look down at them to see their expression, but I refrained. Maybe they didn't want to tell me. And that was okay. They didn't owe me anything. I was just trying to pass the time and distract the both of us with conversation.

"I needed to get away from my life… to forget about it all for a minute because it hurts too much," they finally said in a quiet voice that was full of agony.

My arms instinctively tightened around them. It wasn't to provide more warmth. I needed to shield them from whatever it was that they ran away from. Why that was, I had no fucking clue. Kit messed with my head. One minute I

112

couldn't stand them, the next, I wanted to reassure them everything would be okay.

"But I don't want to talk about that right now."

"Am sorry I made ye bring it up."

"It's okay. You didn't know."

I rubbed a hand over their lower back without thinking about it. I almost stopped when they stiffened slightly, but after a few seconds went by, Kit relaxed again.

"Ye want me tae ask something else?"

"You can do. Although I have to admit, I'm surprised you're being so agreeable right now."

I couldn't help but allow the laugh to spill out from my mouth.

"Mibbe am tired of fighting with ye."

"Is this your way of asking for a truce?"

"If ye wannae think of it that way."

Kit turned their head up to meet my eyes. Their dark hair was messy, and they were wrinkling their nose in that adorable fucking way of theirs. It had me swallowing hard.

"Just while we're stuck together, right? We can go back to disliking each other when we get out of this."

If we get out of this.

There were no guarantees that we would be rescued. Fuck knows how long it would be until I could walk on my ankle without it causing me a lot of pain. I didn't voice that out loud, though. Kit didn't need the reminder that our situation wasn't great.

"Aye."

They smiled at me. It made their icy blue eyes twinkle.

"Okay, well, ask your question then."

I hadn't thought of one yet, but since Kit was staring at me with a face full of expectation, I blurted out the first thing that popped into my head.

"What dae ye dae for work?"

"That might be the most uninspired question ever, but okay."

"Ye know what I dae."

They kept smiling at me. It was the same one they'd worn for Callan. The one that annoyed me because they'd never done it for me. Now they were, and it made my chest ache. Fuck, I was a mess. Why did it have to be over Kit, of all people? Surely the world could have sent someone else. But no, it was this mouthy wee thing who gave me whiplash.

"I'm a tattoo artist."

It took me a minute to respond. Kit didn't have any visible tattoos that I'd noticed. Not that you had to have them yourself in order to be a tattoo artist or anything. I don't know what I expected, but it wasn't that. They'd surprised me yet again.

"Was that something ye always wanted tae dae?"

"Well, I've always drawn stuff, but I kind of fell into it after I started working at reception for a local studio. The owner, Roman, saw my doodles one day and encouraged me to start drawing tattoo designs. Then he offered me an apprenticeship and I guess the rest is history. That was ten years ago. I still work for him now."

I wondered what styles they favoured and what kind of artist they were.

114

"Dae ye have any yerself?"

"Tattoos? Um, yeah." They lifted their hands out of the sleeping bag and showed me their thumbs. "These are the only visible ones I have. Everything else is… under my clothes."

There was a half-crescent moon at the base of their thumb with wee stars trailing up the side. On the other was the sun with its rays curling up the side.

Before they could take their hands away, I caught them with mine and looked at the tattoos more closely.

Kit stared at me with wide eyes.

"They're pretty."

"Roman did them. He's done all my tattoos. I wouldn't trust anyone else."

"Ye must be close."

They shrugged and tried to tug their hands from my grasp. Without thinking about it, I stroked my thumb down one of their tattoos. Their skin was so fucking soft. Kit felt so delicate, but they were stronger than they looked.

"He's a good boss and artist… but I guess he's a friend too. Like not a best friend or anything, though I'm not even sure I have one of those any longer, but a work friend, you know."

Kit looked away as pain flickered in their eyes. It didn't take a rocket scientist to work out that whoever this best friend was they'd alluded to might well be the reason they came on the course.

"What aboot yer other tattoos? Can I see those?"

The way Kit flushed at my words had me suspicious about where they were placed. They hid their face from me a moment later.

"Kind of hard to show you without exposing myself," they murmured.

The possibilities floated through my mind, and all of them had me shifting against Kit.

"Where exactly are they?"

"On my chest." They turned their face back towards mine. "Wait, you didn't think I had them like… down there, did you?"

It was my turn for my face to grow hot.

"No."

"You're lying."

"Am no lying."

Kit narrowed their eyes.

"Not that I have anything against them, but I don't want any there myself."

"I didnae think ye did, Kit."

Their name slipped out of my mouth without me thinking about it.

I let go of Kit's hands. I hadn't realised I was still stroking their thumb. The moment I released them, I wanted to hold their hands again. To feel their soft skin all over mine.

What the fuck is wrong with me? I'm losing my fucking mind here. What are you doing to me, Kit? Seriously… what are you doing to me?

THIRTEEN

Kit

This man and his damn accent would actually be the death of me. There was something about the way he pronounced my name. It sounded like *Khet* rather than *Kit*. And it melted my insides. Coupled with all his touching, I was coming undone at the seams. The way he cuddled up to me, holding me as close as possible, was so at odds with how he'd treated me these past few days. Sure, Thane made it clear he wanted to keep me safe, but this... I didn't know what to make of the stroking and the softness in his green eyes. He always looked so severe, like the weight of the world was on his shoulders, but right then, Thane was, dare I say it, relaxed. It was a sight I didn't want to ruin, not now we'd called a truce.

"Well, that's enough about me. Tell me something about you."

The thought of carrying on our conversation about my tattoos made me nervous. I'd been tempted to show him the one on my chest. And if we kept talking about it, I might well do that. It was an intimacy I was afraid to share with this man.

We were in a set of circumstances neither of us wanted to be in. Forced together by the need to survive. I was already very up close and personal with him. If I bared my sternum to him, we'd cross a line I didn't know if we could come back from. And whether I even wanted to.

Getting close to someone terrified me. I didn't know if I could trust myself. Not after Sienna shat all over our friendship like it was nothing and the past twenty-five years meant fuck all. Loving the wrong person for most of my life made me reconsider a lot of things about myself. Like how could I be so naïve?

I wanted to blame it all on myself, but Sienna had been supportive of me. Had been there for me. But now I was wondering if that was real. If I had mistaken her care for manipulation to keep me on her side. Who the fuck knew. Thinking about it made my head hurt. It made everything hurt, so I shoved it back in a box where it couldn't cause me pain. I would have to open it and deal with the emotions one day, but it wasn't today.

"Me?"

Thane looked perplexed at my request.

"Yeah. Can be anything. Like what you do for fun, but also, I never asked how old you are."

His frown made me close my mouth.

I'd shared things about myself. Wasn't it only fair he did too? Not like we had much else going on. It was snowing outside. We had no phones. Nothing to keep us occupied except for each other. There weren't a lot of things two people could do beyond talking. Any other ideas I might have were most definitely off the table.

"I dinnae like talking aboot mahself."

"You know, I hadn't noticed with your sunny disposition and all."

Maybe I was baiting the bear a little with that one. Thane didn't get to ask me about myself without giving me something in return.

"Yer mooth is trouble."

"No one has ever told me that before."

He blinked before narrowing his eyes as if he didn't believe me.

"No?"

I shook my head and lowered my hands back down now he'd finally released them, resting them in the narrow space between our bodies.

He was so warm. I could stay pressed against him like this forever. There was something comforting about being held by Thane. It shouldn't make me feel that way. As if I was safe. I barely knew him. He'd been a grumpy prick most of the time he was in my presence. It made no sense. And yet I couldn't bring myself to tell him I was no longer cold. Not yet anyway.

"Am no sure whether tae be flattered or offended ye only like tae be a problem for me."

"I haven't been going out of my way to annoy you or anything."

"Ye're a natural."

"Now who's the one laying on the flattery."

I tried not to laugh as he rolled his eyes and let out a huff. And I almost squirmed when he rested his hand on my hip. The way his fingers splayed out, tips touching my thigh and behind, had me taking a breath. His hands weren't exactly small. None of him was. Especially not compared to me.

It had been a miracle that I managed to pull him out of the water last night. Then again, my need to survive had kicked in. Thane was the key to that. Being out here alone without all of his supplies would have left me with worse odds. The ones we had now weren't great to begin with. I hadn't thought about that while we were lying here together. It was nice to forget about our situation for a little while.

"Come on, I've shared stuff about me," I said, wanting to stay in our little bubble, so I didn't have to worry about everything else. "Just tell me one thing."

"Just one?"

"Yeah, but also the age thing. You have to give me that."

He ran his top teeth over his bottom lip as if in deep thought about what he wanted to reveal to me.

"I like tae go foraging… and I turned thirty-two last month."

He wasn't much older than me. I didn't think he was, but I preferred being sure about these things.

"What, like picking wild plants?"

"Aye."

"Can you be any more of a walking cliché for someone who likes the outdoors? You're into mountaineering, you work in forestry, and you like to forage. Next, you're going to tell me you live in a hut in the woods."

The way he grunted and gave me another signature scowl had me trying not to laugh.

"Aye, something like that."

I snorted. That only made him scowl harder.

"Wait, you're not serious? You live in a hut?"

"It's no a hut."

"But you live in the woods."

"Aye."

"Figures."

It honestly didn't surprise me that Thane lived away from other people. He didn't seem the type to want to be around anyone. Except maybe Callan, but they were friends.

"What does?"

"That you're the grumpy old man in the woods that parents tell their kids to stay away from."

"Ye're no as funny as ye think ye are."

I grinned at him.

"Aww, you love it really."

"I shouldnae have said anything."

My fingers rubbed his chest without my say so, wanting to reassure him I was only joking. Actually, I found it endearing that he loved the outdoors so much. And why wouldn't he when he lived in a place like this? It was beautiful in a rugged sort of way.

"I'm just kidding, Thane. Honestly, I thought you were going to tell me you like Geocaching or something, but the fact you like the outdoors so much is cool. I wish I had more time for it."

He gave me an odd look.

"Geo-whating?"

"Geocaching."

His eyes narrowed.

"Is that the thing those eejits who carry around GPS units and look for buried treasure dae?"

"I take it you're not fond of them."

Thane let out another huff and gave me a dark look.

"No, they've always got their noses buried in those fucking rather than looking where they're going. Callan had a bunch of them turn up tae one of his courses, all these posh English cunts who worked in finance and had never gone hillwalking a day in their fucking life, but they're up here in all this expensive gear acting like they're experts. Bunch of fucking posers."

I couldn't help but start laughing at the sheer annoyance dripping from his voice.

No wonder he didn't particularly like me. I came on this course with little experience in mountaineering, but at least I was honest about it. I wasn't trying to pretend I knew everything.

Maybe it pissed him off that I insisted on doing it all myself. The only person I could rely on was myself. And I was feeling especially sore about asking for help from anyone after all the shit with Sienna. I wasn't going to ask a stranger for help when my best friend refused to be there for me.

The only person who had given me any real comfort and understanding over the miscarriage was my dad. It saddened me that the only two people who gave a shit about me were him and my brother. They could only do so much. Olly had his own life to lead. He was a decade younger than me, after all.

"It's no funny."

"No, rich pricks aren't funny, they're definitely cuntish, but the way you're so worked up about it is."

"Ye would be tae if ye had tae deal with those eejits for hours. Told Callan am no helping him on any more courses if those cunts are gonnae be on them."

It was strange how when I first met Thane, his prickly nature really wound me up the wrong way. And yet now, I was enjoying his grumpiness. He didn't like inconvenient and uncaring people. I could understand that. There were too many people in this world who didn't give a shit about anyone else but themselves.

"You helped him on this one."

"Aye, well, that's different. He insisted, said I need tae get oot more, tae dae the things I love again. And he's no wrong."

Thane looked away and his expression grew shuttered.

I got the distinct impression he was thinking about something painful. And a niggling feeling told me it was probably about his wife. It made me wish I hadn't said anything. Considering I hated talking about my own grief, I could only imagine how it felt for him.

"How long has it been?"

Why did you open your stupid mouth? You were literally just thinking you shouldn't have said anything and then you go ask him that. What is wrong with you?

"Almost two years."

I kept rubbing my fingers over his chest, wanting to soothe away that troubled look in his eyes. He'd known I was referring to his wife. And he answered me. That felt significant. My heart ached something fierce over it.

"Normally people would say I'm sorry in this situation, but I kind of hate that. So I'll just say grief is… hard."

"What would ye know aboot grief?"

I tried not to flinch at his accusatory tone.

"A lot. A hell of a fucking lot, actually."

Too. Much. Crushing. Pain.

That was what grief was to me. People don't talk enough about loss. How it consumes every inch of you, makes you want to curl up in a little ball and fade into nothingness, so you don't have to feel for five fucking minutes. But you have to go on with life, so you push it all down, hold it under the surface so no one knows the depth of sorrow you feel.

"But I don't owe you my horror story just as you don't owe me yours, so we should drop this."

I dipped my chin to my chest, so I didn't have to look at him any longer. The lid on the box containing my grief and trauma rattled. My eyes squeezed shut against the onslaught of agony contained within.

I almost let out a little sob when a calloused hand brushed across my cheek.

"Kit."

Don't cry. Don't cry. Don't you dare fucking cry in front of him.

I shook my head. It would be too much. All of it. If I let any of it out, then he would see parts of me I didn't want him to. I barely wanted anyone to see them because of what others thought about people like me.

Push it down. You have to. You can't let this out.

"I didnae mean…" He let out a sigh and rubbed my cheek with his thumb. "I dinnae like talking aboot Jenna, and ye just hit a sore spot. But I didnae mean tae upset ye."

My brain caught on one word in his sentence. *Jenna.* He told me his wife's name. Whether it was on purpose or not, I didn't know, but somehow, that broke through the whirlwind of emotions raging inside me. Maybe I should have been happy he said it, but I wasn't. It only made me care more. Caring about Thane was dangerous. He was clearly complicated. Did I need that in my life? Probably not. It was fucked up enough already. And yet, I really wanted to dive headfirst into a complication with him.

It was that thought that cemented my next words.

"I'm warm enough now. You don't have to keep holding me."

He didn't let go. He didn't even take his hand off my cheek.

"Thane."

"Mibbe am no warm enough, Kit. Ye think of that?"

"Are you?"

"Aye. Am freezing withoot ye, so stay here a wee bit longer with me."

My eyes flew open to meet his green ones. There was a little twinkle in them.

I raised my brows. That made him smile at me, and he finally dropped his hand from my face.

"Well, okay, I suppose I can't have you getting cold on me again. And honestly, I wouldn't mind a nap. I'm still tired from yesterday."

Without letting him speak, I snuggled even closer and buried my face in his chest. Thane didn't object to my burrowing myself against him. In fact, after a few minutes, he settled his hand on my waist again and hummed. It wasn't a tune that I recognised, but it lulled me into oblivion.

Our truce was on very tenuous ground, but I was glad we had kept it. It wouldn't do to be at each other's throats when we were trying to survive in a situation where we didn't know if we would be rescued. Or if we were going to have to get out of here ourselves.

FOURTEEN

Thane

*E*very second I lay there with Kit pressed against me as they slept was another lash of a whip against my back, reminding me that I shouldn't be indulging in such intimacies with another person. Well, technically, I was free to do as I pleased, considering I was a widower, but that didn't make it feel okay. It didn't make it right… did it?

Fuck. Messy. So fucking messy.

That was my inner world right then. So many conflicting thoughts rushed around my brain, making it hurt. And it didn't help that my ankle throbbed as I lay on my side with it propped up on my other one.

I tried to force my mind onto other things, but it all kept coming back to Kit. The way they'd squeezed their eyes shut after telling me they didn't want to talk about their grief. I could hardly blame them when I'd immediately got defensive over talk of my own.

What hurt you, Kit?

And when the fuck did I start caring about them? Kit was still a relative stranger to me. I'd never met a person who challenged me this much within a matter of days.

It was different with Jenna. We'd known each other for a long time before ever embarking on a romantic relationship.

I didn't know how to feel about wanting someone I barely tolerated. How to react to it. To deal with it. I'd never experienced anything like this before. I was so out of my depth, and it showed by the way I kept blowing hot and cold with Kit.

I couldn't help but prevent it when they tried to put distance between us. I didn't want that. But now regret curled around me.

Did that regret temper my fingers, stopping them from tucking their dark hair behind their ear, exposing a black helix ear cuff? No. Nor did it stop me from running one down the bridge of their nose. I brushed my finger over the tip, remembering the way they liked to wrinkle it.

What are you doing?

Indulging in things I shouldn't be. If I could stop, would I? In the quiet stillness of the tent where the world couldn't intrude, I let myself trace lines over their face with the barest of touches. It felt forbidden, illicit almost. And I liked it. Far. Too. Much.

Kit was stunning. I hadn't dared think of them that way before, but it was the truth. Learning more about them had only piqued my interest. A fucked up part of me wanted to rip open the walls they were holding up and find out the truth of why they came up here. What reason did they have to run away from their life?

I was aware it wouldn't be fair of me to ask that of them if I wasn't willing to do the same. Telling Kit about Jenna was terrifying. In fact, telling anyone the whole truth of what happened that night had me shrinking into myself, wanting to hide away from the world and drown myself in whisky all over again. Something I couldn't afford to do. Not when I was fighting my way back out of the hole that I'd found myself in the months following Jenna's death.

I had to find a way to live again. Callan kept telling me that. And this... this situation didn't help me with that goal at all.

Kit stirred.

I immediately withdrew my hand from their face. If they caught me stroking them, I had no idea what they would think.

"Thane?" came their sleepy voice.

"Aye?"

Kit opened one eye. They looked worn out despite being asleep for a few hours. We'd been through quite the fucking ordeal together. It didn't surprise me that this situation was getting to them. It was getting to me too.

"What time is it?"

I looked at the watch on my wrist.

"Just after two."

They let out a groan.

"I slept too long. Fuck, and I haven't even given you more painkillers today."

I hadn't even thought about that since I didn't know how many Kit had brought with them.

"Am okay."

Kit's other eye flicked open. They stared at me for a long moment.

"Don't lie to me. You're hurting."

How they knew that I had no idea. It was disconcerting to have someone see through my words.

"Ye dinnae need tae worry aboot me."

Kit scoffed. Then they were out of my arms and the sleeping bag before I could blink. I turned to find them digging in their pack. They returned to my side with two pills and a water bottle.

"Take them, and don't you dare say I shouldn't worry about you again. I'm taking care of you while you're incapacitated. I want no complaints and no arguments to the contrary."

Rather than opening my mouth to retort, I took the painkillers and swallowed them with the water.

Kit set the bottle down next to the sleeping mat. Then they pulled on their fleece and sat beside me. Their expression was guarded, but I could see the concern bleeding out of them. Concern for me and my injury. For our predicament. For everything between us.

"I need to, uh, go… so I'll be back in a bit." They looked around before reaching out and picking up an empty bottle. "If you need to, then use this and I'll empty it when I get back."

"Aye, right."

They set it down by the water bottle, got themselves dressed, and headed out.

Every second Kit was gone, I replayed the words they'd said over and over in my head. The vehemence in their voice. Did Kit care about me? And why? While I understood we were relying on each other to survive, it felt like more. Like Kit didn't actually dislike me at all. They didn't want *me* specifically to be in pain rather than them merely being a kind person looking out for their fellow human being.

Am I reading into this too much? Am I seeing things that aren't there because of my own conflicting feelings for them?

I had to be. This was why I needed to deal with my feelings. I couldn't go around projecting them onto Kit. That wasn't fair. They had no idea that I didn't dislike them. I hadn't made it clear. They were probably out there cursing me to high hell. Asking why they had to get stuck with someone like me. The thought of that made me smile despite myself.

Kit was so damn fucking adorable. As much as I complained about the shite they said to me, I couldn't help finding it endearing. The fact they weren't scared to put me in my place. Maybe I needed that.

Jenna had never been that way. In fact, my wife was the opposite of Kit. She was rarely combative. We had a harmonious life together until that night. And it haunted me. Every moment leading up to her death was a living fucking nightmare. The aftermath was worse.

But what if I needed a challenge now? Something to break the status quo. I mean, fuck, being stuck in a glen in the snow without knowing whether you'd be rescued was one way of doing it. Then to have someone with you who you didn't know whether you wanted to strangle or... or... I didn't know if I wanted to contemplate the alternative. If I could even think it in my head. Kit was another problem on top of the already dire straits I was in.

By the time Kit came back, I'd used the bottle they gave me and tucked myself up in the sleeping bag. The temperature felt like it had dropped. I could hear the wind whistling outside the fabric of the tent. The barely audible sound of the snow landing on it. It was Kit's stomping feet through the snow that alerted me to their return. The sound of zips followed by them sticking their head into the opening they'd made.

"You have something for me?"

I nodded to the bottle I'd left by the entrance. They picked it up and disappeared for a few minutes. Upon their return, Kit stripped off their coat and boots but kept their trousers on. Then they handed me their hand sanitiser. I squirted some onto my hands, rubbing it over my skin before putting them back under the cover.

"While I was out, I remembered we should probably elevate your ankle, but first I want to check to see if the swelling has gone down."

I let them unzip the bag to check on my ankle. It looked worse than it had done last night, but that was because of the very apparent bruising.

"I usually have a first aid kit, but Callan and Ruairí had it covered for oor trip," I said, wanting to break the tense silence between us.

"It can't be helped. At least we have a way to keep warm and food even if we can't fully treat your injury. Think that counts as a win."

Kit rolled my sock back up and carefully folded their coat to prop my ankles up on it.

"If ye say so."

"If you hadn't been so over-prepared for a single day's walk, we would've been fucked. I'm taking the wins where I can."

They gave me a half-smile before turning and digging at our food supplies. They picked something up out of it. Then they came over and sat on the narrow space I'd left on the sleeping mat. Kit opened the chocolate bar and snapped off a piece that they held out towards me.

"Open."

I stared at them.

"What?"

"Well, your arms are in the bag."

"I dinnae need feeding."

Their smile widened.

"Stop being a grump, Thane."

I opened my mouth to say something, but Kit was faster and shoved the chocolate into it. They were clearly trying not to laugh when they tried to snatch their hand back.

Without thinking about it, I leaned forward and nipped their forefinger with my teeth in retaliation.

Kit sucked in a breath, staring at me with shock. Their pupils dilated until only a thin ring of ice blue around them remained.

The tension thickened in the air, leaving me wanting to do more. To run my tongue over their fingers, suck them into my mouth and taste their skin.

Fuck.

Instead of doing that, my head flopped back against the built-in pillow of the mat, and I bit the chocolate between my teeth. Caramel seeped out of the sides and landed on my tongue. I couldn't fault their taste.

Whenever my mother had boxes of chocolates at home, I would always hoard all the caramel-filled ones before my sister could get a hold of them. Sheona always gave me hell over it when we were kids. I'm not sure she appreciated having a younger brother who got away with everything. I wasn't the favourite child now. I hadn't been for a long time.

Kit's hand hovered between us as if they weren't sure whether to pull away or move it closer.

"Ye gonnae hoard the rest of the bar, or am I allowed more than one piece?"

They shook themself, dropped their hand and stared down at the package in their lap. After a minute, they picked it up, broke off another piece, and popped it into their own mouth.

"Only if you say please."

Kit smirked.

I watched their mouth. Their tongue darted out to lick their bottom lip. My brain fixated on it, wondering what it would feel like against me. How hot their breath would be while their tongue ran down my... *no, no, no! Their tongue is not going near any part of me. Why the fuck can't I control my thoughts around them?*

"Please."

Kit relented and shared the rest of the bar with me. We hadn't eaten lunch, so the food was welcome. We could have eaten more, but I had a feeling Kit was concerned about how much we had. I was too. Three days of food wouldn't be enough if no one came to find us.

The avalanche worried me more than I'd let on to Kit. If our group got caught in it, that worsened our odds significantly. We had no way of knowing. It meant we couldn't exactly rely on rescue. And I would have to make plans accordingly if the weather didn't let up.

When we were done with the chocolate, Kit squeezed onto the mat beside me but didn't get in the bag. They still had their clothes on, so I hoped they were warm enough. As evening fell, the temperature would drop, and they'd have to get in the bag with me. The thought of another night with their body pressed against mine made me want to groan. It wouldn't be a problem if I could control these fucking feelings I had towards them.

The truth was... I couldn't. And that scared me more than our precarious circumstances.

FIFTEEN

Kit

Thane and I had spent the rest of yesterday afternoon in a companionable silence. At dinner, we shared another of his ration packs before I made one last trip outside and then joined him in the sleeping bag. To combat the awkwardness of us being pressed so closely together, I told him about some of the most interesting and unique tattoos I'd done. In return, he explained more about his job. They were safe topics.

We had been walking around the edges of charged conversations about our pasts, trying to navigate a way through this situation without revealing too much. I honestly didn't know how much longer I could keep that up.

It wasn't like me to have such mundane, benign conversations. I hated small talk and the mandatory getting-to-know-each-other topics. What did it matter? If you didn't get to the deep stuff, how would you truly know the other person?

Maybe I was a hypocrite since I didn't let many people see the real me. I'd trusted all the wrong people in my life. It made me withdraw. Be wary about who I interacted with. Too many people abused my willingness to be honest and open. To get along with others and make them happy. I mean, fuck... I'd tried to give my best friend the thing she wanted the most in the world. A baby. And I was a failure at that. At a lot of things. So, why should I open up to anyone else? Why should I make others happy when it had only made me miserable?

People were a minefield to deal with, especially when your brain was wired differently from the vast majority of them. The rules of society I'd meticulously learned weren't always applied universally. It made things confusing and downright frustrating. I muddled through life as best I could, trying to figure shit out until I realised I would never win. So I stopped trying. I started being afraid. And Sienna only made my fears worse. If I couldn't trust the friend I'd had for most of my life, then how could I trust anyone?

However, when it came to Thane, I didn't know what I was so afraid of. I wasn't trying to make him like me. Maybe he could be a bit nicer to me considering I'd saved his life, but I wasn't interested in having him think I was a decent human being.

It was funny how for most of my life I'd masked around people just to get by, but with him, I didn't feel the need to even try. Well, I didn't want to have a meltdown in front of his face, but I hadn't hidden what Sienna liked to call my weird, quirky side from him. But to me, those parts weren't weird or quirky, they were just me. The real me. A me very few people got to see.

"I know ye're awake."

Thane's voice startled me in the chilly morning air. I opened my eyes and stared up into his. I'd been lost in my thoughts, wanting to avoid the very awkward part about waking up on top of him. Neither of us had commented on his erection last night. I wasn't about to start on about it today.

You thought a lot about it last night though, didn't you?

I swear my mind was trying to kill me. Of course, I'd thought about it. It was difficult not to. My brain had conjured up very vivid images of what I could do with said erection. And I'd struggled not to physically react to them. My body might want to get it on with Thane, but my head was having a hard time catching up and getting on board with that scenario.

After he'd been acting a little flirtatious yesterday, what with nipping at my fingers, I thought I was going to expire on the spot. It short-circuited my brain and had me struggling to compose myself. Then I was left wondering about his actual thoughts regarding me. His words and actions didn't match up to each other. It confused the fuck out of me. And I wasn't sure I would get a clearer picture any time soon.

"Being awake doesn't mean I'm ready to get up," I said, as Thane continued to stare at me. "I'm not so great with transitions."

The moment the words left my mouth, I wished them back in. I'd had bad experiences with telling people about my disability. It was never something I blurted out on a whim. I carefully considered whether it was safe before revealing it. I wasn't sure how Thane would react. Whether he would see me differently. And I wasn't sure why I even cared when I wasn't trying to impress him.

"Ye dinnae have tae get up, Kit."

His voice had that gruff quality to it that most people got when they'd just woken up. And fuck me if it didn't sound delicious in that accent of his. Not to mention my name. My fucking name on his lips was deadly.

"No?"

"No."

"Are you saying that because you like having me on top of you?"

What the fuck did you just say to him?

"That's no… that's no the reason," he muttered, looking away as his cheeks flushed.

Your hard dick says otherwise.

I thanked the fucking heavens, which I didn't believe in, that those words stayed in my head.

"No? I swear you said you'd freeze without me yesterday."

The way he huffed had his chest pressing further into mine. My teeth gritted against the sensation of my breasts flattening against the solid expanse of him. Fuck how I wanted to rub them over his bare flesh and revel in the stimulation it would bring being skin on skin.

I rubbed my forefinger against my thumb to seek another form of stimulation instead. There was no way in hell I could ask to rub myself all over this man. He would think I was weird as hell. Who asks a relative stranger if you can rub your flesh on his for reasons that aren't sexual?

I mean, it could be sexual because that would work too. It would scratch that brain itch to help regulate my nervous system. Of course, that wasn't the only reason I had sex. I liked the closeness of it. The release. The feeling of letting go. Being with someone that way made me feel good. But I wasn't going to do that with him. He didn't like me. I wouldn't ask for things he would never be willing to indulge in.

"Ye'll freeze withoot me tae."

"Touché."

Thane scoffed and then looked at me again.

"I wanted tae wish ye happy birthday, no make ye get off me."

That shut me right up. I'd forgotten it was my birthday. My thirtieth turn around the sun. And here I was, stuck in a tent with an injured man I had very inappropriate thoughts and feelings about.

Fuck. My. Life.

"Oh."

"Aye."

I hid my face in his chest as embarrassment licked up my spine.

"In that case, I apologise for teasing you when you were trying to be nice."

"Ye're sorry for teasing me?"

"Yes."

Laughter erupted from his chest. The force of it shook my whole body. My head popped up, and I eyed him warily.

"What's so funny?"

After a minute, he settled down a bit. I froze when he reached out and touched my cheek.

"Ye are. If ye decided tae stop teasing me, I'd think there was something wrong with ye."

"You… you don't mind?"

He bit his lip. Why was that so hot? Why was he so hot? Fuck, I wanted him. I wanted those big hands everywhere, touching, feeling, claiming. It wasn't fair. It was fucked up to feel this way. And yet my body ached. My desire flared. It needed sating somehow.

"Yer troublesome mooth is the least of mah concerns."

"What's the most pressing one, then?"

"Oor survival."

Well, that put a dampener on my libido.

Our survival. Not his, but ours… like we were a team. I suppose in this situation we were. It didn't surprise me, considering how protective Thane had been since the very beginning. It was only now that I felt the weight of it. We'd been here for two nights and there had been no sign of rescue. That didn't bode well for us.

"I mean, that's mine too, but I was trying not to think about it."

I let out a sigh and rested my head back on his chest as my fingers rubbed together again. It was the only stim I could do that wouldn't draw too much attention.

"We dinnae have tae talk aboot it."

"But we should, Thane. This isn't good. You can't walk out of here and I can't leave you."

"Ye could."

I shook my head.

"No, I can't. I have a terrible sense of direction, so I'll get lost and freeze on the side of the mountain knowing my luck."

"Ye didnae let me finish. I wasnae saying ye should leave me here, just that ye could if ye wanted tae."

"There's no wanting to leave you. I can't. You're my best chance of survival, just as I'm yours. And besides, I didn't go to all the trouble of saving you to let you die out here alone."

I shouldn't have said that, but the fact he thought I could go off and leave him here didn't sit well with me. Didn't he know by now that I would do anything to make sure we both got through this?

"I dinnae wannae die when am trying tae live again," he said in a quiet voice that was full of restrained emotion.

My heart squeezed painfully. If I didn't have reason enough to keep him alive, then that would have sealed the deal. How could I walk away from him knowing he was shrouded in grief and was trying to fight his way out of it?

Without thinking about it, I wrapped my arms around him as best as I could and held him.

"I won't let that happen."

"Ye gonnae save both of us from this?"

"I'll try my best."

I wasn't sure how, but I would find a way. There had to be one.

"Am no sure we're gonnae be rescued."

"Me either."

Both of us went silent at that. I didn't stop holding him, even if he didn't hold me back. That was okay. I wanted to offer him my strength, even though I had a limited supply of it.

After a while, Thane coughed and shifted underneath me.

"We should probably eat something," he murmured.

"Yeah," I breathed.

The thought of pulling away from him cleaved me in two, but I did it. I struggled my way out of the sleeping bag into the freezing air.

"Fuck me, it's way colder than yesterday."

Thane shifted and stretched while I set about preparing some semblance of breakfast. When we finished eating, he lay on his side so I could get back into the bag with him. It was far too cold to be outside of it.

"I dread to think how much it snowed overnight."

The sound of the wind whistling outside had me wanting to stay in the tent all day. I would have to venture forth eventually. My bladder wouldn't hold out much longer.

"Winter storms can be absolute shite."

"You must be used to them living up here."

"Aye, but I've never been caught in one like this. Ye can read up on all the advice ye want. Nothing can prepare ye for being in the midst of it."

I fiddled with my top.

"Yeah, not going to lie. When we were up there on the mountain, I was terrified with all the wind and snow. I thought we would slip and fall at any moment."

"It put ye off mountaineering?"

I snorted and pushed at his chest.

"No. I mean, I'm not about to go off climbing the world's highest mountains or anything but bagging a few Munros would be an achievement."

"Pity we couldnae get ye up yer first one this time."

"Maybe next time."

If there is a next time…

There was no point me in contemplating our downfall. We still had supplies and each other for now. I had to hold on to hope that we could get through this.

"We're going to be okay, right, Thane? Like things could be worse."

"Aye, they could be."

I noticed the way he hadn't answered my question. He wasn't sure we would be. I wasn't ready to prepare for the worst yet. Especially not on my birthday. Tomorrow I would consider other outcomes. Tomorrow I would be stronger. But for today, I wanted to stay close to Thane and pretend for a moment that we were friends celebrating my birthday, not strangers who barely knew a thing about each other.

So that was what I was going to do.

SIXTEEN

Thane

I t hadn't been my intention to talk about our predicament today. Not on Kit's birthday. A sense of melancholia fell over the two of us after they'd asked me if we were going to be okay. If I answered that honestly, it would have ruined both of our days. Maybe avoiding it hadn't helped matters, but fuck, I couldn't do that to them today. Couldn't tell them I feared rescue wasn't coming at all.

Our best bet was to stay put and wait out the weather until things improved, then make a plan for what we would do next. I couldn't walk yet anyway, so we weren't getting anywhere fast. And as Kit said, they weren't going to leave me here alone.

I was still wrapping my head around their determination to keep me safe. Was I mistaken in their dislike for me? I hadn't exactly been great company, nor had I given them any reason to be kind to me. And yet they were. I mean, fuck, they'd held me when I told them I didn't want to die. They didn't need to comfort me, but Kit had. They fucking had, and it made me… grateful. I wasn't used to having someone be there for me after two years alone without Jenna. That it was a stranger doing it was even more surprising.

"You know, I'm not that upset about being stuck here on my birthday."

Kit's voice filled the tent, bringing me out of my thoughts.

"I'm not big on the whole celebrating another turn around the sun thing. Maybe it's because I don't like being the centre of attention. I just don't get what the big deal is. Like sure, I came on this trip, but that was my gift to myself. I don't care about gifts from other people or having a party to be like look at me, I'm thirty. And now I'm rambling…"

"Ye can ramble if ye want."

They blinked, looking up at me with a shy smile.

"Oh yeah? You like hearing about my weird view of the world?"

"It's no weird."

Kit's eyebrows shot up.

"My friend said it is. Kind of made me feel bad for seeing things differently."

Whatever made me reach out and cup their shoulder with my hand, I didn't know. Their body heat seeped into my palm. And I couldn't pull away.

"Cannae be a guid friend if they're making ye feel bad aboot yerself."

Kit stared at my hand.

"No, I guess not."

Their voice shook on the words.

I squeezed their shoulder. I hadn't been singing Kit's praises to their face. In fact, I'd been downright disdainful. However, they still deserved people who supported them, not someone who would put them down for being a wee bit different. Everyone did.

"They're not a good friend at all," they whispered a moment later.

"Are they why ye're here?"

The way Kit shuddered at my words made me wish I hadn't said them. Hadn't asked. So much for not wanting to ruin Kit's birthday. Then again, they had just told me they didn't really celebrate it.

Their eyes closed and their nose did that wrinkling thing I liked so much.

"I wouldn't have pegged you as the perceptive type."

"Hard no tae notice ye dinnae like talking aboot yer friend."

Kit let out a puff of air.

"Neither would you if she'd thrown twenty-five years back in your face like it meant nothing to her."

My fingers tightened around them again.

"What did she dae tae ye?"

Kit opened their eyes and scoffed.

"What didn't she do."

They rubbed their face with one hand.

"Ye dinnae have tae talk aboot it."

They shook their head and let out a hollow laugh.

"What the fuck else are we going to do?" Their face fell. "Well, I do need to pee. Maybe I'll feel better after that, but I doubt it."

"Kit…"

They shook their head.

"No, don't. I just… I've not told anyone about what Sienna did, okay? Instead, I hid from it, and then I came here. I thought that would help, but it hasn't. I don't do well if I can't process things verbally, and that's a double-edged sword because it takes me way longer to process shit than it does for other people. So I'm stuck, and it sucks. But you don't have to listen to me either. It's not your job to help me deal with my bullshit life, so don't worry about it."

My mouth stayed shut as they struggled their way out of the sleeping bag and into their clothes. I didn't know what to do when they left to do their business, other than take a piss too. It made me feel so fucking useless knowing they would have to empty the bottle when they got back. Kit was only trying to make it easier on me, but it didn't feel right, me relying on them this much felt so… alien.

And they were wrong. I wanted to listen to them. Wanted to know what this Sienna person did to upset them. If they talked about it, they might feel better, and less burdened. I just really didn't want Kit to be sad or feel alone. No, I wanted to protect them. Had done so from the very moment I met them.

I might not have been able to save my wife, but I could help Kit. I *had* to help Kit. Not to make myself feel better, but because they needed it. Their needs were more important than my own right then.

By the time Kit came back, I'd gone over a hundred different ways to get them to talk in my head. None of them were right. Jenna was better at this shite, at encouraging people to open up and being a good listener. I wasn't bad with people necessarily. I just didn't deal with emotions very well. I would try for Kit. We didn't have anyone else but each other.

They dealt with the bottle before returning and stripping out of their outer layers then setting their glasses down by the mat. Kit got back into the sleeping bag with me, shivering the whole time.

"It's not got any better out there," they murmured, pressing themselves against me for warmth.

The fact they didn't hesitate to get close to me had my heart pumping harder. It made me tuck my arms around them, wanting to share my body heat. It was the only way I could keep them safe in this situation. What a fucking meagre offering it was compared to all they'd had to do for me.

"I cannae remember the last time we had a storm like this."

"Just my luck. The first time I visit Scotland, I get stuck in a once-in-a-lifetime storm."

I snorted.

"Mibbe no once-in-a-lifetime."

"No, I suppose not. I just hope it's only once in *my* lifetime."

My fingers splayed themselves out over their lower back. Their breath hitched. Maybe I was taking liberties, but I didn't really care at that moment. The urge to touch them was far too strong for me to resist. It was as if every passing second chipped away at my resolve. Every moment we spent in this dire situation had me throwing my guilt and worries out of the window. All because I couldn't stop looking at Kit and seeing someone who was carrying a heavy weight just like me. It was unexpected and perhaps unwanted to feel things for them, but what the fuck did it matter when I had no idea if we would escape our snowy prison.

"Tell me aboot Sienna."

Kit's whole body went tense.

"I told you not to worry—"

"Aye, I remember what ye said, Kit. Tell me aboot her anyway."

They stared up at me with those fucking beautiful blue eyes that were so full of sadness, it almost hurt to look at them.

"Why?"

"Why what?"

"Why do you want to know?"

"It's no aboot me. Ye need tae talk, so I'll listen."

They pursed their lips.

"I don't need you to act all selfless on my behalf. I'm not worth that."

Their words stung, but not because it hurt me. They thought they weren't worth listening to. What the fuck had the world done to Kit to make them think so lowly of themselves?

"Am no being selfless. Why would ye think ye're no worth someone's time?"

Kit buried their face in their hands, hiding their features from me.

"No, dinnae dae that. Dinnae hide from me, Kit."

With care, I peeled their fingers away from their face. Their mournful expression had me brushing their hair off their cheek.

"What happened tae ye?"

"No one was there for me," they said in a small voice. "Sienna doesn't care about anyone but herself. I had to hurt all by myself. I'm still hurting. It feels like I can't breathe because it's so fucking painful, and I don't know how to survive it. How to cope with the loss of something I didn't even want in the first place."

The words they said were cryptic, but I could understand them all the same. Loss could be unbearable. It could ruin your life. Turn you into someone you didn't recognise. I knew because that's what had happened to me.

"Start at the beginning," I murmured, stroking their jaw with a light touch so as not to spook them.

Kit lowered their eyes to my chest and nibbled their lip.

153

"I've known Sienna since I was five. She took me under her wing when we met at school. She was outgoing, whereas I was shy, so I guess I looked up to her."

They forced out a laugh.

"Well, it was more than that… when I got older, I found myself loving her as more than just a friend, but I never said anything. Sienna's straight, and there was me, this teenage gender-confused bisexual who had no idea what to do with their feelings other than pretend they didn't exist."

I already disliked this Sienna without knowing exactly what kind of shit they'd put Kit through.

"But she did help me through the gender confusion. She might not have understood it, but she was there. When I came out as non-binary at school, she defended me from the bullies. I know we've never talked about it, but I'm agender, as in I don't identify with having a gender at all. I'm not a woman, I'm a person. I usually just tell people I'm non-binary rather than explain all of my complicated feelings about gender to them."

"Callan mentioned it tae me."

Kit's brow furrowed.

"Oh, he did?"

"Aye."

"So you've always seen me as…"

They glanced up at me.

"A person?"

"Yeah."

"Aye."

154

For a long moment, Kit did nothing. Then tears welled in their eyes.

Without thinking about it, I cupped their face in my hand.

"What's wrong?"

"N-n-nothing. It just… just means a lot to me. Not everyone is so… accepting."

Tears slipped down their cheeks. I wiped one away with my thumb.

"It's no aboot accepting it. Ye are who ye are. Who is anyone else tae say otherwise? And if they dae say shite aboot it tae ye, they're a cunt."

"Then Sienna is a cunt."

I raised my brows.

"I thought ye said she was there for ye."

"She was… until she wasn't. I'll get to that bit later." They put their hand on my chest. "And thank you in advance for listening to this because it's about to get worse."

I almost held my breath as Kit rubbed their fingers against me. It was as if they were soothing themselves while they spoke.

"When we were twenty, Sienna met Lawrence. They got married two years later. I won't say I wasn't happy for her because I was. And I became friends with Law, so I didn't begrudge their happiness."

Despite what Kit said, I couldn't imagine how much it must've hurt to watch the person you loved make a life with someone else. It wasn't anyone's fault, but I hated it for them all the same.

"It's not like I didn't have any of my own relationships. I did, but my feelings for Sienna always lingered in the background. I couldn't rid myself of them no matter how hard I tried, but anyway, that's not really relevant…"

Their expression darkened, and the tears kept flowing. My chest hurt to see them cry, but I didn't tell them to stop. If they needed to let it out, then they could.

"Sienna and Law were happy together, but as the years ticked by, there was one thing missing. They wanted a child, but Sienna can't have a baby herself because she was born with an underdeveloped womb. It's called MRKH syndrome. And it sucks because all Sienna has ever wanted is to have a baby."

Something about Kit's words made me dread what was about to come out of their mouth next.

"So, despite the fact I've never wanted kids, I agreed to be their surrogate. I wanted to make Sienna happy, which I know is fucked up, okay, but you do crazy things for the people you love."

Kit bowed their head, hiding their face from me, but I didn't drop my hand from their cheek.

"It took two tries, but I finally got pregnant. It was progressing just fine, but I hated every moment. It gave me a lot of gender dysphoria, but I told no one about that part because I wasn't doing it for me."

Their body shook at the words. I wanted to hold them and tell them it was okay. That while I would never experience such a thing, I understood it was fucking hard for them to deal with.

"At twenty weeks, I found out it was a boy. Sienna was so excited. I had to pretend I was too, even though my dysphoria was getting worse as the weeks went by. And then…" Kit choked on the words before they took a breath in an attempt to compose themselves. "Two days later I miscarried, and life was never the same again."

With that, Kit broke down into sobs and buried themselves against me. My heart broke into tiny pieces for them. So I held them close and let them cry because I had a feeling no one else had let Kit purge their emotions this way. Let them talk about their real feelings without judgment. I wasn't fucking judging Kit at all. They'd made an impossible choice, and it went to absolute shite.

This was fucking awful, but I had a feeling it wasn't the end of the story. And I was pretty sure it would make me hate Sienna more than I already did.

SEVENTEEN

Kit

*C*rying my heart out on Thane's chest wasn't how I expected to spend my thirtieth birthday. I wanted to pretend we were friends, but at that moment, he felt The fact he'd listened meant so much to me. It meant the whole fucking world. It wasn't just that, though. The way he had reacted to my explanation about my gender... no one had ever made it seem so normal. That it was okay to be me. He didn't ask me how I came to that conclusion. Didn't make me feel like a child who didn't know their own mind. I was so used to being judged and questioned that his reaction completely blindsided me.

I hadn't known how to respond, so I avoided it, but I really fucking hoped he understood how much I appreciated it. Appreciated... him. Crazy to think a relative stranger had more respect for my own individual determinations about my life than people who had known me for decades.

While Dad and Olly had reacted well, they still asked me a thousand and one things about it. Not out of judgement, but the need to understand. I was okay with that since the three of us thrived off logic and a need to get down to the nitty-gritty details of everything. But Thane? Thane didn't have to give me anything. And yet, he gave me everything simply by seeing me not as a woman, but as Kit.

"It's okay," he murmured as he pressed his mouth to the top of my head. "Am here. Ye're okay, Kit. Let it oot. I've got ye."

His voice was so fucking soothing. It quelled the ache inside me just a little bit. Helped me regain my composure enough that my sobs abated. The tears kept flowing, but I was able to speak again without wanting to wail about the horror of losing something I didn't want in the first place.

"Do… do you know what the worst p-part about losing him was?"

His head twisted from side to side against mine as he shook it.

"The guilt I felt over being relieved to have my body back. That I wasn't sharing it any longer and I could be me again. I woke up nauseated every day and all my sensory issues were exacerbated because of it. I hated being pregnant. I never want to experience that again. It was hell."

I sighed as fresh tears slid down my face. Self-loathing reared its ugly head. I'd gone so many years being happy with who I was, only to be pulled back into the confusing mess of gender dysphoria I fought so hard to escape. That was hard to cope with. So fucking hard to get through, but I tried… I tried for Sienna. I was beginning to see it might not have been worth it, given the pain it caused me.

"And to top it all off, I couldn't talk about it to anyone, especially after I lost the baby. I put all my feelings aside because Sienna was so distraught… until she wasn't… until she started asking me when we were going to try again like I hadn't just gone through one of the worst experiences of my life. Even Law was concerned about her sudden turnaround. He didn't want to push me when I was still recovering from it. He didn't think trying again so soon was good for any of us."

A part of me didn't want to tell Thane about the rest of it. Didn't want him to know about the mistakes I'd made in the wake of my bleeding heart. But it was a part of my story. I wasn't infallible. I was messy and chaotic, especially having undergone such a traumatising experience. My life felt like a series of them.

"Sienna didn't want to listen to reason. To either of us. And… and I'm ashamed of what happened next."

"If it's no relevant, ye dinnae have tae tell me."

Oh, I wish it wasn't, but it's just another layer of crap to add to the overflowing shit pile.

Thane's thumb stroked across my cheek, reminding me he was still holding onto my face. Was still grounding me with the touch of his rough fingers, his palm cradling me.

What had I done to deserve such kindness from him? He made me feel like I was a burden when we were on the course, but now… now it was different. It felt different between us.

"Three months after I miscarried, around new year, Sienna had a massive go at Law and me before storming out of their house, saying she was going to stay at her parents for a few days. We had a drink to commiserate with each other. He kept topping up my glass, so I didn't realise how drunk I was until we were suddenly kissing. Like, it wasn't exactly good because he was all tongue and I don't like French kissing, it's kind of icky. Regular kissing with a bit of tongue is fine, but… wow, fuck, I'm sharing way too much information that you don't need to know."

Thane shifted but said nothing to my little revelation. Why couldn't I keep my mouth shut around him? My need to over-explain everything had reared its ugly head and was making me over-share irrelevant details yet again.

"Anyway, I kind of just went along with it all. I was so fucking sad and I wanted to lose myself for a bit, but I didn't have sex with him or anything. It was more like… mutual satisfaction with hands only. I wasn't ready to be *that* intimate with anyone after the miscarriage. I was still trying to deal with the dysphoria, and it was too messy. I'm mostly okay now, like I'd be fine with intimacy if it was with the right person."

Stop telling him things that aren't important to the story! He doesn't need to know that you'd say yes if he offered to fuck you.

My brain was really doing a number on me today. Here I was sharing my horrible story, and my thoughts were on having sex with the man holding me while I cried on him.

"I immediately regretted what happened and left right after. I cried half the night and slept like shit… drinking always does that to me. Law and I never spoke of it. Like fuck, he cheated on Sienna with me, and there we were, pretending like nothing happened. I thought the guilt might eat me alive, but it was overshadowed by how awful Sienna was acting towards me."

I let out a breath. Telling him about the shit Sienna had thrown at me the last time we spoke felt harder than admitting to the cheating. Maybe because she'd been so blasé about her husband's indiscretion. Like it didn't matter. And that made me sick.

"Ye know what all that sounds like tae me?" Thane asked after a minute's silence.

I shook my head.

"He took advantage of ye." He dropped his hand from my cheek and cupped my shoulder instead. "The man plies ye with alcohol, lowers yer inhibitions and ability tae think clearly when he knows ye're under a lot of duress and makes a move on ye. That's no someone acting with pure intentions."

I swallowed hard at the implications of his words. And when I thought about it, they made sense.

"I don't think you're wrong. Sienna told me the last time we spoke that Law has always had a thing for me. She said a lot of hurtful things that day, actually."

"Am no gonnae like this."

"No."

He sighed and tightened his hold on me as if he could protect me from the pain inflicted on me by my so-called best friend.

"She told me I was welcome to his... his dick because that was the only way I'd ever get close to her. Then she said I thought I was more of a woman than her because my body works properly. And when I was like it's not okay to misgender me, she said I was kidding myself about not being a woman. I walked away after that, didn't want to stand there, and be insulted after she spent months pressuring me into something I didn't want to do. Sienna's always had a mean streak. I just didn't think she would ever turn it on me... until she did."

All my energy rushed out of me now that I'd finished my story. Finished unburdening myself. I relaxed fully into Thane's hold, letting the tears wash away the pain. Letting his warmth and comfort soothe my soul. Allowing myself to let my guard down completely. There was nothing to be scared of. Thane gave me something few people had. Safety.

It was a long while before he spoke as if he was processing what I'd told him. Talking about it made me realise how truly awful Sienna had behaved towards me. How little she really cared.

"Dae ye still love her after all that?"

"I'm not... in love with her any longer. She killed that love, but it's hard to stop caring about someone you've known for twenty-five years. I'm trying though. I don't want to see her again, not after the things she said."

"Want mah honest opinion?"

I pulled my head away from his chest, finally looking him in the eyes.

"Go ahead."

His expression was darker than I'd ever seen it before. It scared me a little.

"Ye're better off withoot her. Ye dinnae need someone who doesnae care aboot ye or yer feelings or how something so fucking tragic would affect ye. Sienna's a selfish cunt. She used ye tae get what she wanted and left ye alone when ye needed her the most. And as for her husband, he's no better than her. They both took advantage of ye. Am sorry ye've had tae deal with it all by yerself, Kit. It's no right. Ye deserve better."

I should have known Thane wouldn't mince words. And I couldn't say he was wrong, either.

"Do I?"

His expression grew very serious.

I bit the inside of my cheek when he caught my chin between his fingers.

"Aye, ye fucking dae and dinnae let anyone tell ye otherwise."

"Not even you?"

"Especially no me."

I pressed my hand to his chest.

"Thank you."

"Why ye thanking me?"

A smile played on my lips.

"For listening and for not judging me. It's helped more than you know."

"Am no gonnae judge yer actions when ye were suffering and no one else cared enough tae help ye. They preyed upon ye instead. That's no fucking okay. The only people am judging are those cunts who used ye. I dinnae blame ye for wanting tae get away from their shite. They thought it was okay tae abuse yer friendship… am fucking mad anyone would treat ye that way."

The fact he sounded so incensed on my behalf made my chest ache. Thane had no reason to defend me. I would say he barely knew me, but I'd shared a lot about myself with him. A lot more than most people knew.

"You're mad about it even though you don't like me?"

"Dinnae have tae like someone tae know they've been mistreated." His eyes searched my face for a moment. "But I dinnae dislike ye, Kit. Ye just…"

"Wind you up the wrong way?"

"Aye."

I grinned through my tears.

"I don't dislike you either, you know."

His sharp expression softened. I tried not to hold my breath when he wiped my face with his thumb.

"No? Ye havnae heard mah story yet."

"Are you going to tell me?"

"Am thinking aboot it."

My fingers dug into his chest.

"You don't have to. I'm not expecting anything just because I shared mine with you."

He nodded slowly, his thumb still brushing over my cheek. The way he touched me had my heart pumping harder. It was so gentle and caring. My fucking soul was melting for him at this point. Fuck, I had it bad for this man. There were so many reasons I shouldn't be thinking this way after what just transpired, but I couldn't deny my feelings.

"Ye seem better for talking aboot it."

"I am. I mean, I'm still fucked up about the whole thing if I'm honest, but it doesn't feel quite so... heavy. And, well, I'm seeing it in a different light now. You did that for me."

"I just told ye the truth."

"Can't always see the truth of the matter when you're right in the middle of it."

He looked thoughtful at my statement.

"Aye, mibbe ye're right. Mibbe that's why I should tell ye aboot Jenna."

"You really don't—"

He silenced me with a thumb over my lips.

"If ye dinnae wannae hear it, ye just have tae say it, but I wannae tell ye. I think... I think I need tae."

I pulled his hand away from my face, and without thinking about it, linked our fingers together.

"You can tell me, Thane. I'm listening."

EIGHTEEN

Thane

When Kit entwined our fingers together, I couldn't help staring at them and wondering why they wanted to listen to my story.

If you'd asked me an hour ago whether I would be okay with talking about what truly happened the night Jenna died, the answer would have been fuck no. But something about Kit unburdening themselves to me made me want to share my fucked up story. The true story, not the one I'd given everyone else. There were parts I redacted. The ones that still ate at me. I hadn't forgiven myself for them. For any of it. It was still my worst fucking nightmare.

Kit had been through some shite too. How they coped with it all, I didn't know. They were stronger than they knew.

If I continued to think about how they'd been taken advantage of, I would probably want to smash something. While Kit said it was their choice to be Sienna and Lawrence's surrogate, I couldn't help but feel as though they did it out of misplaced loyalty and love for someone who didn't deserve it. And I hated everything about what they'd told me.

"Thane?" came their whispered voice.

I looked away from them.

"I… I dinnae know where tae start."

Although I wanted to tell Kit, I found it hard to open my mouth and begin.

"Why don't you start with how you and Jenna met."

Them giving me a direction helped. I didn't have to broach the difficult subject of her death just yet. Maybe speaking of the beginning of our lives together would make it easier to talk about the end.

"We were eleven. Jenna's family moved here right before I started high school. We became friends and eventually, when we were sixteen, Jenna admitted she had a crush on me. I hadnae thought aboot her that way until she said it… took me a bit tae agree tae try us oot, but I did, and it worked. We worked."

I vividly remembered the day Jenna admitted she liked me. It was a cold, wet Tuesday. We'd been standing under a shelter outside school, waiting for our parents to pick us up. She blurted it out suddenly. I was so taken aback that I didn't know what to say, so I told her I would talk to her about it the next day.

Callan was the one I confided in after it happened. He was keen for me to try, despite my reservations. Said Jenna would be good for me. And he'd been right in his own way. Jenna wore down my hard edges, made me softer and less… intense, as Callan liked to tell me.

"She was easy tae be with. Always kind, caring, and understanding. She was the one who held us together."

I let out a breath and closed my eyes. It was true enough that Jenna was the glue holding our relationship together. She never made me feel like I had to fight too hard for it. For her. And that was probably why I had no fucking clue things were wrong until it was too late.

"I asked her tae marry me when we were nineteen and a year later, we got married in her parents' back garden under an oak tree with all oor friends and family surrounding us. It was the happiest day of her life. I always knew she wanted the perfect day even though I wasnae really fussed aboot the wedding. Just wanted us tae be together, but I gave her that 'cause I loved her."

Funny that I thought love could carry us through everything. It turned out that wasn't true. A relationship required more than love. It needed open communication and honesty. Something I always thought we had in spades… until we didn't.

"We were happy for many years. She was all I wanted, and I thought I was enough for her. We were enough. We'd talked aboot mah feelings regarding having a family in that I didnae want one. I never have. Am like ye, I dinnae want children. I had a vasectomy when I was twenty-five. Jenna was there with me every step of the way. It was never an issue between us."

Kit's fingers tightened around mine. I swallowed hard. Fuck, how I wished that statement was true. That it was never an issue. It had been the truth for a long time. For years. Until it wasn't.

"I... fuck, I dinnae know how tae talk aboot her death," I whispered. "I havnae told anyone exactly what happened."

"Is it bad?"

"Aye, really fucking bad."

Somehow, I knew Kit would understand why it was so hard for me to tell anyone. Why it hurt so fucking much. It was as if a knife had lodged itself in my chest. Every time I took a breath, it made tiny holes in my heart. They leaked sluggishly, making it feel as though I was slowly dying on the inside. I didn't know how else to describe the pain.

"Then maybe we should take a break and eat something. You can talk about it when you're ready."

"I dinnae think am ever gonnae be ready."

Kit let go of my hand and brushed their fingers over my cheek.

My eyes popped open, staring into their blue ones.

"We'll rip the bandage off together, okay? I'll share the burden with you, so you don't have to be alone in it any longer."

I nodded slowly, not quite believing someone I'd only known for a week would do that for me.

Kit differed from anyone else I'd ever met. And that was why I liked them so very much. All my irritation evaporated when I realised there was far more to them than met the eye. That they weren't out to piss me off on purpose. They were trying to deal with their suffering the best way they could. Just like me.

"It's okay, Thane. I know how hard it is to share your darkest memories. You can take your time. I'm not going anywhere."

Kit gave me a half-smile before slipping out of the sleeping bag and starting to make us lunch.

I watched them, my eyes roaming across their curves and edges, lingering on their neck. Such a delicate wee thing.

Would their skin prickle if I breathed against it?

Would they shudder with anticipation of my mouth on it?

Would they want me to wrap my fingers around their throat while I tasted it?

Why the fuck are you thinking about that?

Here I was meant to be working out how to tell them about Jenna's death and I was too busy staring at their neck like it was a meal. I didn't have a thing about necks in general. In fact, I had never once wanted to encircle Jenna's and use it as an anchor while I did things to her.

It shouldn't be strange to want something different when it came to another person, but it felt that way. My only experience of intimacy was with my wife, and she was the one who led that side of our relationship. It didn't occur to me that I would ever want someone else the way I did with Kit. The way I desired them terrified me. This deep, visceral longing to touch them made my fingers throb. But no one

171

else had sparked this within me. I didn't understand it. How I could feel this way about them when I'd spent a lifetime never experiencing this need for another person.

Even so, the guilt surrounding my feelings towards them lessened with every moment we spent together. I had to restrain myself from acting upon them… but why shouldn't I want Kit?

The answer to that had been so clear before, but now I had a hard time believing it was wrong when we were alone in this glen. When we didn't know if we would be rescued or if anyone even knew we hadn't made it back down the mountain. I had nothing but memories holding me in place. Well, that and the fact Kit probably didn't see me that way at all. They might have said they didn't dislike me, but that didn't mean they were attracted to me.

You're a fucking mess, you know that, right? Stop thinking about how much you want to touch Kit and start deciding how you're going to talk about that night with Jenna.

Maybe my current thoughts were a way of distracting myself from the inevitable pain I had to relive in order to expose my deepest wounds. It was easier to mull over my dilemma regarding Kit than to think about Jenna's death. Although, it wasn't so much of a dilemma any longer. More a case of accepting I liked them in a way I never expected.

"Here you go."

Kit's voice startled me.

I looked up to find them holding out one of the ration packs. Pulling myself up into a sitting position, I took it out of their hands. The cold air made me shiver.

"Yeah, it's pretty fucking chilly," they noted as they slid their legs into the sleeping bag next to mine.

I grunted because saying something was too fucking difficult. Kit being close to me only exacerbated the desire to explore every inch of them. I shut that right down while we ate, trying to keep my mind on the task ahead.

"What was she like?" Kit asked after they put the ration pack away when we were done. "I mean, other than kind and understanding."

I set my arm down behind Kit without thinking about it. The edge of my thumb brushed against them, but I didn't move it.

"She was very serious."

"Serious?"

"Aye. Very competitive and a hard worker. She did have a playful side, it just didnae come oot very often."

Jenna worked for her parents at their bakery. She wanted to run it when they retired. She worked long hours, putting her all into it because that was her ambition in life. To be successful.

"We both enjoyed mountaineering, but it was always more mah thing than hers. She'd always wannae be first tae the top… and I let her. Made her happy tae be number one."

As the years had gone by, Jenna had come out with me less and less, especially after Callan and Ruairí set up their business together. It became the thing I did with them rather than her. I should have realised then how our lives had begun to separate. There were a lot of things I should have realised about our relationship that I hadn't.

"We had different interests, but we had a common life goal. Being with each other through thick and thin. At least, that's what I thought we had. Everyone always said we were perfect for each other."

I rubbed my beard with my free hand as my thumb absently brushed against Kit's thigh.

"Am beginning tae think people saw a perfect marriage on the ootside that was actually crumbling on the inside."

Kit turned their face towards me. Their brow was furrowed, and they had a very serious look in their eyes.

"What makes you say that?"

"The year before she died, things were strained between us. She grew distant, but I didnae realise until it was tae late."

Kit trembled slightly, but they kept their eyes on me.

I wondered what they made of my admission. It wasn't something I had told anyone else, not even Callan. It was hard to admit my marriage was failing long before Jenna died. And, honestly, it was the last thing on my mind in the wake of her death. The pain of losing her overshadowed all of that.

"Are ye cold?"

"Just a bit."

"Come lie doon with me then."

They didn't protest, even if they looked at me with concern. If only I could read their thoughts, I'd know how they felt about what I was telling them. But that wasn't something anyone could do.

I shifted down into the sleeping bag. Rather than turning on my side, I let Kit settle on top of me. It was easier to keep my ankle propped up that way. It hurt less when it was elevated.

My hands landed on their back, one falling at the base of their spine. Neither of us spoke as we lay there. Kit's soft breath dusted across my neck as their head was on my shoulder. I stroked their back, feeling relatively content. I had more to divulge to them, but I wasn't in a rush.

Would it be easier to talk about it when I was concentrating on how close they were to me? Kit made me feel safe somehow. Then there was the fact we were alone out here in a wee bubble of our own. There was no one else around to judge or input their opinion. Kit didn't know Jenna. Had no preconceived notions about our relationship and what happened between us. There was less pressure on me. I didn't have to hide the fact we argued that night in the car or what we had been fighting about.

It was only the guilt of walking out of that vehicle alive when Jenna died that lingered in my mind. And the grief of losing the woman I'd loved for so long.

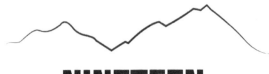

NINETEEN

Kit

L istening to Thane talk about his wife made my heart hurt. There was no fondness in his tone, even when he told me what she was like. He sounded more broken than anything else. That made sense after he admitted their marriage wasn't doing so well. But it didn't sit right with me.

I worried about what he would say next. He'd been building up to her death in his own way. I didn't want to push him or put a time limit on it. Thane had clearly bottled all of this up for a very long time.

"We went tae a wedding for her friend a few hours away."

I rested my hand on his chest and waited for him to continue, knowing this was it. He was going to tell me what happened. Thane hadn't alluded to the circumstances of Jenna's death. I didn't know what I was in for.

"It was early morning when I drove us back. The rain was coming doon hard ootside, so mah attention was mostly on the road. Jenna was unusually quiet. She looked like she was having fun at the wedding, but once we got in the car, she seemed tae deflate, tae withdraw intae herself. It worried me. Her lack of willingness tae communicate had been going on for months, and I was tired of it."

A sickening feeling filled my stomach. If Thane wasn't about to tell me they'd been in a car accident, then my pattern recognition was way off.

I kept silent, not wanting to disturb him as he spoke. My eyes darted up to his face. He stared up at the ceiling with a faraway look in his eyes, as if he was reliving that night right in front of me. His abject misery seeped into me. Sometimes I hated the way I experienced empathy. How I took on other people's emotions. Felt their pain. I'd learned how to disassociate from it if it became too much, but right then, with Thane bleeding out in front of me, I couldn't keep his emotions at bay. Couldn't stop myself from taking them in. Feeling them with him.

"I asked her what was wrong. As usual, she said it was nothing, but I didnae believe her. So I pushed and pushed until she turned tae me and said, 'I want a baby, Thane,' and I swear tae fuck my whole world slammed tae a stop. The car kept going. It was still raining, but it all felt like nothing compared tae the bomb she dropped on me."

I wasn't sure why Thane brought up the topic of not wanting children, especially when he said he and Jenna agreed on that front. Now it made perfect sense. For her to turn around and tell him she wanted a kid after they'd been together for so long… I couldn't even imagine how he must have felt.

"I didnae know what tae say. I had tae keep mah eyes on the road, but mah mind was spinning. Jenna kept talking while I was falling apart. She said she kept it from me 'cause she knew I wouldnae be happy aboot it, but she couldnae stay silent any longer. She wasn't getting any younger, and it had become a necessity tae her. I asked how long she had felt this way… and the answer… fuck."

His voice broke on the last word. Tears welled in his eyes. His fingers dug into my back, but I ignored the pinch of pain that came with it.

The only way I could think to comfort him was to flatten my hand against his chest. My thumb stroked the bare skin above his top at the base of his neck. He let out a shuddering breath.

"I've never said this oot loud before."

His voice was soft, with a touch of weariness to it. The weight of this crushed him. Ate him up from the inside. I felt it in the tension radiating off his body.

"She said she'd always wanted children, but she wanted tae be with me more until it stopped feeling like enough. She wanted something she knew I wouldnae give her."

My chest cracked right open, and the aching void left in its wake crippled me. Tears left my eyes. I'd cried enough for a lifetime today over my pain, but how else could I let it out? The agony of what he had to deal with cut me into tiny pieces. And it was going to get a whole lot worse. I just knew it.

"Before I could answer, she continued, telling me that she'd struggled over what tae dae aboot us, but she knew in her heart, she couldnae deny her need any longer. She wanted a baby regardless of mah feelings. It escalated intae a full-blown argument when I asked her what the fuck that meant. We were practically shouting at each other. She should have talked tae me aboot it. We were meant tae be a team, but she shut me oot. It was awful. My heart was ripping tae shreds over her words and the way she acted like I was the problem when she was the one who hadnae been honest with me."

He wasn't the problem. Thane had been honest with Jenna from the start, judging by what he'd told me. The man had made sure he couldn't have kids. His stance on the matter was pretty fucking clear. And his wife couldn't be truthful about her own feelings on the matter.

At the time they got together, Jenna might not have thought it would become an issue, but clearly, she had misjudged her feelings. I didn't think I could fault her for that. We were entitled to change our minds. However, keeping it from him was wrong. It wasn't fair to him at all.

"The final straw came when she told me she was gonnae have a baby whether or no I was on board with it. She'd dae it withoot me since she knew I wouldnae reverse mah vasectomy and it was uptae me tae decide whether I wanted tae stand by her through it or no. I didnae know what the fuck tae think or dae. My ears were ringing as I stared at the wet road and the wipers going back and forth. She gave me a fucking impossible decision tae make… but it turned oot, I didnae need tae make it at all."

The fact she gave him such a cruel ultimatum made me wrap myself tight around Thane's body. I wanted to shield him from that horror, even though I couldn't. I hadn't known him back then. But I could help him now. I could comfort him and give him my strength and support. It felt woefully small like it wasn't enough, but it was all I had to offer.

"We were driving on this narrow road with limited visibility. Someone clipped the back of mah car as they drove past us. With the road being really fucking wet, the car spun oot and I couldnae get it back under control no matter how hard I tried. There was this crunch as the car slammed intae something and we came to a stop. It all happened so fast, I hardly knew what was up or doon."

He held me tighter like his life depended on keeping me there. The sick feeling was back, making me want to throw up, but I kept my mouth shut. Kept myself from giving into the desire to hurl my guts up.

"All I could hear was the rain pouring doon on the metal and glass. I stared at the windscreen, noting the way it had cracks along it. My eyes followed them, watching them get bigger until I saw a branch hanging over the car. It kept whacking into the glass over and over. My attention caught on the metal around the windscreen. It was crumpled on the passenger side. I turned mah head and saw exactly what happened tae the car."

He choked on the words. His chest shuddered with each of his breaths.

"It buckled in the centre and wrapped itself around the tree. And there was Jenna, her eyes wide and glassy. Her head was all I could bring myself to look at 'cause if I concentrated on her further, I would've seen her crushed body. I tried tae talk, but nothing came oot. And I just fucking knew she was gone."

It didn't feel good that I had been right about them being involved in a car accident. It felt hollow. I didn't know what to say to Thane. My thoughts were chaotic. It had to have been horrific for him to see her that way.

You poor, poor fucking man. Fuck how I wish there was something I could do to make this better. To erase that memory. To make the pain go away.

"There was banging behind me followed by the sound of the car door being wrenched open. Someone was talking tae me, but I couldnae hear them. I felt mahself being pulled from the wreck, but I couldnae speak. Mah wife was dead and the last things we'd said tae each other were in anger. I dinnae really remember what happened next clearly. It was a blur of people talking, flashing lights from the polis and ambulance vehicles. Jenna was pronounced dead on the scene, and I walked away with bruising and a few cuts. It was the worst and longest fucking day of mah life dealing with the aftermath. With the questions and the crying from everyone around me. But I was numb, so fucking numb tae it all."

The fact he not only had a horrible argument with her but then had to deal with her sudden death was almost too much to bear. It didn't surprise me he was numb. He must've been in shock. The utter devastation would come later.

"No one knows aboot oor fight, they just know we got intae an accident. Telling them Jenna wanted children after all these years of them knowing we'd decided no tae have them was tae much for me. All of it was… so I stopped talking tae anyone. I sold oor hoose as I couldnae bear tae be in the space she created. I rented a hoose in the woods tae get away from everyone, withdrew intae mahself, drank tae much so I could sleep at night, and didnae want tae live any longer."

He let out a long sigh as if the weight of it was lifting off him now he'd finally admitted the truth out loud.

"The only person who stuck by me was Callan. He pulled me oot of bed more times than I can remember, forced me tae sober up before I lost mah job and made sure I took care of mahself. I dinnae think I'd be here withoot him. I owe him everything."

"But he doesn't know what Jenna said to you."

"No. Just ye."

A part of me felt honoured Thane had told me about it. The other half understood it was easier to talk to a stranger than the people who knew you best. That was why I told Thane my story.

"I can tell it's been difficult carrying that around all this time. What she did was shitty, Thane, giving you an ultimatum like that. You deserved better than to be blindsided by the truth she kept from you throughout your entire relationship."

He didn't respond for a long while. I was pretty sure he hadn't thought about it that way. Her death likely overshadowed their argument, but I didn't want to hold back on my thoughts when he had made his clear regarding my horrible situation.

"I feel guilty aboot it."

"What part?"

"The argument and her death. I couldnae control the car."

"And you think that was your fault?"

"Aye."

I wiped my tears from my face and pushed myself up to meet his eyes. They were still glassy, and his expression was pained. If he didn't want to talk about their argument further, I wouldn't make him, but we were going to get one thing straight about the car crash.

"It was an accident."

"Aye, but it was mah responsibility tae keep her safe and I didnae."

"No one is at fault for what happened. And assigning blame is a pointless endeavour when it was out of your control. It was out of everyone's control. You didn't demand the rain to fall or the water to be on the road. You were in an impossible situation and that is fucking horrible, but there is not guilt here, Thane. You didn't kill Jenna."

"It feels like I did."

I placed both my hands on his face without thinking about it. He stared up at me with those sad green eyes. It broke something inside me.

"Say it with me… I am not responsible for her death."

"Kit."

"Say it."

I didn't know why I was doing this. I couldn't stand the thought of him beating himself up over her death after all this time. Accidents happened, and it sucked, but he wasn't at fault. Deep down, he had to know that.

"Am no responsible for her death."

He whispered the words, but the fact he said them made my heart hurt.

"Do you mean that?"

"Mibbe."

"Thane."

He blinked, then looked away.

"If we hadnae been arguing, I might've been paying more attention. I should've waited until we were home tae ask her, but I couldnae take it any longer. It had been months of her no wanting tae talk. We werenae intimate. She didnae hug me or kiss me. It was like we were living separate lives but together. I blame mahself for that part. For talking tae aboot it in the car when it was pissing doon with rain. It was a stupid thing tae dae."

If I hadn't known how stubborn he could be, his words would have frustrated me even more. He needed to hear a few home truths about the situation. Just as he had told me that Lawrence had taken advantage of me, I was going to make sure Thane knew he didn't get to take the blame for an accident.

"Well, it wasn't the best idea, no, but you were trying to keep your marriage together. No one can blame you for that. There is never a right time to bring a subject up or talk about things. Sometimes we get it wrong. It's just fucking tragic what happened to both of you, but it's still not your fault. You didn't do it on purpose or make it happen. It just did."

Thane closed his eyes and took a deep breath. When he opened them again, he put his hands on mine, curling his big fingers around my much smaller ones.

"I know ye're right, it's just hard tae reconcile that in mah head. That I didnae dae anything wrong. It isnae fair that I got tae live and she died."

"Life isn't fair."

He gave me a sad smile.

"Aye, it's shite, but thank ye for listening tae me, Kit. I needed that."

He didn't have to thank me, but I would take it. Everything he told me made his behaviour so much easier to understand. Thane had been grieving and suffering alone, living with the guilt, he shouldn't feel over something that wasn't his fault.

I couldn't blame him for being grumpy yet overprotective after what he'd been through. It didn't make me feel sorry for him. I just wanted to help him be okay again because I'd gone and found myself liking him a hell of a lot more than I should. And I wasn't sure what to do with that at all.

TWENTY

Thane

The weight bearing down on me lessened the longer I stared up at Kit. The longer I held their hands against my face.

Talking about Jenna's death was fucking hard, but it helped. Fuck, it helped. The catharsis of finally unburdening myself about our argument. The guilt of walking out of the accident alive when Jenna died on impact. It had been a small consolation at the time, the fact she hadn't suffered. I was the one left hurting. A never-ending punishment. Only I didn't want to be in pain any longer. I wanted to be free of it, even just for a second. For a moment.

"You're welcome," they said with a quirk of their lips.

Kit wrinkled their nose and slipped their hands from my face. I felt bereft of their touch immediately. I wanted it back. I needed it. It had been so long since I'd had any sort of affection that wasn't my family insisting on hugging me and crying on my shoulder. Like it hurt them more than me that my wife died. Not that I was comparing their distress to mine, but I hadn't needed the constant reminders of what I'd lost.

Reaching up without thinking about it, I wiped away the wetness from their cheek. They cried for me. And somehow, that didn't feel wrong the way my family's tears had. Kit made me feel seen. They understood why this hurt so fucking much.

"Sorry, I couldn't help it."

"Dinnae apologise. No one cried for me when it happened. It was only aboot Jenna as it should've been."

Kit let out a choked sound and rested their hand on my heart.

"You lost so much that night. I can… I can feel your pain, the way you bleed, and it's hard not to be upset about it."

They seemed hesitant to tell me that. It didn't feel odd to me that they could feel what I did. It fit Kit somehow.

"Ye feel that, aye?"

Their cheeks blazed red.

"Kind of, but my feelings aren't important right now. How do you feel, you know, after talking about it?"

I dropped my hand from their face, not wanting them to be uncomfortable.

"Better. Still hurts, but it's guid tae get it oot of mah system."

That made them smile.

"Oh good. I'm glad." They let out a sigh. "Well, I don't know about you, but I'm really fucking tired after all that emotional purging."

"Ye can take a nap. No like we have much else tae dae."

"You sure you don't need to talk more?"

I shook my head.

"No, am okay."

What I wanted was for Kit to curl up on me. As terrible as it was, I wanted an excuse to hold them close. To soak up their warmth. To just be with them.

Kit got settled and rested their head on my chest. Their fingers traced lines on it for a long while until they drifted off. I wrapped my arms around them, listening to their soft breathing. They hadn't thought I was a terrible person after what I'd told them. Some days, I felt like a monster for what happened. For being unable to save Jenna from the accident. Save our families from that pain. And for keeping the truth from them. People say the truth sets you free. After telling Kit, I could believe that was true.

I don't think you know what you've done for me.

It was that thought that made me close my eyes and breathe them in. Let myself fully relax for the first time in years. I had a safe place here with Kit against me. An acceptance I never thought I would ever receive.

"Thank ye, mah pretty wee thing," I whispered into their hair and let myself fade away into sleep too.

When I awoke, it was dark in the tent. Kit was fiddling with their fingers on my chest, letting me know they were no longer sleeping.

"Ye been awake long?"

"Not really. Was just preparing myself to get out of the sleeping bag and make us something for dinner."

"I can dae that if ye'd like."

I didn't want Kit to feel like they had to do everything. It wasn't any trouble for me to prepare food, as long as I didn't jostle my ankle too much.

"Okay. I'm not going to say no to that."

Kit unzipped the bag for me, and I slid out from underneath them. Turning the torch on, I noted their messy hair and the sleepy look in their icy eyes. We'd been in the same clothes for days, but at least I had the forethought to bring deodorant. And mouthwash, though I'd forgotten to tell Kit about that part.

Their gaze remained on me as I prepared one of the ration packs using the camping stove. It was likely safer to do this outside the tent, but it was far too cold to be out there. I wouldn't subject Kit to that either.

We ate in a peaceful silence. It was an odd sensation to feel less on edge after talking about my worst memories. I could breathe more easily. My ankle was aching less too. I imagined putting weight on it would be an issue, but that was a worry for tomorrow. Tonight, I wanted to bask in this newfound relief, even if it was just for a moment.

"I've been trying not to think about how worried my dad must be. We usually text every day. He must know something is wrong by now," Kit said as I tidied up our stuff.

"Would he alert the authorities?"

"Probably. I gave him a copy of the itinerary and Callan's contact details, just in case."

"Mibbe there's a wee bit more hope we'll get oot of this."

Kit shrugged.

"I guess so. It doesn't feel like we have much right now. The weather has only got worse. I could barely see a few feet in front of me when I went out earlier."

"We can think aboot that tomorrow. Let's no make yer birthday worse. I have something for ye, anyway."

Their eyebrows quirked up at that.

"Oh yeah? What's that?"

I handed them the bottle of mouthwash. Kit turned it over in their hands with wide eyes.

"Oh my god. I was thinking my breath must be awful. Did you forget you had this?"

"Aye."

"Well, thank you."

They gave me a shy smile before untwisting the cap and using it. They spat the liquid out in the empty thermos cup before handing over the bottle for me to use too.

Kit got up to empty it outside while also relieving themselves. I took the opportunity to do so myself before we bedded down for the night. After they disposed of the contents of the bottle, they came back in with a grimace.

"Fuck me. It snowed even more during the day. The tent is half covered again. Ugh, that's a fucking pain, but like you said, we'll think about it tomorrow."

"Aye, that we will."

They got tucked up in the sleeping bag with me again before turning out the torch.

"I'm not that tired now," they said after a minute.

"Ye wannae talk?"

"Not really. All talked out after today."

They shifted on top of me. I tried not to think about which parts of them were pressing against me. To not imagine myself with my hand around their neck. The guilt surrounding wanting them had all but left me. And yet I couldn't bring myself to act on it. I had no fucking clue how Kit truly felt about me. Besides, it wouldn't be right. We weren't in this situation by choice. They didn't ask to have to lie on top of me at night to stay warm.

"Do you still keep in touch with Jenna's family?"

The question made me tense up.

"No."

"Why not?"

"I dinnae wannae talk aboot them nor mah family, Kit."

I might have been okay with sharing about Jenna, but our families were a sore spot in my life. I was ashamed of the way I treated them. Opening up that can of worms felt like too much after exposing my wounds to Kit.

"Oh, okay… I won't make you. Sorry, I mentioned it."

"Why are ye always apologising? Ye dinnae need tae. Am no mad at ye for bringing it up."

191

They moved again, making me hold back a grunt. Kit rubbing themself against me wasn't helping me stay under control. In fact, it was making things increasingly difficult.

"I don't want to talk about my inability to stop apologising to people."

"Mibbe we shouldnae talk then."

I didn't want us getting into a fight after the way we'd connected today. It would leave a sour taste in both our mouths. We'd called a truce, and I intended to stick by that.

"Fine."

"Guidnight, Kit."

"Night."

Their voice was tight, but I chose not to ask what was wrong. Kit shifted on me again, clearly trying to get comfortable. I fisted my hands at my sides even as my body involuntarily reacted to it.

Just stay still and hope they don't notice.

I closed my eyes and begged my body to stop, but it was impossible when Kit kept wriggling. It wasn't long before I was lying underneath them with an aching cock, wishing I was anywhere else. Wishing they would notice what they were doing to me.

I want you so fucking bad, Kit. I don't know when the hell this started, but I can't hold it in any longer. Pretending this isn't happening isn't working. It's only getting worse. I can't control it. I can't fix it. I don't know what the fuck to do.

My brain kept chanting at me to give in. To allow temptation to overtake all of my senses and bring me some damn relief. My hands clenched and unclenched, desperate to touch them. To make them fucking stop moving to give me peace.

When Kit let out a frustrated sigh, I couldn't take it any longer. Neither of us would get any rest if they kept rubbing against my cock. My very hard cock that I couldn't ignore. And quite frankly, I didn't know how they could either.

Without thinking too hard about what I was doing, my hand came up and gripped their hair, pulling their head back to get their attention. In the dark, I could only make out the outline of their face.

Kit froze, their breathing heavy in the still night air.

"If ye dinnae stop that, am gonnae dae something we'll both regret."

I could feel their eyes on me even if I couldn't see them. We stared at each other for a long moment. Kit said nothing, but I knew exactly what question was on their lips. The one they were desperate to ask.

Like what, Thane?

"Like fuck ye tae stop ye squirming all over mah cock."

The words were out before I could stop them. Before I had a chance to think about the consequences of revealing how much I wanted to push inside of them over and over until we were both panting messes. To relieve the desperate ache of wanting them this much. At least, I hoped this would be how I relieved it because I sure as fuck didn't know how else to fix it.

Kit's response was a choking sound. They weren't expecting me to say that, but I was done pretending I didn't want them. That I hadn't felt the tension between us since the very beginning. It hadn't occurred to me that it could possibly be sexual on my part until I found myself in close quarters with them.

I silently dared them to keep moving as I held them there by their hair. It exposed their neck in the most delicious way. What a delicate wee thing Kit was. How I wanted to taste that skin, taste every part of them and lose myself in their body. Tear their clothes off so I could feel them all over me. Desire choked me, making my control disappear and leaving only need in its place. Desperate, all-consuming need to bury myself inside them.

Do it, Kit. Fucking move again. I dare you. I fucking dare you to move and show me you want it too. Show me it's not just me who feels this. Who wants this. Who fucking needs this. Please, I'm begging you to let me relieve this ache. I can't take it anymore. I need you. Fuck, I need you.

When they shifted, blatantly rubbing themselves against my cock, I quit holding back. I quit denying myself. I gave in.

A growl sounded low in my throat. My other hand gripped their hip, pushing them down on me, making my intention to fuck them very clear.

Kit panted and rocked their hips, encouraging me. That was it. No more waiting. No more stalling. It was done.

"Unzip the bag and take yer clothes off," I demanded. "If am gonnae fuck ye, I wannae feel every inch of ye on me while I dae it."

TWENTY ONE

Thane

It was a long minute before I heard the zip being pulled down. It would be cold as fuck outside of the sleeping bag, but I would keep them warm. They sat up in my lap. My hands went to their thighs. My thumbs dragged up the inner sides of them. Kit's harsh intake of breath made me do it again.

"Thane," they whispered, my name sounding shaky on their lips.

My hands slid to their hips and higher. I pushed their top up, exposing their skin to the air. It was soft as my hands glided along it. Finally, touching them like this made me desperate for more. For everything.

"Take it off."

Their hands met mine, pulling their top from my grasp and lifting it higher. While I couldn't see them clearly, the outline of their body made the breath whoosh out of my chest as they tore off their thermal layer. They weren't wearing anything underneath it. My hands rose higher along their rib cage. They shuddered, their breathing heavier than it had been before. Their moan when my thumb brushed over their nipple had me rocking up into them.

"The rest, Kit, take the rest off."

My hands left their body since I needed to undress too.

Kit let out a noise of protest.

"Don't stop."

"Clothes off first."

That got them moving. They clambered off me and started pulling at their bottoms. I took the opportunity to tear off my top. I barely even felt the pain in my ankle as I dragged my thermals down my legs.

Kit took my clothes from me, dumping them off the side of the sleeping mat along with their own.

I sat up and put my hands on their bare arms.

"Come here."

They swung their leg over me and settled themselves in my lap. My hand instinctively curled around the back of their neck as I leaned down and ran my tongue along the side of it.

Kit trembled as my thumb stroked along their skin.

"Thane."

"Aye? What dae ye want? Am I going tae slow for ye?"

Their wee noise of frustration had me smiling against their neck. My free hand ran down their side and landed on their thigh, tugging them into me until their chest met mine.

"Are ye aching, Kit? That why ye were dry humping me so I'd dae something aboot it? Was that yer way of telling me ye wannae be fucked? Were ye afraid tae ask nicely? Tae use yer words and tell me what ye want? Ye can dae it noo. Say it, Kit. Tell me ye want mah cock in ye."

My hand tightened on the back of their neck.

"Or I'll keep saying yer name until ye dae. I know how much ye like hearing it oot of mah mooth."

Kit gripped my shoulders.

"You're being very unfair right now."

"Am I? Ye wannae play dirty with me, Kit?"

I licked their neck again, letting them consider their options. While it hadn't been my intention to tease them, I couldn't help it. We riled each other up. That was our thing. It would make sense that it translated into the bedroom.

Kit shifted back slightly before taking my hand off their thigh. They pressed it against their sternum.

"You wanted to know where my other tattoo is? It's right here." They dragged my fingers down between the valley of their breasts. "But you can't see it unless you make me come."

"Is that a challenge?"

"Yeah, it fucking is."

"I accept."

They kept a hold of my hand, pulling it lower along their stomach, through a patch of curls before stilling.

"You sure you can manage that?"

My other hand left the back of their neck. I cupped the side of it and dragged my thumb over their lips.

"Aye, am pretty fucking sure I can make ye cry mah name when it happens but am no gonnae until ye tell me what I wannae hear."

Letting go of my hand, they reached down and gripped my cock.

I growled when they stroked it.

"Kit."

"Oh, am I being too slow now?"

My hand dipped to their cunt.

Kit moaned when I stroked them.

"Aye, ye fucking are. Noo, tell me ye want it and I'll give it ye."

They gasped when I circled their clit, rocking into my hand.

"I want you."

"That's no what I told ye tae say."

They groaned and rocked harder.

"I want your cock in me."

"Then take it."

They shifted closer and directed my cock to their entrance. Their wetness coated me. Fuck. I wanted them so much it hurt. I might have been winding them up, but I was just as desperate to have them. To be with them this way.

"Thane," they whispered, "be gentle with me, please."

It reminded me Kit had said they hadn't had penetrative sex since their miscarriage. This was a first for both of us, in a way.

"Be gentle with me tae. I havnae been with anyone else."

Kit paused.

I only told them that to reassure them they weren't alone in being nervous. This was new to me. Being this desperate for a physical connection with another person.

"Only her?"

"Aye."

They leaned closer, pressing their forehead against mine.

"We'll be gentle with each other, then."

I nodded, feeling their skin rub along mine. I wasn't scared of what would happen next. It felt right. Like I needed this with them. Nothing was going to stop me unless Kit said no.

They pressed me inside them. I let out a pant at the sensation. Kit didn't go fast. They took their time as they slid down onto my cock. I didn't hurry them. I held their neck and kept stroking their clit, feeling their fingers tighten around my shoulder.

"Ye okay?" I whispered.

They nodded.

"Ye feel guid."

"Oh yeah?"

"Aye."

Kit let out a snort, which made them sink down further, taking all of me. Their breath whooshed out of them.

"Fuck."

Before I could ask them if it was too much, they rocked themselves on me. I grunted. I wasn't lying when I said they felt good.

Kit rubbed their cheek along mine, continuing to move against me.

"Kit."

They moaned, lifting their hips, and dragging me out of them, only to drop back down. The rhythm they set had me gripping their neck tighter.

"Kit."

They moved faster, panting as they did it.

"Fuck me," they whispered against my cheek, "please. I want you so much."

The vulnerability in their voice had me obeying. As if I could say no. As if I could deny them when they'd already given me so fucking much.

I moved my hips in time with theirs, pressing myself deep with each stroke. Kit's panting and moaning grew louder. My fingers were still circling their clit. I wasn't planning on losing the challenge they'd given me, but it wasn't only about that. They deserved the pleasure.

"Ye want more?" I murmured.

"No, this is perfect. Don't stop, please."

"Am no stopping until ye cry mah name."

"Oh god."

"That's no the right name, Kit."

They slapped my shoulder.

"Shut up."

I tried not to laugh.

"Ye sure ye want that? I willnae be able tae say yer name if I have tae stay silent."

"I'm going to punch you in a minute."

"Dae it, I might like it."

They squirmed, rubbing their nipples against my chest.

"I don't want to hurt you. I want to make you feel good."

"Ye are, have I no made that clear enough?"

I nibbled their jaw, pressing kisses to their skin.

"Ye feel like fucking heaven, Kit. I cannae get enough of ye. If I didnae think it would hurt mah ankle, I'd pin ye doon and fuck ye until ye're a panting mess tae strung oot tae think any longer."

The way they moaned had me squeezing their neck. Fuck, it felt good to give into that impulse. Their throat felt right in my hand. I wasn't trying to cut off their airway or anything. Just wanted a firm grip on them.

"I think ye'd like that. Ye'd get off on being fucked tae within an inch of yer life."

"Fuck."

"Aye, am gonnae fuck ye that way if we get oot of this."

"Since when did you get such a dirty mouth?"

"Only for ye, Kit."

Kit let go of my shoulder and dug their fingers into the bun I'd put my hair in. They tugged at it. I grunted in response. Then I let go of their neck and grabbed their hair.

"Yes," Kit hissed when I pulled it.

I did it again. They moaned and clenched around me. Something told me they were close. I kept pulling their hair and stroking their clit while they rode me. Listening to the low, almost keening sounds in their throat had me wanting to let go myself, but I didn't.

"Thane, fuck! Yes. Fuck."

"That's it, cry mah fucking name, Kit."

And they did. They cried it out as their body shook, trembling with their climax. Hearing it set me off. I groaned, thrusting up twice more before I came inside them. And it was everything. Every-fucking-thing.

Both of us were panting when we stopped moving. I let go of their hair, wrapped my arms around them and buried my face in their neck.

Kit released my hair so they could cling to me. It took a long while for our breathing to even out. We held each other through it. I needed that. To feel close to them in the wake of us crossing over into something else.

Kit finally pulled away and gingerly lifted themselves off me. They shifted off the mat and felt around for something.

"I can turn the torch on," I said.

"It's fine. I'll find it without that."

"What are ye looking for?"

"Something to… to get rid of… I don't want to get it on my skin, so I need to…"

They trailed off. It took me a second to realise what they were getting at. The clean-up after sex. I didn't push them any further, letting them get on with it. Instead, I lay down and waited, worried about how they were feeling in the aftermath of us having sex. Earlier, I didn't think crossing that line was a good idea, but that went out the window the moment Kit started rubbing themselves all over me.

When Kit got back in the sleeping bag, lying down on top of me and zipping it up, they felt stiff against me. I didn't know whether to ask them if they were okay. There was an awkward tension in the air. Neither of us expected to do that with each other. And we were still naked, which I didn't think helped.

Should I suggest we get dressed?
Should I say anything at all if they don't?
Fuck… what do I do now?

I should have been brave and spoken to them about it, but I couldn't bring myself to. It wasn't as if I regretted it. In the moment, it felt so good… so right. I didn't know how to feel now it was over. But I also didn't want Kit to think I was having second thoughts.

So I did the only thing I could think of to reassure them. I gently placed my hand on their back and stroked it. After a minute, their body relaxed into mine. My lips dusted over their forehead, pressing a kiss to it. It occurred to me I hadn't actually kissed their lips. I didn't know how I felt about doing that, especially after Kit had said they didn't like French kissing. It made me nervous that I'd do it wrong, and they wouldn't enjoy it. I couldn't stand it if that was the case.

Kit deserved to have everything done right for them. They'd been so mistreated. They should be with someone who could give them everything they desired.

And that thought scared me because I'd had sex with them when I couldn't give them anything more than this. A relationship was the very last thing on my mind.

Had I fucked it all up by doing this with them? It felt right, but what if they hated me for it? They knew I was still hurting over Jenna's death.

Did I make a mistake?

Fuck, I didn't know. It didn't feel like one, but who the hell knew what was right or wrong any longer. I didn't think I would find an answer tonight. Tomorrow… it was another problem for tomorrow.

Wrapping my other arm around Kit, I held onto them and hoped I wouldn't feel so conflicted come morning. Kit deserved better than that. I just wanted them to be happy. And deep down, I wanted to be the one making them so.

TWENTY TWO

Kit

Waking up felt difficult. Being pulled from dreamland into the real world left me groggy and confused by my surroundings. It took a long minute for me to register that there was a very naked body below me. Two arms banded around me, keeping my body pinned in place.

Why am I naked?

Vivid flashes of sensations flooded me. There weren't many visual reminders since it had been dark, but the touch of skin, pressing of flesh, and pleasure blooming everywhere as my most secret wish had come true.

Oh my fucking god. We had sex. We actually had sex.

A high-pitched squeak left me before I could stop it. I shoved my hand over my mouth, hoping he hadn't heard it.

The rumble of his chest told me Thane was very much awake and aware of me on top of him.

"Ye okay there, Kit?"

Yeah, great, just remembering how amazing your dick felt inside me last night and your dirty mouth saying things no one has ever said to me before and how I got off on it. Just fine, Thane, absolutely peachy.

What did I even say? He hadn't spoken to me after it happened, but then again, it wasn't like I made conversation either.

The whole thing overwhelmed me. There was no universe where I thought for one second he would pull my hair back and threaten to fuck me if I didn't stop squirming on him. I hadn't meant to, but I couldn't get comfortable after our almost fight. My mind kept replaying the way I'd snapped at him. It didn't feel good. But it also hadn't escaped my notice the way he got hard as I did it. That distracted me even further.

My mind had been a mess. Then he had to go threaten me with something I desperately craved. Of course, I'd given in. I wanted him so much it burned. And fuck, had it been worth it.

"I'm fine," I squeaked.

It was a woefully inadequate description of the way I was feeling about everything. I felt too much. It made my skin hot. Pressure erupted at my temples, but I squeezed my eyes shut and willed my body to stay under control. To not lose it on me.

A soothing touch came in the form of Thane running his hand down my bare back. He wasn't too firm or too soft.

The tension dissipated after a few moments, leaving me feeling pretty fucking vulnerable. Anything could set me off, but I couldn't let it happen in front of him. I preferred to be alone when I had a meltdown. Then no one could see the messiness it always brought on. They couldn't make judgements and think badly of me over something I had no control over.

"I think we need tae talk."

Those few words made my breathing falter. Nothing good ever came out of that phrase. At least, not in my experience.

"I guess we do."

Thane let out a sigh even as he kept rubbing my back.

"Kit… I… I feel like I took advantage of the situation last night, and I hate mahself for that. Enough people in yer life have mistreated ye. Ye didnae need me deaing it tae."

What?

"I lost control and am sorry for that. That's no sort of person I wish tae be, someone who cannae control their basest instincts around ye."

My mind whirled with confusion. Why would he think he took advantage of me? I was fully on board with what happened. I told him I wanted him. Did he think I was lying? He didn't coerce me. If I hadn't wanted to sit on his dick, I would have said no. I would have stopped him in his tracks.

"Thane—"

"Am no better than that cunt who got ye drunk and kissed ye."

"That's not—"

"Am so fucking sorry. If ye hate me noo, I'll understand. It's no like ye really even liked me in the—"

I did the only thing I could think of to stop him from talking. From making me feel as though he regretted what happened because I didn't. It would feel shitty if he did. As if the sex between us meant nothing. Because it did. It fucking did.

I kissed him.

Thane froze in place as my mouth landed on his. He hadn't attempted to kiss me last night. I had wondered why at the time, but it didn't seem important when he was being so mouthy about how he was going to fuck me.

I dared move my lips on his as my hand slid up his chest, along his neck and into his beard so I could cup his cheek.

It took a moment for him to relax slightly, to kiss me back. It was tentative as fuck. I had a feeling after he told me he had only been with his wife that it included kissing. He hadn't let anyone else touch him this way and, fuck, if that didn't make my heart clench.

I pulled away slightly, wanting to reassure him with words that he had done nothing wrong. That this was entirely consensual. No one had taken advantage of anyone else.

"What was that for?" he breathed before I could get a word in.

"I wanted you to stop talking… and, well, I wanted to kiss you."

"Ye wanted tae…" he trailed off, a disbelieving look appearing in his green eyes.

I stroked his beard and pressed ahead.

"I don't know where you got the idea that I wasn't very into what we did last night. I distinctly remember telling you I wanted you. Were my words not enough or something?"

Thane stared at me. His disbelief morphed into confusion.

"They were."

"Then why are you saying sorry about what happened? Do you regret it?"

He shook his head slowly. Relief flooded out of me, warming my insides because fuck, I don't know what I would have done if he said yes.

"I don't regret it either."

I pressed another kiss to his mouth.

"I want to do it again."

My free hand stroked his side.

"But only if you want that."

My fingers dug into his beard.

"Also, please never compare yourself to Lawrence again. You're nothing like him."

After what Thane said about Law, it became clear he'd manipulated me into doing things with him. Thane had done nothing of the sort. How he could see himself as the same as Law was beyond me. Behind his gruff exterior, he was kind and protective as hell. He never made me feel anything but safe with him.

"Are ye sure?"

"Which part? That you're not like Law or that I want to fuck again?"

The way he blushed had me holding back a smile. Given how he'd spoken to me last night, I found it endearing that he felt embarrassed now. Besides, did he not realise how attractive he was? How I'd been fighting with myself over wanting him this entire time? I didn't want to hold back any longer. It didn't matter if we didn't get out of this or that if we did, we'd probably not see each other again. Living in the moment and experiencing this with him was far more important to me.

Thane searched my face for a long moment. Then he smirked. He fucking smirked.

"Kiss me, Kit."

"Kiss you?"

"Aye." He dragged his hand down my back and cupped my behind. "Kiss me."

"How about you kiss me, huh? Why do I have to do all the—"

His other hand curled around my throat before he pulled me against his mouth, cutting off my words. His kiss was soft, gentle almost as if he was nervous about it.

"What's wrong?" I whispered against his mouth.

"I dinnae wannae kiss ye wrong."

"Kiss me wrong?"

"Ye said ye dinnae like tae much tongue."

Fuck me… this man remembered what I'd said about Lawrence. About how I didn't really like French kissing. He didn't want it to be bad for me. My chest tightened and my heart squeezed.

You are too fucking sweet for words. The fact you care about it being good for me. That's everything to me.

"Do you want me to show you how I like to be kissed?"

He nodded, his nose brushing over mine.

I smiled at him before pressing my lips to his again. This time, I took control. He let me lead him.

I started off slow, pressing open-mouthed kisses to his lips. He responded in kind, showing me he could follow my instructions. When I deepened the kiss, there was no shoving my tongue down his throat the way Law had done to me. It was soft touches, gentle twirling, and never too much.

After a few minutes, Thane twined his fingers in my hair and stole back the control, kissing me with confidence. Making me melt in a puddle over him as my hips ground into his, seeking more friction. I was already wet, and he was hard. We didn't need more words to tell each other what we desired. What we needed.

"Thane," I moaned against his lips.

His hand left my behind and dug between us, gripping his cock so he could press it to me. I shifted to give him a better angle, letting him push inside me. I sighed, loving the way he filled me. The most delicious sensation that set my whole body on fire.

"Kit," he growled, the vibrations against my lips making me tremble, "ye make me so fucking desperate for ye."

I didn't have it in me to tease him for his words. The feeling was mutual.

"I want yer…" He didn't stop pushing into me, but his voice got all hesitant. "What dae ye want me tae call it?"

"Call what?"

"Yer bits. I dinnae want tae say something ye dinnae like."

I wanted to laugh because his calling it "my bits" was ridiculous. However, I knew he was being serious, so giggling wasn't appropriate. The way he had so much consideration for what I wanted was making me feel so cherished. I'd never had anyone care this much.

"Call it whatever you want. Anything sounds hot coming out of your mouth, to be quite honest."

"Even if I say I like being in yer cunt?"

My mouth went dry.

"Especially that."

"Or I wannae bend ye over and fuck yer cunt so hard ye cry for me."

Fuck me sideways. His mouth.

"Too bad you're incapacitated. I would like that."

The way he growled and kissed me to shut me up had me moving my hips in time with his. Neither of us said anything else, both lost in each other. In the movement of our bodies. Our mouths melding together. The touch of his hands on my skin. Mine shoved between us, stroking myself to completion. Me going off when he pulled my hair. His groans and my name on his lips when he followed me over the edge.

It was just as good as last night, if not better. And as we lay together, him holding me close, I had that overwhelming feeling again. Sex was always a double-edged sword of enjoying the stimulation but knowing it could turn into too much. I would need peace, quiet and calm before doing anything else.

"Kit."

"Yeah?" I whispered.

"When dae I get mah reward for winning yer challenge? I didnae get a chance tae see since ye were so determined tae fuck me."

I'd almost forgotten I told him I'd show him my tattoo if he made me come.

"Soon. I need a minute."

He pressed a kiss to the top of my head. His movement made me hyperaware of how sticky I was. I didn't like that sensation much. The sex had felt so good in the moment, but the aftermath was my least favourite part. I'd got so wrapped up in Thane that I'd forgotten about it.

The pressure at my temples started up again. I shifted against him, feeling uncomfortable in my own skin. It was hot and clammy, and I hated it.

"Thane, I need to… I need to get up."

He moved his hands to unzip the sleeping bag, but it wasn't fast enough for me. I batted his hands away and did it myself.

"Air, I need air," I choked out, feeling tears welling.

Oh god, this can't be happening.

I went to get off him but remembered that the moment I did, his cum could drip out of me. The thought of that made my skin crawl. The sensation of it gave me a huge ick when it got on my body.

No, no, no. Not that. Anything but that.

It was too much. The pressure in my head worsened. I clawed at my throat, feeling myself hyperventilating. Tears fell and I couldn't stop it. I tried to make sounds come out of my mouth, but instead, I found myself gasping for air.

"Kit?"

His voice rang in my ears. The concern in it, but I couldn't focus on that. It was too much. Everything was all too fucking much. The tension. The sensations. Everything. And I couldn't hold it back any longer... so I gave in.

TWENTY THREE

Kit

Tears streamed down my cheeks as I pushed myself up into a sitting position, dislodging Thane from inside me. I didn't even care at that point if stuff went everywhere. All my focus was on the pressure in my head.

My body trembled. One hand went back to my throat as the other clenched and unclenched. My chest rose and fell in a shuddering motion. Breathing was difficult. Thinking was even worse. My head was so full. I couldn't see properly through my watery eyes. I could hear my heart pounding in my ears, but nothing else.

If Thane said anything further, I had no fucking idea. All my focus was on my panicked state. On how everything felt so overwhelming. I wanted out of my head. Out of my skin. Out of my fucking body.

"I can't… I can't… I can't."

I pushed at my thighs with my hands, dragging my blunt nails across them. Then slapped the sides of my head. Anything to let the overwhelming pressure out.

Make it stop. Make it stop. Make it fucking stop!

I could feel my chest heaving, my breathing erratic and out of control. My nails cut across it, trying to free my lungs from their cage. To find a way to breathe.

Two large hands banded around mine, pulling them away from my chest. They let go, only to grip my shoulders and tug me down. Thane wrapped me up in his arms, holding me tight against his chest.

I cried harder, my body jerking in his embrace as my attempt to speak came out in panicky gasps of air. He had no idea what was happening to me, and yet he held me close, giving me a much-needed anchor to grip onto as I drowned in the horror of overstimulation.

I don't know how long I cried and hyperventilated. It felt like forever until I started to calm down. Until the pressure in my head lessened. Until my body stilled.

I gulped in air as my eyes continued to stream. They always did in the aftermath. My hand wrapped around his shoulder, squeezing lightly to steady myself, and perhaps let him know I was more in control of myself now.

The way he kissed my hair and whispered, "It's okay, Kit, am here, I've got ye," had my heart in knots.

A cross between a sob and a hiccup was my only response. The only one I was capable of giving.

I didn't extricate myself from his embrace. Usually, I didn't want anyone to touch me when this happened, but Thane represented safety for me. Having him close was comforting rather than too much. Besides, I would have probably hurt myself if he hadn't put me against his chest. It wouldn't be the first time I clawed my skin, and it wouldn't be the last.

After a while, he removed his arms from around my back. He brushed my hair off my wet face, looking down at me with concern.

"Will ye let me clean ye up?"

I nodded, my bottom lip trembling from the softness in his voice.

Thane had me sit up with him but kept me in his lap as if wanting me close. He dug around for the toilet paper, pulled off a few sheets and gently wiped my tears before having me blow my nose. Without asking, he tore more off and cleaned up the space between my legs. He didn't even look put out by it.

"Dae ye want water?" he asked when he was done.

I nodded again.

He picked up the water bottle and handed it to me, watching me take a long gulp. The cool water soothed my throat. I finished the rest of the bottle without thinking about it, needing the hydration after expelling all of those tears.

"Can I dae anything else for ye? Ye want clothes?"

217

I pointed at my underwear that was sitting in the pile of our clothes on the floor.

Thane grabbed them and helped me into them. He slid his boxers on but didn't attempt to dress himself further.

I indicated I wanted to lie down. That prompted him to shift down on the mat and lay on his side, leaving me room to tuck myself up next to him. Thane covered us both with the sleeping bag before gently stroking my shoulder.

Despite knowing he was watching me, I remained with my face tucked against his chest, not wanting to look up. I closed my eyes and breathed, letting the stillness and quiet fold over me. It had a calming effect, along with his soft touch.

"Thane," I whispered when I felt ready to talk after our peaceful silence.

"Aye?"

His hand was splayed out over my back, his arms caging me in, but I didn't feel enclosed. I felt secure… protected. That was a rarity in my life.

"Are you going to tell me off if I say sorry?"

"I'd ask what ye're apologising for."

"Having a meltdown in front of you."

Now it was over, embarrassment flooded my veins. I hated how out of control I'd been. It wasn't like I had any choice in the matter, but it didn't make it any better.

He said nothing as if waiting for me to elaborate.

I'd revealed so many things to this man. He hadn't looked at me differently because of it, but fear clung to my skin. This wasn't just a shitty thing that had happened to me.

My disability affected every part of my life. It was there in my everyday experiences. The way I went through the world. It was why I thought about things differently. Why I said things like they were and didn't have any hidden meaning behind my words. And why I had so many struggles navigating around a society that wasn't built for the way my brain operated.

I ran my fingers over his bare chest, brushing along the light dusting of hair there. My eyes fixed on the freckles covering it, trying not to be afraid of his reaction. Of him seeing me in another light and hating it.

The fact I cared so much about his opinion when I hadn't been trying to impress him before was indicative of my changed feelings towards him.

Be brave, Kit. You have to do this. He should have an explanation for what happened.

I squeezed my eyes shut and took a breath.

"I'm autistic."

I paused, trying to work out how much else I should reveal about it. How much I should explain. Then I dived right in.

"I have meltdowns, and I take longer to learn how to do things, and that's why my coordination is shit, and sometimes I struggle to do everyday tasks. I have sensory issues. I'm not good at social events or in large groups because it's too loud and my auditory processing is all messed up."

Thane stroked my back and hummed as if letting me know he was paying attention.

It didn't feel like I had enough words to encapsulate the effect my disability had on my life, but I wanted him to know what the cause of my meltdown was, so he didn't think it was him. There was no blame here. It was just something I had to deal with.

"I don't like the feeling of cum on my skin and that's what set me off, the thought of it. But that's only a part of it because I was overstimulated from us having sex, and don't get me wrong, I like sex because it's an amazing sensory experience, but sometimes it's too much. I need peace and quiet and calm afterwards, so I don't get overwhelmed. But I've been so overwhelmed with everything that we've been through, and I've been trying to push it down. I couldn't do it any longer, so I lost it, and I couldn't explain that to you because it's hard to talk or focus on anything else but what's happening to me. So... so that's why I'm sorry because you had to deal with that without knowing what was going on."

I let out a long breath.

"And now I feel like I'm rambling and over-explaining everything, which is probably really fucking annoying, so I'm sorry about that too."

His hand moved from my back to my hair, fingers tangling in the strands.

"It's no annoying. Ye can over-explain as much as ye want. I like listening tae ye."

No one had ever said that to me before.

"You do?"

"Aye."

I tore my head away from his chest and turned my face up to his. There was nothing but rapt attention there, his green eyes intent on me.

"I don't tell many people about my disability because there's so much stigma and I've had a few not even believe me since I appear so normal to them. I get nervous talking about it to someone new because of that."

"Ye think I wouldnae have believed ye?"

"No, but… I never know what reaction I'm going to get."

Thane gave me a half-smile.

"It doesnae change how I see ye if that's what ye're worrying aboot. Ye're still Kit, a mouthy wee thing who winds me up and keeps me on mah toes."

He leaned closer until our faces were inches apart.

"Am no gonnae claim tae know a lot aboot autism, but what I dae know is ye confiding in me aboot it helps me understand ye better."

He cocked his head to the side.

"Did I dae anything wrong when it happened? Did ye no want me tae touch ye or…?"

I shook my head.

"No, I mean, usually I don't like being touched when it happens, but when you held me, it helped. The pressure helped. I felt safe with you… I feel safe with you and that's not something I can say about anyone but my dad and Olly."

Thane's eyes darted between mine, staring at me with such reverence that it grew hard to breathe.

"I wannae kiss ye," he whispered, "but no if it's tae much for ye right noo."

I've cried so very much today already, but I want to cry happy tears this time.

Thane had to be one of the most considerate people I'd ever met.

"You can."

He pressed his mouth against mine for the briefest of kisses that almost didn't feel like enough.

"After what we've had tae deal with, there's no shame in it being hard for ye, Kit. It's a lot tae cope with."

"Yeah… this situation hasn't been easy."

We'd avoided discussing what we would do about our predicament long enough. I didn't feel like I was emotionally ready to speak further about my disability with Thane. Meltdowns wore me out. And I was still trying to wrap my head around the fact he'd been so understanding about it.

Thane shifted back, putting some space between us. His expression was cautious as if he knew the time had come to make a decision regarding what to do next.

We couldn't stay here forever. Our food supplies were going to run out. I didn't know how long a human body could survive with only water to sustain it. And allowing my mind to go towards the worst-case scenario wouldn't help matters.

"What are our options here, Thane? Tell me honestly."

He folded his lips inside his mouth and looked away from me.

I gave him a minute. There was no point in demanding he answer me immediately. We weren't in any urgent need right at that moment, but we would be soon. I could feel it.

"Well, ye know we can continue tae stay here and hope we get rescued."

"We'll call that option one."

"Aye. Option two is that ye walk oot of here and get help."

"What exactly would that entail?"

He sighed.

"Ye cannae get oot of this glen withoot a four tae five hour walk in either direction, but likely longer after all the fresh snow and the conditions. That's why I said ye would have tae go. With me, it'll take twice as long, if no more."

"And you'll be in pain the whole time. I don't want to do that to you."

His eyes grew soft at my words. Did he not realise how much I cared about him? That causing him pain would only hurt me too.

"Are those the only options we have?"

"Aye."

They both sounded horrible if I was honest. Well, not that being with Thane was a chore, but I felt gross after wearing the same clothes for days. I wanted a hot shower, warm food, and a real bed. I wanted that for both of us. The thought of him being alone out here felt wrong. We'd been in this together from the beginning. And yet we couldn't stay either. Not forever.

"Which one do you suggest?"

Thane's eyes grew dark, and his expression was grim.

"I dinnae wannae send ye oot in the snow. I cannae keep ye safe if ye leave me, but the chance of rescue is feeling very fucking slim at this point. Mah head tells me I should let ye go tae give us both the best chance of survival as we're gonnae run oot of food soon."

"But you don't want that."

He nodded.

My heart hurt. It fucking hurt at the impossible situation we were in. But I had always been honest with Thane, and I wasn't going to stop that now.

"I don't want that either. I don't want to leave you at all."

TWENTY FOUR

Thane

here was a desperate note in Kit's voice as they told me they didn't want to leave me. I wanted nothing more than to soothe their fears and tell them we would be okay. To make that worry in their beautiful blue eyes disappear. I wanted to save them from this so badly, it almost crushed me into tiny pieces.

Was the world fucking testing me again? Hadn't I suffered enough? I couldn't save my wife and now history was repeating itself with Kit.

Just when I realised how fucking amazing they were, reality intruded and crushed my moment of happiness after all the shite I'd been dealing with for years. Maybe that was all this was. A moment. A point in time to show me that life was worth living. That I could find joy where I never expected it to be. That going through the motions wasn't going to fulfil me.

Trying to work it out felt exhausting. I was fucking tired of feeling so alone, lost at sea without a tether or something keeping me afloat. So what if I wanted to stay here with Kit and pretend the world outside didn't exist? I wanted to hold on to them and hope to fuck that I could survive long enough to smile again without reservation. Without feeling as though my life should have ended the day my wife died. Those feelings needed to go away. I wanted to live. I wanted to fucking live without this weighing me down.

But I didn't have time to wallow. I didn't have time to wish for things I couldn't have. Reality stared me in the face and told me I had to do what was practical. Had to do the necessary to keep Kit alive. I couldn't forgive myself if they didn't survive. To see their vibrant being snuffed out would be a fucking tragedy. And yet… everything inside me screamed not to let them go out there in the cold. The idea of them walking hours upon hours without me, fighting against the weather and the snow, cut me to the very core.

"I cannae let ye go, Kit. Ye have tae stay with me. I have tae know ye're safe. I wouldnae be able tae forgive mahself if something happens tae ye."

I might know in my head that them leaving for help would be the best option, but it didn't make it so in my heart. If anyone was coming for us, they were probably concentrating on the avalanche, thinking we'd got lost in it. That would be the logical explanation. If they didn't find us there, then they would expand the search, but who the fuck knew how long it would take. Callan wouldn't know where I'd gone. He could guess, but there were too many options. While he knew I had my camping gear on me, no one could fully prepare for the storm we'd been in. If they couldn't find any sign of us, then they would be preparing for the worst. For bodies. The thought of that made my chest seize up.

"Then I won't go."

Kit said it like it was simple. As if they weren't condemning us to waiting and not knowing if they would ever find us. Mountain rescue wouldn't stop searching, but I couldn't help feeling as though it would be too late. We would be found too late.

My mind wanted to prepare me for the worst because the worst had happened to me before. It stole my hope from me. I no longer felt optimistic or looked forward to the future. I was stuck in a cycle of worst-case scenarios. Probably why I jumped to the conclusion that Kit was sent to piss me off. It stopped me from looking deeper and seeing that they were just as traumatised as I was by what had happened to them. And what a fucking tragic way to live that was. To expect everything to go wrong and nothing to go right… ever.

I wouldn't allow myself to bring Kit down with this shite. They should have hope, even if I had none.

"But we have to do something."

Kit extracted themselves from my arms and got up. I said nothing as they put their clothes on before handing me mine. They chucked me one of the flapjacks for breakfast. After unwrapping their own and stuffing half of it in their mouth, their hands went to my outdoor clothes.

"Well, your clothes are finally dry. We should go outside for a bit, get the lay of the land. It seems like the wind has died down, so maybe it's stopped snowing too. Plus, I'm sure both of us need to relieve ourselves. And we can test out how your ankle is doing."

The determination in their voice had me keeping mine shut. I ate instead, watching Kit potter about in the tent, checking everything over before they got their outdoor clothes on. Then they approached me with a small smile on their face.

"Let me help you get your things on, yeah?"

I wanted to say no. To not bother. Kit likely saw the reluctance in my expression as they cocked their head to the side and wrinkled their nose.

"We're not going to get all awkward about this stuff again, okay?"

"Am no being awkward."

They snorted.

"You look terrified of me helping you dress, or was it because I mentioned the fact we need to relieve ourselves? I thought we were over that. We're humans, we shit and piss, that's just life. Now, get out of that sleeping bag and quit scowling at me or I'll have to kiss it off your face."

I stared at them. It shouldn't come as a surprise they were being mouthy again, but it did. And the way they so casually mentioned kissing me had my stomach in knots.

"I don't have all day. I'm fucking tired, Thane, that meltdown took it out of me, so I'd rather get this done now so I can rest."

That spurred me into action. The mention of what happened earlier had me worrying all over again. I didn't want to be the cause of more stress for them. It scared me to see them that way. I didn't know what to do or how to help them.

When they told me why it happened, it only made me want to do better for them. I wanted to learn how to read the signs of when things were becoming too much. To know what to do when they had a meltdown and how to take care of them afterwards. To do what I could to mitigate things. To help them through it.

Funny that I wanted to do all these things for someone I'd not known for long. But to be honest, I would do anything for Kit at this point. They'd given me so much more than they knew. From the way they'd talked about it, I could tell that some people they'd encountered viewed their disability as a burden. It only gave me a clearer picture of Kit. I understood them better. That was the only difference it made to me.

After I got dressed, Kit put the spade and toilet paper into my pockets before helping me out of the tent.

"I dinnae wannae make things harder on ye," I said, my attention on them rather than on our surroundings.

"You're not. If I sound irritated, it's not you. I get grumpy when I'm tired. This whole situation is wearing on me and keeping a lid on everything was hard."

I reached out and pushed their hair behind their ear.

"Ye dinnae have tae hide that from me, Kit."

"I know that now."

They tucked themselves under my arm and let me lean on them. Tipping their head back, they met my eyes.

"How is your ankle?"

I tested putting weight on it. The pain wasn't as intense as it had been a couple of days ago, but it still hurt. It made me wonder how bad the sprain was. Had I torn ligaments in the fall? How long would they take to heal? There was no point in speculating.

"Sore, but I can walk."

"I'm still helping you."

I didn't dispute that, knowing it would be easier if they did.

Kit didn't move off immediately. They looked around, their eyes scanning the landscape.

"Well, it looks like the storm is over."

"Aye."

They gave me a smile, then tugged me toward the trees. We found a suitable spot to get our business done and made our way back to the tent. Kit helped me sit down outside to let me rest while they set about digging around the tent to clear the snow.

The air was bracing, but now I was back in my warm clothes, it wasn't too bad. It was nice to get some fresh air rather than being stuck in the tent. It was less oppressive, but seeing all the snow made desolation set in. Even if my ankle was doing better, I still couldn't see me or Kit walking through it back to civilisation. Not that we would as they agreed to stay here with me.

By the time Kit was done, their cheeks were flushed pink from the cold. They stood by the tent with their hands on their hips, surveying the land.

"Your tent doesn't really stand out against the snow."

It was dark green, matching the pine trees next to us. Tents came in all shapes, colours, and sizes, but I didn't want something outlandish. And I rarely camped out in it when it snowed.

"We need something bright if they're going to see us."

"Who?" I asked.

"Mountain rescue. Now the storm has cleared, it'll make it easier for them to find us."

"I dinnae think they're coming."

They frowned.

"Well, I know our chances are slim, but I'm not going to rule it out completely."

Before I could say another word, Kit dived back into the tent. They made a lot of noise as they rummaged around in it. They emerged with a triumphant look on their face brandishing a bright blue scarf.

"What are ye daeing with that?"

Kit grinned.

"Well, this is the brightest thing we have, so I'm going to tie it to the tent."

"Why?"

"Because it'll stick out against the snow, and they might see it if they fly overhead."

I wanted to tell Kit that it was pointless doing that, but if I did, they might question why I had lost all hope of rescue. They'd ask why I didn't think anyone would come for us. Ruining Kit's optimistic outlook felt wrong. So I said nothing as I watched them tie the scarf to one of the guy ropes on the tent. I sat there while they went off to refill our water bottles and wondered how long it would take for them to give up all hope. That depressed the fuck out of me even more and left a sour taste in my mouth.

Kit didn't notice my low mood when they returned and helped me back into the tent. I got tucked up in the sleeping bag with them again and held them tight, wishing I could see us getting out of this.

Kit wriggled against me after a few minutes. In response, I turned their face up to mine and kissed them. It was the only way I could distract myself. And to stop Kit from seeing how fucking bleak my thoughts were. Their soft mouth was the only thing saving me from drowning.

"I'm sleepy," they murmured against my mouth.

I let them go so they could rest. And sank further into desolation. So much for wanting to live. I was already acting as though I was going to die.

The storm was over. That should give me hope, but I had none left. This was my punishment for my wife's death. I'd found a small piece of happiness, only to have it ripped away cruelly.

"I dinnae wannae die," I whispered to my sleeping Kit, "I dinnae want ye tae either, but am scared we willnae survive this. Am terrified, Kit. This feels worse than when

Jenna died 'cause I know it's gonnae happen this time. Ye deserve so much better than this… than me. Am no enough. I cannae save ye."

Hot, wet tears slid down my cheeks at the injustice of it. I cried as Kit slept, hating myself, hating everything. And wishing for a fucking miracle so I could spare Kit from the inevitable pain of losing it all.

TWENTY FIVE

Kit

A strange noise woke me from a deep sleep. It sounded like whump, whump, whump. I found it rather disorientating after only hearing the wind for days on end.

Yesterday, after I had a nap, Thane had been very subdued for the rest of the day and into the evening. His mood plummeted the moment we started talking about what we should do regarding our situation. While I had tried to remain optimistic, he seemed to withdraw into himself. I didn't know what was up with him, only that he didn't want to talk about it. That much was clear by his one-word answers. So I left it alone, letting him stew in whatever he was thinking. If he'd wanted to tell me what was up, he could, but he hadn't.

We went to bed early, considering it had been a tiring day for me in particular. I hadn't expected a kiss from him, but I got one, which helped set my mind at ease. At least he wasn't upset with me. Not sure I could take that after what happened between us.

I rubbed the sleep from my eyes and looked up at Thane. He had his eyes shut and his breathing was steady. The whumping noise grew louder. There was a whirling quality to it as well.

Wait, I think I recognise that sound.

I scrambled to unzip the sleeping bag, rushing out of it, and pulling on my clothes haphazardly.

"Kit?" came Thane's groggy voice.

I had no time to tell him what was going on. He could hear it himself if he listened hard enough. I had to see what was going on.

My fingers unzipped the inner tent. I crawled out, digging around for the outer zip, and almost ripped it open. I dashed out, my head turning up to the sky, and sure enough, I could see the source of the noise. My arms immediately went up. I started waving at the red and white helicopter in the sky. The one hovering overhead.

"It's a helicopter, Thane," I shouted, practically laughing with glee. "It's a fucking helicopter!"

We're saved. We're actually fucking saved.

There had been many times I worried we would never get out of this. That we would die out there together because they couldn't find us. Maybe if we had managed a few more days, Thane might have been able to walk, but I hadn't liked those odds. It didn't matter now. Rescue was here. And I could've cried from relief. But I didn't. I had to keep my cool for now.

A few minutes later, a couple of people descended from the helicopter on a line nearby. I rushed over to meet them. They introduced themselves as being from the coastguard rescue team. I told them what had happened to Thane since I was more concerned about getting him medical attention than anything else.

Once I finished explaining, I led them over to the tent. Thane was dressed by that time. We helped him out of the tent so I could pack everything up. I heard them talking outside with him, but I didn't listen to what they were saying.

One man helped me take down the tent and pack up our backpacks before we were winched up into the helicopter. It all happened so fast that I barely had time to process the fact we were no longer stuck in a snowy valley.

Thane and I sat together in the helicopter. He had a pensive look on his face. Without thinking about it too hard, I reached out and took his hand, lacing our fingers together and squeezed. He didn't turn to me, but his features relaxed a fraction.

I stared out of the window for the rest of the way until we touched down at the hospital in Inverness. I had vaguely heard one man explaining that they couldn't fly over the mountains for the past couple of days because of the low clouds and the storm, but they were called out once the weather had cleared up to look for us.

While Thane was taken inside to be seen by the doctors, they helped me with our bags. I sat in the waiting room of accident and emergency, surrounded by our things, staring at my hands after they handed us over to the hospital staff. I'd been assured that someone was on their way to pick us up but hadn't thought to ask who.

Everything seemed so surreal. I hadn't paid all that much attention to what was going on. My mind had been trying to process the fact we were back in civilisation. That we hadn't been left out there to die.

"Kit?" came a voice I recognised.

I looked up, finding Callan moving towards me with a concerned expression on his face. Jumping up immediately, I gave him a smile.

"Oh, hey, are you our ride?"

He bit his lip before grinning at me.

"Aye. Where's Thane? Is he okay?"

"He's all right. He twisted his ankle, so he's being seen by the doctor, I think. They didn't tell me much since I'm not family."

"And are ye okay?"

I nodded.

"I think so. Kind of overwhelming this whole being rescued business. I wasn't sure if we would make it out."

"Well, ye and Thane can tell me everything on the way back tae the lodge, aye? All yer stuff is still there. I packed it up for ye as we had other guests. I hope that's okay."

"Oh yeah, of course. Thank you, I appreciate it."

237

"Did ye wannae speak tae yer dad? He's been in contact with me every day since we realised ye and Thane were missing."

Callan drew his phone out of his pocket, unlocked it, and swiped it a few times before handing it to me.

I nodded at him in thanks, seeing that he had already brought up my dad's number from his contacts. I clicked call and stuck it to my ear.

"Hello?" came my dad's voice when he answered.

My throat got tight at the sound of it. I'd tried not to think about him while I was stuck in the tent, but I missed him. Having my routine of speaking to him via text every day disrupted made things a lot harder. In fact, having all of my routines thrown out the window was an issue. It surprised me that I've only had one meltdown. All that change was hard. I managed, though. I had no other choice but to make it through. Thane had been relying on me, so that had given me an incentive to keep it together when I thought I might fall apart.

"Dad, it's Kit."

"Oh, sweetheart, I'm so thankful they found you. Are you okay?"

The relief in his voice made me smile. Dad quite often spoke in monotone, but when emotions stirred him, you could hear it in his voice.

"Yeah, I'm okay. Just at the hospital, but I didn't get hurt. The guy I was with did. We kept each other safe."

"That's good. I'm sure you'll tell me all about it when you get back."

Dad didn't like speaking on the phone. Neither did I, but this was one of those times when it was a necessity.

"Definitely."

"Well, I'll let Olly know you're okay, and Sienna, of course."

My heart seized at the mention of her name. Dad didn't know about my argument with her. I hadn't wanted to worry him while I was still working out what the fuck to do about my fractured friendship with Sienna. While I didn't want to speak to her, I knew I would eventually have to deal with it.

"You told Sienna I was missing?"

"Of course I did. She's very worried about you."

That was something I didn't believe for a second. More like worried that her walking womb was no longer available. I immediately scolded myself for the thought. I wasn't a mean person like Sienna, but I didn't feel like being nice about her, either. She didn't deserve that after the way she'd treated me.

My gaze darted away from the floor towards the double doors leading into the ward. They opened and there he was, walking gingerly through them. Thane had a pained look on his face, but at least he was walking. That had to mean his injury wasn't too bad.

The sight of him made my heart thump in my chest. Even with us both being dishevelled and in need of a wash, he was still so damn handsome. Arresting almost. I couldn't help wanting to go to him. To be near to him. Everything changed between us during our time in the tent. And all I could focus on was the fact I wanted him with an ache that threatened to tear me apart.

"Listen, Dad, Thane's done with the doctor, so I have to go."

"Oh okay, well, let me know when you're coming home."

"Sure, will do. Love you."

"Love you too."

I hung up and handed the phone back to Callan. There was curiosity in his brown eyes. I didn't stop to say anything to him. Instead, I rushed over to Thane to see if he needed help.

"You okay?" I asked when I got close.

Without waiting for a reply, I tucked myself under his arm so he could lean on me. Being next to him gave me a sense of safety. The unfamiliar surroundings and noises didn't feel so scary and overwhelming knowing I had him to shield me from them.

"Aye, am fine, Kit," he mumbled, staring down at me with those dark green eyes of his.

His cheeks went slightly red, making me hide a smile.

"What did the doctor say?"

I led him over to where Callan was standing with our stuff.

"I had an x-ray tae make sure there's no a break. Just have tae rest it and see how we go. I cannae drive though, no yet."

Callan must've overheard that because he grinned.

"Shame, ye hate other people driving ye around."

"Fuck off, Callan."

I untucked myself from Thane just as Callan dragged him into a hug.

"Ye scared the shite out of me, Thane."

"Am alive, ye get."

"Dinnae pull a fucking stunt like that again, ye hear? Ye're making me sprout more greys with all the worrying I dae aboot ye."

Thane let out a grumble and extricated himself from Callan's arms.

"Dinnae let yer husband hear that."

Callan snorted and rolled his eyes.

"Aye, he's happy ye're back. Says I can shut up aboot ye noo."

Thane gave him a nod and scratched his beard.

"Tell him am no sorry for stealing all yer attention."

"Get."

Their back and forth amused me. It was clear as day how close the two of them were. I would have known it without Thane telling me that Callan saved him after Jenna died.

I tucked myself under Thane's arm again. The anxiety at being separated from him made me do it.

Thane squeezed me, almost as if he recognised I was feeling a certain type of way. No matter the reason was, I was grateful for his support.

Callan eyed us with a raised brow. Whatever he saw made him smile.

"We going?" Thane asked.

"Aye, I'll bring the car around so ye dinnae have tae walk far."

Callan gave us both a nod before walking away to the doors that led outside. I turned to Thane. He stared at Callan's retreating back.

"It doesn't feel real."

"What doesnae?"

"That we're here and not stuck in the tent."

"Aye. I didnae think they were coming."

Thane kept his eyes averted from mine as if he didn't want me to know the extent of his loss of hope that we'd get out of there alive.

"Maybe it was a miracle."

"Feels that way."

There were so many things I wanted to ask him, but I couldn't find the words. They got stuck in my throat. The thought of walking away from him after everything we'd been through left my chest hollow.

It wasn't enough time. I hadn't had enough time with Thane. There were so many conversations left to be had. So much I had to say. To do. I was desperate not to have to go home yet. To face Sienna again because I wasn't ready for any of it. And most of all, I wanted to stay close to Thane.

What happens now?

TWENTY SIX

Thane

*E*verything about our rescue had happened so fast that I barely had time to process it all. One minute we were stuck in the snow, the next we had the coastguard rescue team taking us up in a helicopter and we were arriving at the hospital in Inverness. It was only when I was waiting to be seen by the doctors that I could take a minute to breathe.

I didn't want to dwell on the dark thoughts I'd had last night about dying out there. Not when I was back in civilisation. It didn't feel real. That someone had come for us. I hadn't wanted to tell Kit that the chances of rescue via helicopter had been slim because of the low cloud in the area. The fact they were able to find us was quite something. And I begrudgingly had to admit Kit's idea to tie their scarf on the guy rope had turned the tide. One of the rescuers told me that's what caught their attention.

Kit saved you.

A part of me thought it should have been the other way around. I couldn't bring myself to give that any credence. The overwhelming feeling I had was one of gratitude. And I could never repay them for that. They ensured I got my wish to live. To keep going.

How can I ever thank you adequately enough?

Kit stood under my arm, looking up at me, but I couldn't meet their eyes. There were too many emotions in them. Ones I was afraid of. Fuck knows why. Kit had given me so much of their trust. They had mine in return. And now, we would go our separate ways.

That's what you're scared of.

I shoved the thought away. What happened out there didn't automatically translate into the real world. Just because we had connected on an intimate level didn't make it mean something more.

That idea messed with me. I gave into my desire for them, knowing it might be the last chance I had to explore such a thing. I didn't do it lightly. I wasn't the impulsive sort, but Kit had opened up a whole new fucking world for me. A whole new part of me I never knew existed. And, honestly, being back in reality made that a terrifying prospect. To be alone with the newfound knowledge and not have Kit by my side to go through it with me.

You have to let them go, you know. You both have lives to get back to.

When Callan came back, the silence between Kit and me was awkward. He eyed us with some concern, but rather than saying anything, he handed Kit their pack and picked up my stuff. He led us to his car, placing everything in the boot before he opened the passenger side door for me.

My eyes went to Kit. They had this nervous look in their eyes. When they glanced at me, desperation filled their features. My heart ached at the sight of it.

"Am gonnae sit in the back with Kit," I said to Callan.

The way he blinked and bit his lip told me everything. He was putting two and two together. I didn't want him to see that, but I knew better than to expect anything less. Callan was the most astute person I'd ever met. He saw all.

"Aye, let me pull the seat forward for ye."

He ducked into the passenger side to move it forward. I opened the door behind us and slid in, putting my seatbelt on. My ankle throbbed, but they'd given me painkillers in the hospital. I'd have to get more, especially since they advised me to return to normal activities as much as possible. I still needed to rest it as well.

Kit got into the back with me. Their relief was palpable. They told me they didn't do well in social situations. The unfamiliar surroundings were likely not helping either.

Callan got into the driver's side and set off.

I turned my attention to the window outside.

"Am gonnae take ye tae the lodge. Yer car is still there, and Kit needs tae pick up their stuff."

"Ye gonnae get off home?" I asked Kit without turning my head.

"Um, I hadn't decided. Kind of still reeling from the whole being rescued business."

You still have some time with them then.

I told my brain to shove it.

"If ye dinnae wannae leave today, am sure we can find ye somewhere tae stay," Callan said.

My head twisted to find Kit shrugging. There were a lot of reasons why they might not want to leave yet. Sienna came to mind first. They wouldn't want to see her, and I didn't blame them. But they'd been here longer than they planned. They couldn't stay indefinitely. They had a job to get back to and so did I.

"Can I borrow yer phone? Mine likely took a dip in the stream I fell in," I asked, rather than make Kit reply to Callan about what their plans were.

"Ye fell in a stream?"

"Aye, that's how I twisted mah ankle. Am sure Kit can tell ye the details. I need tae call mah boss."

Callan grabbed his phone off the dash holder and shoved it at me.

"I told yer parents ye're safe. They're worried aboot ye."

I took his phone.

"Aye, I hope ye told them tae leave me be."

The look in his eyes spoke volumes.

"I said they should let ye get yer bearings today, but I cannae promise they willnae drop by."

A huff escaped my mouth. Dealing with them was not what I wanted to do right then. It might seem callous, but honestly, it would only fill me with guilt if I had to speak to

246

them right after the ordeal I'd been through. I needed a minute to breathe, to get my shite together before seeing them.

I dialled my boss's number rather than respond to Callan. He asked Kit to regale him with our wee adventure while the phone rang. When my boss answered, we spoke for several minutes. I'd already had time off to go on Callan's course, but with my injury, she agreed it was best I stay off for a wee bit longer. After all, I had been stuck in the snow for several days. I needed time to recover.

By the time I finished talking to her, Kit had got to the part about us being rescued. I set Callan's phone down between us, watching Kit's animated face.

"It was like a fucking miracle seeing that helicopter in the sky. We were losing hope that someone would come."

In the rearview mirror, I could see Callan's serious expression.

"We wouldnae have stopped looking no matter what."

I should have known that. Hope was in limited supply for me, but I knew Callan. He would have moved the damn mountain to get to me.

"What took so long, if you don't mind me asking?"

"The avalanche. Several of the group got caught in it. We didnae realise ye were missing while we were looking for survivors. Dinnae worry. No one perished, but it was only after we got them oot that I realised the two of ye hadnae come back. The storm made it difficult tae mount a search for ye, but I knew Thane had his supplies with him. I was certain we'd find ye alive."

I dreaded to think about what Callan would have done if I hadn't made it. Probably cursed my grave. We'd always been inseparable. The best of friends. He made sure I got through Jenna's death. And me? Well, I'd been there for all of the big events of his life. His first crush. When he came out. The day he met his husband. I coached him through the proposal. We were best men at each other's weddings. Our lives were inextricably linked. I don't think he would have forgiven me for losing my life in the mountains we both loved so much if he wasn't going with me.

"Ye'd have killed me again if I died on ye," I put in.

"Aye, ye're fucking right, I would. We dinnae need more tragedy in oor lives."

His words stabbed at a sore spot. I rubbed my chest, trying to dispel the pain radiating from it.

Kit noticed the movement. Their icy eyes softened. That look almost decimated me. They knew the total extent of it. More than I'd revealed to Callan.

That means something.

No, it doesn't. I had to get it off my chest, and I trusted Kit to understand. That's it.

Keep fooling yourself there, Thane. You'll come around soon enough.

"Well, at least we're all here, hey? Best not dwell on things that haven't come to pass."

Kit's words had Callan eyeing both of us through the rearview mirror.

"Aye, right. Am surprised the two of ye are so… civil with each other," he said with a smirk.

Kit's entire face went a bright shade of red. They ducked their chin and wrinkled their nose.

"We called a truce, that's all."

It was so much more than a truce. Admissions of liking each other followed by baring our souls and… sex. I couldn't forget that part even if I wanted to. Which I didn't. The memories were burned into my brain. The way it felt. The rightness. The need. And the screaming desire inside of me to do it again. No matter how much I wanted to pretend it meant nothing, I couldn't avoid the truth. I wasn't ready to be done with what happened between us.

"Easier tae survive if ye're no at each other's throats," I said.

"Aye. I wouldnae have blamed Kit for leaving yer grumpy arse in the stream."

"I could never!"

The vehemence in Kit's tone wasn't a surprise to me, but it was to Callan. He glanced back at us with wide eyes before turning to the road again.

"I wasnae being serious."

Kit didn't look at either of us. They weren't the sort of person to leave anyone behind. That kind heart of theirs wouldn't allow it. And they cared about me, as misguided as that might be. I wouldn't hurt them on purpose, of course, but they already knew I was stuck in an inescapable grieving cycle. They weren't under any illusions about the two of us. At least, I hoped not for their sake… and mine.

Callan pulled up to the lodge a wee while later. The rest of the journey had been silent. Kit seemed uncomfortable, and I didn't want to make it worse.

"If ye cannae drive, ye want me tae take ye home?" he asked, turning towards the back of the car after he switched the engine off.

"And leave the Defender here? No."

"Ye got someone tae drive ye?"

He knew very well I didn't. The wee shite was up to something. I could tell by the twinkle in his eyes.

"I can drive you."

My head whipped around to Kit.

"I dinnae wannae put ye oot if ye're gonnae get home."

They shrugged before eyeing Callan. Kit didn't want to have this conversation in front of him. Neither did I.

"How aboot I leave ye two tae decide amongst yerselves?" Callan said, clearly knowing he wasn't wanted.

He got out before either of us could say a word.

I let out a breath the moment he slammed the door shut.

Kit shifted in their seat, their fingers struggling to unclip the belt. I leaned across and did it for them.

"Going home isn't on the top of my list of priorities," Kit said slowly as they met my eyes. "A hot shower and a change of clothes are more pressing."

My throat got all tight as I thought about them naked in my shower. Hot water spilling down their skin.

"Okay, look, Dad told Sienna about me going missing and I'm not ready to deal with that shit yet. You said you can't drive, so let me help you until you can. I'll speak to

Roman. I'm sure he'll rearrange my schedule. He'll understand why I need a few more days."

"Are ye asking tae stay with me?"

I had to be sure.

"Yes."

How on earth could I say no after everything Kit had done for me? Would this go some way to repaying them?

I leaned back in my seat and rubbed my beard.

"Ye wannae ask Roman first?"

Kit bit their lip.

"I suppose so."

"Let's go get yer stuff then."

I unclipped my seatbelt and got out of the car. Callan was leaning on the bonnet.

"Ye made a decision?"

"Help Kit take their stuff to the Defender."

I almost rolled my eyes at his smirk.

I hate you.

They set off towards the lodge, leaving me to round the back of Callan's car and open the boot. I dug through my pack to find my keys. There was no point in me taking anything over there myself. Callan would tell me off. I hobbled over to the car to unlock it and got in the passenger side.

By the time Kit and Callan had finished loading stuff into the Defender, I was impatient to get home.

"Ye keep him safe," Callan said to Kit before they shut the door after they got in.

"I will."

I handed Kit the keys, feeling a wee bit apprehensive about someone else driving my car.

"Don't worry, I have insurance," they assured me as they adjusted the seat and mirrors.

"Aye."

It hadn't crossed my mind. Kit wouldn't have offered to drive if they were uninsured.

"You'll have to direct me, though we probably need to stop at the shop to get some food in."

"What did Roman say?"

They started the engine and put the heating on.

"He gave me a week and will sort out my bookings. He's just glad I'm okay."

I have you for a week.

It wasn't much in the grand scheme of things, but it was more than I could have hoped for. It was a good thing I had that amount of time off work too.

"I turned my phone off when we hung up. There's a bunch of messages from Sienna I have no interest in looking at. Callan kept it charged for me."

"Ye dinnae need tae think aboot her. She's no worth it."

Kit nodded slowly and set off. I directed them to the shops. They disappeared inside with instructions about which painkillers to get. When they got back, we drove to my place. Kit didn't go fast as the back roads were a wee bit ropey in places, especially the track up to my place.

We pulled up outside. Kit stared at the place with wide eyes.

"This is where you live?"

"Aye," I replied before I got out.

It wasn't mine. I merely rented it, but it was away from people and that suited me. It was good to be home, even if I was worried about sharing it with Kit for a week. Not because I would hate it. I was worried I would like them being here a wee bit too much.

TWENTY SEVEN

Kit

hane's house sat on the edge of a wood. We had to drive up a dirt track to reach it.

I sat in his car, staring at the place as Thane got out. It had light wood cladding and a metal roof. There were two huge floor-to-ceiling windows on the front. One to the left-hand side and one in the middle. Through the windows, I could see an open plan living/dining area. There was a deck surrounding three sides and a little wooden staircase leading up to it.

This isn't how I envisioned his place, but somehow, it's so fitting.

Shaking myself, I stepped out of the car and met Thane, who was waiting for me on the other side. Immediately cursing myself for dawdling, I tucked a shoulder under his arm and helped him up the stairs onto the deck. He unlocked the front door, sliding it to the side and stepped in.

The floor was oak and there was a wood-burning stove sitting between the two large windows. The living room area had a corner sofa with a rug and a coffee table in front of it. The dining table sat in front of the kitchen area near the front sliding door. To the right was a small corridor with two doors leading off it. I assumed they would be the bathroom and bedroom.

One bedroom… wait… ONE bedroom. Is he intending to let me sleep with him? I mean, I don't want to assume anything about the state of our relationship. He might not want to sleep with me again.

"This is nice," I said to distract myself from those thoughts.

Thane sat down on the small bench by the door that had hooks above it for coats.

"Aye. It's no mine. I rent it from one of the local farmers. Wasnae in the right headspace tae buy anywhere after… well, ye know."

After his wife died, he sold their house. I didn't blame him for not being ready to settle down anywhere again after that. At least he wasn't still there, surrounded by their things. That couldn't have made things easy for him.

Thane took his boots off and rubbed his face. He looked as exhausted as I felt. The time we'd been stuck in the tent had worn us both down. Not to mention it brought up a lot of emotions. It had been a very draining experience all around.

"I'll just bring the stuff in."

I practically ran out of the house before he could reply. It took several trips for me to get everything inside. I locked the car and left the keys on the dining table before closing the front door. Thane hadn't moved from his spot.

"Ye mentioned wanting a shower."

I bent down to take my boots off.

"You can go first. It's your place, after all."

"Or ye can join me."

I froze in the process of untying my laces.

"Join you?"

"Aye. Ye owe me a reward."

My mind went blank at that. I finished untying my laces and kicked off my boots as I tried to think of what he might mean by it.

"A reward."

I looked over at him. Thane wore a smirk that made me shiver.

"Ye said I could see yer chest tattoo. Well, I already saw it, but I didnae get a guid look."

The memory of us having sex came back to me. The challenge I issued. I owed him since he had succeeded.

"Oh yeah, that totally slipped my mind. Um, sure, let me get my stuff."

I took off my coat before moving over to my suitcase, setting it down and unzipping it to dig out my toiletries.

"There is one small issue, though."

"That is?"

"I can't shower without music. It keeps my mind distracted from the sensory overload of water pounding on me and, well, I don't want to switch my phone on."

It felt odd to reveal that piece of information to him. No one else knew about my coping methods when it came to my sensory issues. It was something I kept to myself. No one needed to know about the little routines I'd created to help me do daily tasks that seemed to come so easily to everyone else.

"No bother. Mah tablet is on the coffee table. We can play ye something through that."

My heart squeezed. The fact that he accepted it so readily left me reeling. Being around Thane made me feel less… othered. I didn't have to be ashamed of myself for the way I was built. The way my mind worked. And I didn't know how to process that.

I put my toiletries down on the dining table and took a deep breath.

"Thane."

"Aye?"

"Are you going to judge me if I cry over how nice you're being to me?"

He blinked.

"Am no being nice, Kit. If ye tell me ye need something, I'll give it ye if I can. Ye deserve tae have yer needs respected."

Tears welled in my eyes at his words. I wanted to run to him, curl up in his lap and sob. But I didn't. I sniffled and rubbed my face.

"Let's get in the shower before I make a mess of my face, then."

He smirked and got up off the bench, peeling off his coat before he hung it up.

I gathered up my things and his tablet from the coffee table. The door on the right-hand side of the corridor opened into the bathroom. It had a huge rainfall shower with a big glass screen separating it from the sink and toilet. I handed Thane the tablet after I followed him in. Taking out my shampoo, conditioner, and razor, I put them in the holder by the shower before retreating to undress.

As I peeled everything off, a sense of relief flooded me. I could get clean and wear something comfy. When I looked up after leaving my clothes in a pile in the corner, I noted Thane had already stripped and was un-braiding his hair. My fingers itched to touch the red strands, but I stayed where I was.

"Dae ye have a preference for what I put on?" he asked, indicating the tablet with his head as he looked at me in the mirror.

"Not really."

I'm too busy thinking about how hot you are right now.

I rubbed my arms, while Thane put some music on. I recognised it as Lofi as the soothing sounds erupted from the tablet's speakers.

Thane turned around, leaned against the sink counter, and cocked his head to the side as his eyes went to my chest. I dropped my arms and stepped closer to let him look at my tattoo. He reached out, his fingers hovering over the spot between my breasts where a full moon lay. Above and below were more moons in different stages of its cycle. Crescents of waxing and waning moons. Tiny stars and lines connected them.

"You can touch it if you want."

The warmth of his fingers seeped into me as he gently placed them on my skin. He traced the lines. I let out a shuddering breath at the delicate touch.

"Ye like the night."

I nodded.

"It's quieter than the daytime. Plus, the sky is pretty with all the stars out. Suppose they're far more visible here than at home with the lack of light pollution."

"Aye."

He smiled and dropped his hand. I watched him hobble into the shower and turn it on. After a minute, he beckoned me over. I took my glasses off and set them on the counter before I stepped in. Thane made room for me under the spray. Maybe it should have felt uncomfortable to be naked in front of him, but I only felt safe. Not like he hadn't seen it all before.

As Thane was the injured one, I let him get cleaned up first. I had a routine that I preferred not to diverge from. Being with Thane might make me feel comfortable, but I was in a place I didn't know. It made my anxiety spike, but it wasn't as bad as when we'd been at the hospital. It wasn't like I had a fight for survival to distract me from the unfamiliar surroundings like I had done in the tent. If I could stick to the things I knew, it would make it easier to remain regulated.

After Thane was done, he leaned up against the wall to take the weight off his injured ankle. I set about washing, running through my normal steps without worrying about what Thane would think. There was nothing unusual about what I was doing, but self-consciousness about my routines and the way people perceived me was a constant struggle.

As I finished rinsing the conditioner out of my hair, I turned my attention to him. Thane was staring at me with a look I didn't recognise. My hand reached out to turn the shower off as I tried to discern what he might be thinking. The way his pupils had blown made me slightly nervous.

"What?" I asked, rubbing my hands over my arms.

"Ye done?"

"Yeah."

"Come here."

My body instinctively reacted to his demand before my brain had a chance to catch up with it. As I stood before him, his hand darted out and tangled in my wet hair. He tugged my head back the same way he had done in the tent and leaned towards me, hovering his face over mine.

"Kit," he breathed.

I held back a squeak as my hands went to his chest automatically, not to push him away, but I had to anchor myself somehow. My knees wanted to buckle from the way he pulled my hair and said my name.

"Ye're so fucking pretty. It almost kills me tae look at ye."

"I don't really want you to die."

He let out a huff of air as if he was trying not to laugh and looked between us. His lips curved up into a smile a moment later.

"I'll try mah best no tae expire on ye."

"You think I'm pretty?" I whispered.

His other hand came up to rest on the side of my neck. I shuddered when his thumb stroked down my throat.

"Aye. I watched ye shower and listed in mah head all the places on yer body I wannae put my tongue."

My mouth went dry, and I had absolutely no idea how to respond. Well, other than I'd let him put his tongue anywhere he wanted now I was clean.

"Unless that's no something ye're comfortable with…"

I must have let the silence go on for too long. I unstuck my tongue from the roof of my mouth and blurted out the first thing that came into my head.

"You can lick me."

"Aye? What else can I dae tae ye?"

"With your mouth? Kiss me… oh and bite me. I'm more than good with biting."

He grinned.

"Can I lick, kiss and bite ye right noo?"

My eyes darted between us, noting that Thane was very much aroused before I looked up at him again. I wasn't opposed to that at all, but we weren't exactly in the best place for it.

"In the shower? I don't know if that's a good idea with your ankle. I don't want to cause you any unnecessary pain."

Thane dusted his lips over mine.

"What aboot in mah bed?"

"I was going to ask about sleeping arrangements, but yes, bed is good."

"Did ye think I wouldnae want ye sleeping with me?"

I shrugged.

"I didn't want to make any assumptions. I need you to spell stuff like that out for me. I'm not good at reading between the lines…"

He eyed me for a moment as his thumb continued to stroke my neck.

"After what we went through, ye deserve a bed, Kit. I wasnae gonnae make ye sleep anywhere else but with me. That stands regardless of whether we dae more. I wannae dae a lot of things tae ye, but if that's no what ye want, then ye just have tae say."

"I want to do more. All the things really. I want to do all the things with you."

I said it so fast after he stopped talking, he barely had time to blink. If he thought I didn't want him after we got out of our dire straits, then I hadn't done a very good job of making my feelings clear.

"All the things?"

"The kissing, licking, touching, and fucking things. I want you everywhere, all over me because in case you haven't noticed, I like you a lot and I'm very turned on right now. Can we get dry so we can get to the licking part of the program already, please?"

Thane chuckled and pressed his mouth against mine, kissing me thoroughly before releasing me.

"Aye, we can."

And with that, he hustled me out of the shower. While I hadn't been expecting Thane to want to continue what we'd started out there in the mountains, I certainly wasn't going to complain about it. I'd appreciate it while I could have it since I was well aware I had to go back to my life in a week. Forgetting that would likely only end in disaster. I wasn't going to make the same mistakes I'd made in the past. Those had only got me heartache and pain. As much as I liked Thane, I wasn't going to delude myself into thinking this could be more than what it was.

What exactly is it, Kit? You don't even know the answer to that.

I told my brain to get lost and followed my instincts instead. They were leading me into Thane's bed for today.

One day at a time until I had to go home. That's how I would deal with this. It was the only way I could or risk hurting myself. I wasn't willing to do that. Not any longer. Not now I knew better. That was something I was learning from Thane. I deserved more than what the people closest to me had shown me. And I would try to remind myself of that when I eventually had to deal with the shit my life had turned into. But not now. Not when I was about to get licked all over by a man hotter than sin who told me things like I was pretty, and he wanted me.

He's who I want to focus on. The only person I want to think about for the next seven days. And hope that when I do go home, I won't be wishing we could be so much more.

TWENTY EIGHT

Kit

Thane grabbed us some towels from a shelf in the bathroom. Once we were both suitably dry and our hair was no longer dripping, he took my hand and led me across the hallway to his bedroom.

It was a large room with a big bed against the wall that was opposite the corridor. There was another of those huge windows that looked out across the woods. It had two sets of curtains, light-blocking ones which were open and sheer curtains that were drawn. To the left of the door was an entire wall of built-in wardrobes with dark, wooden double doors.

He brought me over to the bed, took the towel out of my hands and set it over the pillows so our wet hair wouldn't make them damp. I lay down at his encouragement, situating myself in the centre.

Thane crawled over me, careful of his ankle, and kissed me. It grew heated quickly, our bodies grinding against one another, seeking friction.

Maybe I should have questioned this more. Asked what his intentions regarding me were, but I was too busy being consumed by desire to care. We'd survived. Kissing and touching him felt life-affirming in a strange sort of way.

"Kit," he groaned, pressing his mouth to my jaw, and trailing his tongue down my neck.

My hands were at his back, keeping him as close as possible. Cocooning myself in his embrace gave me safety. I could ignore everything else and be in this fully without worrying about what any of it meant.

When his tongue met my collarbone, he nibbled at it, leaving soft bites across my skin. I trembled. His touch was maddening in all the best ways.

"More," I moaned. "More, please."

Thane licked my sternum, trailing his tongue down the valley of my breasts where my tattoo lay.

"So fucking pretty," he muttered, kissing each moon in turn. "Desperate, that's what I am for ye, fucking desperate tae feast on ye."

It didn't feel like he was merely touching me. There was a reverence to it like I was an altar he worshipped at. I basked in it, knowing in that moment I was precious to him.

My back arched when he ran his tongue over one of my nipples. I moaned when he bit me, my hands tightening around him.

Thane licked a path down my stomach before settling between my legs. His eyes were on me, but I couldn't look at him. It would be too intense. Instead, as he bent his head lower, I put my arm over my eyes and my attempt to breathe turned into a moan. His tongue was on me, circling around my clit and making me grip the sheets below us with my free hand. Two of his fingers speared inside of me. His other hand slid up my stomach, holding me down on the bed as my back arched off it.

"Oh fuck."

Thane didn't respond. He kept licking me and fucking me with his fingers. As good as it felt, I found it difficult to let go enough to climax. My brain was too full now he was no longer surrounding me completely. I kept thinking about what I must look like to him. Whether I was moving right.

A lifetime of being self-conscious because of other people constantly criticising me was hard to undo. Didn't matter if Thane was kind and never made me feel like I was a weirdo, I was having trouble focusing solely on the pleasure. It wasn't like in the tent where I was mostly hidden from view. When we were lost in each other. Now it was only about me, old habits were rearing their ugly heads.

My arm dropped from my face. I reached out and tugged on his hair to get his attention.

Thane looked up at me, eyes searching mine for a moment. Then he raised his head and frowned.

"Ye okay? Am I daeing it wrong?"

I shook my head.

"No, no, fuck no. It's me… I'm really self-conscious right now, and that's not your fault. I can't come when I feel like this."

Embarrassment at admitting the truth flared inside me. It shouldn't, but the vulnerability of the position I was in made it hard not to feel it. I had never been *this* honest with anyone in my life, despite valuing truth and honesty above most other things.

Thane pressed a kiss to my inner thigh and slid his fingers from me.

"Dae ye wannae stop?"

"No."

He kissed my thigh again.

"Dae ye want me tae pin ye doon and impale ye on mah cock while I pull yer hair until ye stop thinking so hard?"

I nodded, biting down on my bottom lip. If he consumed me entirely, I might well forget about anything but him.

He smirked and pushed himself up onto his knees.

"Turn over."

I did as he asked, settling myself on my hands and knees. His big hands curled around my hips, pulling me into him as his cock slid along the length of my cunt. I whined in response. Thane chuckled and did it again.

"Please."

"Mah needy wee thing."

I want to be entirely yours and no one else's.

The thought was so sudden that I barely had time to process it before Thane pushed inside me. He didn't go fast, more like achingly slow to make me feel every single inch. I panted and closed my eyes. He leaned over me, one hand landing by mine and the other sliding into my damp hair. His breath dusted over the tip of my ear, sending a shiver down my spine.

"I can tell ye like that, Kit," he murmured, his voice low and gravelly, "ye wannae be fucked until ye're a mess on mah bed, desperate for a reprieve, but I willnae give ye one. Am gonnae enjoy hearing ye beg."

He pulled back and slid into me again. I whimpered because everything he said sounded so good. His hand made a fist in my hair, and he tugged on it.

"This is how I wanted tae fuck ye when we were in the tent. Tae have ye at my mercy. I havnae been able tae stop thinking aboot it. How ye'd feel. The way ye'd moan. Yer body trembling every time I say yer name."

His thrusts became harder. It was growing increasingly difficult to keep thinking about anything else but him, the way he fucked me, and the things he was saying in my ear.

"Kit… Kit… Kit," he whispered, punctuating each one with the thrust of his body into mine.

"Thane," I cried out as he tugged my head back and met my eyes.

"Aye, that's it, pretty wee thing. Cry for me."

His mouth is going to be the actual death of me.

If you'd asked me whether I was into dirty talk before I met Thane, I would have said absolutely not. Something about his voice, his accent, and the things he said were hot rather than cringe-inducing. It was just Thane in general that I found attractive. Everything he did and said was addicting.

"I'll cry," I choked out.

"Ye will, Kit. I'll make ye."

The idea of Thane making me do stuff had me trembling with need.

"Please."

With all of his weight, Thane pressed my body down onto the bed. I collapsed onto it. He went with me, continuing to fuck me with increasingly ruthless strokes. He kept one hand in my hair, tugging at the roots. His other hand slid up my arm before he entwined our fingers together and pinned my hand on the bed.

"Beg."

The single word had me immediately obeying.

"Fuck me until I cry, please... please don't stop, I want it to hurt."

He didn't even falter in his strokes. The way he was pressing me down had the bedsheets rubbing against me. The friction was perfect. This was exactly what I needed. To feel utterly consumed and at his mercy.

"Thane, please."

"So needy."

"Yes, yes, I am. I want you everywhere."

"Everywhere..."

I shifted against him but found I couldn't move a whole lot.

"Yes, everywhere."

"Ye want me tae hold on tae yer hair while I shove mah cock in yer mooth?"

I moaned as I pictured myself on my knees with him towering above me in full view of the windows in his living room. The way his green eyes would darken as he used me for his pleasure. How he wouldn't let me touch myself, only him as he did it. I would be such a mess if he did that, desperate to please him so he would fuck me afterwards.

"Are ye imagining it, Kit?"

"Yes."

He practically growled and tugged at my hair, making me wince from the way he held it. Then he licked my ear. I whimpered, too overwhelmed by it all to utter another word.

"With yer troublesome mooth, I didnae think ye'd want me tae be in control, but ye're desperate for it, aren't ye?"

A tear leaked out of my eye as I moaned in response.

"Aye, I see ye, Kit. I fucking see ye."

It was all too much. The pounding of his cock inside me. The way our flesh rubbed together. How my clit was constantly being stimulated by the covers. I cried out as a wave of pure pleasure crashed over me. My body clenched around his, making Thane groan when he realised what was happening. I came so hard that I saw stars behind my eyes as I kept them squeezed shut against the intensity.

The moment I came down, I panted and lay there, allowing him to continue fucking me. I didn't want it to stop. The joy he gave me was everything.

"Kit," he ground out through gritted teeth, "can I come in ye or dae ye want it somewhere else?"

It took a bit for me to figure out why he was asking me that. Last time we had sex, I'd had a meltdown over the thought of his cum getting on me. I would be able to get to the bathroom and deal with it afterwards with ease, so it didn't worry me.

"In me. I want it in me."

He groaned, increasing the speed of his thrusts. It was only a few minutes more before he erupted, moaning my name in my ear as he did it.

I squeezed his fingers between mine when he stilled on top of me. He made sure not to fully put his weight on me, so I wouldn't get squished on the bed. I was content to have him on top of me.

Thane pressed a kiss to my cheek and released my hair.

I sighed in happiness. Who would have thought we could be *this* compatible in the bedroom. At least, I hoped he enjoyed it as much as I did. That this was what he wanted, and he wasn't doing it just because I liked it.

"Thane…"

"Aye?"

"Do… do you…"

"Dae I what?"

"Like being the one in control?"

He nuzzled the side of my face with his nose.

"With ye, I like it." He pressed kisses to my shoulder. "Am finding I like a lot of things with ye I havnae tried before."

It didn't entirely surprise me this was new for him, considering he'd only been with one other person. I wasn't the most adventurous type in the bedroom, but I knew I liked it when someone else was in charge. Not having to make the decisions or think about what I was doing was something I appreciated. It quietened the part of my mind that always criticised me for getting it wrong.

"So you'd be okay with taking charge whenever we have sex?"

"If that's what ye want."

"I want to know what you want."

He was quiet at that. Thane pulled away, being gentle as he slid out of me and rolled onto his back next to me. I turned my face to look at his profile. He stared up at the ceiling with a pensive expression on his face.

"I want tae explore this 'cause it makes me feel guid, Kit. Am no deaing it just 'cause ye want it even if that's a big part of it. I want it tae."

"That's all I needed to know."

His words reassured me. I didn't want this to be all about me. Although he had instigated the sex, so I guess I was worrying for no reason. I was so used to trying to make other people happy that I often forgot about myself. But with Thane... he made me think of myself and how things affected me. I wasn't used to being catered to by another person so freely.

I lifted myself up onto my knees and pressed a kiss to his shoulder before slipping off the bed and making a mad dash for the bathroom.

After cleaning myself up from our session, I dug my brush out of my toiletries bag and carefully brushed my hair out. It would be messy when it dried if I didn't.

As I set my brush down, I noted another one sitting on the sink counter. I scooped up my glasses and slid my glasses on my face as I stared at it.

Surely, he needs to brush his hair too.

Without thinking too hard about what I was doing, I picked it up and took it with me into the bedroom.

Thane was sitting up against the headboard, clearly having cleaned himself up too.

I stood at the end of the bed with the brush dangling from my fingers. His gaze went to it, and he cocked his head to the side.

Before he could ask what was going on, I opened my mouth and asked him the question burning in the back of my throat.

"Would you let me brush your hair?"

TWENTY NINE

Thane

None of what occurred since we got to my place had been in my plans. Then again, nothing had really gone to plan since the start of the course. Maybe that was a good thing. It had certainly shaken my life up in a huge fucking way.

As we stood in the shower, all I could think about was how I didn't want to live in the past any longer. I wanted the here and now with Kit, even if it was only for a week. My need for them made me reckless. Made me ask for something I should have thought more about before jumping headlong into bed with them. But I didn't really care about that at the time. Kit happened to be an all-consuming force I couldn't deny.

Now, staring at them after they'd asked to brush my hair, I had no idea what to say or do. I was still wrapped up in the warm afterglow of the intense sex between us.

Kit was always saying the most unexpected things to me. That was part of their charm. I liked the fact they could surprise me. It was refreshing to be around someone who told you exactly what they were thinking.

"I'd just find the repetitive motion soothing," Kit continued when I didn't respond. "It would help me calm down after, well, that." They waved a hand at the bed and blushed. "And I'd like to take care of you if that's okay."

Their earnest expression had me hiding a smile.

"Aye, it's okay with me."

The way their face lit up at my acquiescence made saying yes more than worth it. Kit wearing a genuine smile and the way their body almost vibrated with excitement was a sight to behold.

"Okay, great, thank you. Um, but first, I don't want to be naked and well, I'm not that keen on being out in the open in your living room. Those windows are big."

No one would come up my drive, but I didn't want Kit to be uncomfortable. We could bring their suitcase in here later, so they no longer had to worry about such things.

"If ye open those doors…" I waved at the ones closest to the doorway. "Ye can grab us some t-shirts."

Kit set the brush on the bed and went over to them. They took both bronze handles in their hands and pulled them open together. Inside the wardrobe were floor-to-ceiling shelves. The second set of doors had some hanging space, and the third had more shelves. I didn't use the last set as I didn't have that many clothes. They'd been built with a couple living here in mind.

Kit looked through the shelves and picked up two t-shirts.

"Do you want, um, underwear too?"

"Aye."

They selected a pair of boxers before closing the doors and coming over to the bed. Kit handed me my things. They then proceeded to pull a dark green t-shirt over their head. It was big enough to land a third of the way down their thighs.

I got dressed, being careful as I tugged the boxers over my ankle.

Kit grabbed the brush and made me scoot forward so they could sit behind my back up against the headboard.

They picked up the towel we'd brought in and dried my hair further. Then they got to work, starting from the bottom. My hair had been a mess after all that time we spent in the tent. I was glad to be clean now. Not that I minded camping in the wild and not being able to wash for a couple of days but doing it in the winter was no fun at all.

Kit hummed as they brushed my hair. As the minutes ticked by, my shoulders relaxed and the tension in my body faded away. It had been a trying time. Being somewhere safe hadn't felt like an option before. Now I was home, I could let it all go under Kit's gentle touch.

"Your hair is really soft," they said after a while. "I've kind of been desperate to run my fingers through it but asking felt weird."

My hair was relatively thick and naturally wavy. I'd done my best to take care of it since I started growing it out after asking for some advice from my barber. I saw him regularly as my undercut took some upkeep.

"I dinnae mind if ye dae. It feels… nice."

"Oh? You like this?"

I nodded, feeling embarrassed about admitting that.

Kit continued and said nothing else about it, maybe sensing that I was feeling a wee bit vulnerable. They reached the top of my head and were able to brush through the entire length of it over and over. After a few minutes, their hands dropped from my hair. I turned my head to see them set the brush down on the bedside table.

"There… though, I'll be honest. I kind of don't want to stop."

"Dae ye know how tae braid?"

Kit stared at me with those fucking beautiful icy eyes of theirs.

"Yeah. Sienna used to make me braid her hair all the time when we were kids."

The mention of their friend added tension lines to Kit's face. I didn't want them thinking about Sienna. A part of me wanted to replace all their memories of them with ones of me, so they wouldn't have to associate things with her.

"Would ye braid mine?"

Kit nodded as their face cleared slightly.

"My comb and elastics are on the sink counter."

They jumped off the bed and went to get them. When they got back, Kit sat crossed legged on the bed.

"It might be easier if you put your head in my lap," they said with a shrug, giving me a half-smile.

Without thinking too hard about it, I laid down on my side and put my head in Kit's lap. No one had ever braided my hair for me. It was something I taught myself to do. It took months of practice to get it perfect, so the braids weren't wonky on the sides of my head.

Kit carefully sectioned out the hair by my hairline, making use of the comb before starting on braiding. They hummed again as they did it. I closed my eyes, soothed by the sound and the motion of their hands.

"Would you let me do this every day while I'm here?"

"If ye want."

Having someone else do this for me was a novelty. Having Kit want to take care of me was one too.

"Jenna didnae like it when I started growing mah hair oot."

I don't know why I told Kit that. Maybe to help them understand that this was really fucking new for me.

"No? How long ago did you start?"

"Five years. She always preferred it short, but I wanted a change. Just one of the things we didnae see eye tae eye aboot, but she didnae stop me even if she would make cutting remarks aboot it from time tae time."

Kit paused in their braiding for a moment. They were going slow, but I figured they wanted to get it all lined up nicely. It had probably been a while since they'd done this.

"Well, I like it. It suits you a lot. Like you're super handsome as it is, but this, in my opinion, makes you all the more so."

Getting complimented by Kit made my face grow hot. When was the last time anyone said something nice about me who wasn't Callan? Although, half the time, he said less than pleasant things about me. I let him get away with it since he was my best friend and had every right to give me shite after what I put him through in the wake of Jenna's death.

"Super handsome?"

"Yeah, I couldn't think of the right word, so super will have to do."

You are so fucking cute, Kit. Sienna doesn't deserve you. She doesn't appreciate your humour or the way your mind works... but I do. I fucking do, and I'm afraid of what that means.

"It works."

I opened my eyes. Kit looked down at me with a smile before they reached over and grabbed one of the clear elastics I used to tie off my braids. They wrapped it around the base of the braid at the back of my head.

"All done on this side. Do you want me to do the same on the other?"

"Aye."

I turned over, wincing at the ache in my ankle. How long had it been since I had painkillers? Maybe I needed some more. I would worry about that after Kit was done.

Kit started sectioning out the second braid. I watched their face as they did it. The way they concentrated with that wee wrinkle in their nose was adorable.

"We should probably eat after this. I just realised we haven't had anything all day. With the rescue and all the madness after that, I forgot."

We also had to put all the food they bought away. I was sure it would be okay for now. Kit's wanting to wash had been more important to me than that.

"Aye."

"I hope you don't mind something plain. I bought a lot of my safe foods."

"Safe foods?"

They nodded and bit their lip.

"The foods that I can eat that don't cause me any issues and I never really get bored of. I have trouble eating some stuff as the textures and tastes don't sit right with me. It's a part of the sensory issues I mentioned."

"Aye, right. I dinnae mind. Make whatever suits ye best. I'll eat it."

I wasn't going to make Kit eat anything they didn't enjoy. And there weren't a lot of things I didn't eat.

"Okay, thank you. It's just with all the changes and new environment, I want to stick to things I know." They scrunched up their face. "I'd rather avoid another meltdown, but if it happens, I can't really help it, you know."

I raised my hand and placed it on one of theirs, stilling their movements.

"It's fine. Whatever ye need is fine."

They started braiding my hair again despite my hand being on theirs. I noted the way their eyes misted over.

"Kit…"

"Please don't," they whispered. "Just let me finish this. I can't… no one has ever been so good to me and… and I'm having a really fucking hard time with that."

I took my hand off theirs and did as they said, letting them finish the braid. The moment they tied it off, tears slipped down their face.

I pushed myself up out of their lap, twisted around, and immediately pulled them against me.

Kit gripped my t-shirt and let out a sob as they buried their face in my neck. I stroked their back, letting them purge their emotions without interrupting them.

When their sobs abated, I pressed my mouth to the top of their head and cuddled them closer.

"It's okay," I whispered. "We've been through a lot. It's okay tae be overwhelmed by it all."

"I'm… I'm not used to this."

"Tae what?"

"I'm always the one taking care of everyone else. No one has ever wanted to take care of me."

"I dae."

"I don't know how to deal with that."

"Ye let it happen."

"It's that easy, is it?"

I gently pulled their face away from my neck and wiped their cheeks with my thumbs.

"Never said it's easy, Kit, but ye're clearly exhausted and am no gonnae let ye keep pushing yerself until ye break. That's no healthy."

They sniffled and nodded slowly. I pressed my lips to their forehead and stroked their face with my thumbs, clearing more of their tears.

"What dae ye wannae eat?"

"I can make it. You're still hurt."

I shook my head.

"Am no so injured I cannae make us something tae eat. Ye've been taking care of us for days. Let me take care of this."

I could tell Kit wanted to argue with me further, but they didn't.

"Pasta with butter and cheese, please."

"That everything?"

They nodded and released my t-shirt from the tight grip of their fingers.

"Yeah. Safe foods, remember?"

I smiled and kissed their forehead again.

"Aye."

So that's what I did. Made us plain pasta without a fuss. Took more painkillers to help deal with my ankle while we ate and afterwards, I let Kit curl up between my legs on the sofa while we watched TV for the rest of the afternoon. And we went to bed early that evening, so Kit could get some much-needed rest. They slept pressed up against my chest. It would have felt weird if I wasn't touching them in some way after we'd spent several nights together in a single sleeping bag.

I appreciated that Kit wanted to look after me. It felt good to let them brush and braid my hair. However, they needed someone to care for them as well. They deserved that. While I could, I would be that person for them. It was the very least I could do after everything they'd done for me. But I wasn't just doing it because of that... I wanted to. I really fucking wanted to. Kit meant something to me. And even though that scared me, I wouldn't let my fears get in the way of being there for them in the short time they were with me.

You deserve the world, Kit. And I'll prove it to you... if you let me.

THIRTY

Thane

As the sun peeked out through the clouds, I noted a car coming up the track towards my house from my perch on the sofa. It was a vehicle I instantly recognised. They'd stayed away yesterday after our rescue, but I had no such luck today. And that was going to be a fucking problem.

I should have known they wouldn't listen to Callan.

"Kit."

A head of dark hair appeared around the wall separating the living room from the kitchen. Kit pushed their glasses up their nose, stepping out further. They had a mug between their fingers. They'd made me a coffee and disappeared to finish brewing their tea.

"Yeah?"

"Mah parents are here."

Kit glanced towards the windows where a dark grey car was pulling up in the driveway next to my old Defender.

"Oh… uh, I…"

The slight hint of fear in their expression gave their feelings away.

"Ye dinnae have tae deal with them."

"No?"

I shook my head. It was bad enough that I did.

Kit had been quiet since we got up, but it didn't worry me. I figured they needed some time to adjust to being here. And it wasn't as if I had any plans other than daily exercise for my healing ankle. We were playing everything by ear until they had to leave. That was the only permanent part of this. Kit going home. They booked their train ticket while we were having breakfast. I didn't expect it to feel so final. I shoved away the disquiet it brought on since there was no point in dwelling on it until the day came.

"Okay, I'm just going to…"

They dashed towards my bedroom without finishing their sentence. I couldn't help but smile.

Kit didn't even hesitate to run away from a situation they didn't want any part of. And I didn't blame them.

I waited as my parents got out of the car. I took after my father, who stood tall above my mother as they walked up the steps onto the deck. They didn't bother ringing the doorbell. My mother slid the front door open and stepped inside. Her eyes went to me immediately and tears welled in them.

"Thane."

She rushed over and wrapped her arms around me without waiting for me to get up off the sofa. I hadn't been planning on it, as my injured ankle was propped up on a cushion. My father followed more slowly after he slid the door shut.

"I've been so worried," Mum said into my shoulder. "Ye gave us both such a fright."

"Am fine, Mum."

"Ye're no fine. Callan told us ye've hurt yerself."

I rolled my eyes, not that she could see, and patted her back.

"It's just mah ankle and it'll heal."

She finally pulled away and looked me in the eye.

"Ye let yer mother worry over ye."

"Margie, leave the poor lad alone," my father said with a shake of his head as he came over and gave my shoulder a squeeze. "Ye're all right, son."

He moved away and took a seat on the end of the sofa. Mum sat beside me and took my hand.

"I dread tae think what would've happened if they didnae find ye," she said with a sigh.

"They did, and I had company. It wasnae just me oot there alone."

"Aye, Callan mentioned that. They werenae injured, were they?"

"No, they saved mah life."

Her eyebrow curled up.

"Saved ye?"

"They dragged me oot of a stream after I fell in. That's how I twisted mah ankle. They took care of me, made sure I got warm and dry. If it wasnae for them… well, we dinnae need tae think aboot that."

I probably shouldn't have told my parents I almost died, but lying to my mother wasn't going to do me any favours. Our relationship was strained enough as it was.

"Ye almost died?"

Her voice took on an alarmed tone.

"I wasnae at death's door, Mum. Am just saying they made sure I stayed alive."

Her other hand went to her neck.

"I dinnae think I could stand it if ye never came back, Thane. It doesnae even feel that long ago since we lost Jenna."

I flinched at her words. Why she always had to remind me of Jenna's death whenever I saw her was a mystery to me. It felt like a punishment. Not something I would have ever said before I exposed the whole truth of that sorry night to Kit. But now I had some very different feelings regarding my dead wife and our relationship. Difficult feelings I would eventually have to work through. However, I didn't want to do that when I only had a week to spend with Kit. Focusing on them and this connection we shared felt like the right thing to do. Dwelling on my past was something I did all too often. And I didn't want to be that person any longer. The one who drowned in misery and pain. He didn't feel like me.

"Dae ye always have tae mention Jenna?"

Mum blinked.

"What?"

"Every time we see each other, ye always bring up Jenna."

What are you doing?

"She was a big part of oor lives."

"Aye, but she's no here noo. She's gone and I dinnae wannae be reminded of that all the fucking time."

I rarely said fuck around my parents, despite having no compunction about doing it around anyone else. It didn't come as a surprise that they both looked taken aback by my words.

"Thane—"

"Ye talk aboot it like ye would rather have her here than me. Am tired of it. I wannae live withoot feeling guilty for it when she fucking died. Ye're no helping me dae that. I thought I was gonnae die oot there in the mountains and here we are talking aboot Jenna yet again. Is it any fucking wonder we're barely on speaking terms when ye keep bringing up mah dead wife every chance ye get?"

Two years of bottled-up resentment came out without me wanting it to. I hadn't been very good to them in the aftermath of the accident, but they didn't make things easier on me. Maybe they didn't know the right things to say. I tried so hard not to take it out on them when they were trying their best with me. But it was fucking difficult when they kept throwing the subject I wanted to avoid in my face time and time again. And I guess this was the final straw. The one occasion where it was time to focus on me and it had still come back around to Jenna.

I ground my teeth together to stop myself from saying more, from making it worse.

My mother looked horrified at my outburst. I didn't even turn my gaze to my father, knowing I would only see disappointed in his features.

Mum swallowed and blinked back tears. Then she slowly stood up.

"Right, well, we should get going. Ye need yer rest. I hope yer ankle heals up soon."

She awkwardly patted my shoulder and moved away towards the front door.

"Son," came Dad's voice as he stood too, "we'll see ye soon."

I balled my hands at my sides and tried not to hate myself even more for upsetting them. And yet it needed to be said. I couldn't go on listening to them talk about Jenna forever. It was wearing on me too much.

Their footsteps echoed on the wooden floor. The sound of the door sliding open and shut had me holding my breath. I let it out when the car started up. Then I leaned forward, put my face in my hands and let out a sigh.

"Fuck."

A few minutes later, the soft pad of feet alerted me to their presence. I didn't look up or move from my spot. What I was not expecting was for Kit to crawl onto the sofa, squeeze themselves in the wee space behind me and wrap their arms around my front. They rested their head against my back and breathed with me.

I don't know how much time went by as we sat there. The tension in my body lessened with their touch. Their gentle support. They gave it freely, without words. I didn't feel like I deserved it, but I took it anyway.

"I saved you, huh?" they whispered.

"Aye."

There was no doubt in my mind that Kit had heard every word between me and my parents. Shame bubbled up inside me. I'd treated Kit to harsh words when we first met and here I was showing them that side of me still existed. That I wasn't immune to losing my temper. Then again, who was? Human nature dictated we all had emotions regardless of the narrative society liked to spin about controlling them. About not feeling them. I'd pushed mine down long enough to know that wasn't healthy or productive. And yet... I still felt ashamed of the way I'd behaved.

"Ye shouldnae have had tae hear that."

"You think I'm judging you for what you said to your parents?"

I dropped my hands from my face and closed my eyes.

"Aye."

"I can't imagine it's easy when everyone ignores what her death did to you and only focuses on what it did to them. It's especially difficult when it comes from your own mother."

"She means well."

"People can mean well and still do the wrong thing, Thane."

When it came to my parents, that statement was entirely accurate. But I hadn't helped matters either. This wasn't my first outburst, and it wouldn't be the last. It was why they'd left rather than have it out with me. The walking around on eggshells clearly needed to stop. I had things to apologise for, but they had to understand they were making mistakes too. Was it so wrong to want them to see me as myself rather than as part of a package deal? It wasn't Thane and Jenna any longer. It was *just* me. And I needed them to see that.

"They dinnae see me… in their heads, Jenna and I go hand in hand. They cannae separate me from her."

"I think that's a mistake a lot of people make when others get into relationships. They no longer see the individual, they just see the couple, but we're all still individuals regardless of whether we're with someone else. At least, that's what I believe."

I'd never looked at it like that before, but what Kit said resonated with me.

"And there's nothing wrong with you wanting them to see you. They should. I hope they seriously think about what you said to them."

I nodded slowly, unsure of whether that would happen. Hope wasn't something I had much of these days. What I did have was the will to live again. And Kit had helped me with that. Just as they were helping me with this.

I keep owing more and more to you, Kit. I don't know why you do all of this so freely. Why you care so much, but I appreciate it.

"Kit…"

"Yeah?"

291

"Can I... I can I hold ye?"

They let go of me without a word, sliding out from behind me and crawling around to my front. I sat back to let them settle in my lap.

Kit smiled as they wrapped their arms around my neck. My hands hesitantly went to their waist. I ran them up their sides. One hand moved higher, across their breastbone until it rested at the base of their neck. The other went to their hair, threading through the strands, enjoying the soft feel of it against my fingertips.

They leaned closer and rested their forehead on mine. I closed my eyes and breathed out.

"Thank ye."

"For what?"

"For being here, listening tae me, understanding me. No one else bar Callan has ever wanted tae look deeper, but ye dae and I... I... am trying tae say I appreciate ye more than ye know."

I heard rather than saw Kit swallow. The brush of their lips over mine came a moment later.

"I hope you know I appreciate you too," they whispered before kissing me.

My heart squeezed almost violently. I wanted to clutch my chest, but my hands were on Kit. Removing them would leave me feeling worse.

I slid one further up their neck and loosely clutched it, feeling their pulse thump against my palm.

I waited for the guilt to set in as I deepened the kiss. Waited for my mind to tell me I shouldn't be indulging in my desire for Kit when I was still so messed up over the death of my wife. But nothing came. My mind was perfectly content.

Is this what wanting someone is meant to feel like? Is this what it feels like when it's right? How am I supposed to know when I've never experienced this before?

These were questions I would have to ponder later. Questions I should ask Callan because fuck knows, I had no clue what I was doing when it came to Kit. Acting on instinct and need would only sustain me for so long. I didn't want to fuck up the only good thing to happen to me in two years... perhaps longer.

"Kit," I whispered into their mouth. "Kit."

Don't leave me.

That's what I wanted to say, but it came with ramifications I didn't think either of us would be ready to deal with. So I kept quiet and kissed them until we were both breathless. Until the world faded away to just Kit and me the way it had been in the tent. That was easier than owning up to the truth. That I wasn't sure if I could let them go when the time came for them to go home.

THIRTY ONE

Kit

As much as I wanted to spend all day kissing Thane, I kept replaying his interaction with his parents over and over in my head. It wasn't because I judged him for the way he spoke to them or anything. It merely reminded me of my own broken family.

Well, there was nothing wrong with my relationship with my father, but my mother was a different story. I told Thane she was dead to me. That was the truth. It might seem callous to many people, but they didn't have the full picture. It was hard to talk about. My memories of her were worse than anything Sienna had done to me.

I released Thane's mouth and rubbed my cheek against his bearded one before resting my forehead on his shoulder. He let go of my neck, placing his hand on my back instead.

"Ye okay?"

I sighed as I nuzzled his jumper.

"Yes, and no."

"Ye wannae tell me aboot the no part?"

Did I want to discuss my mother with him? Thane wouldn't judge. If anything, he would likely be horrified. It wasn't a pretty tale.

"The thing with your parents made me think about my non-existent relationship with my mother."

I slid my fingers into the messy bun he'd put his hair up into this morning, needing something to do with my hands.

"And before you ask, no, I don't want to change that."

"Am I allowed tae ask why?"

It shouldn't surprise me that he would ask that question. Telling him before we opened up to each other about our traumatic pasts had felt too invasive. I didn't want a stranger knowing my business. Things were different now. We weren't the same and what we shared scared me, but I was trying not to think too hard about it. The fact I would have to leave him when I was catching serious feelings for him. It was too soon and too fast, but when you've gone through a terrifying experience with someone you barely know it forms a bond. We had no choice but to rely on each other. And now… I wanted to rely on him all over again. On his kindness. On his care. On knowing he had me, regardless of what I threw at him.

I took a deep breath, unable to remember the last time I spoke about what happened with my mother out loud.

"She's in prison."

Thane stiffened underneath me. I doubt he expected that. Nobody ever expected it. That was the thing about her. She appeared fine to the outside world, but that was never the case at home, behind closed doors where no one else bar her family could witness her true nature.

"What did she dae?"

"She was convicted of three counts of attempted murder. She's serving her sentences concurrently, but it basically amounts to life with a minimum term of thirty-five years."

It was typically quite difficult to prove attempted murder, but there was no trial because my mother pleaded guilty to all three counts. In fact, she told the judge during sentencing if they let her out, she would do it again. Unless she started showing remorse in the intervening years since her sentencing, I doubted they would let her out on parole. And even if they did, she would be on licence for the rest of her life. They could recall her to prison at any time.

"Who did she try tae kill, Kit?"

His voice was hesitant, as if he already knew the answer to that question, but had to ask it, anyway. Had to be sure of what he suspected.

"My dad, Olly and… me."

Thane said nothing. He merely wrapped both arms around me and pressed me tight against his chest.

"I don't remember a time when she wasn't abusive towards Dad. A lot of it had to do with him being autistic. It steadily got worse after Olly was born until Dad kicked her out. Olly was six, and I was sixteen. Dad was given full custody. My mother had supervised visitation because of her history of domestic abuse."

My parents should have never been together, but Dad didn't know any better at the time. I didn't blame him for staying with her for so long. It was hard to get out of an abusive relationship. And things had been a lot better for the three of us after we were free of her. That only lasted for a couple of years. Then things went very wrong.

"It happened a few days after Olly's eighth birthday. She arrived at the house saying she wanted to give him a present. Dad stupidly let her in and that's when she attacked him with a knife. She left him bleeding in the hallway and came after Olly. I tried to stop her, to protect him, but she managed to get both of us. The neighbours called the police after they heard screaming. It took five of them to restrain her. The three of us were taken to hospital. Olly and I only had minor injuries, but Dad now walks with a cane and has a carer who comes in to help him with daily tasks."

I turned my face into Thane's neck. Talking about it didn't make me upset. I'd already dealt with my feelings towards her years ago after she was convicted. Cutting her out of my life was for the best. I'd never visited her in prison and lived my life as if she didn't exist.

"She hated me and Olly, resented having us because we turned out like our father. She refused to accept that I'm non-binary, and she's the only person who still uses what used to be my full name. Dad started calling me Kit after I told him I hated the name Katherine. I legally changed it when I was eighteen."

Drawing my fingers out of Thane's bun, I ran them across the soft hairs at the back of his head where his undercut was.

"So that's why I refuse to have anything to do with her."

"I dinnae blame ye. That's fucking awful. I dinnae understand people who want tae take away another person's life. It's no right."

"She had a shit upbringing, but it doesn't excuse her behaviour towards us. I'll never forgive her for what she did."

I pulled away from him. Thane let me out of his arms, but he kept his hands on my waist as if he didn't want me to escape completely. I didn't want to be anywhere else but with him.

My fingers went to my clothes, tugging up my jumper and t-shirt. Thane moved his hands to my thighs. I twisted to the side and pointed out the small puncture-shaped scar on my left side. He stroked it with two of his fingers. Then I showed him my fingers where there was a faint slashing scar across them.

"This is where I stopped the blade going into Olly. I was lucky it didn't go too deep. I had a few more cuts and scrapes, but none of the others scarred."

Thane took my hand and pressed kisses to each of my scars. I trembled at his gentleness. At the soft look in his beautiful green eyes.

"She doesnae deserve yer forgiveness. She doesnae deserve ye full stop."

He pressed my palm to his cheek.

"Thank ye for confiding in me. We didnae start off on the right foot, but I truly appreciate every part of ye that ye've allowed me tae see."

Some people might think it should have been talking about my mother that set me off, but it was the man in front of me. His reaction to it. The way he understood me. I squeezed my eyes shut to stop tears from forming.

"You're doing it again."

"Daeing what?"

"Being nice to me."

He let out a snort.

"Aye and am gonnae keep deaing it until ye realise it's no me being nice, but me treating ye with decency and respect."

A tear leaked out of my eye. We'd been put through the emotional wringer time and time again over the past week. I was exhausted. Mentally and physically exhausted. No wonder I kept crying. There was only so much one person could take, and I was way over my limit.

"Kit…"

"I'm so tired. It's too much, you know. Everything we've had to deal with, it's too much. I feel like I'm drowning. I can't swim anymore. I want it all to stop. All of it for just a little while so I can recover my strength."

The soft pads of two fingertips brushed away the tear streaking down my cheek. Gentle hands removed my glasses from my face.

"Come lie doon, and rest with me."

I opened my eyes to find Thane reaching over to place my glasses on the coffee table. Then he encouraged me to lie with him on the sofa. He turned on his side. I curled up in his arms with my face buried in his chest. He stroked my hair and didn't say a word, letting me rest.

I couldn't remember a time when another person's touch had brought me so much comfort. He would give me the peace I so desperately craved. I could fall apart next to him, and Thane would help me fix my broken parts back together.

It didn't seem real that a person like him existed. Maybe I was far too used to being mistreated by others. I was waiting for the other shoe to drop. But it already had, in a way.

Thane wasn't over his relationship with Jenna. I wasn't expecting him to move beyond her at the drop of a hat. I had my own unresolved issues, anyway.

We were two broken people who had an expiry date on whatever this was between us. Maybe that made it easier for him to be with me right now. Besides, I wasn't brave enough to ask him what we were doing. What would happen when I went home. If we said goodbye and that would be it. The very thought of having that conversation made my anxiety spike. And that wasn't what I needed right then.

"I was planning on moving out before she tried to kill us," I said in a quiet voice to distract myself from those thoughts. "I was eighteen, had just changed my name and wanted to do something with my life."

Thane's arms tightened around me.

"I stayed to take care of Olly and Dad. I didn't move out for another six years and even then, I only moved across town, so I was still close by if they needed anything."

I tucked a hand under his top to rest on the bare skin of his waist.

"It's only been in the last two years since Olly moved to Manchester that I've felt like my life is my own if that makes sense. Only I don't really know what I'm doing with it."

"Can I be honest with ye, Kit?"

"Always."

He let out a breath against my hair as he pressed his face to the top of my head.

"From what ye've told me, ye've spent yer life putting everyone else first and neglecting yerself along the way. Ye cannae keep that up indefinitely. I think ye need tae put yerself first and if what ye need is a rest, then take it. It doesnae matter what other people need if ye're no okay."

I didn't stiffen at his words as they settled over me. He wasn't wrong. And maybe that was just what I needed to hear.

The tension in my limbs melted away. I relaxed into his hold, rubbing my fingertips over his bare skin to soothe myself further.

"I feel like you just gave me permission to rest."

He chuckled.

"Did ye need someone tae tell ye that ye can?"

"Maybe."

"Then while ye're here with me, ye're gonnae take it easy."

"But you still need—"

"Am fine, Kit. The only thing I need ye tae dae is tae drive if we have tae go oot. I dinnae want ye worrying aboot anything else."

I shut my mouth. Thane could be stubborn when he wanted. And I had a feeling this wasn't going to be an argument I would win. Rather than disturbing our peace, I closed my eyes and allowed myself to let it all go because right then, that was exactly what I needed.

THIRTY TWO

Thane

The look in Kit's eyes when their phone started ringing on the dining table as we were finishing breakfast spoke volumes. I almost stopped them from answering it, but Kit had to make their own choices. Not sure they would appreciate me interfering.

"What do you want, Sienna?"

Kit's voice was off, almost robotic in nature. My fingers clenched around my mug of coffee, but I said nothing.

Why the fuck is she calling Kit?

"What do you mean, you're here?"

Their eyes widened and their free hand curled around the edge of the table as if to steady themselves.

"I'm fine, you don't need to worry about me… I don't want to see you… well, I'm not in town, I'm staying with someone outside of it… okay, okay, hold on…"

Kit put their hand over the phone, bringing it away from their ear.

"Sienna's in town. She flew up here to see me and she's not taking no for an answer. Dad must've told her where I am."

The thought of Kit having to see Sienna filled me with anger. And the fact she'd come all the way up here was suspicious. I couldn't imagine a person like Sienna doing anything out of the kindness of her own heart after the shite Kit had told me about her. This was to serve her own self-interests.

"What dae ye wannae dae?" I asked quietly as I tapped my fingers on the wooden table.

"To get this over with… but I'd also like it if you were with me when I speak to her."

"Invite her here then."

As much as I would rather not have Sienna at my place, the pleading look in Kit's eyes was more than I could take. There was no fucking way I would let them face their friend alone. Not when they'd specifically asked for me. They told me back in the tent that they felt safe with me. So I'd keep providing that for them as long as I was with them. Besides, it was probably better for them to have a conversation with Sienna in private rather than out in the open in a café in town.

"Thank you."

Kit stood and continued talking to Sienna.

I got up and moved into the living room to sit on the sofa.

I wondered what would happen when she turned up. If she would upset Kit and how I would handle that. There was no point in trying to predict it. I would do what was necessary depending on what occurred when she got here.

After Kit got off the phone, they grew more and more anxious with every passing minute. They paced the living room, wringing their hands and looking as though they'd rather be anywhere else.

This wasn't what we needed. Not after my parents turned up yesterday and Kit told me how exhausted they were. What I wanted was for both of us to rest, but that wasn't going to happen today. Other people were determined to disrupt us.

Hadn't we dealt with enough already? When would we get the time to decompress and process everything we'd been through? I had no fucking clue at this point.

"Kit."

They waved me off.

"I'm fine."

"Ye're no fine."

"No, but I have to do this. I just can't believe she came all the way here, that she couldn't wait until I got back. It's not like her, you know, she always puts herself first."

Kit said no more and continued to pace until a car pulled up in the driveway. Sienna must've hired it at the airport. It made me wonder what she did for a living if she could leave at the drop of the hat and afford to come up here. But it wasn't important enough that I would ask Kit about it.

When Sienna stepped out of the car, I took in the tall, slender woman with long red hair and brown eyes. She looked far too perfectly polished against the background of the snowy landscape surrounding my house. As she glanced around, she wrinkled her nose. Then she walked up the steps to the deck. Kit rushed to the front door, sliding it open for her.

"Hey," they said with hesitancy in their voice.

Sienna's haughty expression changed to one of fake concern at the sight of Kit. Her eyes darted over them, checking every inch before her lips pressed into a thin line.

"You're okay."

"Of course I am. Didn't Dad tell you?"

She crossed her arms over her chest.

"He did, but I had to see for myself."

Kit stood in the doorway, looking incredibly awkward.

"Are you coming in?"

They stepped back as Sienna walked into my place. My hands fisted at my sides, wanting to throw her right back out of here. I kept my cool as Kit led Sienna further into the living room. They rolled their feet as they stood near the coffee table, looking anywhere else but Sienna.

"Why are you still here, Kit? You should be home with your family and friends."

Kit rubbed their arms.

"I went through a lot out there. I just needed some space." They looked up at their friend. "And I told you I didn't want to see you."

Sienna stared them down. She looked at Kit like they were nothing more than an inconvenience. That pissed me off, but I stayed on my perch on the sofa, waiting for it to play out.

"Did you expect me to stay away after my best friend went missing in the middle of winter? Do you think so little of me now? That I wouldn't care?"

Kit's hands fell to their sides. They rubbed their fingers together. They were agitated. I'd been learning to read the subtle signs. Kit might keep a straight face a lot of the time, but their body language gave so much away. It was clear as day if you knew what you were looking for.

"Honestly, Sienna, I don't know any longer. You said some pretty cruel things to me the last time we spoke. And I'm not sure I can forgive you for that or if I even want to."

"So that's it, huh? You want to throw away our friendship over some things I said in anger? You looked like you were about to jump off the cliff. How do you think I was meant to feel seeing that?"

Their fingers rubbed against each other harder. Kit paced away and their expression grew grim.

"How you were meant to feel? It's always about how you feel, isn't it? It's never about me. It's always Kit did this to me, or Kit did that, but you don't think about what you do to others. I was hurting, and you weren't there for me even though I tried to be there for you."

307

They sighed and closed their eyes, coming to a standstill in front of Sienna.

"I have no interest in fighting with you over this. Tell me the real reason you're here, and no bullshit, okay? I don't want to hear fake platitudes any longer."

"Fake? You think I'm fake?"

"Sienna."

She let out a huff.

"Fine. I need you home because it's time we tried again. You've had long enough to deal with whatever it is you're feeling. Come back with me and we can get ready for it."

Kit opened their eyes and stared at Sienna with no emotion on their face.

"Are you for real right now?"

"What's that supposed to mean?"

"I almost fucking died out there in the mountains and all you can think about is your need for a baby. God, you are so selfish. It's always the Sienna show with you. All aboard the fucking Sienna train. You never think about anyone but yourself. You didn't come here because you care about me. You came here to make sure I do what you want and give you a baby. Well, I've got news for you. That's not happening. I'm not getting pregnant again. Not for you. Not for anyone."

Sienna blinked rapidly, and then her expression turned to one of consternation.

"All right, Katherine, tell me how you really feel, why don't you." She scoffed. "I should have known you wouldn't follow through with it. You never do with anything. You're always making excuses and using your" – she made air quotations with her fingers – "disability as a way of getting out of things. No fucking wonder you're too scared to do anything with your life. You're too busy thinking everything and everyone is against you rather than actually making the effort to do better."

Kit froze in place.

I stood up the moment Sienna called them by their previous name, unable to contain myself any longer. Then she kept pulling punches, and I was done. My eyes went to Kit, who looked more upset than I'd ever seen them be before. Sienna took the knife and dug it deep, twisting it several times to play on all of Kit's insecurities and fears.

"That's enough."

Sienna took me in then as if she hadn't noticed I was there before.

"Who are you?"

I marched over to them and put myself between Kit and Sienna, wanting to shield them.

"Me? Am the one who got lost in those mountains with Kit. The person they've been staying with tae recover from it."

Sienna looked me up and down like I was nothing but a piece of dirt on her shoe.

"Funny that Flynn didn't mention you when he told me Kit went missing."

I assumed Flynn was Kit's father. They'd never mentioned his name.

"It doesnae really matter who I am. What does is the shite ye've said tae Kit."

"I only stated the truth."

I stepped towards her, forcing her to give ground. I wanted her away from Kit, so she couldn't hurt them any longer.

"The only truth here is that ye're a selfish cunt. How fucking dare ye come here and expect them tae bend tae yer will after they told ye they didnae wannae see ye. Dae ye no understand the word, no? Or are ye tae fucking up yer own arse, ye cannae listen tae a word anyone else says?"

Her mouth flew open.

"And ye have the fucking gall tae call Kit by their deadname, knowing why they hate it. Dinnae even get me started on ye fucking misgendering them and making them feel like they're worthless. If ye fucking listened tae them for one minute, ye'd know they went through hell when they were pregnant. Ye'd know they suffered gender dysphoria, but ye're so wrapped up in yer own self-interest that ye didnae even see yer friend crying oot for help. Ye didnae see the pain they were in. No, ye see Kit as less than fucking human, dinnae ye? Just a tool for ye tae use and discard when ye're done with them."

I took another step towards her. I didn't care if I was intimidating Sienna, nor did I feel the pain in my ankle. All I could focus on was making sure she knew what she'd done to Kit.

"Well, that's no happening anymore. Ye dinnae deserve tae be anywhere near them. Ye dinnae appreciate Kit for who they are, but I dae. I see how fucking amazing they are. And am no gonnae let ye dim their light any longer. Get the fuck oot of mah hoose and the fuck oot of Kit's life. Never contact them again or I'll hunt ye the fuck doon and make ye understand why ye messed with the wrong person, ye hear? Am no joking. Ye're no allowed within ten feet of them again."

Sienna stood there, clearly shell-shocked by what I'd thrown at her. Well, I didn't give a fuck. She deserved worse, but I was holding back for fear Kit would get upset with me for shouting at their friend.

"Leave or I'll fucking make ye."

She tried to look behind me at Kit, but I stepped into her eyeline, making myself bigger.

"Are you going to let him speak to me like that?"

I crossed my arms over my chest and glared at her. Then I felt a hand on my arm as Kit came to stand next to me.

"You should leave, Sienna," they said in a quiet voice.

Kit's eyes were on me. I could feel them, but I didn't look down. I kept my gaze on Sienna, waiting for her to move.

"I always knew you were a coward, Kit. Cowering behind a man because you can't handle anything by yourself. Consider me gone from your life. Who would want to be friends with such a spineless bitch, anyway? I only kept you around because I felt sorry for you. Well, more fool me."

Sienna spun on her heel and walked out. I would have given her hell for what she called Kit if she hadn't gone. But it didn't stop my anger. It didn't stop the rage from swelling inside. Sienna was so much worse than Kit made out. Then

311

again, I was pretty sure Kit had rose-coloured glasses on when it came to their friend… well, hopefully ex-friend now. And I need them to take those glasses off. For them to see Sienna for what she really was. They deserved so much more than to be treated like they were nothing.

My hands clenched into fists as the car peeled out of my driveway and back down the track. I had to get my rage out somehow before I spoke to Kit. I didn't want to take it out on them, but by fuck did I want to hit something until my fists bled. That wouldn't do me any good. So I would go do the next best thing and deal with my anger the only way I could.

THIRTY THREE

Kit

hane stood next to me, his chest heaving after he laid into Sienna for what she said to me. After she used the name she knew I hated more than anything.

I stared up at him. This beautiful man who protected me and called me amazing. No one had ever come to my defence that way before. No one had threatened to go after someone for me if they didn't do as they were told. That shouldn't be as hot as it was. In fact, I should probably not be feeling like I wanted to jump on him and kiss him for all he was worth. But I was so awestruck by Thane that I couldn't help myself.

"Fuck," he ground out before he pulled his arm out of my grasp, stomped over to the door, shoved his feet into a pair of shoes and stormed out of the house.

I stood there for a second, wondering where the hell he was going. Then I chased after him.

He walked down the steps with determination in his stride. I stayed on the deck as I hadn't put any shoes on. He made his way around the side of the house. When I walked around the corner, I found him picking up an axe that was leaning up against the deck. He stood next to what looked like a woodshed with a large slice of a tree trunk in front of it. Thane then propped a log up on the trunk before bringing the axe down and chopping it. He did it again and again, leaving a messy pile of chopped wood around the trunk.

I rubbed my arms, feeling the cold seeping into my bones.

"What are you doing?"

"Go back in the hoose, Kit."

"No, you come back in. You're going to hurt yourself doing that."

"Am no gonnae fucking hurt mahself. Am fine."

I dropped my hands and stepped up to the edge of the deck.

"You'll hurt your ankle and it'll take longer for it to heal. Come inside and we can talk about this."

"No, am tae fucking angry tae talk. That friend of yers is a terrible fucking person."

"So what? You're taking out your anger on the wood?"

"Aye, I fucking am."

I stared at him for a long moment, watching the way his muscles flexed as he brought the axe down again. I shouldn't have found him so attractive when he was angrily cutting wood, but I did. I wanted all of those muscles on me, pushing me down and forcing me to do whatever he wanted.

"Take it out on me instead."

Thane paused mid-swing, his head whipping up to me.

"What did ye just say?"

"Come take it out on me."

He blinked several times. His mouth thinned and his eyes grew concerned.

"Am no gonnae hit someone. Chopping wood is safer for all of us."

I cocked my head to the side.

"I'm not asking you to hit me. I'm asking you to fuck me."

He blinked again, still holding the axe in the air.

"I would never hit ye, Kit, that's no what I was saying. I was talking aboot Sienna. I wannae hurt her for the shite she said tae ye but am no gonnae dae that. That's no the kind of man I am."

I crossed my arms over my chest.

"I know you wouldn't hit me or anyone else. And that's beside the point. I still want you to fuck me. Like really, would you rather be chopping that wood or forcing me to my knees and making me take it?"

He slowly lowered the axe to the ground.

"Ye want me tae fuck ye?"

"Yes."

He set the axe against the tree trunk and took a step towards me.

"Get in the fucking hoose."

He didn't have to tell me twice. I ran across the deck, rounded the corner, and dived into the house. I could hear his footsteps as he came after me. As I turned and backed into the table, Thane walked in. He kicked off his shoes and shut the front door. Then he stalked towards me like a predator coming up on his prey. My back bowed over the table as he leaned down, pressing his hands onto it on either side of me, caging me in.

"On. Yer. Knees."

All thoughts and words disappeared from my head. I lowered myself to the ground and knelt at his feet.

Thane straightened and stared down at me with heat in his eyes. He dug his hand into my hair, pulling my head back further. He dragged the fingers of his other hand over my lips. I parted them on instinct. He pushed two fingers into my mouth before dragging them out to the tips. When he pushed them in again, I moaned in response. He smirked and kept fucking my mouth with his fingers.

"That's it, Kit, show me how much ye want mah cock in yer needy wee mooth."

I sucked his fingers and ran my tongue along them. He growled in response, tightening his grip on my hair. I'd provoked him and now I was reaping the rewards. I could get upset about what Sienna said later. Right then, I wanted to show him what his coming to my defence meant to me. I could reward him for it in a way that would please both of us.

Thane drew his fingers out of my mouth and used his hand to tug his clothes down. He was wearing black joggers, both of us preferring casual attire since we weren't planning on leaving his house. The moment his cock sprang free, I licked my lip.

"Open."

I lowered my jaw, letting my lips part for him to slide his cock between them. He wasn't rough with me, merely kept a firm hold of my hair and pushed deeper into my mouth. Then he pulled back and thrust in again.

"Fuck."

The longer he fucked my mouth, the more I squirmed in his hold. I reached out and gripped his clothes when his thrusts grew harder. My eyes watered, but I didn't care. The look in his eyes had me captivated. Anger, lust, and desire clashed in those green depths. I rubbed my thighs together, wanting to touch myself, but I kept my hands on him. This was about him expelling all of those negative emotions. I was just along for the ride.

"Look at ye squirming, ye're so desperate for me."

I hummed in response since I couldn't speak with his cock sinking deeper into my mouth. Touching my throat. I gagged a little, which made him pull back. Thane didn't want to make me take more than I was capable of.

"Get up," he demanded, pulling me by my hair.

I scrambled to my feet. Thane removed my glasses from my face and placed them on the far end of the table. Then he dragged me around to the other end where there was no chair in the way and lifted me up, seating me on the edge. He tugged off my joggers and underwear, leaving them in a pool at our feet.

Thane stepped between my legs and wrapped his hand around my throat. He stared at me for a long moment. A voiceless conversation happened between us. I dared him to be rough. To use me in ways he never had before. He wanted to know that I was onboard with it. That I wanted what he was about to do. I gave a soft nod, reassuring him I desired it as much as he did.

Thane's free hand landed on my thigh, tugging me into him before using his thumb to direct his cock to my entrance. One sharp thrust had me panting. I gripped his biceps as he pulled back. Again, he pushed into me, rougher this time. I was ready for him. For everything he had to give. My leg hooked around his hip, encouraging the pounding I was about to receive.

"Do it," I hissed, "make me scream."

He leaned closer, pressing his forehead to mine as he kept a tight hold on my neck. The harsh breaths erupting from his mouth had me parting mine, breathing with him. He didn't speak. He stared into my eyes, gripped my hip, and gave it to me.

It wasn't the thrust of his cock inside me that overwhelmed me, but the way he looked at me, as if he saw everything I hid behind high walls with a multitude of spikes barring the way up. He scaled them without a care for his own safety and dropped down on the other side. And I was utterly at his mercy in all the ways that counted.

Being perceived by others could be physically painful for me. It was especially that way right then, but the way he fucked me counteracted it. The brutality of his strokes. I couldn't stop him from seeing me. Nor did I wish to. He could bleed me dry, and I wouldn't care. I was so wrapped up in him. In the duality of his nature. The way he could be so kind and yet fuck me with a viciousness that had me spiralling. Then he kissed me and that lit a fuse inside me. Spurred me into fucking him back with equal measure.

I clawed at him. He bit my lip. I tugged on his luscious hair. He squeezed my throat. We taunted each other with our actions until our movements blurred together. Until I was holding onto him for dear life as he fucked me into oblivion. Until time stood still and I was screaming his name, wishing for it to go on forever and wanting it to end at the same time.

"Kit," he grunted in my ear before he bit down on the lobe.

"Don't stop," I panted, "don't you dare fucking stop."

He let go of my neck and gripped my face with both his hands instead. He kissed me for all he was worth. It was messy, saliva going everywhere as he licked my face, but with him… messy was okay. Messy was good. Our tongues duelling felt as though we were fighting for control. We both knew he had it all, but the illusion that I could take it from him was intoxicating.

Thane pressed my back down onto the table. He pinned me there with his body over mine.

"Am gonnae come in ye," he growled in my ear. "Ye're gonnae take it all."

"Please."

"Aye, that's it. Beg for it."

His hips pounded into mine. His body tensed. There was no doubt he was close to exploding.

"I want it. Give it to me, please. Come in me. Fill me up."

His hand slammed down on the table by my head.

"Fuck, Kit."

Thane groaned as he emptied himself inside of me. His whole body shuddered as he tangled the fingers of his free hand in my hair.

I closed my eyes and stroked his back, feeling contentment wash over me.

For some people, the lack of climax would be a deal breaker, but I wasn't someone who cared about that. The act of sex was the pleasurable part for me. Not that I would say no to an orgasm. It wasn't the most important factor in my book. And Thane had just rocked my world completely.

He slumped on top of me, pressing kisses to my neck as he buried his face in it.

"Ye okay?" he whispered.

"More than." I kissed his hair. "That was out of this world."

He let out a snort.

"Aye?"

"Yeah, I wouldn't lie about that. Was it okay for you?"

"If ye think that wasnae okay for me, ye werenae paying attention."

He pulled his body away from mine, leaving me with an empty feeling, bereft of his presence inside me. Thane placed his hands next to my head to hover above me. There was a dark look in his eyes as he took me in, but it didn't scare me.

"Sex with ye is everything I didnae know I wanted, so dinnae doubt that am enjoying mahself when am with ye."

I turned my head, finding it hard to meet his eyes.

"I must come across as being so insecure."

"No, ye've just lived a lifetime of people putting ye doon for being yerself. But I like ye just the way ye are."

Those words made me feel so exposed, but I didn't try to hide from Thane. He wasn't going to make me feel bad about myself.

"What... what Sienna said... about me being a coward... that I hid behind you..."

"Dinnae listen tae a fucking word that cunt said."

Thane gently caressed the side of my face with his hand but didn't force me to look at him.

"Ye dragged a grown man oot of a stream and put him in his place when he gave ye a hard time aboot it. Ye made sure he stayed alive. Ye never gave up, even when he'd lost all hope of rescue. I dinnae think those are the actions of a coward."

"No?"

"No. Ye've put up with so much shite from this world trying tae drag ye doon, but ye're still standing. Ye're the bravest person I know, Kit."

And with his kind words, I promptly burst into tears.

THIRTY FOUR

Thane

as I surprised Kit was emotional after what they'd just been through? Not at all. It wasn't about us or the sex. It had everything to do with Sienna's appearance and the nasty things she said about Kit.

The only thing I hadn't been expecting was for them to want physical intimacy. That had taken me by surprise.

It was the roughest I'd been with Kit, and they'd encouraged every moment of it. Getting to explore this side of me with them was a revelation, even if I wasn't sure what it all meant. Going thirty-two years without ever feeling this way about another person made it hard to know what was happening, whether it was how it was supposed to feel or if I was just… different.

Kit sniffled and wiped their face with their sleeve, bringing me out of my thoughts.

"This is so embarrassing," they sobbed, "I keep crying every time we have sex."

I kept stroking their face.

"I hope ye're no crying 'cause am bad at sex."

Their head turned back to mine, their eyes wide, and they reached up to shove my shoulder with one hand.

"No, don't be ridiculous. You're the best at sex. I'm just overwhelmed, and I knew this was coming after all those things Sienna said."

"Am no gonnae tell ye no to cry over that cunt, even if she doesnae deserve yer tears."

"I'm not really crying over her but losing a friendship I held onto for twenty-five years. I'm more upset about that than anything else. Well, what she said wasn't nice either."

I nodded slowly as I pushed myself up to a standing position. Now the adrenaline rush was over, I could feel the dull ache in my ankle. Reaching over, I pulled out one of the dining chairs and seated myself in it to take the weight off it.

Kit sat up and swiped their hands over their face.

"I'm going to go clean up and then I'll make us a drink."

"Ye dinnae have tae dae that."

"I want to."

Kit slid off the table, picking up their clothes before they ran to the bathroom.

I shook my head and closed my eyes. It would take them time to shed the idea that they didn't have to look after everyone else. That putting themself first wasn't being selfish.

I got up from the chair and went into the kitchen, cleaning myself up and straightening out my clothes while the kettle boiled. Then I made Kit a cup of tea and myself a coffee. I brought those into the living room, setting them on the coffee table before I sat down on the sofa. Propping my legs up on it, I waited for Kit to finish up.

When they walked into the living room, they eyed the mugs for a second before they came over and crawled into my lap. I wrapped my arms around them as they laid their head against my chest.

"Even though I know Sienna isn't a good friend and I'm better off without her, it's still hard to wrap my head around it. To stop feeling something for her… it's not love, but it's something. I don't know how to turn it off."

I stroked their back.

"Ye cannae turn them off, Kit. It's no that simple. If it was, people wouldnae grieve the loss of someone precious tae them. And love isnae just the romantic kind. Ye loved her as a friend, even if it was also something more at one point. That love doesnae disappear overnight."

I knew that all too well. Although now I thought about it, I wasn't sure if love was what I felt for Jenna. Not anymore, at least. There were so many other emotions there. Ones I wasn't sure I was allowed to feel about someone who died.

"I suppose you're right. Grief isn't linear. You don't just get over it in a direct way, even if I wish it was that simple.

My life would be easier if the world was simpler... I mean, you saw how Sienna misinterpreted what I said and added hidden meanings to my words. She brought up my disability when that wasn't even a part of the conversation. I don't think I've ever once used that as an excuse. It's an explanation of why, not a justification."

I thought about what it would feel like to go through the world with everyone around you misreading everything you said to them. How damaging that could be to a person. I'd never had to navigate the world that way, but it didn't mean I couldn't understand how hard it made things for Kit.

"Ye just say it like it is and folks dinnae see that."

"Yes. Exactly. It's so exhausting. I feel like I have to explain what I mean over and over... and they still don't get it."

"I like yer over-explaining."

"You're the only person who does."

"I like everything aboot ye."

Kit turned their head up to look at me.

"You do?"

"Aye. Even when ye're giving me a hard time."

They grinned and bit their lip.

"So if I said that you already had plenty of wood next to the stove and that you were simply throwing a man tantrum by storming out to chop wood, you'd like that?"

I shook my head and snorted.

"I told ye, chopping wood was safer than anything else I wanted tae dae."

"What exactly did you want to do?"

"Throw Sienna intae the snow tae ruin her expensive coat and shoes."

Their smile grew wider.

"She'd have hated that so much."

"Aye, I didnae like the way she was looking at mah place like it was some kind of hovel."

Kit put their hands on my chest and pushed themselves up to sit on my lap. My hands instinctively went to their thighs.

I was obsessed with touching them. It wasn't even about sex. I like their closeness more than anything else. The way they felt against me. It was comforting. Kit was a safe place for me. And losing this when they went home? That was going to hurt.

"I love your place. It's cosy and peaceful."

I couldn't help but smile at Kit's earnest expression.

"And ye gave me shite aboot living in the woods."

"That was more about you being grumpy and hating people."

I squeezed their thigh.

"Aye, ye just like tae give me shite."

"You make it far too easy."

"Says the person who cries after sex."

Kit looked indignant at my words.

"Hey!"

"Ye dish it oot, but cannae take it."

"Shut up. Just shut up."

"Make me."

327

They shoved a hand over my mouth. I licked their palm in response. Kit immediately pulled their hand away and wiped it off on my jumper.

"Gross."

"I thought ye liked me licking ye."

A blush spread across their face before they hid it behind their hands and let out a groan.

"Only under very specific circumstances."

"Like when I licked yer cunt?"

They dropped their hands, only to shove both of them over my mouth. Their face was incredibly red, and their eyes were wide.

"Shhh."

"I thought ye liked it when I say dirty things," I said, although it was muffled by their hands.

"Oh my god, I don't even know whether to be annoyed or turned on by you right now."

They were so fucking cute when they got all flustered. Especially when it was over me.

I tugged their hands off my mouth and held them between us.

"I can dae something aboot that."

"Which part?"

"Both at the same time."

They raised their eyebrows.

"How do you propose to do that?"

I smiled at them as I let go of their hands before digging one of my own underneath their clothes. Kit looked between us as my fingers slid along their cunt. A gasp left their mouth

328

as I stroked them until they were wet. Then I slid two fingers inside them and ground my palm against their clit.

"Like this," I whispered as I dug my free hand into their hair and tugged them closer. "Am gonnae make ye come, and ye can decide if ye're still annoyed after that."

Their hands landed on my shoulders. When a groan left their mouth, I smiled and planted kisses down their jaw.

"This isn't fair."

"When I fucked ye on the table, that was for me. This is all for ye. That's fair."

I caught Kit's mouth so they couldn't respond to me. They moaned as they kissed me back. Kit rocked on my fingers, encouraging me to fuck them harder. It hadn't been my intention to turn this sexual, but watching Kit come alive under my playful teasing was intoxicating. Something about them giving control to me in an intimate setting made me feel good. I wanted more of it. Wanted more of them. Wanted... everything.

"That's it," I murmured as I tugged their head back by their hair, "let me make ye feel guid."

Kit had their eyes closed with their mouth parted slightly.

"Thane," they sighed.

My name on their lips was an addictive sound. Had anything else ever sounded this good? I didn't think I would ever get bored of it... or bored of them. They were funny, smart and everything I didn't know I wanted in another person. And that made me think about the fact they were leaving. About how it could never work because they lived so fucking far away from me. I had too much baggage to deal with, anyway. So did Kit. We might like each other, but it didn't mean this would work. There were too many obstacles to overcome. I couldn't ask them to give up everything for me. That wouldn't be right or fair.

Stop dwelling on this. You've got time. You still have some time.

It wasn't enough. It would *never* be enough. A few days ago, when we were back in the tent and I thought we might not survive, it would have been enough to spend my last moments with them. But not now. Now I wanted Kit more than I wanted to breathe. But they were so far out of reach that having them permanently was an impossibility.

Shaking myself internally, I focused back on the here and now. On the moans and gasps Kit made as I continued to press my fingers inside them. As they kept grinding their hips into me. They were so fucking pretty. So unabashed in taking their pleasure now their embarrassment had faded. Nothing could top this view.

"Oh god, yes, yes, yes."

Their back bowed as they came all over my fingers. Their hands tightened on my shoulders. I watched their body shaking and the moans spilling out of their mouth. Then Kit slumped forward on my chest and buried their face in my neck. I let them catch their breath as I removed my fingers from them. Kit didn't notice me sticking them in my mouth to taste them. I wasn't sure how many times I had left to do that.

"Ye still annoyed with me?" I asked after a minute.

"No."

"Then I fixed both problems."

330

Kit snorted and rubbed their face against my neck.

"Guess you did."

Neither of us spoke after that, both content to just be with each other in the aftermath of Sienna's presence at my house. I think I liked that best, having Kit in my arms, their body pressed to mine. It was peaceful and comforting. Kit gave me all the affection I didn't realise I needed in the exact way I needed it.

Why did I have to meet you? I don't regret it, but the fact you live so far away, and I can't have you is just… devastating.

It didn't matter what way I looked at it, I couldn't make Kit mine. How I wished our circumstances were different. However, the one thing meeting Kit had done was make me very aware of the changes I had to make in my life. How I had to work past my grief and pain. As much as Callan kept pressing me to do it, it had taken meeting this vivacious soul and almost dying out there in the mountains to realise that I had so much to live for.

For the very first time in almost two years, I no longer wished I'd died in that car crash with Jenna. I was grateful to be alive. And I owed all of that to Kit.

THIRTY FIVE

Kit

As I stood on the platform waiting for my train, I fidgeted and tried not to think too hard about what was about to happen. I'd put off dealing with my emotions regarding leaving because I knew if I started down that road, I would end up in a crying mess on the floor. That wasn't going to be good for anyone.

Thane and I had spent the last few days resting and talking about our lives. Getting to know more about him had only cemented my feelings for him. He was, quite frankly, the kindest and most protective person I'd ever had the pleasure of being around.

As we talked, I shared more about my autistic traits. I told him what it was like for me to go about in a world full of barriers and overstimulation.

He told me more about his love of the outdoors, what types of things he foraged, and how many Munros he'd bagged. Sixty out of two hundred and eighty-two, to be precise. All the ones in the Cairngorms National Park, plus a few others. He wanted to travel further afield to do some more, but since Jenna's death, he hadn't done a whole lot of walking up mountains.

I didn't blame him, considering his grief had been all-consuming for a long time. I hoped going forward he would find a way to live for the now and not be stuck in the past. That was something I had to do too. Work past my grief and loss to live a more fulfilling life that didn't revolve around people who were bad for me.

My eyes darted up towards the board, checking the time, and noted the train should be arriving in a few minutes. That prompted me to look at Thane, who was staring at the platform on the other side of the tracks. We hadn't said all that much to each other this morning as we had breakfast and I finished packing up my stuff.

His ankle was a lot better now, and he'd insisted on driving me here. I expected him to drop me at the entrance to the train station, but he'd come onto the platform to see me off.

I didn't know how I would deal with being separated from him. What had been around two and a half weeks had felt like a lifetime. Everything inside me kept screaming, telling me to speak up and let him know how I felt, but I couldn't. He gave no indication he wanted to continue this. I was too afraid to put myself out there like that.

My whole life had been a series of rejections from other people. And while I trusted Thane wholeheartedly, I was very aware of the obstacles that stood in the way of this working out in the long run. They were hurdles I wasn't sure I could face knowing how much change that would entail. I didn't do well with change, especially not the huge, life-altering type.

Knowing I only had minutes left with Thane, I stepped in front of him. He looked down at me right before I pressed myself against his chest and wrapped my arms around his back. He hugged me, resting his chin on the top of my head. I breathed him in, trying to commit to memory his scent and the way his body moulded to mine.

There had been more sex between us while I was at his, but last night, we had merely cuddled in his bed before we went to sleep. There was so much more to us than a sexual connection. We had a powerful emotional bond forged in the worst circumstances. And I didn't want to let that go.

You have to.

"Thank you," I whispered into his chest.

Those words weren't enough to explain how grateful I was to have met him, but they were the only ones I knew.

"Thank ye tae," he murmured back.

The rumble of the train on the tracks vibrated through me. My arms didn't want to release him. My body cried out to stay in his embrace. But I didn't listen to either of them. Slowly, I untangled myself from him, stepping back as the train pulled into the station.

Thane had a guarded expression on his face. I didn't know what he was thinking, how he was feeling about me leaving. He hadn't said. We hadn't talked about today at all.

"Have a safe trip," he said with a nod.

I forced myself to smile.

"I'm sure I will."

I couldn't find it in me to say the word goodbye to him. That had so much finality to it. I wanted to leave the door open for something more, even if it was a possibility that didn't feel obtainable. Instead, I nodded slowly and turned. My eyes went to the train carriage. Luckily, it was the one on my ticket. I took hold of the handle of my suitcase and started towards the door, dragging it behind me.

You're just going to leave it like that, Kit? Is this it? Are you going to walk away without giving him any indication of your feelings towards him?

I paused a foot from the door. My fingers released the suitcase as I turned.

Thane wasn't watching me. He had his hands dug into his pockets and his gaze was on the floor in front of him. He had his auburn hair up in a messy bun and was bundled up in a big winter coat.

My eyes imprinted his handsome features in my brain as I dashed towards him, unable to leave without one more thing.

My mouth didn't form words when I got to him. I reached up with one hand as I went up on my tiptoes. My mouth landed on his, while my hand went to his shoulder.

335

Thane let out a startled grunt. I closed my eyes and kissed him. When his lips moved with mine, I almost cried. He wasn't rejecting me. That simple movement told me all the things he couldn't. He was going to miss me as much as I was going to miss him.

Before tears could fall, I pulled back and left him, rushing over to my suitcase and hauling it onto the train. Only after I'd stowed my suitcase and found my seat did I look out of the window.

Thane stood there with a stunned look on his face. He hadn't been expecting that kiss. I would have kicked myself if I hadn't done it. There had been so many things I regretted in my life but kissing him one last time wasn't one of them.

I watched him as the train pulled away from the station. He hadn't left. He kept watching the train until we disappeared from sight. I sat back in my seat and stared at my hands. And that was when regret finally sank its claws into me. Not for kissing him. No, it was for not telling him how I felt. How in the short time I'd been with him, I'd come to adore everything about him. Even his grumpiness... actually, especially that.

Adore wasn't the right word, of course, but I was terrified of the true feeling sitting in my chest. Was it even possible to fall for someone this fast? I mean, I knew it was, but I had never experienced such an intense situation with another person before. A part of me wanted to put it down to the circumstances we'd been in, but every other part knew better. What we shared was real. It was so fucking real. Nothing I'd had before could compare to what I had with

Thane. But I didn't have it any longer. It had been temporary... fleeting.

I put my headphones over my ears and stuck some music on to distract myself from thoughts about us because they were only making me upset. But that didn't work. I stewed the entire way to London over my feelings towards him. It was a direct service, so I didn't have to make any changes. Hours flew by and I hardly noticed them. My mind was stuck replaying each and every moment we shared.

When we reached Kings Cross, I had to walk over to St Pancras to get a train to Brighton. From there, I changed to another train to get to Seaford. I'd booked this route because I only had to make two changes. That was less stressful, and I didn't have to go on the underground. Travelling through London was always a little bit overwhelming for me with the crowds and noise, especially at rush hour.

It was past seven in the evening by the time I arrived home after getting a taxi from the station. I hadn't felt like lugging my suitcase halfway across the town to my studio flat.

The first thing I did after I got in the door was order a takeaway. There was no fucking way I was cooking for myself after that long journey. Then I methodically unpacked everything, knowing if I didn't do it straight away, my suitcase would sit there for a week or more. Having that reminder of my time in Scotland wouldn't help me in the long run.

After I ate my takeaway pizza in front of the TV, I got ready for bed and curled up under my duvet. I was truly alone for the first time since I'd got stuck on that mountain. It didn't feel good. While I loved and needed my solitary time to recharge, nothing about it felt right.

I buried my head under the covers, wishing I had Thane right there with me. And that's when I finally let my tears fall.

Ugly sounds erupted from my throat as I sobbed my heart out. My hands clawed at my sheets because if I didn't, I would hurt myself. The emotional pain was overwhelming.

I kept it all together while I was on the train for fear of what people would think if I had a meltdown in public. In the safety of my home, I couldn't hold it in any longer. I let go of that tightly wound control, allowing it to flood through me.

I shook and cried harder, hitting the bed below me repeatedly until my fists hurt.

"I can't... I can't... I can't."

It hurt so fucking much. Everything did. The agony of leaving him hit me at full force, along with all the overstimulation from the past few weeks. It shouldn't be this damn hard. I hated losing it. Hated how out of control I felt whenever it happened. And I wished I could be different. That my brain didn't work this way. No matter how many times I told myself it was okay to be autistic, there were days I wished I wasn't born this way. I wanted to turn it off and be like everyone else for just once. But that wasn't how things worked. I had to live with this. Be this every day of my life. And sometimes, like right now, it sucked.

By the time the intensity of my meltdown faded away, I was completely drained. My pillow was soaked, but I couldn't drag myself out of bed to change the case. Instead, I curled up into a ball and rubbed my chest, wishing away the loss building inside me.

I miss you already. I miss you so much it hurts my whole damn soul.

I fell asleep with the admission to myself that I'd fallen in love with another person I couldn't have. And that was the worst part about this of all.

THIRTY SIX

Thane

My fingers went to my lips as the train disappeared from sight. I stood on that platform trying to keep hold of the touch of their mouth against mine. And it worked for a few minutes. Then the sensation faded, and I was left alone, shivering in the cold, and wondering what the fuck to do next.

It was Sunday. I only noticed that when I checked my phone this morning. The new one I had ordered earlier in the week turned up yesterday. After I got it synced up to the cloud, I was happy to see that I hadn't lost anything. However, looking through my photos only made my chest ache, so I refrained from checking those.

My head fell back. I stared up at the cloudy sky and sighed. It felt so final. Kit going back to their life and leaving me here to get back to mine. Except I didn't want to do that. A part of me wanted to chase after that train, but it would be futile. I couldn't outrun a train any more than I could run away from my past.

Why didn't you give them your number?

I thought it would be easier to cut ties this way, but I was wrong. It had barely been five minutes and my chest already hurt from missing them. Why did I think I could let them go without it causing me pain? Why did I trick myself into thinking it would all be okay? It wasn't. Not by a long fucking shot.

I dropped my chin and dug my phone out of my pocket. Then I dialled my best friend's number.

"Ye got a new phone, did ye?" came Callan's voice when he answered.

"Aye."

I rubbed my beard with my free hand. Now I had him on the phone, I didn't know what to say.

"Ye okay?"

I shook my head.

"Am no sure."

"Where are ye?"

"At the station. I dropped Kit off."

Saying their name made it hurt more. Being with Kit this week was everything. I didn't want it to end. Now it had, I regretted not saying anything. Not telling them I wanted more. But it wouldn't have been fair of me to ask for that. Not when my head was so messed up. And we lived hundreds of miles apart.

"Ye dinnae sound tae happy aboot that."

"Ye can tell that over the phone, can ye?"

"Aye."

I wanted to grumble, but it would do me no good. Callan always knew when something was wrong.

"And I know something happened between the two of ye on that mountain," he continued. "Ye wannae enlighten me, or should I take a stab in the dark?"

"I'll tell ye, but no over the phone."

"Ye gonnae drag yerself over here then?"

I rolled my eyes and started off in the direction of the entrance to the station to get back to my car.

"Aye, but dinnae give me any shite. Am no feeling okay."

"Yer ankle still hurting ye?"

"A wee bit, but it's no that."

I wasn't going to elaborate right then. He could wait until I got to his place. There was too much to say and too many feelings knocking around in my head. Ones I'd been ruminating over for the past week. I needed help making sense of everything. Callan was the only person I trusted with all of this.

"Ye'll tell me when ye get here."

"Aye."

"See ye in a bit, then."

He hung up, not that it bothered me. There wasn't much left to say.

Once I got to my car, I drove over to Callan and Ruairí's place just outside of town. They'd bought a plot of land, hired an architect and builders to create their perfect home

342

and had moved in last summer. It wasn't a big place, but it was very similar to mine, with wood cladding and huge glass windows on one side overlooking the glen.

I knocked on the front door. Callan answered it with a grin before insisting on hugging me. I patted his head since he was shorter than me as he let me go. He scowled but waved at me to follow him into the kitchen. I took a seat at the island to take the weight off my ankle as he moved over to the other side and popped the kettle on.

"Coffee?"

"Aye," I replied with a nod.

He got mugs out of the cupboard and then leaned back against the counter, eyeing me with uncertainty.

"Where's yer husband?"

He bit his lip.

"Still in bed."

"Lazy fuck."

Callan snorted.

"He had a late one doon the pub last night with the lads."

I sat back on the stool and crossed my arms over my chest. I hadn't come here to talk about Ruairí. My eyes darted away to the window, taking in the landscape spread out before us.

"I have a lot tae say. Am gonnae need ye tae listen and no interject until am done. This is no just aboot Kit… it's aboot Jenna tae."

"Ye're no aboot tae tell me ye're letting her get in the way of whatever it is that happened between ye and Kit?"

I waved a hand.

"It's no that simple, Callan. Hear me oot, and ye can share yer damn opinion afterwards."

I glanced over to find him putting his hands up. Sometimes he wasn't good at keeping his mouth shut. Usually, I didn't mind, but I wouldn't be able to get it all out if he kept interjecting.

When I was sure he was going to do as I asked, I started with my tale. I explained what happened with Kit on the mountain, keeping parts of their story to myself. Kit wouldn't want me sharing their trauma with someone else without their consent. And I wouldn't do that to them regardless.

I went on to tell Callan about the argument I had with Jenna in the car, and how Kit was the only person I shared that with. His eyes widened at that part, but he didn't say a word even as I told him what went on this week while Kit was at my place. As I got to the end, I could tell he was having issues holding back. His hands were fisted at his sides, and he had a troubled look in his eyes.

While I talked, he'd made me coffee and pushed it across the kitchen island towards me. I finally took a sip and stared down at the dark granite top, awaiting his opinion on everything. It took Callan a few minutes before he spoke. He leaned his arms on the counter and stared at me.

"Ye kept that fucking quiet."

"Which part?"

"Jenna. Ye should've told me what she said tae ye."

"Why? What difference would it have made?"

He slapped a hand on the countertop, making me jolt.

"Ye wouldnae have been carrying that around for two years all by yer lonesome."

I shrugged and fiddled with the mug handle.

"It didnae feel relevant after she died."

He let out a sigh.

"How is it no relevant, Thane? Ye're telling me that yer wife wanting a baby after ye spent fourteen years together, knowing that whole time ye didnae want children is nothing, is it?"

"It's no nothing. It fucked me up, but how can I be angry with her when she died?"

He shook his head and rubbed his face with both hands.

"What she did was no okay. Her death has nothing tae dae with the fact she gave ye an ultimatum. Am no saying she's no allowed tae have changed her mind over having kids, but tae keep it from ye is fucked up. And then tae dump it all on ye like that… I cannae even imagine daeing that tae someone I love."

Kit had very similar sentiments about what Jenna did. And I'd had long enough to think about it. To know that they were both right.

"Ye're allowed tae be angry with her. Yer grief is separate tae that."

Picking up my mug, I took another sip of coffee and allowed his words to sink in. Maybe that was my problem. I'd never let myself be truly angry with what she'd done. It didn't feel right when she died, but how could I ever let go when I had unresolved emotions towards her?

"I would've lost her even if she hadn't died," I said after a moment. "Oor marriage was done. And am no sure I've let mahself feel that."

Callan nodded slowly.

"Am beginning tae see why her death messed ye up so much. The accident was bad enough, but this… well, it puts a new spin on things."

I was aware of how much Callan had to put up with from me over the past two years. How he saved me from myself when no one else would or could. He knew how grateful I was for it, even if I never said it. Some things didn't need to be put into words.

"I feel bad noo."

I frowned.

"Why?"

"I pushed ye and Kit together, but I didnae know ye were dealing with this on top of the rest."

My eyes darted to the counter.

"I knew ye were meddling."

"And ye let me? If ye'd said something, I wouldnae—"

"Ye did nothing wrong, Callan. I like Kit even if we didnae get along in the beginning."

He scoffed.

"I think ye more than like them."

This man always liked to state the obvious. I'd got used to it over the years even if he did drive me fucking nuts with it.

"Aye, ye're no wrong." I set my mug down and rubbed my chest with one hand. "It wasnae like this with Jenna. Am no trying tae compare them but I… I've never felt this way before."

"What way?"

I tried to put it into words, but it was hard for me to explain despite ruminating on it for days on end. Callan was the only person I could share it with, even if it didn't make sense to me.

"Like I was gonnae lose mah fucking mind over them."

"That narrows it doon."

"I loved Jenna, but I didnae feel the way everyone says ye're supposed tae feel aboot her."

Callan cocked his head to the side.

"Ye mean ye werenae attracted tae her?"

"I thought she was beautiful, but…"

Why the fuck was this so hard to say? It made me feel strange to discuss such intimate things with my best friend. I barely even talked about them with Jenna.

"I never felt desire towards her. Have never felt that for anyone."

"But ye dae with Kit?"

I shook my head.

"Am attracted tae Kit for who they are, and they've shown me things aboot mahself I didnae realise I wanted… intimate things. While I dinnae think I'd want them with anyone else, I still dinnae feel that desire that am supposed tae be feeling. I just want Kit." I sighed. "I dinnae think am explaining this right."

Callan smiled at me in a knowing way.

"No, I understand. Ye dinnae have the right language for what ye're feeling."

"Aye."

He rolled his shoulders.

"Have ye ever considered that ye might be asexual?"

My brain stumbled over the word asexual for a moment. It wasn't that I didn't understand what it meant, but it never occurred to me that might explain things about myself.

"Am no trying tae put a label on ye, Thane, but that's what it sounds like tae me. A limited or lack of sexual attraction doesnae mean ye cannae want and like sex, which by yer own admission ye clearly dae with Kit."

My face burned. It shouldn't embarrass me to admit to wanting to sleep with Kit but laying it all out there wasn't something I was used to. It had been hard enough when Kit kept asking me what I wanted in the bedroom. I didn't begrudge them that, but it forced me to think about it in ways I hadn't before. And consider whether I was doing it for them or for me. It was both.

"Why dae ye know so much aboot it?"

Callan looked up at the ceiling.

"Ruairí is ace. Have had tae dae a lot of learning for him, but oor relationship is better for it. I can give ye some books if ye wannae look intae it more since I know ye wouldnae be comfortable asking him."

The thought of asking Ruairí about it did not fill me with enthusiasm. It wasn't that we didn't like each other, but talking about sexual attraction or my lack of it with him was not something I was willing to do.

"Aye, mibbe I should read them."

"It might help ye explain yer feelings a wee bit more, even if it's just tae yerself."

I nodded slowly before I stared out of the window again. Clearly, there were things I had yet to discover about myself. And maybe Callan was right. It would explain why I never understood when people talked about wanting to sleep with people they didn't know. It felt weird to me, but I never voiced that out loud for fear of being seen as abnormal.

"So, ye like Kit," Callan said after a minute.

"Aye."

"And ye let them leave withoot telling them ye have feelings for them."

"Am no ready for another relationship. And they live in England."

"Are ye sure those are no just excuses?"

I turned my gaze back towards him.

"It wouldnae be fair of me tae ask them tae be with me when am still so fucked up aboot Jenna. I need time tae deal with it."

"Ye left yerself no way tae contact them when ye are ready."

"Kit's no ready either. Even when I am, there's no guarantee they'll want something with me. And they still live in England, Callan. That willnae work in the long run and I could never ask them tae uproot their life for me. Am no worth that."

He gave me a look that spoke volumes. I tried not to flinch.

"Ye will be worth it for the someone who loves ye for ye."

"I thought I was for Jenna."

"Dinnae let what she did make ye feel like ye're no enough. Am betting Kit thinks ye're enough. I saw the way they looked at ye. How badly they wanted tae be near ye that they'd stay a whole week taking care of ye withoot a second thought."

My hands curled around the mug as my brain desperately tried to disprove what he'd said. It couldn't. I saw the way Kit looked at me. The things they'd said made it clear too. They liked me for me, just as I liked them for them.

"They didnae tell me they wanted more."

"Aye, well, mibbe they were afraid… just like ye are."

"Am no—"

"Ye are, and I dinnae blame ye. Putting yerself oot there is terrifying, especially after what ye've been through. Just dinnae let that fear hold ye back forever. Work through yer stuff and we'll see where ye are after that. I have their contact details, so ye've no lost yer chance with them. Ye just need tae ask when ye're ready."

I was about to reply that I didn't think that was a good idea when Ruairí walked in, looking a wee bit worse for wear.

"Morning, when did this grumpy fuck get here?" he asked, looking at me as he walked over to Callan and pressed a kiss to his forehead.

"A while ago, ye were asleep. He needed some girl talk."

Ruairí looked between us.

"Did he?"

"Shut the fuck up, Callan," I grumbled.

"Am surprised this one willingly talked aboot his emotions." Ruairí pointed a thumb in my direction. "Ye said it was like pulling teeth."

I shoved away from the counter and got up, finishing off my coffee.

"And that's mah signal tae leave."

"We're no done," Callan said.

"Aye, we are. I have a lot tae think aboot. Thank ye for listening."

And with that, I walked out, leaving the two of them to stare after me. I didn't really feel like being around people any longer. Not when I needed to unpack all of my feelings regarding Jenna… and my sexuality. Perhaps if I did that, I might take Callan up on his offer to give me a way to contact Kit. Perhaps not. I didn't know how long it would take. And if Kit would even be open to more with me.

Callan wasn't wrong. I was afraid. I just didn't know if I was more scared of their potential rejection or the other possibility… them actually wanting a relationship with me.

THIRTY SEVEN

Kit

T hree weeks, two days, nine hours, and twenty-eight minutes. That was how long it had been since I'd left Scotland. Since I'd last seen Thane. And it sucked.

Two and a half weeks shouldn't be long enough to fall in love with someone, but most people didn't spend several nights trapped in a tent in the mountains, forced to rely on a stranger for survival. They didn't get to dig into each other's darkest secrets and worst memories. Those things showed a lot about a person.

The bond I formed with Thane was deeply emotional. And without it, I didn't know what the fuck I was doing with my life. It wasn't like I was thriving before I left for Scotland, but meeting him, and being shown how I could be treated well and have my needs met, was eye-opening. Getting back to reality had proven to me that my life had been about taking care of others and never myself. But changing that was scary... downright terrifying, to be honest. And I had no idea how to do it.

I had the keys to Dad's flat, so I didn't bother knocking. He downsized after Olly moved out. The house got to be too much for him.

"Dad?" I called out.

It was almost six, which meant dinner time. I could hear noises coming from the kitchen, so I wandered into the room, finding Dad chatting with his carer, Janice. She had dinner on the go while he was sitting at the small table in the corner.

"Oh hello, sweetheart," Dad said as he saw me come in.

"Hey, Dad."

I went over and pressed a kiss to the top of his head before shedding my coat and bag. Then I sat down across from him. He was all smiles, but I didn't feel like being cheerful. In fact, I was wallowing in misery. Dad didn't expect me to pretend I was okay, anyway. There was no need to put on an act when we were together.

He continued talking to Janice as she finished up dinner before putting a couple of plates in front of us. I'd told her several times that she didn't need to make me anything during my weekly after-work visits to my father, but she paid me no mind. Said it was nice that his kid came over every week.

Dad didn't work due to his mobility issues, but he went out with a local group regularly. He had friends and people to see other than me, but apparently, family was most important, according to Janice. I kept my mouth shut about that, knowing our values differed. My so-called mother had betrayed us, so I wasn't inclined to believe that family mattered above all. Not when I had proof to the contrary.

After Janice left, Dad and I ate in a peaceful silence before I washed up and he went into the living room. I joined him, taking a seat on the sofa while he reclined in his favourite armchair with his feet up.

"Are you ready to talk about it?" he asked after I kept sighing as the two of us watched TV.

"Talk about what?"

He turned the volume down and looked at me. While I had mostly taken after my mother, I had my father's blue eyes. He didn't always make eye contact, but when he did, I knew it was serious.

"Whatever it is that's been bothering you since you got back from Scotland."

It didn't surprise me that he'd noticed I wasn't happy. Dad could pick up on my emotions quite easily, just as I could with his. Affective empathy did that to a person.

"For instance, you haven't mentioned Sienna," he continued when I didn't speak. "Is that a part of it?"

"Sienna and I aren't friends anymore."

His face remained impassive at my declaration. My eyes darted to my hands as I fiddled with the hem of my jumper.

I hadn't thought about her in the past three weeks. While I mourned the loss of a life-long friendship, I didn't miss Sienna herself. I thought about all the ways I had sacrificed my own morals to be friends with her. How I would ignore the discomfort I felt at her meanness towards other people. And I wasn't willing to do that any longer. Not having her around to make me feel bad was freeing.

"She isn't a very nice person. I didn't see that before, but I do now… Thane helped me see it. She came up to Scotland while I was there, said some really horrible shit to me before Thane told her off and kicked her out of his house. I haven't seen her since, and I don't want to."

"Thane's the bloke you got stuck with?"

I hadn't talked about him a great deal to my dad. Even saying his name made my chest ache.

"Yeah. No one has ever defended me the way he did. He's a good person."

I let out yet another sigh and rubbed my fingers together.

"Is he the reason you're so down in the dumps?"

"Dad…"

"I'm not trying to pry, but since you've sacked off Sienna, who else are you going to discuss this with?"

He had a point, even if I didn't like it. I had other friends, but we weren't that close. I sometimes found friendships with allistic people difficult to manage. We got our wires crossed too often. I guess that's one of the reasons I was so close to my dad. Our brains worked in the same way, which made it easier to communicate and understand each other.

It didn't matter if we didn't share all the same autistic traits. There was enough common ground between us.

"I don't think I could have talked to Sienna about Thane even if we were still friends."

"Then I really am the only person you can talk to."

"It's just hard to put into words."

"Tell me what happened between you, and we'll go from there, okay?"

I nodded. When I got back, I'd given Dad the bare minimum details of what went down in Scotland. I left out all the stuff about how my relationship with Thane developed and kept to the facts. This time I told him everything except for the sex parts. No matter how open I was with my dad, I wasn't willing to discuss that. And I was vague about Thane's relationship with Jenna since that wasn't my story to tell.

"So you love this man, and you didn't tell him that?" Dad asked when I finished.

"Yes."

"Are you scared he doesn't feel the same way?"

I shrugged. Thane liked me, but love wasn't something I allowed myself to hope for under the circumstances. Whether or not someone loved you was out of your control, so I tried not to worry about it.

"Even if he did, I don't think he's ready for another relationship. I didn't want to pressure him. And he didn't say anything about his feelings, so what was I supposed to do?"

Dad gave me a look.

"Maybe he was scared you didn't feel the same way too. You didn't give him all the facts. How was he meant to make a decision about the two of you without knowing you love him? Did you think of that?"

"No… but even if I did tell him, what was that going to do? I can't do a long-distance relationship. I'm not built for that. One of us would have to uproot our life for the other person, and that's a huge commitment to make."

I would never ask Thane to leave his beloved home for me. He belonged in the mountains where he grew up. It left me to do the big thing and that was scary.

"Is that what this is about? You're scared to move up there?"

"How did you know it would be me?"

"I know you. And the way you described how much he loves where he lives made it sound like he wouldn't leave willingly."

"No, he wouldn't, and I couldn't ask him to, anyway."

Dad watched me for a long moment before his eyes went back to the TV.

I continued to fiddle with my clothes, feeling agitated by this conversation, even though it was necessary. I had to get this shit out of my head. It had been driving me up the wall for weeks. I was sad all the time and it sucked to have to put on an act at work. Even Roman had noticed I wasn't myself. I'd been very busy with all my rescheduled clients, which distracted me to an extent. But it wasn't enough to keep my misery at bay. I wasn't happy in my life any longer. I didn't think I had been for a very long time.

"What's keeping you here, Kit? And don't say me. You know I would support your decision to leave, just as I did with Olly's."

I turned my attention to the window, staring at the houses across the road from my dad's flat.

"I would miss working with Roman. He understands me. And I'd have to get a whole new licence to tattoo in Scotland."

"I'm sure you can find someone else who understands you, and doing paperwork isn't fun, but it's necessary. You've done it once, you can do it again."

"Change is hard for me. I don't know how I would cope with a whole new place by myself."

"You wouldn't be by yourself. You'd have Thane."

"That's only if he wants to be with me."

I knew Dad would find a way to counter all of my arguments. He was a very practical man. And my reasonings were beginning to sound more like excuses now that I'd said them out loud.

"You'd go even if he didn't want to be with you?"

"Doing it for him feels like it would be putting too much pressure on us to make it work. If I move up there, I'd want it to be for myself, even if he's also a big part of it."

"Did you like it there?"

I nodded slowly and turned back to him.

"It's a really beautiful place. I liked the quiet. It's much less overstimulating, but that didn't help with all the shit I went through, hence why I kept having meltdowns and crying all over him."

Dad gave me a sad smile.

"Yes, well, that's to be expected under the circumstances."

"He was really good about it, though. Even after I explained why, he was the one who told me that I should have my needs met. That I deserve it. He never made me feel like I was less than because I'm disabled. That meant a lot to me…"

Tears welled in my eyes. I missed him so fucking much. The way his green eyes twinkled when he made a joke. How he looked at me as if I was the prettiest thing he'd ever seen. The way he cared. It was devastating to be without him when he made me feel so damn much. He made me better.

"God, I love him so much. He's not perfect, but he's so considerate and kind. I never knew how much I needed someone who likes me for me until I met him. What we had felt so real, and now it's gone, and I miss him, Dad. I'm so fucking unhappy. My heart hurts all the time and I'm going through the motions, but I go home and cry because I hate it. I hate pretending when I didn't have to pretend with him."

Without a second thought, I got up off the sofa and went to my dad. I fell at his feet, put my head in his lap, and cried. He stroked my hair, giving me space to purge my emotions.

We weren't particularly affectionate. Dad wasn't always a fan of being touched, but I needed it at that moment. I missed being held by Thane. I didn't even care about sex. All I wanted was to curl up in his arms and listen to him breathe. Hear his heart beating in his chest. He was my safe space.

When I'd let it all out, I sat up and stared at my dad. His eyes were misty. I knew he found it hard not to feel it too when I got emotional.

"I'm not going to tell you to go, but you need to think about what you really want for your life, Kit. Don't waste it being somewhere you don't want to. Change is hard, but sometimes it's for the better. Remember that when you're deciding what next. You and I both know you can't stay in limbo like this forever. You'll only make it worse for yourself if you do."

I nodded and got up to get a tissue to wipe my eyes. When I came back, I sat down on the sofa.

"Thank you, Dad. I'll think about what you said."

"I'll support you no matter what, sweetheart. You deserve to be happy."

We went back to watching TV together until it was time for me to go home to get some sleep before work in the morning. He'd given me a lot to consider. I'd known talking to him would help me, but I was afraid. So fucking afraid of everything. But Dad was right. I couldn't spend my life in misery. So I had a decision to make… and it was going to be a difficult one either way I looked at it. There were so many risks involved, but maybe, just maybe, this one would be worth taking.

THIRTY EIGHT

Thane

A beam of light shone through my windows as a car pulled up outside in my driveway. As it was dark, I couldn't make out who it was. I stared at the car from the kitchen, watching as someone got out from the backseat. They dragged what looked like an overnight bag with them. They waved at the driver, who backed out of the drive, before turning towards the house.

My heart just about stopped in my chest when they walked up onto the deck and into the light. My feet were carrying me over to the front door before my mind could catch up. I slid it open before they had a chance to knock.

"Hi."

My mouth refused to open. I thought for a second my eyes might be deceiving me, but they weren't. Standing on my doorstep was the object of my heart's desire. The one person I wanted most in the world.

What are you doing here, Kit?

"Can I come in? It's cold out here."

I stepped back on automatic. They walked in, set their bag down and closed the door before rubbing their hands together.

"So, um, I'm really sorry to just turn up unannounced like this, but I kind of decided on this trip last minute and I didn't know how you'd feel about seeing me again."

My hands itched to reach out and touch them. To make sure they were real. It had been almost a month since Kit had been here. It was all I could do to look at them as my heart thundered in my chest with want and need.

"There's a lot I need to say to you. I spent the whole way up here rehearsing it in my head, and I'm hoping it comes out right, but I'm not that great at words, so yeah… um, here we go…"

I fisted my hands at my sides and licked my bottom lip.

Kit fiddled with the hem of their jumper. Their eyes were focused on something behind me.

"I…"

They closed their eyes and took a deep breath.

"God, now I'm here in front of you, I can't fucking think any longer."

Kit shook out their hands.

"Okay, okay."

They opened their eyes and looked at me. I could tell from their expression this was incredibly difficult for them.

I wanted to reach out and reassure them it was okay, that I was so fucking happy to see them, I barely knew what to do with myself.

"I shouldn't have left without telling you how I feel. I was scared. I'm still really fucking scared, but I don't want fear to dictate my life choices. And well, the thing is… I… I want more than just a week. I want… you. I want you so badly it hurts. The time I spent with you was everything to me. You are everything I never knew I wanted or needed in another person, and I want to be with you."

They rubbed their chest and took another breath.

"I've been fucking miserable this last month without you, though, honestly, I wasn't doing too great before we met. But when I got back, I did a lot of soul-searching and wondering what I was doing with my life. Being with you made me see that I've been living for other people, doing what they expected of me to make them happy rather than myself. And I don't want to do that anymore. I want to make my own choices for me."

I was glad they'd finally realised that. Kit should be living for themselves, doing what they wanted.

"So I'm in the process of quitting my job, giving up my flat and I'm going to move away from my hometown. It's a huge change and it's really, really terrifying because I don't do well with change, but it's like my dad said, sometimes change is for the better."

I didn't want to interrupt them with questions, but I had so fucking many right then. Kit said they wanted me. Well, I wanted them too... desperately. But what did they mean they were moving?

"It's going to take a while, but I want to be here. It might sound like I'm doing it for you, but I came here knowing that you might turn me down and that's okay. I'm still going to move anyway. I don't want to be somewhere that is making me unhappy. This is for me. I'm doing it to make my life better."

Turn you down? How could I turn you down, Kit?

I supposed they had no clue how I felt. And it made me realise how brave they were to come here and say all of this without any guarantee that I would reciprocate their feelings. How much courage it must have taken them to face me like this. They were one of the strongest people I knew.

"But I really, really, really hope that you'll give us a chance because I think we're good for each other. You make me happy and I... I..."

Their voice broke as they tried to hold back their emotions.

I took a step towards them but kept my hands at my sides, not knowing whether to do something.

"I love you, Thane. I know that probably sounds nuts and it's really, really fast, but I... I just love you."

They shrugged helplessly, staring at me with tears welling in their eyes.

"I really l—"

I surged forward, grabbed hold of their face with both hands and kissed them. Kit froze as I did it, but I didn't care.

They loved me. And I knew they wouldn't stop talking if I didn't shut them up.

I kept kissing them until Kit let out a wee whimper and gripped my arms. Releasing their mouth, I closed my eyes and rested my forehead against theirs.

"Kit," I breathed.

"Y-y-yeah?"

I opened my eyes and stared at them.

"If ye want me as much as ye say ye dae, then ye should be kissing me back."

"I wasn't expecting you to kiss me."

"Was the only way I could shut ye up. Ye didnae seem like ye were gonnae at any point."

They blinked.

"You stole my move."

I smiled.

"Aye, noo, ye gonnae be angry aboot it or kiss me?"

"Kiss you."

"Guid."

I caught their mouth again and this time, Kit kissed me back with as much passion as I gave them. I let go of their face to wrap my arms around them, hauling their body against mine. Fuck, it felt so good to have them close again. There was no scenario I'd imagined where they turned up at my doorstep to declare their love for me. Kit made the grandest gesture ever by telling me they were going to move here. And that meant the world to me.

You picked me despite knowing everything you know about me. You chose me, Kit. I don't know if anyone has ever picked me before. I'm... enough. I'm really enough for someone. Fuck.

"Am so fucking happy ye're here," I told them as my mouth left theirs and I hugged them tighter against my chest. "But as much as I wannae talk aboot everything, we dinnae have time right noo, so it'll have tae wait until later."

"No?"

"Callan and Ruairí will be here in a wee bit."

Kit pulled their head away from my chest to stare up at me.

"Ruairí from the course?"

"Aye. He's Callan's husband."

"They're married? I had no idea."

I grinned.

"They like tae keep work and their private life separate."

"So they're coming over?"

"For dinner. I have a steak pie in the oven but can make ye something different if that's no something ye eat."

"That's okay for me."

They looked away.

"Ye are staying with me while ye're here, aye?"

"I mean, yeah, that was my intention, but... but..."

I moved one hand up to their head to thread my fingers in the hair at the back of it. I rubbed Kit's scalp, wanting to reassure them that they could talk to me about what was going on in their head.

"You said we'll talk later, but I need to know one thing now or I'll be worrying the whole time your guests are here."

"What is it?"

"I said all that stuff about wanting to be with you, and I know you kissed me, but that's not enough. I need… I need you to say it."

I leaned closer to them.

"Say what?"

"That you want this too."

Their face went red with their words. I tried not to smile.

"Ye wannae hear that I want ye?"

They nodded.

"I want ye, Kit."

"Are… are you mine? Like, is this real? You want a relationship with me?" they whispered.

They were the most adorable human being on the planet in my eyes. The way they said what they were thinking all the time was probably one of my favourite things about them.

I licked my bottom lip and tugged on their hair lightly.

"Am yours. Are ye mine?"

"Yes, yes, a million times, yes."

"Say it," I whispered, leaning ever closer.

"I'm yours, Thane."

Hearing those words out of their mouth settled something deep inside me. These weeks without them hadn't been particularly enjoyable for me. I'd missed them something fierce. And while I wanted to get in contact with them, I'd been working on myself. I wanted to be in a place where I could wholeheartedly say I was ready to be with them without the burden of my past hanging over me. Now they were here, I realised I didn't care about any of that. All

I cared about was Kit. Besides, I was in a better place than I had been a month ago. The rest of the work I could do with Kit by my side. I couldn't wait any longer. Not when they showed up here and told me they loved me.

I didn't have to lean down any further because Kit surged up on their tiptoes and kissed me. They wrapped their arms around my neck and showed me they were mine with their mouth. I almost groaned when their body rubbed against mine. If my best friend wasn't coming over, I would have picked them up and taken them straight to bed. Although, we probably needed to have a conversation about that before I did anything sexual with them.

I had to set them down when I heard a car pulling up outside. Kit looked dazed when I pulled back.

"They're here. Why dinnae ye put yer stuff in mah room before they come in?"

They nodded before shedding their coat and shoes. Kit took their bag into my room and returned as Callan and Ruairí were walking up the steps of the deck.

This dinner was meant to be a thank you to them for helping me work through things regarding my sexuality over the past few weeks. As much as I hadn't wanted to discuss it with Ruairí, he had been very understanding and answered the questions I had that I couldn't ask anyone else.

The fact Kit was here to share it with us was just the icing on the cake. They'd paved the way for this discovery after all. If it wasn't for them, I might never have spoken to Callan about my confusing feelings and discovered a whole new side of myself.

Before Kit could move away, I tucked them up under my arm as I went to open the front door. Now I had them back, I didn't want to let them go. A part of me needed to touch them, and I wanted to give them my strength to get through this dinner. Kit would be anxious, no doubt.

I slid open the front door, finding Callan staring at the two of us with wide eyes, and Ruairí had a raised eyebrow.

"Look who turned up no long before ye did," I said, grinning down at Kit.

They gave me a look as if to say this wasn't funny.

"Hullo, Kit," Callan said, as his eyes began to twinkle.

"Hey, Callan, Ruairí, it's nice to see you again," Kit replied as they turned towards our guests.

I moved back to allow them both inside, taking Kit with me. They curled into me, wrapping both arms around my middle. Leaning down, I pressed a kiss to their forehead, not even caring about the looks I got from Callan and Ruairí for my casual display of affection.

"Beer?" I asked the two of them without straightening.

"Ruairí will have one. Am driving, so a juice for me," Callan said as he took off his coat and slid out of his shoes, while Ruairí did the same.

"Kit?"

"Water is fine," they mumbled.

I kissed their forehead again and pushed them in the direction of the living room. Kit looked at me for reassurance as they walked towards it. I gave them a nod before moving into the kitchen to sort drinks and finish getting the food done.

I noted that Ruairí followed Kit, but Callan came towards me with eyes as wide as saucers. He had no intention of waiting until later to get an explanation for Kit's appearance. I just hoped Kit would be okay with Ruairí for a few minutes until dinner was ready. If not, I'd rescue them in an instant.

I'd do anything for Kit because while I hadn't said it yet, I was in love with them too. And I'd tell them that later when we were alone, along with everything else I'd discovered about myself while we were apart.

THIRTY NINE

Kit

As I sat down on the sofa, I noticed Callan following Thane into the kitchen and heard the hushed words he directed towards his best friend.

"What was that?"

"What dae ye mean?" came Thane's response.

"Ye and the forehead kisses. Have ye been replaced by an alien or something?"

Thane's snort echoed around the room. I had no idea why Thane kissing me on the forehead was so surprising. He did that a lot when we were together.

Ruairí took a seat on the other side of the sofa from me, setting his arm down across the top of it. He was burly, with a bald head and a beard. His hazel eyes shot to mine, and he gave me a grin.

"Dinnae mind mah husband. He's just surprised tae see Thane willingly engaging in public displays of affection," he said with a dismissive wave towards Callan.

"He didn't do that with Jenna?"

Ruairí raised a dark brown brow.

"No. He told ye aboot her, did he?"

I shrugged.

"Yeah. I know all about Jenna."

He nodded slowly and gave me another smile.

"He was a fucking mess after she died. Callan dropped everything tae take care of him. Was a time when I wasnae sure I'd get mah husband back."

I laced my fingers together in my lap and kept my mouth shut, not knowing where Ruairí was going with this.

"I did eventually, but he came home with a new houseguest. He was with us for almost a year. Thought he'd never leave, but Callan set him up here. Thane's still a grumpy fuck but am glad he's met someone new."

"He lived with you?"

Thane hadn't told me about that part. I knew he was grateful to Callan for helping him through it, but I had no idea what lengths Callan had gone to.

"Aye, after he sold the hoose. Well, Callan did it for him. He just signed the paperwork. I dinnae blame mah husband. Thane's parents were fucking useless and his sister's in the Outer Hebrides with her kids and husband, so she couldnae help him. Surprised he got back on his feet. Callan never gave up on him, even if everyone else in his life did."

He looked up in time to see his husband approaching with a pair of drinks in hand.

"What are ye telling, Kit?" Callan asked with a suspicious look in his eyes.

"Never ye mind."

Ruairí gave me a conspiratorial wink. I tried to keep a straight face and not let on that he'd told me something I wasn't sure I was meant to know.

"I dinnae trust ye."

"Would I, yer beloved, tell yer best friend's new partner something I shouldnae?"

"Aye, ye fucking would."

"I cannae believe ye'd think so lowly of me."

"Am warning ye."

He stood up and gave his husband a peck on the cheek.

"We heard ye giving Thane a hard time. Mibbe learn tae keep yer voice doon."

Ruairí walked away towards the table, where Thane was placing down plates filled with food. Callan followed after him with a stormy look on his face.

"Ruairí!"

Thane ignored the two of them as Callan caught up to his husband and dropped the drinks on the table before he dragged Ruairí away into the corridor where the bathroom and bedroom were.

Thane waved me over. I got up off the sofa and quick walked towards him, letting Thane catch me up in his arms and rest his chin on the top of my head.

"Ye okay?"

I pressed my cheek to his chest, listening to his heartbeat. That gave me comfort.

"Yeah, I'm good. Are those two going to be okay?"

"Aye. They're always like that. What did Ruairí say tae ye?"

"Um…"

I didn't want to lie to him, but I wasn't sure now was the right time to bring it up.

"Just some stuff about how you stayed with them for almost a year. And that Callan did everything for you."

I hugged him tighter as he tensed.

"But it's okay, I'm not judging. I know how hard Jenna's death was for you."

"It's no mah proudest moment."

"We all go through rough patches. I'm just glad you had someone who never gave up on you."

Thane let out a breath that disturbed my hair.

"Aye, Callan is a guid friend."

He let me go only to hold my face in both hands. The soft look in his eyes had me locking my knees together to stop from melting on the spot. He held me there for several minutes. I tried not to fidget, but I couldn't stop my fingers from rubbing together.

"Am just reminding mahself ye're real," he told me with a smile as if he noticed my slight agitation at being stared at for too long.

"I'm not a figment of your imagination."

"Aye, ye are mine though."

I nodded and smiled at him. Before I could speak again, Callan and Ruairí returned to the table. Callan looked a little flushed and his husband had a wide smile on his face.

"Ye two done with yer little tiff?" Thane asked.

"Aye," Ruairí said as he took a seat. "Callan's forgiven me."

"Am gonnae take it back if ye tell them how ye made me forgive ye," Callan said, plopping himself down in the chair next to his husband.

"Wouldnae dream of it."

Ruairí winked at me again. Thane rolled his eyes and let me go to retrieve the rest of the dishes from the kitchen. I took a seat across from Callan. Thane had set down a glass of water for me. I took a sip while I tried to think of something to say. Thane, thankfully, saved me from having to do anything when he returned and sat down. He put a hand on my knee and gave it a squeeze before telling Callan and Ruairí to help themselves.

Having that casual affection from him made me feel good. Knowing he wasn't like this before only made it clear Thane had changed since his wife's death. And that was okay. We all evolved depending on what life threw at us. I was grateful all the same that he chose me to bestow his affection on. I loved that he wanted to be close to me. I wanted that with him too.

Dinner was actually way less terrifying than I thought it would be. I had fun getting to know more about Callan and Ruairí. Since I was going to move here, I would be seeing a lot more of them. At least I'd know three people in town.

Made the prospect of leaving my hometown behind a little less scary.

By the time they left, I was ready to be alone with Thane. We had a lot to talk about, and, honestly, I just wanted to be held. So when he took a seat on the sofa, I stood awkwardly staring at his lap.

"Come here," he murmured, reaching a hand out to me.

I took it and let him pull me down. My knees fell on either side of his thighs as I straddled him. He dug his hands into my hair and pressed his forehead to mine. Then he closed his eyes and sighed.

"I've missed ye, Kit."

"I missed you too."

"I know ye probably have questions." He opened his eyes and sat back against the cushions. "Will ye let me talk first?"

I nodded.

"Of course."

He reached out and took one of my hands, entwining our fingers together. He pulled them towards his face and kissed my fingertips. I shivered at the touch.

"I wasnae okay when ye left. A part of me wanted tae tell ye how I felt, but I wasnae ready for… us. I wanted ye, really fucking wanted ye, but mah head was all tangled up and I needed time. Ye deserved more than I could give ye, Kit. Ye deserve everything."

He kissed my fingers again. The way he looked at me made my chest tight. The adoration in his green eyes was almost overwhelming, but I tried not to focus on that. His words were more important.

"I went tae see Callan and finally told him aboot mah argument with Jenna… and he made me see I needed tae deal with mah anger towards her. That it was okay tae be angry at her for what she did. I would've lost her even if she lived. And that's changed a lot for me."

He squeezed my fingers.

"I wanted tae contact ye, but I was really fucking scared that I wasnae ready… and I wasnae enough. Callan keeps telling me that am an eejit for thinking that."

Fuck, you were always enough, Thane. You always will be.

With my free hand, I cupped his bearded cheek and stroked my thumb along his mouth. He'd done so much work on himself while we'd been apart. I was so fucking proud of him.

"You're more than enough," I whispered, "you're everything to me."

He didn't say anything, but I could tell from his expression he needed to hear that from me. So I pressed a kiss to his mouth before I pulled back and smiled.

Thane bit his lip and looked away.

"That's no the only thing I discussed with Callan."

"No?"

"I told him how I felt aboot ye… how it confused the fuck oot of me 'cause I've never felt this way aboot anyone before. I spent mah whole life being told how ye should feel if ye like someone, but it's never been that way for me. Then ye came along and I knew I was attracted tae ye, but it still wasn't like how they said, so I didnae know what tae dae with that."

I stilled in his lap. He looked incredibly nervous about saying this to me.

"Callan asked me questions and I tried mah best tae answer them… then he made a suggestion that made a lot of fucking sense the more I thought aboot it. That's why they were here for dinner. Callan and Ruairí helped me work through all of this and I wanted tae say thank ye."

He looked down at my legs. I didn't know what he was about to tell me, but he had to know that it wouldn't change anything. I would love Thane no matter what.

"Am asexual, Kit."

"Okay."

He looked up at me.

"Okay?"

I nodded.

"If that's your sexuality, then that's fine. I'm glad you worked it out and you're not confused any longer."

He blinked.

"Ye're okay with it?"

"Why wouldn't I be? I mean, I have questions, but they are more about the practicalities of our relationship and not me having an issue with you being ace."

"What are yer questions?"

I cocked my head to the side.

"Well, what are your feelings about sex? It's okay if you don't want it. We can deal with that together."

His face was a picture. Thane clearly wasn't expecting me to accept it so readily. As someone who had been given a lot of shit for being non-binary, queer and autistic, I would never do that to anyone else. And it wasn't a problem for me, anyway. I understood attraction worked differently for every individual person, and that it came in many different forms.

He swallowed and squeezed my fingers again. Thane was going to have to get comfortable talking about this stuff with me. I wanted us to be clear about our boundaries.

"I enjoy sex with ye, Kit. I dinnae know everything I like, but I wannae continue exploring that 'cause ye make me feel safe. Ye always have." His bottom lip trembled. "Ye're so fucking special tae me. Ye have no idea how much I want and need everything aboot ye."

Before I knew what was happening, he'd let go of my hand, grabbed a hold of my face, and kissed me so hard, I thought I might drown in his passion. His other hand gripped my hip, tugging me closer until our bodies were pressed together. I could feel him growing hard the longer we kissed. My hips ground into him on instinct as I whimpered. Then I remembered that we weren't done talking yet.

"Wait," I gasped, trying to pull away, "we still have a lot to discuss."

"That can wait until after I've made ye a naked, panting mess," he practically growled at me. "I want ye noo, Kit, and ye're gonnae dae exactly as I say 'cause we both know how needy ye get when am in charge."

Well, fuck, that told me.

FORTY

Thane

While I was very aware that Kit and I had things to talk about, I couldn't wait any longer. The fact they accepted my sexuality meant so much.

It wasn't like I thought Kit would see me differently because of it, but it hadn't stopped me from being nervous. It was all so new to me and sharing it with others was a scary prospect. But Kit knowing that I was ace was important. It needed to be said before things progressed between us. Now, it felt like nothing was holding me back from reconnecting with them on a physically intimate level.

When they didn't protest, I kissed them again, digging my hand in their hair and tugging on it. Their responding moan had me struggling not to rush this. I wanted them bare, their skin touching mine, the feeling of being inside them. I wanted it all, but only with them.

Some people wouldn't understand that my desire for Kit had nothing to do with sexual attraction, but it made sense to me. I wanted Kit for them, and sex was just one way of expressing the need to connect with them.

As I let go of their hair, my hands went to their clothes instead, tugging at them to get them off Kit. They helped me, putting their arms up so I could get rid of their top half.

Kit peeled off their bralette the next moment. There was arousal in their icy blue eyes. A lust-drunk look that had me kissing them again. My hands dragged down their sides, revelling in the feel of their bare skin.

"Thane," they moaned in my mouth.

I know, I want you too. I want you everywhere, Kit.

My hand went to their throat. I dragged my thumb down it, feeling them swallow.

"Clothes off, Kit," I demanded. "I need tae see ye."

They struggled to get off me. As they stood, their hands went to their jeans to undo the button. I took the opportunity to remove my shirt, throwing it away and not caring what direction it went in.

Since I had the wood-burning stove going, the house was pretty warm. Still, Kit's skin pebbled as they stood before me completely bare. They took their glasses off and placed them on the coffee table before turning back to me.

"Ye're so fucking pretty."

Kit blushed but didn't attempt to hide themselves.

I unbuckled my belt and lifted my hips to pull off the rest of my clothes.

They stared at me with their bottom lip caught between their teeth.

I reached out for their hand. Kit let me take it. I kissed their fingers and palm, watching them shiver with need. Then I dragged them into my lap. I caught Kit's throat with one hand again and kissed them. They ground themselves against me, coating my cock in their arousal.

"Dae ye want it, Kit?" I whispered. "Are ye needy for me yet?"

"Yes, yes, please, I want you."

Hearing the breathiness in their voice and the way they held onto my shoulders had me aching. I gripped my cock and lined myself up. Then I caught their mouth as I pressed inside them, kissing them for all I was worth. I fucking missed this. Having them close. Feeling them against me.

How the fuck did I think I could ever live without Kit? That I was going to be okay if they weren't in my life. I wanted to contact them so badly, but the distance and everything else held me back. Having them here was a fucking miracle and a half. One I would never take for granted.

When they were fully settled in my lap, Kit rested their forehead against mine and closed their eyes. Their hands slid around the back of my neck and into my hair.

"Are ye okay?"

They rubbed their head against mine before opening their eyes.

"Yeah, I'm just thinking about how lucky I am that you're mine."

"That makes ye lucky?"

"Of course it does. You're kind, considerate, and everything I could ever want, why wouldn't that make me lucky?"

"Ye're being very free with yer compliments today."

"It wasn't supposed to be one! I'm just telling you the truth."

I didn't think I would ever get over Kit's blunt honesty. It really was one of their most endearing traits.

"I know ye were."

Kit tugged my hair and scowled at me.

"Don't make me hurt you."

"I told ye I might like that."

"Just… just… just shut up and fuck me."

I grinned at them.

"Ye sure ye dinnae wannae find oot?"

They narrowed their eyes. Then they pulled back and looked me over. A sly smile spread across their face.

I released their throat and waited to see what they had planned, having no intention of stopping them.

Kit leaned down while keeping their eyes on me as they stuck their tongue out and licked my nipple.

"That's no—" My words got cut off when they bit me. "Fuck, Kit."

They had a wicked smile as they pulled away and straightened.

"Did you like it?"

I rubbed my nipple.

"No really."

"Maybe think about that next time you decide to tease me. I bite."

They snapped their teeth at me.

I raised my brows before looking down at their nipples and back up at them.

Kit didn't get a chance to say another word. I had them by the shoulder as I pushed them to the side and down onto the sofa. I twisted around to settle back between their legs, pinning them against the fabric with a hand around their neck. I smiled at their wide-eyed stare before licking a path down their chest.

They gasped when I bit them right back in the same place they had me. Then they moaned and I knew I had them.

Pressing myself back inside them, I set a sedate pace, watching them squirm beneath me. Their hands went to my shoulders, squeezing my flesh between their fingers.

"Thane," they whimpered.

"Aye?"

"Faster."

"No, ye'll take what I give ye."

"Please."

They tried shifting their hips, but I held onto them with my free hand, keeping them still.

"So needy."

"Please."

"Ye beg so sweetly for such a moothy wee thing."

They gave me such a sad look that I couldn't help but give in. Leaning down, I pressed open-mouthed kisses to their jaw as I increased my pace. They curved their legs over mine, bringing me even closer. Words were lost between kisses, thrusts, and moans of pleasure.

It was the perfect reunion between our bodies. I couldn't get enough of them. I reminded myself I could have this every day once Kit moved here if I wanted. Sex between us was special but just holding Kit was my favourite thing to do. If I could lace my fingers between theirs and lay together for hours without speaking, it would be enough. But I was glad I could have more. That Kit wanted to share everything with me.

You're the best thing that ever happened to me, my pretty wee love.

Kit pushed their hand between us. I adjusted my weight on them to give them enough space to touch themselves. Their eyes were closed, and their breath came out in spurts as they rubbed their clit.

"Thane…"

"Aye?"

"My hair, pull my hair."

I did as they asked, using my free hand to tug at the roots. My other hand was still wrapped around their neck where it belonged.

Kit squirmed as their back bowed off the sofa.

"Fuck," they cried out right before they came.

It was a sight to behold. Their flushed face and neck. One of their hands wrapped tightly around my shoulder. Their blunt nails digging into my skin. The way their mouth parted on a silent moan. Kit was beautiful in every single way. And I was in awe of them.

They slumped back against the sofa cushions when they came down. Kit opened their eyes, looking up at me with a small smile. I slowed down to a gentle pace, wanting to make sure I didn't overwhelm them.

"Okay?"

They pulled their hand away from their clit and stuck their fingers in my mouth. Without missing a beat, I sucked them clean. Their smile grew wider.

"I am now."

"That another thing ye dinnae like on yer skin?" I asked when they pulled their fingers out of my mouth.

"No, I just like watching you taste me."

I didn't get a chance to respond to that. Kit grabbed a hold of my head and kissed me. I groaned and increased my thrusts, wanting to find my end too. They moved with me, encouraging every press of my body against theirs.

"Kit," I panted, "am gonnae…"

"In my mouth."

"What?"

"I want you to come in my mouth."

I faltered in my movements, my brain short-circuiting at their request. While Kit had gone down on me a couple of times, it was never to completion. I didn't think they'd want that, but apparently, I was mistaken. Maybe I should have asked rather than assumed it wasn't on the table.

"Ye dae?"

They nodded as they pressed both hands on my shoulders, pushing me back. I got off them and sat down.

Kit slid onto the floor and knelt between my spread legs. They took hold of one of my hands and placed it on their head as they bowed it over me. My breath shuddered when they slid their mouth over my cock.

After a minute of them sucking me on their own, I took over, directing the pace with my hand on their head. Kit hummed with pleasure. Even in this, they wanted me to be in control.

It didn't take long for me to explode in their mouth. I was pent up from fucking them. I groaned with my release, staring down at Kit's head.

When I was done, they pulled back and swallowed. I smiled and stroked their cheek.

"What a guid wee thing ye are, taking it all so well."

Their mouth dropped open.

"Thane!"

"Ye dinnae want me tae praise ye?"

Kit hid their flushed face behind their hands and squirmed.

"I… I wasn't expecting it."

I took hold of their hands and used them to pull Kit up into my lap. Then I wrapped my arms around them, cradling them against my chest.

"Mibbe am no the only one who needs tae explore their… interests."

"Clearly," they mumbled, pressing their face into my neck.

I chuckled and stroked their back. Then I pushed off the sofa, getting up with them still clutching me. Kit let out a yelp.

"Oh my god, what about your ankle?"

"It healed up all fine. Dinnae worry aboot me."

They stared at me as I carried them into my bedroom.

"I'll always worry about you because I care."

And I love you for that, so fucking much.

I'd realised I was in love with Kit not long after they left. My feelings became clearer after my initial conversation with Callan regarding Kit. They'd shown me so much of themselves in the short time we had been around each other. Everything about them fascinated me and had me in awe. With them, I could be myself in every way without fear of misunderstandings and judgment. Kit got me and I got them.

Rather than questioning how I could fall in love with someone so fast, I asked myself how could I not love them? Kit was everything.

I pulled back the covers and set Kit down in bed. Then I disappeared to clear up our clothes, lock up and turn out the lights. When I got back, I slid in next to them, pulled the covers over us and curled myself around their back. Kit let out a contented sigh.

"Did ye wannae get dressed?" I asked knowing that Kit didn't often like being naked and hated going to sleep without anything on.

"Maybe later before we go to sleep."

They snuggled deeper into my embrace. I pressed a kiss to their hair and breathed them in. Contentment washed over me. This was what I missed the most, holding Kit at night. Not having them there to sleep next to had been an odd experience. I hadn't got used to it no matter how much time passed. I never had to worry about that again. Sure, there were going to be times when we were apart, but most nights, I would get to fall asleep with this beautiful human being who gave me everything I never knew I needed.

"Kit," I whispered in their ear.

They stroked my hand but didn't say anything.

"Kit."

"Mmm?"

"Kit."

They turned their head to meet my gaze.

"Yes?"

I ran my eyes all over their face, taking in their eyes, their nose, their lips, and every freckle.

They wrinkled their nose and nudged me with their shoulder.

"What is it?"

I smiled before cupping their face and running a thumb over their bottom lip. It might not be the perfect time, but there was no such thing as perfect timing. Kit coming here had taught me that. And in my head, there was no better moment than right then to tell them exactly how I felt.

"I love ye."

FORTY ONE

Kit

It took a long minute for the words Thane spoke to register. And when they did, my emotions threatened to overwhelm me. I couldn't speak as my throat got all clogged up. But what I could do was kiss him. So that's what I did.

I turned around completely, cupped his cheek, and pressed my mouth to his. Thane responded immediately, kissing me back with such tenderness, I thought I would burst into tears. But no, I wasn't going to cry. I was happy. He loved me back. It wasn't something I expected, but I was ecstatic he felt the way I did all the same.

When he released my mouth, he brushed my lip with his thumb again.

"Ye okay?"

I nodded, still struggling to speak my thoughts out loud. It happened sometimes when things got a little too much. Rather than force myself to verbalise my feelings, I pointed at myself, drew a heart with my fingers and then pointed at him.

"Ye love me tae."

I nodded again. He smiled, clearly understanding that I was struggling to communicate. And I loved him even more for that. Thane would never make me speak for his benefit. He'd shown me that he would accommodate my disability in whatever way I needed.

"I didnae think it was nuts or tae fast when ye said it earlier, no when I feel the same. Nothing aboot us is tae fast, no after what we went through together."

He had a point. We had gone through a lot together in a short time.

"But we can talk aboot all of that when ye're ready. Am just gonnae hold ye."

I buried my face in his chest and appreciated how much patience he had. The way he cared. How could he have ever thought he wasn't enough when he was everything I could have ever wanted? Although, I supposed I did know why. His family hadn't been all that great to him in the wake of Jenna's death, not to mention the things she said to him before it happened. By his own admission, he was still working through that stuff. I'd do what I could to support him now that we were together, but it wouldn't have mattered if we weren't. I'd have done it anyway.

When my racing mind calmed down and my emotions were less intense, I pulled back and rested my head on Thane's arm. He had his eyes closed. I watched him for a long moment. The way his eyelashes fluttered slightly against his cheeks. Those freckles all over his face made him more attractive in my eyes. His hair was glinting in the low light since he had only turned on a bedside lamp. He knew I wasn't a fan of the big light. This man was beautiful through and through. I loved his mind. I loved his kindness. I just loved him.

"How are things with your parents?"

I wanted to check if he'd made any progress with them. I could tell it weighed heavily on him after our conversation about what I had overhead when they were here.

He slowly opened his eyes. The soft look in them had my heart racing.

"They're better. We had a long talk and they apologised for making me feel like they didnae see me. They've been trying, and that's improved oor relationship… and I told them aboot ye."

"You did?"

"Aye. Dad didnae understand why I didnae just ask Callan for yer number tae tell ye how I feel. I didnae tell him I wasnae feeling like I was enough for ye."

"You're not just enough, you're more."

He blushed, which I found incredibly adorable.

"Aye, well, I know that noo."

"I'm glad you figured things out with them."

He pressed a kiss to my forehead.

"How is yer dad? He okay with ye wanting tae move here?"

"He's the one who told me to not fear change and do what makes me happy, so yeah, he supports this. And he wants to meet you at some point."

"We can arrange that."

"Yeah?"

Thane grinned and bit his lip.

"Aye. Am gonnae help ye move yer stuff up here, dinnae want ye deaing with that all by yerself. So, I'll have tae go doon tae Seaford to bring ye home. And we'll visit him. I know ye're close tae yer dad. Dinnae want ye missing oot on seeing him."

Why are you so perfect? It's like you'll do anything for me… actually… I'm pretty sure you would. But I'd also do anything for you.

"Bring me home?"

My brain snagged on those words.

"Aye, ye're home is here with me."

I didn't know what to say for a long moment. Where I would live hadn't been something I had given too much thought to. I figured I would work it out after I talked to Thane, as then I would know where we stood.

"You want me to move in here?"

"Only if ye want tae. If ye're no ready for that, then we can find ye a place in toon, but tae be very clear, I want ye tae live here with me."

"Thane…"

"It's tae soon? That's okay. I'll talk tae Callan, he'll know somewhere we can set ye up. I just didnae want ye tae think ye had no support. I know ye dinnae like change and this willnae be easy for ye. If ye're here with me, I can take care of ye. I wannae dae that."

I put a hand on his chest. I couldn't with this man.

"It's not that… I'm just trying to wrap my head around the fact you'd do that for me."

"I'd dae anything. Ye're the one uprooting yer life. This is the very least I can dae for ye. But that's no the reason. I truly want tae live with ye. I know what being apart from ye feels like. I dinnae want that again."

There I had it, confirmation that Thane would, indeed, do anything for me.

"It's going to be a little while before I realistically can move."

"It's enough for me tae know that ye are."

"So you just suddenly decided that you want me to live here?"

Thane grinned.

"No, have been thinking aboot it since ye told me ye wannae move. I weighed up the options in mah head over dinner and then made a decision."

"But we've only spent like two and a half weeks together. I'm a lot to deal with, you know."

His eyebrows raised slowly.

"Ye're no a lot tae deal with, Kit. I love ye the way ye are. Ye dinnae have tae worry ye're gonnae be tae much for me. Ye could never be."

In all fairness, Thane had seen me at one of my worst points. He witnessed the varying degrees of intensity when it came to my meltdowns. He listened when I explained my specific autistic traits to him since no two autistic people were the same. He didn't make me feel like I was a burden or that I was ever too much. Sure, he teased me about crying after sex, but I knew he was joking. That was how we were together.

"Okay."

"Okay?"

"I'll move in with you provided you promise me that you'll be honest if it doesn't work, and we need to figure something else out."

It wasn't that I didn't want to live with Thane. I really did, but I was nervous about the whole thing. Living with another person was a big deal to me. But I loved him and being apart from him had been tough. The transition from living in Seaford to living here would be easier if I had him to support me through it. There would be a lot of bad days mixed in with the good ones. It was something I had to prepare both of us for.

"I swear I'll always be honest with ye."

"Then okay… wait, won't your landlord have something to say about this?"

"Baird? No, he'll no make any issue of it." Thane shrugged. "He's said in the past that he'd sell the place tae me."

"Would you want to buy it?"

"Mibbe in the future if that's something we want. There's no rush."

We… he said we. He's already seeing us as a couple who makes these decisions together.

"Well, I like it here, but you're right, we can decide that when we're ready."

Thane pressed a kiss to my lips and gave me a soft smile.

"Guid. Am happy ye wannae come live with me. I wouldnae have asked ye tae move away from yer home tae be with me."

"I appreciate that, but I don't want to be away from you. And, honestly, I don't want to live anywhere near Sienna and her bullshit. I ran into her a couple of days ago and she pretended I didn't even exist. Not that I tried to talk to her or anything because fuck her."

"Aye, fuck her. She's no worth yer time or energy."

I smiled.

"Dad told me that he never liked her and is glad we aren't friends any longer. He put up with her for my sake. I wish he'd said something earlier, but it's like he said, I have to make my own choices."

He stroked my hair back from my face.

"Aye, we all make mistakes. I know I've made a lot of them, but ye'll never be one."

"You'll never be one for me either."

Thane pressed his forehead against mine and just breathed with me with a smile on his face.

My heart felt so full right then. I couldn't have asked for a better outcome when I came up here to tell Thane how I felt. It had been the scariest thing I'd ever done. But I trusted him enough to be vulnerable. I'd shown him my worst parts and he accepted me for who I was. He loved me. And he was mine now.

We would have a lot of challenges ahead of us, but we'd be together, supporting each other through them. I never thought I would find someone who cared the way Thane did. Who made me see that I was worthy of having my needs met. He didn't think I was difficult or too much. He didn't view my disability as a problem, but as something to accommodate to help make things easier on me. He was perfect in my eyes. And I couldn't wait to continue on this adventure we called life with him.

After a while of us just holding each other, we got up to get ready for bed. He gave me one of his t-shirts to wear and said I could take it home with me. He wanted to give me something of his to keep while we were apart. When we were dressed and our teeth were brushed, we got tucked up in bed together again. Thane held me against his chest and kissed my forehead.

"I love ye, Kit," he whispered.

I kissed his chest and snuggled deeper into his embrace.

"Love you too."

I fell asleep with him, finally back in my safe place with the man I'd shared the scariest experiences of my life with. But we got through that together. We would get through whatever life threw at us too because we had each other. And that was all that mattered.

EPILOGUE

Thane

Kit walked ahead of me. Their hands were tucked into the straps of their daypack. The sun glinted off their dark hair. They'd braided it down both sides and tied off their neck, leaving wee tufts of hair sticking out of the hairbands. They had a light fleece on top of their t-shirt with walking trousers and boots since it was a wee bit colder up here. There was a spring to their step, and they hummed a tune.

It had been a year since they'd moved in with me. It took them three months to get everything sorted so they could move up here, so it was mid-June by the time we started living together. And what a year it had been.

Things weren't easy for Kit in the beginning. They struggled with the transition and all the change. I was there for them every step of the way, taking care of everything so they didn't have to worry. I made sure they had all the support they needed with help from Callan. We'd made him aware of Kit being autistic, so he understood their disability and could be there for them when I was unable to. That was the wonderful thing about my best friend. Just as he would do anything for me, he was the same way with Kit.

Once Kit became more settled, they found a studio where they could work part-time. After sorting out their licence, they got back to tattooing, and now, they were thriving.

I'd been their first client up here. Kit was nervous about tattooing me, but I told them not to worry. That I trusted them. They'd been so meticulous about it, wanting to get it just right. They gave me a small line tattoo of a mountain range with wee snow caps on my wrist. It signified our time on the mountain together, something I'd wanted to immortalise on my skin. It was a turning point in my life. No matter how hard that time had been, it had also brought me Kit, who I couldn't imagine being without.

No matter how difficult things got, Kit and I were solid. They knew they could lean on me, and I could do the same with them. We were each other's biggest supporters and safe spaces. The understanding and connection we shared made it easy to be with each other.

"Oh my god, I can see the top," they called back to me, their icy blue eyes shining with happiness.

The next thing I knew, Kit had dashed off up the slope. I shook my head as I walked after them. I couldn't fault Kit's excitement. This was a big moment for both of us.

When I crested the peak, Kit had taken their pack off and was standing there with their arms spread out and their face turned up towards the sky. They looked so free and happy that I had to pause for a moment to take it in. My heart thumped and my chest expanded with all the love I had for them. It was quite something to see them express their joy without any reservations.

"We fucking did it!" they shouted as they spun around and spied me standing several feet away. "This fucking mountain couldn't beat us twice!"

I smiled back at them. My beautiful, vivacious partner who was so full of life and love. Their infectious happiness spread through my veins. I dumped my pack down on the ground and ran towards them. Kit squealed when I picked them up and spun them around.

"Thane!"

I didn't put them down even as they held onto my shoulders and squealed again, spinning them around and around until we were both dizzy. We almost fell in a heap together, but we held onto each other to get our bearings back. Kit hugged me close and buried their face in my chest, squishing their glasses against me.

"Aye, we did," I murmured, pressing my face into their hair, "we made it, mah pretty wee love."

We had talked about this for months, our attempt on the damn mountain we never managed to conquer together almost a year and a half ago. Kit and I decided it would be better to do it in the summer. Neither of us was keen on summiting mountains in the snow ever again.

It was the first time I'd been up a mountain since I injured my ankle. We'd done a lot of walking over the past year to get Kit's stamina up. And today was the culmination of all that hard work. Our summit attempt had gone to plan. Kit had finally conquered a Munro.

Kit pulled away to look at me.

"And to think, Callan was betting with Ruairí that I would want to turn back before we got here."

"He did what?"

Their eyes widened.

"I don't think I was meant to tell you that."

"Am gonnae throw that wee shite off the next mountain we summit together. He should have more faith in ye."

Kit laughed.

"Ruairí refused to take the bet. Said Callan was being too harsh on me."

Oddly enough, Ruairí and Kit had become fast friends. They both enjoyed winding Callan up. I thought he deserved it after all the interfering he did in other people's lives, but he wasn't too impressed by their antics. Nevertheless, he loved Kit like they were his long-lost sibling. And had told me on multiple occasions that if I fucked anything up with Kit, he would kick me to the kerb on their behalf.

"Am the one who believed in ye first. Those two are eejits."

"Aww, are you jealous that Ruairí likes me so much?"

"No, am no jealous of anyone. I know ye're mine, Kit."

They blushed and gave me a shy smile.

"Yeah, I am. Always."

Kit went up on their tiptoes, indicating they wanted a kiss, which I gave them willingly. When we pulled apart, Kit remained on their toes as I rested my forehead against theirs.

"Am proud of ye," I murmured, "mah brave wee thing."

"I thought I was your pretty wee love."

"That tae."

Kit grinned. I don't know when I started calling them that, but it fit. They were smaller than me, pretty and I loved them. The first time I said to them, Kit had raised an eyebrow but didn't comment on it. Only after the third or fourth time did they ask me if that was my new nickname for them. And then it became a thing.

"Am I allowed to be proud of you for getting up here as well?"

"Aye."

They dropped back to their feet and turned to look out over the landscape stretching out for miles around us. I stood behind them with my arms wrapped around their front. Kit leaned their head on my arm and sighed.

"It's beautiful up here."

We were lucky that the sky was relatively clear of clouds and the sun was out.

"Aye. Almost as beautiful as ye."

"Oh shush, you'll make me blush again."

"I like it when ye blush."

Kit squirmed in my arms.

"Don't say that."

"Why no?"

"Three months ago you admitted that you liked it when my skin gets all flushed after you make me come and now every time you talk about me blushing, that's all I can think about."

I laughed remembering that exact moment now they'd mentioned it. Kit nudged me with their elbow.

"Don't laugh."

"Ye're adorable."

"Oh my god, stop. I am not."

I leaned down, hovering my mouth over their ear.

"Aye, ye're the most adorable person I've ever met, and when we get home, am gonnae make ye flush several times over as a reward for climbing yer first Munro."

Kit went very quiet for a long moment. They didn't try to escape my grasp, so I waited until they were ready to talk.

"Okay, I'd like that," they whispered, "but can we stay up here a little while longer? It's so pretty and I'm still in awe that we made it."

"We can stay as long as ye want."

"Thank you."

So Kit and I remained where we were, me holding them as they took in the view. The two of us had been through a lot on this mountain and the glen below us. Now we were in better place. We conquered so much. And we would continue to because we were together.

Kit turned their head up towards me with a smile.

"I love you, Thane."

"Love ye tae, Kit."

Our love and respect would see us through everything because we had each other.

Forever and always.

ACKNOWLEDGEMENTS

To one of my most treasured friends, Allison. The thing is, I don't know how to thank you enough for your friendship and support. I've never been good at putting my gratitude into words. The way you have accepted me for who I am and make the effort to understand my struggles is something I've not experienced with many people. I never feel anything but safe with you. When I told you about this story, you were immediately onboard and encouraged me to tell it in the most authentic and raw way. You fell in love with Kit and Thane alongside me, helping me tell their story and make it the best it could be. You know how scared I was to put my own experiences into words through Kit. How hard it was to be so open about being autistic and what that looks like on the inside. I never wanted to sugarcoat the autistic experience. And you told me how proud you were of me for that. I don't know how I would have got through writing The Edge of Never without you. Thank you for being there for me through the highs and lows of this book. Thank you for being in my life. Thank you for being you.

To my wonderful PA, listener of my long, full of various tangents voice notes and fellow member of the redheaded man fan club, Amber. I'm not sure what I would do without you helping me with the publishing process. In fact, I have no idea how I coped before you came on board! We make a good team and knowing you have my back once I set a release date makes everything easier on me. Thank you for going on this journey with me. When it came to writing The Edge of Never, you were there for me during my 'I have no idea what I'm doing' moments and helped me work through stuff. Your support is invaluable.

To my bestie, Ash. What can I say? You're always there for me. You tell me to go for it when I come to you with my ideas no matter what they are. You encourage me to tell authentic stories in my voice. I've improved myself as a writer and storyteller tenfold just by having you in my life. Thank you for being here for me during The Edge of Never.

To my mother. Thank you for proofreading all of my books. I know this one was particularly difficult for you to read!

To Kaitie. Thank you for sensitivity reading The Edge of Never and being an amazing friend. Thank you for putting up with my crazy ass. You have no idea how grateful I am to have someone who doesn't misunderstand me or misconstrue my words and who gets me without having to explain the whys. Thank you for being you.

And finally, to my husband. He doesn't read my books and will probably never see this, so I'm safe to admit things he doesn't need to know. I tell him that I don't base my book men off him, and while that is true in most cases, it doesn't apply to The Edge of Never. Thane has my husband's kindness and his considerate and caring nature. My husband is a nurturer but only with me. I'm forever grateful to be the one who gets to see his sensitive side. He's the one who puts up with me on a daily basis and deals with my disability firsthand. He knows my struggles and no matter how he's feeling, he's there for me when I need him. I'm not sure what I would do without him even though he drives me crazy. I love him more than words could say. So thank you, husband, if you ever do read this. You're one of the good ones.

ABOUT THE AUTHOR

Sarah writes dark, contemporary, erotic and paranormal romances. They adore all forms of steamy romance and can always be found with a book or ten on their Kindle. They love anti-heroes, alpha males and flawed characters with a little bit of darkness lurking within. Their writing buddies nicknamed Sarah: 'Queen of Steam' for their pulse racing sex scenes which will leave you a little hot under the collar.

Born and raised in Sussex, UK near the Ashdown Forest, they grew up climbing trees and building Lego towns with their younger brother. Sarah fell in love with novels as a teenager reading their aunt's historical regency romances. They have always loved the supernatural and exploring the darker side of romance and fantasy novels.

Sarah currently resides in the Scottish Highlands with their husband. Music is one of their biggest inspirations and they always have something on in the background whilst writing. They are an avid gamer and are often found hogging their husband's Xbox.

Printed in Poland
by Amazon Fulfillment
Poland Sp. z o.o., Wrocław

33599642R00238